"You were beautiful that night," Alec said, giving her figure a slow once-over.

Charlotte couldn't contain herself. "I was twenty-two that night."

"You didn't have to take the key."

"I was confused." It had taken her a moment to realise the card he'd handed her was a hotel room key.

"You were tempted."

"I'd known you for two minutes." Other women might be tempted by a dashing aristocrat with money to burn, but Charlotte wasn't interested in a fling.

"I'd been watching you for a lot longer than two minutes. You were attractive. You seemed interesting and intelligent, and by the way you were making all those other men laugh, I knew you had a sense of humour."

"Giving me your room key was supposed to be funny?"

"I wanted to get to know you better."

"It didn't occur to you to ask me for coffee?"

"I'm not a patient man."

* * *

**Don't miss the exclusive in-book short stories by
USA TODAY bestselling author Maureen Child after the
last page of *Transformed Into the Frenchman's Mistress*
and *Bargained Into Her Boss's Bed*!**

Transformed Into
The Frenchman's Mistress
by Barbara Dunlop

Bargained Into Her Boss's Bed
by Emilie Rose

The urge to kiss Max awake was almost too strong for Dana to resist. Too bad *almost* didn't count.

"Max," she called quietly. He didn't stir.

"Max," she tried again, a little louder this time. Dana eased onto the cushion beside him. The warm proximity of his leg beside hers made her heart race. "Max, wake up."

His eyelids slowly lifted and his unfocused gaze found hers. "Morning." The groggy, rough timbre of his voice made her stomach muscles quiver. Wouldn't she love to wake up to that every day?

His hand painted a hot path up her spine. She gasped. Then his fingers cupped her nape and he pulled her forwards. Warm lips covered hers. Shocked but thrilled, she responded for just a second before reality hit her on the head.

Who does he think he's kissing?

**Available in March 2010
from Mills & Boon® Desire™**

The Moretti Heir
by Katherine Garbera

&

Billionaire Extraordinaire
by Leanne Banks

Transformed Into the Frenchman's Mistress
by Barbara Dunlop

&

Bargained Into Her Boss's Bed
by Emilie Rose
Mini-series – THE HUDSONS OF BEVERLY HILLS
Featuring two bonus stories by Maureen Child

In the Argentine's Bed
by Jennifer Lewis

&

Secret Baby, Public Affair
by Yvonne Lindsay

TRANSFORMED INTO THE FRENCHMAN'S MISTRESS

BY
BARBARA DUNLOP

BARGAINED INTO HER BOSS'S BED

BY
EMILIE ROSE

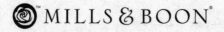 MILLS & BOON®

First published in Great Britain 2010
Harlequin Mills & Boon Limited,
Eton House, 18-24 Paradise Road, Richmond, Surrey TW9 1SR

The publisher acknowledges the copyright holders of the
individual works as follows:

Transformed Into the Frenchman's Mistress © Harlequin Books S.A. 2009
Bargained Into Her Boss's Bed © Harlequin Books S.A. 2009

Special thanks and acknowledgements are given to Barbara Dunlop and
Emilie Rose for their contribution to THE HUDSONS OF BEVERLY HILLS
series.

ISBN: 978 0 263 88161 5

51-0310

Harlequin Mills & Boon policy is to use papers that are natural, renewable
and recyclable products and made from wood grown in sustainable forests.
The logging and manufacturing processes conform to the legal environmental
regulations of the country of origin.

Printed and bound in Spain
by Litografia Rosés S.A., Barcelona

TRANSFORMED INTO THE FRENCHMAN'S MISTRESS

BY
BARBARA DUNLOP

Dear Reader,

Is there anything more romantic than a château in the south of France, with picturesque gardens, a well-stocked wine cellar and hot hero? And who doesn't love the thought of being whisked away to Paris, Rome and London in a private jet?

French aristocrat Alec Montcalm has it all: the looks, the pedigree, the money and all those gorgeous women. And Charlotte Hudson doesn't trust him for a single second. Unfortunately, the favour she's forced to ask is a test of her loyalty to her family. It's a favour Alec is willing to grant her – for a price.

I hope you enjoy the newest instalment in the Hudsons' saga!

Barbara Dunlop

For Susie Ross

One

Slightly windblown, and more than a little jet-lagged, Charlotte Hudson found herself in France. A phone call from her brother, Jack, yesterday had cut short her tour with their grandfather, Ambassador Edmond Cassettes. The diplomatic contingent had been in New Orleans, where Charlotte and the ambassador were being wined, dined and entertained by the governor, a couple of senators and every Louisiana mayor with aspirations of doing business with the wealthy Mediterranean nation of Monte Allegro.

Then Jack had called, and now she was in Provence, pulling up to the Montcalm family château with a favor to ask. Her college friend Raine would be surprised to see her, but Charlotte was couting on Raine's good nature to help her secure the favor. It was the first time her brother, or anyone on the Hudson side of the family, had included her in Hudson Pictures' film-making business. And she desperately wanted to impress.

Charlotte had been raised in Europe by her maternal grandparents, while Jack was raised an ocean away in Hollywood by the Hudsons. She mad met the film-making dynasty of a family on only a couple of occasions. They were perfectly polite to her, but it was clear they were close-knit, and she was very much the outsider.

But now, terminally ill matriarch Lillian Hudson was determined to honor her late husband's wishes by having Hudson Pictures bring their wartime romance to the big screen. The entire family had rallied around the project and decreed Château Montcalm was the perfect location.

Charlotte finally had a chance to participate in the Hudsons' world.

She drew a breath, giving her straight skirt and matching ivory blazer a final tug as she approached the main doors of the Montcalm's stately, three-story stone mansion. The doors were intimidating oversize planked walnut, inset with vintage beveled windows. The château was old-world and impressive. She knew it had been in the Montcalm family for a dozen generations, ever since some fiery warlord of a Montcalm ancestor had taken it in battle. Her friend Raine had quite the pedigree.

Charlotte took a breath and reached for the ornate doorbell, waiting only a moment until a formally dressed butler drew the door wide, his expression a study in formality and courtesy.

"Bonjour, madame."

"Bonjour," Charlotte returned. "I'm looking for Raine Montcalm."

The man paused while he considered Charlotte's appearance. "Do you have an appointment?"

Charlotte shook her head. "I'm Charlotte Hudson. Raine and I are friends. We were together at Oxford."

"Mademoiselle Montcalm is unavailable."

"But—"

"I do apologize."

"Could you at least tell her I'm here?" She hoped Raine would become available if she heard Charlotte's name.

"The mademoiselle is not currently in residence."

Charlotte struggled to decide if she was getting the brush-off. "She's really not here?"

He didn't answer, but his expression became crisper and even more formal, if that was possible.

"Because, if you could just let her know—"

"A problem, Henri?" came a gravelly, masculine voice.

Oh no. Not Alec.

"Non, monsieur."

Charlotte reflexively drew back as a tall, aristocratically handsome man moved into the doorway, displacing the butler. Raine's brother was supposed to be in London. Charltte had seen his picture in the tabloids just yesterday, dancing at some posh nightclub on Whitehall.

"I'm afraid Raine's away on—" He suddenly stopped speaking. A wolfish smile grew on his lips. "Charlotte Hudson."

She didn't answer.

"Thank you, Henri." Alec's dismissal was polite but clear, his gaze never leaving Charlotte.

As the butler drew back, Alec leaned indolently against the doorjamb. He wore a charcoal Caraceni suit, a classic white shirt and a dark silk tie that was scattered with bright red flecks. The flecks, it seemed, were miniatures of the Montcalm family crest, painstakingly embroidered into the fabric.

Her heart pounding with a mixture of awareness and trepidation, Charlotte decided to bluff. She held out her hand and gave him a breezy smile. "I don't believe we've been formally introduced."

At least that part wasn't a lie. There'd been nothing remotely formal about their one and only meeting. It had been humiliating, and her only defense was to pretend she'd forgotten all about it.

"Oh, we've been introduced, Ms. Hudson." His warm, callused hand closed over hers, sending a shiver along her spine.

She painstakingly schooled her features, raising her brow in question.

"Three years ago." He cocked his head to one side, clearly challenging her to acknowledge him.

She held her ground.

"The *Ottobrate Ballo* in Rome," he continued, eyes mocking. "I asked you to dance."

He'd done a lot more than ask. He'd nearly derailed her career in under five minutes.

Rome had been one of her first official assignments as her grandfather's executive assistant. Becoming his official E.A. had been a big step for her, and she'd been nervous all night, anxious to do well.

Alec's smile widened as he watched her expression. "It's etched very firmly in *my* mind," he told her.

"I don't—"

"Sure you do," he countered softly, and they both knew he was right. "And you liked it."

Too true.

"But then Ambassador Cassettes stepped in."

Thank goodness for her grandfather.

"Charlotte?" Alec prompted.

She pretended she'd only just remembered. "You tried to give me your room key," she accused with a stern frown.

"And you took it."

"I didn't know what it was." She'd been twenty-two years old, a neophyte on the diplomatic circuit, and he'd been right there, poised to take advantage of her.

He chuckled his disbelief, and she glared at him.

Then he sobered. "You were beautiful that night." His gaze went soft as he gave her figure a slow once-over.

She couldn't keep the outrage from her tone. "I was twenty-two that night."

His shoulders went up in a careless shrug. "You didn't have to take the key."

"I was confused." It truly had taken her a moment to realize the card he'd handed her was a hotel room key.

"I think you were tempted."

Her brain warned her mouth to shut up. But her emotions overrode the instruction. "I'd known you for two minutes." Other women might be tempted by a dashing, urbane aristocrat with money to burn, but Charlotte wasn't interested in a fling.

"I'd been watching you for a lot longer than two minutes."

His words caused her thoughts to stumble. He'd

been watching her? In a complimentary way, or in a creepy, stalker sort of way?

He moved subtly closer. "You were attractive. You seemed interesting and intelligent, and by the way you were making all those other men laugh, I knew you had a sense of humor."

"Giving me your room key was supposed to be funny?"

His brown eyes turned to molten chocolate. "Not at all. The ball was ending. I wanted to get to know you better."

Charlotte couldn't believe his gall. Aside from being young and naive, she'd been on official business that night, and she'd never dishonor her grandfather nor the ambassador's office by leaving the party with a strange man, particularly a man with Alec Montcalm's reputation. He was still one of France's most notorious bachelors. His dates were lucky to stay out of the tabloids.

"It didn't occur to you to ask me for coffee?" she asked tartly.

"I'm not a patient man." He paused, and she checked an impulse to gaze into his dark eyes, or to contemplate that rakish slash of a mouth, or the tilt of his square chin. Which left her his nose—straight, aristocratic, slightly flared, as if he was drinking in her scent.

He continued speaking. "The direct approach is sometimes the most effective."

"You're telling me that room-key thing works?" She couldn't really be surprised. There had to be plenty of women who'd give their eye teeth to hop into Alec Montcalm's bed. Charlotte simply wasn't one of them. And she never would be.

His quirk of a smile confirmed her suspicions. But then he seemed to tire of the game. He straightened, his expression turning more businesslike. "In my sister's absence, is there anything I can do for you, Ms. Hudson?"

Charlotte instantly remembered her mission. She also realized she'd made a colossal error by arguing with him. She forced herself to calm down, to step back from the web of emotions he seemed to evoke, and to focus on the reason she'd come.

"When is Raine expected back?" she tried.

"Tuesday morning. She was called to a photo shoot on Malta for *Intérêt.*"

Charlotte knew *Intérêt* was the Montcalm Corporation's fashion magazine, and Raine was editor-in-chief. Tuesday morning wasn't going to do it. Jack needed to know this weekend if he could send the film's location manager to Château Montcalm. Principal photography was set to start at the end of the summer, and they were already behind schedule.

Charlotte supposed she could fly to Malta and talk to Raine there. But she knew the magazine wouldn't call out the editor-in-chief unless there was a problem. The last thing she wanted to do was catch Raine at a stressful time. It wouldn't help her cause, and it wouldn't be fair to Raine.

That left Alec. She had *so* hoped to avoid asking him directly. But she wasn't in a position to be choosy.

She took a bracing breath. "There's something I'd like to discuss with you."

Alec's eyes instantly twinkled, and an anticipatory smile transformed his slash of a mouth.

Charlotte battled a spontaneous sexual reaction.

There was a reason women from Milan and Prague accepted his room key on the dance floor. The man was sexy as sin.

"Entrer," he offered, gesturing with his arm and making a small space between his body and the door for her to enter the foyer.

She hesitated, then took the invitation, brushing past him, a tingle invading her shoulder where it contacted his chest.

"Dinner is casual tonight," he told her. *"La pissaladière.* And I'll bring up a bottle of 1996 Montcalm *Maison Inouï* from the cellar."

"It's not that kind of a discussion," she warned, turning back to face him. Bringing out the big guns from his family's winery wasn't going to make her fall into his bed.

"You're in Provence," he countered smoothly, closing the door. "Everything is that kind of a discussion."

She blinked to adjust her eyes to the interior light. "This is business."

"I understand." But his expression didn't change. *"Do* you?"

"Absolument."

She didn't believe him for a second. But she had no choice but to stay for dinner. Jack needed the location. She needed the credibility with the Hudson family. And she wasn't about to blow this chance.

Alec had been handed a second chance.

Three long years later, the sexy woman he'd admired across the dance floor was in his kitchen, looking sexier than ever. If he'd known Raine's friend Charlotte and his *Ottobrate Ballo* Charlotte were one and the same, he'd have made this happen a whole lot sooner. But patience was good. Anticipation was good.

And now, gazing at her crystal-clear blue eyes, her dark lashes, her full lips and porcelain-smooth skin, he was glad he'd waited. Her neck was long and graceful, decorated with a delicate, moon-shaped diamond and gold pendant that telegraphed taste rather than extravagance. The suit's skirt fit her like a glove, emphasizing the curve of her waist, the flare of her hips and her long, sleek, toned legs that ended in a pair of sexy heels.

On the butcher-block island in the terra-cotta tiled kitchen, he popped the cork on the *Maison Inouï*. It was his family's signature label, their finest vintage, bottles he saved for very special occasions.

He reached up to the hanging rack, sliding off a pair of crystal red-wine goblets.

Having initially gazed around with interest, Charlotte was now standing uncertainly at the center of the large room.

He nodded to one of the low-backed bar stools on the opposite side of the island. "Hop up."

She hesitated for a split second, but then slipped gracefully into the leather-upholstered seat, setting her small clutch bag on the lip of the counter.

"Thank you," she said primly as he placed one of the glasses of wine in front of her.

Alec remembered that intriguing expression, the shield of formality, covering what he was certain was a fiery rebel, chafing beneath the bounds of propriety. He'd tried to test the theory in Rome, but her grandfather, the watchful ambassador, had stopped him cold.

Back then, he'd shrugged the disappointment off

philosophically. Women came; women went. Sometimes it worked out. Sometimes it didn't.

He lifted his wineglass, swirling the small measure of wine, taking an experimental sip and letting the deep, sweet, woodsy flavor of the wine glide over his tongue.

Sometimes a man got another chance.

The wine was perfect, so he filled their glasses.

Charlotte tasted hers, and her eyes went wide with the experience. "Nice," she admitted with respect.

"From our vineyard in Bordeaux."

"I'm impressed."

He smiled in satisfaction at her reaction.

"Not *that* impressed," she drawled.

"That was pride of craftsmanship," he told her.

"My mistake." But her sea-foam eyes told him she knew it was lust.

Of course it was. But not a problem. He'd back off and let her relax.

"*La pissaladière,*" he decreed, retrieving a steel mixing bowl from beneath the countertop. He then assembled flour, yeast, sugar and olive oil.

She watched wordlessly for a few moments. "You can cook?"

"*Oui.* Of course." He sprinkled sugar into the bottom of the bowl, adding the yeast and a measure of water. French children learned to bake almost before they learned to walk.

"You do your own cooking?" she pressed in obvious surprise.

"Sometimes." He nodded to her wineglass. "Enjoy. Relax. Tell me what you wanted to talk about."

The invitation seemed to sober her, and she took a slow sip of the wine.

Stalling.

Interesting.

"That is one exceedingly fine wine," she commented.

"I applaud your good taste, *mademoiselle*," he told her honestly. Then he retrieved a heavy skillet and drizzled olive oil into the bottom.

"You've lived here a long time?" she asked. Her gaze was on her wineglass as she rubbed her thumb and forefinger over the stem.

He watched the motion for a moment. "I was born here."

"In Provence or in the château?"

"In the hospital in Castres."

"Oh." She nodded then turned silent.

"Is that what you wanted to ask me?"

"Not exactly." Her white teeth came down on her bottom lip. "My family in America…the Hudsons. They make movies."

"You don't say," he drawled. A person would have to be dead not to know of Hudson Pictures. Their awards were numerous, their reputation stellar and they'd launched the careers of half the Hollywood elite.

"I wasn't sure you knew," she defended. "They're successful in America, but—"

"You're far too modest."

"It's not like I had anything to do with it." She flicked back her hair, gaze still focused on the burgundy wine. "They're filming a new movie."

"Just one?"

That made her look up. "A special one."

"I see."

"I don't…." She glanced around the spacious kitchen.

Alec set down his chopping knife. "Is it getting any easier with these delay tactics?"

"I'm not—" Then she caught his eyes and sighed. "I really was hoping you'd be Raine."

"Sorry."

"Not as sorry as I am." Then she gave her head a little shake. "I didn't mean that the way it sounded."

If she didn't look so serious, he might have laughed. "Is it some kind of women's thing?"

"No."

"Boyfriend break up with you?" That wouldn't be such a bad thing. She could stay here while she got over the guy. And Alec would be on hand to lend a sympathetic ear, or shoulder, or anything else that was required.

"No," she said. "It's not that."

Too bad. "Am I likely to guess?"

She fought a half smile and shook her head.

He picked up the knife, bringing it down to chop off the stem of an onion. "Then shall we get on with it?"

"You're not making this easy."

He chopped again. "Well, it's not from the lack of trying."

Her lips compressed, then her shoulders drooped. "Okay, now there's been too much buildup."

He rinsed his hands in the small square sink in the middle of the island. *"You,"* he enunciated, "are impossible."

"Fine." She braced her hands on the countertop. "Here goes. The Hudsons would like to use your château as a movie set." She clamped her jaw and waited for his reaction.

Alec stilled.

Was she joking?

Was she crazy?

He'd spent years avoiding the press—years of fighting tooth and nail for a scrap of privacy. To invite a movie crew, cameras, actors, an entire Hollywood cartel into his home for weeks on end?

He gathered the thinly sliced onions onto the knife edge, then dumped them all at once in the hot olive oil. They hissed and sizzled, steam rising to the ceiling.

"No," he said, with absolute finality. There was not a chance in hell.

Okay, Charlotte had expected resistance. Alec wasn't going to say yes immediately. Who would? It was an inconvenience and a disruption in his life. She understood that.

"It's my grandparents' love story," she put in, trying to stress the significance of the film. "They met during the war. In occupied France."

Alec didn't say a word.

"All of Hudson Pictures' resources will be behind it." The quality would be unparalleled.

He lifted a spatula and stirred the sizzling onions.

"My grandmother was a cabaret performer, and they were secretly married under the noses of the Germans."

Alec looked up. "And this makes a difference how?"

"Cece Cassidy is attached to the project. It's sure to be a contender for best writer—"

"Like the screenwriter's the problem."

"Is it about money?" she probed. "They'd absolutely compensate you for the inconvenience. And they'd leave everything exactly as they found it. You wouldn't—"

"It's about my home not being a movie set."

"They wouldn't need your entire home." Charlotte

searched her brain for more ammunition. "You'd be able to stay in residence. Jack sent me a script breakdown. They'd need the kitchen, the great room, one of the libraries and a couple of bedrooms. Oh, and the grounds of course. They'd need the grounds. Maybe your back deck for one scene."

"And that's *all?*" Alec drawled, his sarcastic tone playing havoc with her confidence.

"I'm fairly sure that's all." She kept her voice even.

"They wouldn't need access to my private study? Or my bathroom?" he continued, voice going up. "Or maybe they'd like to take a peek inside—"

"You could designate some areas off-limits," she rushed in. "And you could even stay at one of your other houses during filming."

His eyes darkened, and he brandished the spatula like a weapon. "And give a pack of Hollywood hooligans free rein over my home?"

"It's not like they're some biker gang." Sure, some stars had a reputation for bad behavior, but the Hudson Pictures producers were very professional. And Raine was a friend. Charlotte wouldn't fill her house with a bunch of wild partiers.

"I never said they were."

"Then what is it?"

"Do you have *any* idea how hard I have to fight for privacy?"

"Well, maybe if you didn't—" She stopped herself.

"Yes?" he prompted, cocking his dark head to one side.

"Nothing." She shook her head. This was turning into enough of a disaster without her insulting him.

"I must insist," he said, seeming to grow even taller.

"We could cover any privacy concerns in the contract." She attempted to distract him. "You'd really have nothing to worry—"

"I'll decide what I worry about. Now what were you about to say?"

She gazed into his probing eyes. "I forgot."

He waited.

Her brain scrambled, but she couldn't for the life of her come up with a good lie.

Oh, hell. She might as well go for it. The battle was all but over, anyway. "Maybe if you didn't make yourself such an attractive target for the paparazzi."

He paused. "You're suggesting it's *my* fault?"

"You don't have to escort supermodels to every A-list party in Europe."

His brown eyes darkened to ebony. "You think a plain Jane on my arm would stop the gossip? You think a woman who didn't fit their mold would do *anything* but guarantee me the front page?"

Charlotte quickly realized he had a point. Being seen with anybody out of type would cause even more speculation. But he'd missed her point entirely. "You could skip the parties."

"I don't attend that many parties."

Charlotte scoffed out a laugh of disbelief.

He frowned at her. "How many did *you* attend last month? Last week? Lost count?"

In fact, she had. "That's different," she pointed out primly. "I was on business."

He gave the onions another stir and reduced the heat. "What is it you think I do at parties?"

He washed his hands while she thought about that. Then he retrieved a mesh bag of ripe tomatoes.

She tried to figure out if it was a trick question. "Dance with supermodels?" She stated the obvious.

"I make business contacts."

"With supermodels?"

He sliced through a tomato. "Would you rather I went stag? Danced with other men's dates?"

Charlotte wriggled forward on the high seat. "You're trying to tell me you *suffer* the attentions of supermodels in order to make business contacts?"

"I'm trying to tell you I like my privacy, and you shouldn't make assumptions about other people's lifestyles."

"Alec, you hand out hotel room keys on the dance floor." She knew from firsthand experience. He'd tried it with her.

His knife stilled.

She sat back, not even attempting to mask her satisfaction. "You are so busted."

"Really?" He resumed slicing. "Well, you are *so* not making a movie in my château."

Two

Round one had gone to Alec, and Charlotte had no choice but to back off and regroup as they moved to the veranda for dinner. The sizzling *pissaladière* was now on a round glass table between them.

Flickering light from the garden torches highlighted the planes and angles of his face, while the freshening breeze picked up the scents of lavender and thyme. He seemed relaxed enough. While the *pissaladière* had baked, their conversation had ranged from vacation spots to impressionist painters to the monetary policy of the European Union.

But now, it was time for round two.

"You could hide anything personal," she opened conversationally, transferring a slice of the delicate tomato pie to her plate. "You could stay out of sight. I doubt any of the crew would even know it was your château."

"Please," he drawled, lifting the silver serving spoon from her hand. "There's a big sign over the gate that says Château Montcalm."

"Take it down."

"My name is etched into five-hundred-year-old stone."

Right. "Surely you're not the only Montcalm in Provence."

"I'm the only one who makes the front page." He settled on two slices of the pie.

"I think you're overestimating your fame."

"I think you're overestimating your powers of persuasion."

"More wine?" she asked, topping off his glass while treating him to the brilliant smile her grandfather's image consultant had insisted she learn for photographs.

He watched the burgundy liquid rise in his crystal goblet. "It won't work, Charlotte."

She finished topping his glass. "What won't work?"

"I was weaned on *Maison Inouï*."

She feigned innocence. "You think I'm trying to get you drunk?"

"I think you're entirely too fixated on my château." He moved the bottle to one side so that his view of her was unobstructed. "What gives? There are plenty of other châteaus."

She tried to stay businesslike. But his mocha eyes glowed under the soft torchlight, making it look like he somehow cared.

"It's perfect for the story," she told him honestly, gazing around the estate. "The family thinks—"

"You're not even involved in the business."

Charlotte squared her shoulders. "I am a Hudson." She found herself battling a stupid but familiar sense of loneliness. Her Cassettes grandparents had given her a wonderful life, a dream life. If her heart had ached for her brother, Jack, in the dead of night, it was only because she'd been so young when they were separated.

"Charlotte?"

She blinked at Alec.

"There are many châteaus in Provence."

"He...*they* want this one."

"He?"

"The producers." She was doing this for the good of the film, not specifically for Jack.

"Something going on between you and the producers?"

"*No.*"

Alec gazed at her in silence. The wind kicked up a notch, and the stems of lavender rustled below them in the country garden.

"What?" she finally asked, battling an urge to squirm.

He lifted his wineglass. "You want it too bad."

She huffed out a breath. "I don't see why this has to be such a big thing. What do you want? What can we do? How can we persuade you to give up your precious privacy for six weeks?"

He sipped the wine, watching her intently. Then he set down the glass, running his thumb along the length of the stem.

"There is one thing I want." His molten eyes told her exactly what that one thing was.

"I am not sleeping with you to get a film location."

Alec tipped back his head and laughed.

Charlotte squirmed. Had she completely misread his signals? Made a colossal fool of herself?

No. She couldn't have been that far wrong. The man had once tried to give her his hotel room key.

"I'm not asking to sleep with you, Charlotte."

She took an unladylike swig of her own wine, struggling desperately not to blush in humiliation. "Well. Good. That's good."

He grinned. "Although, I definitely wouldn't say no if you—"

"Shut up."

He clamped his jaw.

She waited as long as she could stand.

"Fine. What is it—"

"Charlotte!" came Raine's delighted voice. She rushed through an open set of French doors, dropping her purse and a briefcase on a lounger. "Why didn't you *tell* me you were coming?"

She wore a slim, tailored black dress and charcoal stockings, and her high-heeled shoes clattered on the stone deck. Her dark hair was cut in a chic bob, and her bright red mouth was sliced in a smile of delight.

"The trip came up suddenly," said Charlotte, coming to her feet, as did Alec beside her. "But I thought you were away until Tuesday." She cursed her stupidity at rushing the conversation with Alec. If only she'd waited a few hours!

"I talked to Henri. He told me you were here." There was a clear admonishment in the tone.

But then they embraced in a tight hug, Raine laughing with delight in Charlotte's ear.

When they finally separated, Alec broke in. "*Bonsoir, ma soeur.*"

Raine glanced over, feigning surprise. "Alec? I didn't see you there."

He shook his head and held out his arms.

She walked into a warm hug and an affectionate kiss for each cheek.

Watching them, regret twitched reflexively inside Charlotte. She glanced away, wishing she could have such an easy relationship with Jack.

"So," said Raine as she settled into the third chair. "What are we eating?" She sniffed at the *pissaladière*. Then she lifted the wine bottle, brows arching at the label. *"Très bon."*

"I know how to be a good host, even if you don't," said Alec.

"I didn't even know she was coming." Raine tipped the bottle up, and up. "It's empty."

Alec reached behind him, exchanging it for a full one while Raine helped herself to a slice of the pie.

"What are we talking about?" she asked, glancing from one to the other.

Alec deftly drilled into the wine cork. "Charlotte wants to use the château as a movie set."

Charlotte cringed at the bald statement.

But Raine looked intrigued. "Really?"

Charlotte nodded.

"That's *fantastic*."

"I didn't say yes," Alec warned.

"Why on earth not?" asked Raine.

He popped the cork. "Because you interrupted us."

"But you were about to," she prompted.

"I was about to suggest a compromise."

Charlotte reminded herself it wasn't sex. Though there was still a nervous churning in her stomach.

What would Alec want? More important, what was she willing to give?

Not sex. No. Of course not. Still…

He continued speaking, and she forced herself to pay attention to the words. "I was going to say yes—"

Raine clapped her hands together in delight.

"Provided," Alec put in firmly, and Charlotte listened closely. "Provided we have an understanding that the third floor is off-limits. As is the south gallery."

"Done," Charlotte quickly answered, sticking out her hand to shake.

"Nobody goes in the rose garden." He didn't shake her hand.

She nodded vigorously. Easy. Piece of cake. According to Jack, landowners always had a list of stipulations.

"Or any of the outbuildings. Shooting stops by ten every night. My staff are *not* part of the production crew. And you stay in residence to make sure it goes smoothly."

"Abso—" Charlotte snapped her jaw shut, dropping her hand to the table. *"What?"*

"I don't want any extra work for my staff," he repeated.

"Not *that* part."

"It's perfect," Raine sang, grasping Charlotte's forearm in a friendly squeeze. "We can hang out, visit. It'll be like we're back in college."

"I can't move in," Charlotte protested. "I have a job back in Monte Allegro. My grandfather needs me. There's a summit in Athens on the twenty-fifth."

Alec pinned her with a look. "So you're willing to inconvenience *me,* but not yourself?"

"I'm not…" She gazed into his mocking eyes.

He raised a brow.

Instinct told her to grab the yes before he could change his mind. But here? With Alec? For weeks on end?

She thought back to the hotel room key, and to the way her stomach had quivered in daring anticipation for the split second when she'd thought about accepting it. She was older now, wiser, and she knew full well the importance of leading a perfectly circumspect life—one that didn't include a stint on the front page of the tabloids.

But the quiver was still there. And she knew that he knew. She could fight it all she wanted, intellectualize it all she wanted, but the bald truth was that she was attracted to the man. She and several thousand other women fantasized about a night in Alec Montcalm's bed. And Alec would take advantage of that in any way he could.

But then she pictured Jack's joy, her pride when she told him she'd succeeded. She thought about her grandmother and the whole Hudson clan. For once, she'd be part of the team.

"I'll stay," she told Alec.

Raine squealed in delight.

Alec reached for his wineglass, raising it in a mock toast while his dark, molten eyes told her the chase was on.

"They will *hound* you," said Kiefer, as he geared his mountain bike down for the incline.

"She's a friend of Raine's," Alec defended, following suit, putting more power to his pedals.

They were on a dirt road that wound along the ridgeline above the Montcalm estate. The tires bumped beneath Alec, and sweat began to form at his hairline as the sun cleared the eastern horizon, lighting up the river and the patchwork of fields and woods below.

"So?" Kiefer demanded. "It's a Hollywood movie. There'll be press all over it. You know how the Japanese are going to react—"

"It's under control," Alec cut in, even though the venture wasn't anywhere near under control. He was attracted to Charlotte, and he'd let that attraction overrule his logic. Filming a movie in his living room? Kiefer, his vice president, was right to be ticked off. They'd met with a high-priced image consultant only last week, and Alec had agreed to try to be more circumspect in his personal life.

"Kana Hanako wants a business partner, not a playboy."

"It's a business deal," said Alec, taking a swig from his water bottle, refusing to acknowledge Kiefer's point. "They're renting the château."

"Who's the star?"

"Ridley Sinclair."

Kiefer snorted. "You know what I mean."

"Isabella Hudson. I've never even met her."

Kiefer gaped at him. "*The* Isabella Hudson?"

Like there would be another. "She is a member of the family."

"You're going to have Isabella Hudson staying at the Château Montcalm. Good God, Alec, why not just go ahead and murder someone? Even the Japanese tabloids will pick up you and Isabella Hudson."

"I'm not going near Isabella Hudson. There'll be no pictures, nothing whatsoever for them to report."

But Kiefer wasn't listening. He was inside his own

head, obviously dreaming up one dire scenario after another. "You're going to have to move out."

"No," said Alec.

"Go stay in Rome. Better still, go to Tokyo and work with Akiko on the prototype."

"They don't need me in the bike lab." If the one he was riding was anything to go on, R & D had made great strides with the frame alloy.

"Well, I need you out of Provence."

They crested the hill, and Alec grabbed a higher gear, putting his frustration into muscle power that produced speed. Let a film crew invade his house yet *miss* his chance with Charlotte? No way.

"I am staying in my home," he told Kiefer, bending his head into the wind.

"We need a mitigation strategy," Kiefer called, falling slightly behind.

"Mitigate this!" Alec sent back a rude hand gesture.

"Don't let the press catch you doing that." Kiefer caught up. "Could you maybe get married?" he huffed.

Alec rolled his eyes. He'd yet to meet a woman who wasn't after his money or his status—usually both.

"At least find a girlfriend? Not forever, just while Isabella is there. Somebody who's a nobody, a plain Jane who won't get you into any trouble."

Alec didn't want a plain Jane nobody. And he had zero interest in Isabella Hudson. He wanted Charlotte.

And then he realized he'd missed his big chance. "Damn," he spat out.

"What?" Kiefer glanced from side to side.

He could have made that a condition of the movie location deal. What was he thinking? Charlotte could have played his girlfriend for a couple of months.

"What?" Kiefer repeated.

But it was too late now. She didn't strike him as the kind of person who would renegotiate.

"I almost had a girl we could bribe," Alec admitted.

"Who?"

Alec shook his head. "We missed the boat on that one."

"Who is she?"

"Nobody."

"Perfect," said Kiefer with enthusiasm.

"I lost my leverage." Alec slowed his bike, taking a right-hand turn into the pullout beside Crystal Lake.

"Well, what was your leverage?" Kiefer's voice was eager.

"Oh, no, you don't." Alec braked to a halt and put his feet down, taking in the view of the lake while they took a breather.

"Oh, no, I don't what?"

"She's smart, tough and unreasonable."

"At least give me a shot." Kiefer squirted a stream of water into his open mouth.

"There's no real problem," said Alec. "The Kana Hanako brass aren't going to give up my Tour de France connection, no matter what the tabloids write."

"Yeah, but they can make my life hell in the meantime. Do you know how much time I waste being yelled at by Takahiro's translator?"

"Do you know how much I pay you to get yelled at by Takahiro's translator?"

"Not nearly enough," Kiefer grumbled. Then he recapped his water bottle and ran spread fingers through his short hair. "Who were you talking about?"

Alec shook his head.

"I swear I won't even talk to her."

Alec paused. "Charlotte Hudson. She's the friend of Raine's."

"Ah." Kiefer instantly caught on. "You could have bribed her with access to the château."

Alec nodded.

"She's not Isabella's sister or something?"

"Maybe a cousin. I'm not sure. Raine says Charlotte grew up with her maternal grandparents, mostly in Europe. Her grandfather's the U.S. ambassador to Monte Allegro. She works for him."

"Sounds tame enough," Kiefer mused.

"The plan's off the table. I had a hard enough time getting her to stay at the château for the shoot."

Kiefer came alert. "She's staying at the château?"

"Don't touch it." Alec's tone was flat.

"I'm just sayin'—"

"You are *not* leaking her to the press."

"Well, somebody's going to 'leak' something. Better it's her than Isabella."

"In whose opinion?"

"Mine."

"You don't count. You're the hired help." Alec snapped one foot back onto the pedal and pushed off.

Kiefer quickly followed suit. "Will you at least ask her?"

"I will not."

"If she says no, she says no. But she might—"

"She'll never agree."

"How do you know?"

Alec pulled onto the rough road for the return trip. "It's like this," he explained with exaggerated patience. "You're executive assistant to an ambassador. You like your job. In fact, the ambassador is your own grand-father. A man with a public reputation like mine asks you to pretend to date him in order to protect his reputation. You say…what, exactly?"

"Point taken," Kiefer admitted.

They rode in silence to the crest of the hill, where Alec's thoughts turned to the croissants his cook had been putting in the oven when they left the château.

"Still," Kiefer continued, as their speed picked up and the morning air whipped past, "the worst she can do is say no."

"No, no, no," Charlotte emphasized into the cordless telephone. "You *can't* put Syria next to Bulgaria. Put them next to Canada, or the Swiss—"

The telephone handset was summarily tugged out of Charlotte's hand.

"Hey!" She twisted her head to Raine, who was lying back in the next deck lounger.

"Charlotte has to go now, Emily," Raine said into the handset. "She's in the middle of a pedicure."

"You can't do that," Charlotte protested.

But Raine calmly hit the off button.

"You need to hold still," warned the esthetician working on Charlotte's toes. "Or you'll have purple passion streaked halfway to your ankle."

"You listen to her." Raine gestured with the phone.

"You hung up on Emily."

"You've been on the phone with her for half an hour."

"It's the summit dinner. She was about to put Syria next to Bulgaria."

"Will it cause a war?"

"Maybe," said Charlotte, glancing down at her toes.

The purple passion sparkled in the sunshine. She'd borrowed a sea-blue two-piece bathing suit from Raine, and they were lounging on thickly padded lounge chairs next to the Montcalm pool. An emerald lawn stretched out in front of them, while lush cypress trees and flowering shrubs screened them from the house, offering dappled shade.

"They're cultural attachés," Raine pointed out. "I doubt they have the launch codes."

"Maybe not. But I can't just walk away from my responsibilities on a moment's notice." Charlotte had spoken with her grandfather this morning, and he'd been more than gracious in giving her the time off, telling her not to worry. But there were about a thousand details she had to make sure were passed on to other staff members.

"I did," said Raine. "When I heard you were here, I walked right off the shoot in Malta and onto the corporate jet."

"Is that a problem?" Charlotte quickly asked.

"I guess we'll find out when the October issue hits the stands, won't we?"

"No, seriously—"

"The magazine will survive, and so will the ambassador. You need to relax."

"You should not move for at least half an hour," Charlotte's esthetician advised, admiring Charlotte's toes as she rose from her chair.

"Thank you," said Charlotte, raising her newly polished fingernails and fluttering them to compare to her matching toes.

Raine's esthetician finished a final topcoat, and the two women began to pack their things.

Charlotte leaned over to whisper to Raine. "Do we tip or something?"

"All taken care of," Raine whispered back. "Shall I ring for strawberries and champagne?"

"It's still morning."

"You're on vacation. And you're in Provence." Raine grinned and hit a speed-dial button on the phone.

"At this rate, I may never leave," Charlotte muttered, sighing and relaxing back into the soft lounger.

While Raine talked to the kitchen, Charlotte closed her eyes, letting the soft breeze caress her face and listening to the gentle hum of the cicadas fill in the background.

"Quick!" Raine's elbow jolted Charlotte back to reality. "Take a look."

Charlotte blinked against the bright sunshine, scanning the lawn beyond the pool and coming to two male figures.

Alec. And he was dressed in bicycle shorts and a spandex shirt that clung to every sculpted muscle.

"Isn't he the hottest thing you've ever seen?" asked Raine.

He was, but it seemed an odd thing for Raine to notice. "Alec?"

"*Nooo.*" Raine grimaced. "Kiefer. The guy with him."

"Oh." Charlotte hadn't paid the least bit of attention to the slightly shorter man with short, sandy-blond hair striding down the brick pathway next to Alec.

"He's our vice president," Raine elaborated. "The girls in the office go ga-ga over him."

"Sounds like you do, too." Charlotte chuckled, watching the man named Kiefer saunter closer. He was probably six foot two. Though a slighter build than Alec, he was well muscled with an angular face, square jaw and an easy, self-confident stride.

"Don't you dare say a word," Raine warned.

"You don't want to date an employee?" Charlotte asked, her gaze moving involuntarily to Alec. Now *that* was a gorgeous man. Everything about him moved in perfect symmetry.

"I don't want him to think I'm one of his groupies," Raine corrected.

"It's that bad?"

"Just look at him," Raine scoffed.

Charlotte glanced back for a split second. Sure, he was attractive enough. But she wasn't sensing the animal magnetism she saw in Alec. If the girls in the office were going to go ga-ga, she would have thought Alec would be their target.

The two women halted their conversation as the men came within earshot. They stopped in front of the two loungers. Kiefer's gaze swept Charlotte without sparing a single glance for Raine.

"*This* is your plain Jane?" Kiefer asked Alec, astonishment clear in his tone.

Charlotte shot Alec an exaggerated expression of offense. "I'm your *what?*"

Alec's jaw tightened. "Smooth, Kiefer." He drew a breath. "Charlotte, this is my vice president, Kiefer Knight. He's just come up with the most ridiculous idea in the world."

Three

Kiefer pulled a deck chair up next to Charlotte's lounger, angling away from Raine. She could feel Alec's gaze on her honey-brown skin. Maybe a bikini hadn't been such a good idea after all. His attention was raising goose bumps, and she couldn't help imagining his fingers trailing over her stomach, down the length of her legs…

"I'm concerned about Alec's reputation," Kiefer began in a gentle, cajoling voice.

Charlotte forced herself to concentrate on Kiefer's words.

"I understand Isabella Hudson is starring in your movie."

"My family's movie," Charlotte corrected. All she'd done was secure the location. Well, and she was going to babysit the shoot. But that was only because Alec was being obstinate. She really had no role here except pandering to his need for power and control.

"If they're together here, rumors about Alec and Isabella are bound to circulate."

Her gaze shifted to Alec, who still stood indolently at the foot of her lounger, taking in the color of her toenails.

"You're involved with Bella?" she asked him. For some reason, the idea put a cramp in her belly.

"You're botching this," Alec growled at Kiefer.

Kiefer held up his hands in surrender. "Be my guest."

"Kiefer wants you to pretend to be my girlfriend to forestall any gossip about me and Isabella."

Charlotte tried to sort out his words. "You're dating Bella?" Why hadn't Isabella asked for the use of the château? Why had Jack sent Charlotte? And what was Alec doing flirting with *her?*

"I am *not* dating Isabella," he huffed in exasperation.

"But she's high profile," Kiefer put in. "And beautiful. And the press will invent their own headlines."

Charlotte got the picture. They wanted to throw her to the wolves to save Alec's reputation. Like there was any hope for Alec's reputation.

"Is this a joke?" she asked.

"Sadly," said Alec, "Kiefer is completely serious."

"He's been gracious enough to let you use the château," Kiefer put in.

"Here's a thought," suggested Charlotte, an edge to her tone. "Alec can keep his hands off Isabella, and then there'll be no reason for a ruse with 'Plain Jane.'"

"I am not going to have my hands *on* Isabella," Alec practically shouted.

Charlotte barely glanced at him then turned to Kiefer. "Problem solved."

"The tabloids don't rely on the truth," said Kiefer.

"Apparently," Charlotte shot back, "neither do you."

"Has anyone thought about Charlotte's reputation?" asked Raine.

"Charlotte has," said Charlotte.

"He could have made it a condition of the contract," Kiefer pointed out.

"He didn't," Alec said flatly.

Charlotte turned to Alec once more. "Do *you* think it's a good idea?" Not that she'd go along with it in any event. And thank goodness Alec hadn't asked for it before they closed the deal.

"I think it's an idea," he said, obviously choosing his words carefully. "Good? Not sure. But it might deflect speculation."

"Since when have you cared about speculation on your love life?"

Kiefer jumped in again. "Since the president of Kana Hanako, our Japanese partner, expressed concern."

"Something I should know about?" asked Raine, her alert, businesslike tone at odds with her bikini-clad pose on the lounger.

Kiefer's attention went to her for the briefest of seconds, but then he blinked and focused on the small pool house behind her. "It's not that serious."

"Then why are we having this conversation? Charlotte's not going to trash her reputation by being seen with Alec—"

"Hello?" Alec tossed in.

Raine waved a dismissive hand. "You made your bed a long time ago, *mon frère.*"

"Just don't make a bed with Isabella," Charlotte advised.

"I have *no interest* in Isabella." His eyes darkened to walnut, pinning Charlotte in place. "Can I talk to you in private?"

Not when he looked like that. Not when the predatory set of his jaw made her skin tingle and her spine turn to jelly. "I'm letting my toenails dry."

Both Raine and Kiefer stilled, while Alec stared at her in silence. Clearly, people didn't normally turn down Alec's requests.

"Later, then," he finally said with a tense nod, turning on his heel.

Later proved hard to come by for Alec. Raine and Charlotte took a shopping trip into Toulouse. The location manager, set designer and second-unit director all arrived, followed quickly by carpenters, set dressers and lighting technicians.

The main floor of Alec's house quickly turned into a construction zone. There was more than one moment when he contemplated moving out for the duration. But then he'd catch a glimpse of Charlotte.

The more he saw of her, the more determined he was to get to know her better—much, much better.

He finally caught her alone, leaning on the rail of the third-floor hallway, staring down to the rotunda foyer where the grips were setting tracks for a camera.

"*Bonjour*," he opened, resting his forearms on the polished wood, matching her pose.

She glanced over at him, then her gaze darted worriedly from the staircase to the front door and to either side of them.

"No photographers," he assured her.

"I don't trust Kiefer," she responded.

"My apologies," Alec offered. "I shouldn't have let him make that request."

"That I fake being your girlfriend?" she clarified.

Alec nodded. Though his only true regret was that she'd said no. It would have given him a perfect excuse to spend time with her. It was also regrettable that the experience had left her suspicious and jumpy. "I promise he won't jump out of the bushes with a camera."

"How do I know I can trust you?"

A piece of equipment crashed in the foyer below. The noise was followed by an exchange of shouts.

"How do I know you won't destroy my home?" Alec countered. "I guess we're both taking a leap of faith."

She turned her head to gaze at him, and he was struck once again by her beauty. Her crystal-blue eyes sparkled in the sunshine that streamed through the stained-glass dome ceiling. Her lips were deep red as they curved up in a wry smile. And her cheeks were rosy highlights to her creamy skin.

"You can rebuild the château," she told him.

"That's three-hundred-year-old limestone on the floor."

Her glance was drawn downward. "So, it must be pretty much indestructible," she offered in a perky voice.

Alec couldn't help but chuckle. "I'm not going to harm your reputation," he promised.

She gave a small nod. "Thank you."

But then a camera flash went off below, and Alec quickly grasped her hand, tugging her through the open door behind them and swiftly closing it against the world.

"Reference shots for the crew back home," she explained, a grin growing on her face. "But thanks for the effort."

"I didn't want to break my word within the first two minutes."

Their hands were still joined as they stood next to the arched, oak-plank door of the third-floor library. Shelves were lined with leather volumes and heavy, green-velvet drapes were pulled aside with gold cording, letting a beam of morning sunshine stream through paned windows. The room was slightly dusky, cool, quiet and still.

Her small hand was soft under his, the skin of her palm warm, hinting at the texture of other regions of her body. He inhaled the clean floral scent of her shampoo. It reminded him of the lavender plants blowing softly in his country garden.

Everything about Charlotte was sweet and fresh, from her white flash of a smile, to the breezy, shoulder-length style of her blond hair. Her figure was lithe and streamlined. He'd watched her play tennis with Raine yesterday, and he knew she was in fabulous shape.

His thoughts trailed back to the way she'd looked by the pool. The aqua bikini had revealed a light, glowing tan. Her belly was flat, with the sexiest navel he'd ever seen. Her shoulders were kissable, and the curve of her breasts had invaded his dreams every night since.

"Alec?" Her voice was soft, in keeping with the atmosphere of the room.

He tugged gently on her hand, drawing her toward him. His gaze fixed on her full lips. "Tell me you haven't been curious," he whispered.

"I—" But then she stopped, her gaze fixed on his lips, apparently unable to lie but unwilling to be honest.

He smiled. "Me, too."

"We can't do this," she warned.

"We're not *doing* anything."

"Oh, yes, we are."

He tugged her closer still, so that she brushed up against him. "At the moment, we're merely talking."

"We're talking about kissing."

"Nothing wrong with kissing."

"You got a camera in your pocket?"

"That's not a camera."

She scrunched her eyes shut. "I can't believe you said that."

"I can't believe it shocked you." He chuckled low. "You're blushing." For some reason, he found her reaction completely endearing.

"I'm embarrassed because the joke was so bad."

"You're embarrassed because you're attracted to me and, for some reason, you think you should fight it."

"Of course I should fight it."

"Why?"

"You're a playboy and a philanderer."

"You say that like it's a bad thing."

"You'll destroy my reputation."

"By kissing you in private? I'm flattered you think I have that kind of power." He drew a breath and held her with a frank gaze. "Charlotte, kiss me, don't kiss me. But at least be honest. Your reputation is in absolutely no danger at the moment."

Her shoulders dropped. "You're right," she admitted.

But she didn't make a move.

It was more than tempting to wrap his arms around her, dip his head and take her lips to his. But he held back. She was still jumpy, and the last thing he wanted to do was scare her off.

He wanted this kiss. Of course, he wanted more than just a kiss, but at least a kiss was heading in the right direction.

To his surprise, she placed a hand on his shoulder.

"It's mere curiosity," she warned.

A half smile crept out. "But of course."

She pulled up on her toes. "I might not even like it."

"You might not," he agreed, holding himself still by sheer force of will.

This time, it was Charlotte who smiled. "Do many women not like kissing you?"

"I can't recall any specific complaints. But I've sure never had one give it this much thought before-hand."

"I'm a planner."

"Evidently."

They both sobered, staring at each other in silence.

"Oh, man." Charlotte moaned a surrender, closing her eyes and stretching up toward him.

It was all the invitation Alec needed.

He immediately leaned in, parting his lips, pressing them to her heated mouth.

An explosion went off at the base of his brain, obliterating everything but the taste, scent and feel of Charlotte. He deepened the kiss, flattening her against the oak door, pressing his body flush against hers.

His hands cupped her face, caressing her skin while holding her in place as his tongue plundered shamelessly. She moaned, opened her mouth wider, and her arms wrapped around his waist. He pushed his thigh between her legs, lifting, bunching her short skirt, the fabric of his slacks meeting the satin of her panties.

His body flushed hot, tense, rigid with desire, and

a freight train roared in his ears and the world contracted to the two of them.

"Charlotte?" came a faraway voice.

Raine.

Charlotte tensed, and Alec groaned, reluctantly taking his mouth from hers. He eased back, knowing they might have only seconds before Raine tried the door.

"Charlotte?" Raine repeated.

"Let go," Charlotte whispered.

Alec took a step back, rasping deep breaths, trying vainly to put his raging hormones back under control.

"You okay?" he asked.

"Fine," Charlotte shot back, smoothing her pleated, navy skirt and straightening the white, sleeveless blouse.

He reached out to fix her mussed hair, and she drew in a sharp breath. There was nothing he could do about the just-kissed puffiness of her mouth—except try like hell not to get turned on by it.

The doorknob rattled, and Charlotte jumped back. "Why are we in here?" she frantically whispered.

Alec drew open the door. "Raine?" He gazed at the quizzical expression on his sister's face. "I'm glad it's you," he continued. "There was a photographer downstairs, and Charlotte got a little freaked out." He gave Charlotte a teasing wink. "I told her there was nothing to worry about. Did you see anyone skulking around with a camera?"

Rained glanced at Charlotte, then back to Alec. "No."

"Good," he said heartily. "I'll be in my office. Kiefer should be here in an hour or so. If you see him, could you have Henri send him straight up?"

With Raine suitably distracted by erroneous details,

and having given Charlotte at least a couple of minutes to recover, Alec exited the room.

Then, three steps down the hallway, he put a hand against the wall to steady himself. It was a kiss, he reminded himself, a simple kiss.

Except that it hadn't been simple. It had blown his expectations right out of the water. If he'd been attracted to Charlotte before, he was nearly wild for her now. The chemistry between them was nothing short of mind-blowing, and he wasn't going to be able to focus on Kana Hanako or anything else until he investigated it further.

"I don't blame you for being paranoid," said Raine, as Alec left the library.

"Hmm?" Charlotte stalled, not yet capable of producing actual words. Her skin was tingling, her heart was thumping and her knees felt as if they'd been turned to gelatin.

"Kiefer can be devious."

"Right." Charlotte nodded, telling herself to snap out of it. The kiss had been good—well, great, actually. But she'd expected it to be great. If she hadn't, she wouldn't have bothered kissing Alec, would she? What woman would embark on a kiss she thought would be boring?

"One picture of you and Alec, doing something as innocent as having a conversation, and Kiefer gets his nefarious wish. You want me to talk to him?" Raine paused. "Charlotte?"

"What?"

"You want me to talk to Kiefer? Or maybe you should steer clear of Alec. Just to be on the safe side."

Charlotte drew a deep breath and gave herself a

mental shake. "Yeah. Good idea." Steering clear of Alec was better than the alternative—hauling him into the nearest bed and kissing him until her brain exploded.

"Mademoiselle Charlotte?" came a new voice from the hallway. Henri.

Raine turned to meet him. "*Oui,* Henri?"

"A Jack Hudson has arrived."

"Jack's here?" The words jumped from Charlotte as a familiar little knot grew in her stomach. She loved her big brother. But their relationship was complicated.

She couldn't help remembering Alec and Raine's greeting embrace. Charlotte hadn't hugged Jack in more than twenty years—not since she'd been torn from his arms in the airport at four years old, after her mother died, after her own father gave her away.

The next time they'd seen each other, he'd felt like a stranger. She wasn't sure how to act, and neither was he.

He didn't seem like the strong, protective big brother she'd fantasized about at night. Their visits grew further apart, and the awkwardness became acute in their teenage years. And now, as adults, neither seemed to know how to break the barrier.

Or maybe Jack didn't want to break the barrier. He was a grown man with his own life. Why would he need a little sister hanging all over him?

She squared her shoulders and headed to the hallway. Once she got through the initial hello, it was always easier.

Raine fell into step beside her. "You okay?"

"I'm fine."

"You look a little pale."

Better pale with anxiety than flushed with sexual desire, Charlotte supposed.

"Everything's moving smoothly," Raine offered. She knew of Charlotte's desire to impress the Hudson side of the family. "Even Lars Hinckleman is happy today."

Charlotte couldn't help but smile at the mention of the temperamental second-unit director. Raine was right. Things were going—

"I said *dramatic,* not *appalling!*" Lars shouted from the bottom of the stairs.

"Spoke too soon," Raine muttered, as Charlotte quickened her steps on the curved, wrought-iron-railed staircase.

The stocky man was waving his arms, an unlit cigar clamped between his teeth, his dark hair curling over his forehead.

"It's authentic Stix, Baer & Fuller," the costume assistant dared, causing the entire room to hush and collectively suck in a breath.

Even Charlotte missed a step. Lars had been at the château for only three days, but she'd quickly learned the near-military command-control structure of the film set.

Lars leaned into the hapless young woman, his dark, round eyes narrowing. "Lillian Hudson will *not* wear a bird's nest on her head."

"She was Lillian Colbert then."

The man's face turned purple.

The costume designer quickly stepped in. "We'll come up with other options, of course." She latched on to the younger woman's arm and deftly drew her away.

"Fire that thing," Lars huffed to an assistant.

The assistant made a note on a clipboard and said something into his walkie-talkie. Charlotte fervently hoped the command was all bluster. Then she spotted Jack.

He was talking to the director of photography, ignoring the commotion on set, while everyone around him continued with set preparation.

"That's your brother?" asked Raine.

Charlotte nodded, putting one foot in front of the other as she made her way across the foyer.

"You look alike."

Charlotte disagreed. Jack was much darker. He was dignified, where she was decidedly cute. "No, we don't."

"It's your nose, and the eyes," said Raine. "That vivid blue. Gorgeous."

Charlotte gazed at Jack as they drew near. Did they look alike? Did people notice? Could there be other things they had in common? Thoughts, opinions, emotions?

"Hello, Charlotte." He greeted her with a broad smile.

"Good morning, Jack." As always, she felt like there was something she should do. A hug? A kiss? A handshake?

He glanced around the huge rotunda. "Well done," he told her, sounding sincere.

At least she had that. "This is Raine Montcalm," she introduced.

The director of photography was drawn into another conversation and turned away.

Jack reached out to shake Raine's hand. "On behalf of the family, allow me to express our gratitude for opening up your home."

A brief pain shot through Charlotte's chest. Clearly, Jack didn't see her as a representative of the Hudsons. She'd already thanked the Montcalms, but that obviously wasn't good enough.

"Alec Montcalm." Alec's deep voice startled Charlotte.

He moved up beside her and shook Jack's hand.

"Jack Hudson." Jack introduced himself before she could get her bearings. "My grandmother sends her thanks."

Alec's fingertips touched ever so lightly on the small of Charlotte's back. "You sister made a convincing argument."

Jack smiled down at Charlotte. "We were hoping her connection to Raine would help."

Alec's hand tensed almost imperceptibly. "Yes. Well, I hope you're happy with the results."

"We'll also need a couple of rental houses for the VIPs and stars," said Jack. "Any suggestions?"

"I can make a couple of calls."

"I don't want to put you to any trouble."

"No trouble," said Alec. "Charlotte?" He glanced down, his palm warm on her back. "Maybe you could give me a hand?"

More time with Alec?

Her mind screamed no. While her body shouted yes. Then her reflexive nod broke the tie.

To her surprise, instead of taking her back to his office for privacy, he said goodbyes and ushered her out the front door.

"I thought we were making a few calls?" she said as Alec cut toward the garage. She scrambled to keep up in her heels. The sunshine was warm on her bare arms and legs, and the sweet smell of the estate's flowers and herb gardens invaded her nostrils.

"I brought my cell," said Alec.

"Where are we going?"

He hit the button on a small remote and one of the garage doors glided open, revealing a burnished copper Lamborghini convertible. The top was down, showing off a black and copper interior, a sexy console and low-slung leather bucket seats.

"Nice," she acknowledged.

"Thanks." He popped open the passenger door then offered a hand to steady her as she climbed in.

"Where are we going?" she repeated, even as her body all but sighed into the soft leather. It would be nice to get away from the chaos for a while, clear her head, remember there were other things in life besides the approval of the Hudsons.

In answer to her question, Alec grinned and gestured to the sky. "A day like this? In the south of France? In a Murciélago? Who cares?"

He made a good point.

Charlotte shrugged both in agreement and capitulation. The seat surrounded her body like a glove. Alec leaned in, pulled out the seat belt and reached across to click it into the buckle. She couldn't resist inhaling his scent, fresh and clean like the region where he lived.

He shut the door, then rounded the hood to the driver's side, removing his jacket and rolling up the sleeves of his white dress shirt. Next, he untied his tie, slipping it off and setting it behind the seat.

Charlotte glanced around at the classy interior. She couldn't help a smile at the thought of zooming through the countryside in such a magnificent vehicle.

Henri magically appeared and retrieved the jacket. "You have everything you need, sir?"

Alec nodded, perching a pair of sunglasses on his nose.

"You ready?" he asked Charlotte.

"I don't have my purse," she remembered.

"Sir?" asked Henri.

"She won't need it," said Alec, turning the key. The powerful engine roared to life, rumbling the seat beneath her. He clicked the car into gear and pulled smoothly out of the garage. They passed semitrailers containing warehouses of filming equipment, one that was a wardrobe room, and another containing a full, industrial kitchen.

"I thought you might like to get away from the circus for a while," said Alec, picking up speed down the long, concrete driveway.

"That Lars makes me nervous."

"I don't know why people put up with him."

"I guess he's in charge for the moment." The second-unit filming was scheduled to take place before the stars and director arrived.

The car came to a smooth stop at the end of the driveway, and Alec turned it toward Castres.

"Being in charge is no excuse for being a jerk."

"Not an excuse," Charlotte agreed. "But it's a reason."

"There's never a reason to abuse power," said Alec, bringing up the revs and changing gears as the road straightened out.

Charlotte considered his profile for a moment.

He glanced over. "What?"

"You have power," she observed, wondering what he was like with his own employees, remembering how he'd insisted the film crew not cause them any additional work.

"At the moment." He winked, gearing down and pulling into the oncoming lane to pass a truck. "I also have speed."

The sports car stuck to the road like glue, accelerating effortlessly past the truck and another car in front.

Charlotte's hand automatically gripped the door handle.

"Nervous?" asked Alec.

"Not exactly." There was something about Alec that oozed confidence behind the wheel. Well, actually, there was something about him that oozed confidence about *everything*. She trusted him not to push himself or the car past their limits.

"I won't hurt you," he assured her in a solemn tone.

She'd have to be blind not to catch the double entendre. "How can you be sure?"

"With power comes responsibility," he said, easing back into the proper lane. "I was born to both."

Did she dare trust him with her sexual attraction? And was that what this was about? Was he whisking her off to some discreet inn where they could spend the afternoon in bed exploring it?

Pretty bold of him not to ask her. She should tell him no. Just to thwart his arrogant self-confidence, she should tell him she wasn't interested in a tryst.

He flipped on his signal and left the main road.

And maybe she would.

Soon.

In the meantime, she watched the businesses roll by on the tree-lined boulevard, keeping an eye out for possible hotels and inns. They passed one, then another, then a small bed-and-breakfast.

But, to her surprise, Alec pulled into the parking lot of a real-estate office.

She raised her brows. "Here?"

"My friend Renaldo," said Alec. "He'll let us know what's up for rent."

"Oh." Didn't Charlotte feel like a fool. "A real-estate office."

A knowing light came into Alec's eyes. "What were you expecting?"

"This," she quickly responded with a nod.

He grinned, and she felt her face heat.

Four

Alec wanted to sleep with Charlotte—so much so that it was beginning to feel like an obsession. That kiss this morning told him they would all but combust together, and the confused looks she'd been giving him said she'd felt it, too. And now they were alone. They had several hours to spend together. And there were endless possible locations to make love in town. They had everything but a set of runway lights guiding them to paradise.

But something was holding him back. And he couldn't begin to imagine what it might be. Guys like him could talk women into bed without breaking a sweat. Half the time it was about his money, of course. But then half the time he didn't really care.

Maybe he was getting old. Or maybe he wanted to

pretend it was different with Charlotte—that there was more to it than sex on his side and manipulation on hers.

Which didn't make sense. He barely knew her. She could be as susceptible to his millions as every other woman he'd met in this lifetime. Just because she was Raine's friend, and just because she was bright and witty, with an endearing dash of vulnerability, didn't make her any different from anyone else.

Still, instead of rushing her to the nearest hotel room, he found himself winding his way through Castres to the first of three houses available for rent.

The first one was an old, converted mill set next to the river on a few acres of lawn.

"Gorgeous," sang Charlotte, tipping her head back and turning in a circle as they entered a boxy, high-ceilinged main room. A polished wooden staircase was set against the stone wall and led up to the landing on the second story. The wood floors gleamed, and the furniture was big and comfortable.

"You think it might be too small?" asked Alec.

"It's charming," said Charlotte, passing beneath the staircase, past the stone fireplace to the arched doorway that led to a restored kitchen. Bright enamel pots hung from the ceiling, and a giant white sink dominated the counter below a window that looked out over the water. The cupboards were worn, and the floor tiles had definitely seen better days.

Alec tested the table for dust. "We're talking about bigwigs and movie stars."

Charlotte frowned at him. "I'd stay here," she declared, wandering to the big sink.

He followed. "Yeah? Well, apparently, you're not all that fussy."

She turned suddenly, and they were nearly nose to nose, her back trapped against the sink.

"How would you know that?" she asked.

He held up his finger to show the dust, rubbing it off with his thumb.

She watched the motion, and he felt a flicker of warning heat build up inside him.

"Nothing a little elbow grease won't fix," she said.

"I'm guessing stars don't do windows," he countered, attempting to keep the mood light.

"Of course not. They have people who do it for them. But then, you'd know all about that, wouldn't you?"

"Got a problem with my money?" Sarcasm wasn't the female reaction he normally experienced.

She paused. "I like your car."

"You have good taste."

"You like to go fast?"

He digested the statement for a second, wondering which tack to take.

A flicker of unease crossed her face.

"I like to go fast," he agreed softly, keeping his expression steady, allowing her decide whether to let it drop or pick it up and run with it.

They stared at each other in silence. The river rushed by below the window, and a songbird serenaded them from a nearby tree branch. The house itself was still and silent. It seemed to be holding its breath along with them.

"I thought the kiss would get us out of this," she finally said.

"I guess it didn't," he responded.

Another minute went by.

"Shouldn't you be doing something?" she asked.

"Like what?"

"I don't know, something decisive one way or the other."

He smiled. "I thought about that. And then I thought I'd let you make the first move."

She shifted against the cool ceramic sink. "And if I don't?"

He shrugged. "Then I guess it's like a staring contest. We'll see who blinks first."

"And you think that would be fun?"

"I think it would be fascinating." And he did.

He had a will of iron when he wanted it. Not that he necessarily wanted it in this case. But toying with Charlotte was like stomping the accelerator of his Lamborghini. It was always exhilarating to see which would come first, disaster or delirium.

"In that case." She slipped sideways, dancing away from him, across the kitchen. "I'm betting I can hold out longer than you."

"You think?"

She snagged his attention with a sultry, sexy look. "I guess we'll find out. Where's the next house?"

"Rue du Blanc. Top of the hill."

It was a modern stone villa with twelve rooms and a pool overlooking an olive grove. Charlotte liked it. So did Alec. The kitchen was clean and modern, and there were plenty of bedrooms and enough baths for an entourage.

Their final stop was a full-on castle, with bleached stones, hewn ceiling beams, a formal dining room and seven bedrooms with king-size beds. A gilded fountain dominated the driveway turnaround, while acres of emerald lawn stretched out front. The furniture was

French provincial, with many valuable antiques dotting the impressively large rooms. Out back, there was a swimming pool and a meticulously maintained garden maze that was a work of art.

"I hope they're not a party crowd," Alec observed as they moved from the patio back into the formal dining room. Too many highballs, and somebody was going to get hopelessly lost in that maze.

"Okay, now I envy your money," said Charlotte, making her way back to the grand entrance hall with its octagonal windows, antique rugs and tapestry. "I'd love to pick up something like this on a whim."

"You like it that much?" asked Alec.

She nodded. "I'd buy it."

"The kitchen's a little small."

"I'd renovate."

He chuckled. "You'd actually knock out a stone wall?"

She flung open the double doors to the great room. "It's my fantasy," she pointed out, walking through the furniture groupings, past oil portraits and a massive, rolltop desk. "I guess I can knock out whatever I want."

At the far end of the great room, there was a balcony overlooking a duck pond. Charlotte wandered into the sunshine and leaned on the wide rail. "If I lived here, I could name the ducks."

"You could," he agreed, moving next to her. "Though I'm not sure how you'd tell them apart."

"I'd buy a dog. Put up a swing for the kids."

"Kids?"

"Sure. I wouldn't use all seven bedrooms myself."

A wistful expression came over her face as she gazed

into the distance, obviously imagining a picture-perfect family.

"So, what's with you and Jack?" Alec ventured, reminded of her real family.

She kept her eyes straight forward. "What do you mean?"

Alec had seen the expression on her face. He'd watched their body language, and the distance they kept between them. "It seemed like there was some kind of tension—"

"I don't know what you're talking about."

"Are you angry with him?" It seemed like the most logical explanation.

"Why would I be angry with him?"

"I don't know. It was—"

"I barely know him."

Alec took in her profile for a moment. "He's your brother."

"We didn't grow up together."

Alec had heard as much from Raine. "What happened?"

She brushed a speck of sand off the concrete rail, then scratched her thumbnail over a flaw. "When I was four, my mother died. Jack stayed with the Hudson grandparents, and I went with the Cassettes."

Alec found his heart going out to her. His parents had died when he was in his twenties, and that was enough of a blow. And he'd always had Raine. Charlotte, on the other hand, had her entire family ripped away when she was little more than a baby. No wonder she fantasized about home and hearth.

"Did you ever ask why?"

"Ask Jack?"

"Your father."

She shook her head. "David Hudson and I don't talk much."

Alec stilled her small hand with his own. "I guess not."

She shrugged her slim, bare shoulders. "It was hardly *Oliver Twist*."

"But it hurt you just the same."

She smoothed back her hair, raking spread fingers through the tangles. "It's just…sometimes…" But then she shook her head.

"Tell me," he prompted.

She turned to look at him. "Like you and Raine. You hug, you tease." She moved her hands in a gesture of confusion.

"That comes from years of learning exactly how to push each other's buttons."

"That might be how you tease her, but that's not why you hug her."

Suddenly, Charlotte looked so vulnerable and confused and alone on the windswept balcony that he couldn't help himself. He wrapped his arms around her and drew her against him, cradling her head against his shoulder and smoothing her tousled hair.

"Be patient," he advised. "Relationships are complicated."

"I'm twenty-five," said Charlotte. "And we live on different continents."

"Some are more complicated than others."

Her body trembled against his.

"Hey," he soothed, rubbing his palm across her back, trying desperately to keep his perspective. But she was soft and sexy in his arms. She smelled like a spring garden, and the vivid memory of her taste was pounding inside his head.

She drew back, and he was surprised to see she was laughing instead of crying.

"What's funny?" he asked.

"I guess Jack and I would be on the complicated end of the spectrum."

Alec gazed into her bright eyes, her flushed cheeks, the wild hair begging to be smoothed out of the way.

"No." He shook his head, and she sobered under his expression. "You and *I* would be on the complicated end of the spectrum." And he bent his head to kiss her tempting lips.

The instant Alec's lips touched hers, Charlotte knew how he did it. She knew why dozens if not hundreds of women fell head over heels for him, knew why they clambered into his bed and made fools of themselves in public.

He wasn't just gorgeous, wasn't just sexy, wasn't just a rich man who could wine them and dine them all over the planet. Alec Montcalm was magic.

It was in his eyes, in his touch, in his voice that made a woman feel like she was the only person on earth.

Her arms wound around his neck, and she tipped her head to better accommodate his kiss. His hot lips parted, and she invited him in, parrying with his tongue while his arms tightened. Her breasts pressed against his chest, and she could feel a tingle start within her nipples, radiating out to touch every fiber of her being.

He whispered her name, then kissed her deeper, backing her against the rail. His hands cradled her face, thumbs stroking her cheeks, fingertips burying in her hairline. It was, hands down, the most sensual kiss she'd ever experienced.

Their bodies were plastered together, and his lips began to roam. First to her cheek, her temple, her eyelids. Then he kissed the lobe of her ear, making his way down the curve of her neck.

She struggled to breathe, her lips still tingling. Her hands found his short hair, tunneling their way through its coarse softness. His kisses found her mouth again, and she moaned her appreciation.

Her clothes suddenly felt stifling, and the waning sun was hot on her back. Sweat prickled her skin and she longed to tear off her clothes to get some respite from the suddenly humid air.

Then he clasped her to him, lifting her right off the patio, turning, breathing deeply in her ear.

"We have to stop," he rasped, even as she kissed his salty neck.

She wasn't sure why, so she kept right on kissing.

"Not here," he elaborated with obvious strain.

Of course.

Not here.

They were in a stranger's house.

What was she thinking?

She stopped kissing, burying her face against his shoulder. His skin was superheated, the cotton of his shirt damp against her cheek.

"Sorry," she managed between breaths.

"Hell, I'm sure not."

"We can't keep doing this." She was warning herself as much as she was warning him. If they kept it up, sooner or later, they were going to make love, even if they didn't find the perfect time and location.

"We can," he argued. "But sooner or later, we'll get caught."

"The tabloids," she confirmed, appreciating his concern for her reputation.

"I was thinking of your brother," Alec admitted, still holding her tight. "But, yes, let's go with the tabloids."

"There's only one of Jack," Charlotte noted, not exactly sure of her point. What was she suggesting?

"You saying we can outsmart him?"

"I'm saying he can't be everywhere." She paused. "But the tabloids can." And they were definitely worth worrying about.

"So, what do we do?"

"You might want to put me down."

He gently loosened his arms, letting her slide sensually along his body until her shoes met the deck.

"Damn it," he gasped.

Passion ricocheted along her nerve endings, and she silently echoed his curse. She forced herself to take a step back, and he let her go.

She laughed weakly, turning her attention to the fields, the duck pond and the distant orchard, struggling valiantly to bring her emotions under control. "You do have a way with women, Alec."

He was silent for a long moment, and when he spoke there was a distance in his tone. "Not all women."

Maybe not. But she was willing to bet it was with most women. "We need to get back," she managed.

"Of course," he agreed.

Then he waited for her to start back through the great room. He followed more slowly, locking up behind them.

In the Lamborghini, Charlotte tipped her head back and closed her eyes, letting the wind buffet her senses while Alec sped back to Château Montcalm and normal life.

There was nothing remotely normal about Alec's world. He'd expected a disruption in the château, but nothing had prepared him for five semitrailers in the front yard, a hundred crew members, several dozen extras, one temperamental second-unit director and two demanding stars.

The worst part was, his very reason for doing this, Charlotte, had all but disappeared. Claiming Alec had monopolized too much of Charlotte's time when they checked out the rental houses, Raine had latched on to her and stuck by her side round the clock. Not that Alec begrudged them their tennis and spa visits, but was a few minutes alone with Charlotte so much to ask? Sure, they had breakfast and dinner together, but Raine was always there, and sometimes Kiefer, Jack or even Lars joined them.

Suddenly, there was yet another crash in the front yard, followed by shouts and the booming voice of Lars. Alec stood up, crossed the room and pulled his office window shut, securing the latch. The barrier dampened the noise, and he breathed a sigh of relief. Then he settled back into his desk to review the marketing strategy Kana Hanako was proposing leading up to the Tour de France.

So far, none of the tabloids had made a link between Alec and Isabella, even though she'd arrived in Provence two days ago. She and costar Ridley Sinclair had chosen the modern villa in the olive grove, and were sharing it along with a few entourage members.

The growl of a motor buzzed its way through the wall. It grew louder and louder, actually shaking the foundation of the château.

Alec threw down his pen, jerked to his feet and stomped his way through the hallways to the entry, ducking under booms and avoiding cameras and light stands as he made his way to his front door.

He cut through the open doorway in time to see a massive, truck-mounted crane come to a halt on his driveway turnaround. Huge, hydraulic arms whined out to smack into the ground, stabilizing the unit. The key grip shouted directions to the crane operator.

"What the hell?" Alec asked to no one in particular.

"An aerial shot of the balcony scene," a crew member offered.

Just then, the crane shifted. One of the arms broke the concrete with a deafening boom, and the ground shook.

A few people shrieked, but then most settled to laughing nervously as the disturbance subsided.

Alec wasn't laughing. His driveway was ruined.

"Where is Charlotte?" he growled. This was her job. She'd promised to keep the film crew from destroying his home.

"Where is Charlotte?" he asked in a louder voice.

The three closest crew members turned to look at him.

"I want to speak to Charlotte Hudson," he enunciated.

One of the crew members spoke into his walkie-talkie.

"Alec?" came Raine's voice.

He turned to find the two women, small souvenir bags

in tow, jaunty hats on their heads and pretty tans on their perky faces.

"Where the hell have you been?" he demanded, making a beeline to Charlotte.

Her eyes widened. She opened her mouth, but no sound came out.

"This was *your* job," he shouted, gesturing at the chaos around him. "We might as well be having an earthquake. The château is shaking off its foundation. The driveway is destroyed. And I can't even hear myself think."

"I'll—"

"I want that crane gone," he roared. "And I want it gone *now.*" He caught Jack in his peripheral vision.

"But—"

"And no more sightseeing. No more spas. No more fun and games with Raine while I suffer this noise and destruction alone." He was ranting now, but he couldn't seem to stop himself. All he'd asked was that she hang around and make sure these people didn't ruin his life. Even that seemed to be too much trouble.

"They need the crane shot," she tried, but her mouth was pinched and her skin was going pale under the tan.

"And I need my château to be standing when this is all over."

She shrank back, and Alec could have kicked himself.

Instead, he turned on Jack. "And *you?* What the hell's the matter with you? I'm standing here screaming at your sister."

Jack blinked in obvious confusion.

"Why don't you hit me?"

Now everybody within earshot looked confused.

Alec cursed under his breath, stomping back into the château, thinking seriously about an extended trip to Rome until this was all over.

* * *

Charlotte stared at her brother, but his gaze slid away, and he became instantly interested in a list on one of the production assistants' clipboards. The noise level in the immediate area went back to normal, as everyone's attention went to their jobs.

Raine shifted toward Charlotte. "That's not normal," she intoned.

"Thank goodness," said Charlotte.

"I don't know what got into him."

"He's not wrong," said Charlotte. "I did promise to make sure everything ran smoothly."

"Alec doesn't yell," said Raine. "He stews. He plots. He might methodically bankrupt you. But he doesn't yell."

"So, I've pushed him over the edge." Charlotte needed to go clear the air. She couldn't leave things hanging between them like this. She subconsciously started toward the front door.

"It appears you have," Raine mused, giving Charlotte a considering look as she fell into step beside her. "Is there something you're not telling me?"

"Like what?" Charlotte stalled, not wanting to lie to her friend, but *really* not wanting to admit she was attracted to Alec. It was so cliché, so tiresome.

"Like maybe he made a pass at you? And you turned him down. Alec's not used to hearing the word no."

"I guess not," Charlotte chuckled.

"So, did he?" asked Raine, keeping her voice low. "Make a pass at me?"

Raine elbowed her in the ribs. "Are you avoiding the question?"

"Pretty much."

"He *did*." Raine linked her arm with Charlotte, steering her down the walkway, through a wooden gate and into a secluded garden where they sat down at a white-painted, wrought-iron table next to a trickling fountain. "So, you said no?" There was a fiendish glee in Raine's wide grin.

"Not exactly," Charlotte admitted, setting down her purse and the small bag.

Her friend's eyes went wide. "You said *yes?*"

"I didn't really say anything."

"Oh my God. You two—"

"No!" Then Charlotte lowered her voice. "No. We didn't."

"I don't understand."

"We kissed." Charlotte sat back in the straight-backed chair. "We kissed, okay?"

"So, why's he mad at you?"

"I'm guessing it's because the crane broke your driveway."

Raine toyed with a tiny leaf that had blown onto the grid-work table. "Trust me when I tell you Alec doesn't yell over broken driveways. And what was that thing with Jack hitting him?"

"You got me," said Charlotte, more than happy to move off the kiss. "Does Alec beat up anyone who yells at you?"

"No one's ever yelled at me. At least not in front of Alec." Raine paused. "And, actually, no, people don't tend to yell at me."

"That's because you're sweet and kind," said Charlotte, only half joking.

"I'm starting to think it's because I have a pit bull for a brother."

Charlotte laughed. "You think he warned them off?"

"Maybe. But let's get back to the kiss. Tell me about it."

"Nothing to tell," Charlotte lied. It had been a kiss for the record books, and she'd been avoiding Alec ever since.

"Where were you? How did it happen?"

"We were on the balcony at one of the rental houses."

"And he just up and kissed you?"

"He thought I was crying."

Raine frowned. "That doesn't sound right."

"I was actually laughing," said Charlotte, forcing her mind to back away from the memory.

"Alec doesn't give sympathy kisses."

"You know about *all* his kisses, do you?"

"I have heard tales."

"Well, you're not going to hear any more tales from me." Charlotte sighed and got to her feet. "I'd better get out there and see what's going on. Alec's right. I did promise to take care of things." She picked up her purse. "I guess our fun's over."

"Uh-uh." Raine shook her head in denial. "I'm definitely going to talk to him."

"Oh, no, you don't," Charlotte protested. She had a job to do here, and she was going to take care of it.

"You don't need to watch every move they make," said Raine. "I'm not going to let him keep you prisoner here for weeks on end."

"*I'll* talk to him," said Charlotte. "Later." After Alec had a chance to calm down, they'd have a discussion and set out the parameters of her role in the film. She had an obligation to him, and she was going to live up to it.

Five

Filming went on until eight o'clock that night. Alec requested dinner in his office, not wanting to inflict his foul mood on anyone else. He'd signed up as a film location—a stupid decision, obviously. But it was a decision he'd made, and now he was going to have to live with it.

Things hadn't turned out exactly as he'd planned, but that was life. He'd leave for Tokyo in the morning. Might as well roll up his sleeves and ensure the new bicycle line launch came off without a hitch. He could also make a stop in New Delhi and touch base with the high-tech division.

There was always a long list of social events he should attend. Maybe he'd find a plain-Jane date, get his picture taken, make Kiefer happy. He might as well make somebody happy, because it sure wasn't going to be him, not if he stayed here.

There was a light tap on his office door.

"*Oui,* Henri?"

The door cracked open.

"It's Charlotte."

Oh, good. Now he could apologize on top of everything else. He sighed and came to his feet. *"Entrée."*

She slipped into the room, closed the door behind her and leaned against it. She was drop-dead gorgeous in a jazzy gold spaghetti-strap cocktail dress. Its vertical streaks shimmered against her toned thighs.

The wide, mahogany desk and two padded guest chairs formed a barrier between them. Just as well.

"They're going to replace the driveway," she finally said.

He moved around the desk, drawn to her. "It wasn't about the driveway."

She nodded her understanding. "Still. They broke it, they'll replace it."

"I take it you've been doing your job this afternoon?"

"I was."

"I appreciate that." What he really appreciated was that she was standing here in front of him, and they were alone for the first time in days.

"It was part of the deal."

"I was angry because you stayed away," he admitted, moving closer still, marveling that she grew more beautiful with each step.

"I've been here every day."

"With Raine glued to your side. Where is my sister, by the way?"

"She had to do something with Kiefer."

"At the office?"

Charlotte nodded.

Alec came to a halt in front of her. "And Jack?"

"At the hotel. With the crew."

Tokyo faded from his mind as Alec stroked his thumb over the fabric of her dress. He discovered the shimmer came from ribbons, beads and sequins. There was a weight and fullness to the dress that felt good under his hand. It had a double hem—scalloped over straight. It was a perfect dress for dancing.

Her long legs flowed down into strappy gold sandals. And the gold hoops dangling from her ears set off her shiny blond hair.

"You know," he told her softly, reframing his mood. "We all did something wrong."

She tipped her head questioningly.

"You shouldn't have stayed away. I shouldn't have yelled. And Jack should have decked me."

That got a smile from her. "Jack thinks you're crazy."

"He needs to learn how to be your brother."

"I can only hope that doesn't involve too many fist-fights."

Alec closed his hand around her rib cage, feeling the texture of the dress tickle his palm.

"I missed you," he admitted.

She closed her eyes for a long second. "Are we deep into the complicated end of the relationship spectrum?"

"It's simple from where I'm standing." He gazed at her creamy shoulders, the delicate straps of the dress, thinking how easy it would be to roll one off and press his lips against the warm fragrance of her skin.

"You're gorgeous," he elaborated. "I can't keep my hands off you. And there's *finally* nobody else here."

He slipped his index finger under the strap, sliding it back and forth. "What could be simpler than that?"

"I came here to talk to you about expectations."

He smiled. "I hope you won't be disappointed."

"I mean my job here. For the film. I don't want to let you down again."

"Forget it."

She searched his expression. "I don't know what that means."

"It means I wasn't angry about the driveway. I wasn't angry you had fun with Raine. I was angry because you weren't in my bed. And that's not a fair reason to be angry."

She stilled. Not breathing, staring up at him with desire, trepidation and anticipation all mixed up together.

His hand tightened, drawing her in. He bent his head, parted his lips and met hers in a slow, gentle exploration.

Last time had been too hurried. He'd behaved like a teenager, not giving a thought to savoring the moment, to making sure she felt cherished, to kissing her the way a Frenchman should kiss, the way a Frenchman ought to approach everything in life.

She tasted of fine wine, his own vintage. Her lips were soft and smooth, warm and malleable under his. She was kissing him back, and passion uncoiled within him. His forearm went to the small of her back, pressing her soft curves against his firm body. She was ambrosia, a gift from the gods, an angel set down on earth for him and him alone.

Her tongue flicked against his lips, kicking a jolt of desire from his body to his brain. He struggled to keep it slow, but his mouth was moving of its own accord, delving deeper, kissing harder, bending her backward so that her body arched into his own.

Blood rushed through his system, priming his body, challenging reason. Her hands gripped his shoulders, while small moans worked their way from her chest to her mouth. His lips moved to her neck, and she arched back farther. Her breasts were taut against the dress, cleavage bursting from the V-neck, her nipples outlined against the fabric.

His hand covered one breast, and they both gasped in wonder. He drew his thumb over the peak, and her knees buckled. He held her steady, whispering words of endearment and encouragement.

He lifted her, wrapping her legs around his waist, pushing her dress out of the way and pressing her against the solid door. He took her mouth once more, kissing her deeply. His hands roamed from her breasts to her waist to her bare thighs revealed by the bunched dress. When he touched the lace of her panties, she hissed out a yes.

Her hands cupped his face, and she covered him with tiny kisses. She drew his earlobe into her hot mouth, and his body nearly jackknifed in shock. He slipped his thumb between her legs, over the silk of her panties. She was hot and moist and delectably sweet.

There were condoms in the bathroom adjoining the office. He cradled her bottom, lifting her away from the door, carrying her to the en suite, all the while kissing, caressing and assuring her she was the most beautiful woman in the world.

Inside, he perched her on the counter, stripped off his slacks and the scrap of her panties, donned the condom, then stepped between her legs. The counter was the right height, and their bodies touched intimately.

He smoothed back her hair and gazed into her eyes. Then he drew his thumb along her swollen bottom lip, following it up with his mouth, drawing her lip inside, tasting her essence as his hands roamed lower.

She squirmed forward, bringing his fingers in contact with the fire between her legs. Her hands fisted in his hair, and her moaning little pants heated his ear.

He parted her flesh.

"Now?" he asked.

"Right now," she gasped in return, and he pushed inside.

She arched back, and he anchored his hands at the base of her spine, pressing her forward, refining his angle, savoring the feel of her body for long moments before he withdrew. Then he pushed in again, swifter, harder.

Her eyes were closed, and sweat dotted her hairline. Her skin was slick and fragrant against his. Her dress rustled against the counter. He drew down the neckline, revealing her breasts, closing his mouth over one pert nipple, laving it, drawing hard, eliciting a groan as her hands tightened and her fingernails dug into his upper arms.

He moved to the other breast, repeating the motion.

Her eyes were scrunched tight. Her hips arched, her body matching his motion. He wished he could rip off the dress and see her naked. But there was no time for that.

His speed increased of its own accord, and her keening cries made his brain buzz with need. There was nothing left but a roar of desire and a primal need to take them both to the clouds and over the edge and straight into eternal paradise.

He wrapped his arms around her, holding her close as the tremors shook both of their bodies and heat drenched their skin.

Charlotte lay in the tangled sheets of Alec's big bed. Her cheek rested on his chest, and his breathing was even and strong. A breeze flowed through the open, third-floor window, billowing sheer curtains and revealing the garden lights below.

"I guess we should probably keep this a secret," she ventured.

"You think?" He trailed his fingertips lightly down her bare arm. "Or should we let Kiefer in with the camera?"

"Or we could hold a press conference right here in the bed like John and Yoko?"

"I can guarantee you the front page."

She turned her head, resting her chin on his shoulder. "Seriously."

He gazed into her eyes. "Seriously. It's our secret."

She nodded.

"What about Jack?"

Charlotte frowned, not understanding.

"Are you going to tell Jack?"

"No." Her brother had never been privy to her love life before. "Are you going to tell Raine?"

Alec shrugged. "Your call."

"She's suspicious, you know."

"Really?"

"After you yelled at me this afternoon, she asked if

you'd made a pass at me. She thought you were mad because I'd turned you down."

"She's not far off the mark," he said.

"I told her we'd kissed." Charlotte settled more comfortably against Alec's chest, toying with the edge of the white sheet.

"Are you going to tell her…" His voice trailed off.

Charlotte didn't exactly know what to call it, either. A one-night stand? A fling?

But one thing she did know, she wasn't going to get all needy on him and start demanding to know what this meant and where it was going. She'd gone into it with her eyes wide open. She knew what and who Alec was, but she'd hopped into his bed anyway.

"It's better if she doesn't know," Charlotte admitted. "But I don't want to lie to her. My grandfather—" She stopped.

She wasn't going to start borrowing trouble here. Her grandfather didn't need to find out. Nobody needed to find out. Unless Alec was a complete cad, and she certainly didn't think he was, this interlude would remain locked in her heart forever.

"How long have you worked for the ambassador?" Alec asked, obviously prepared to move on.

She followed his lead. "Since I was a teenager. I started off helping in the office. Then, after college, I worked full-time. And when his executive assistant quit to get married, I stepped in temporarily."

"When was that?"

"Three years ago. Right before I met you the first time."

"Ahh." He nodded. "Rome. You should have taken my key that night."

"Right. And I'd have made the front page, scandalized my family and been fired from my job."

Alec paused. "That's altogether a worst-case scenario, isn't it?"

"It's a likely-case scenario. You nearly ruined my life."

"Good that we waited, then." He placed a gentle kiss on her forehead, gathering her close. "Honestly— right now, I'm very, very glad we waited."

Charlotte didn't know what to say to that. He made it sound as if they'd done it deliberately, as if they'd had some kind of connection, as if they'd been thinking about each other over the past three years. Had he thought about her after Rome? Did he even remember her in the long line of women he flirted with?

She gave herself a mental shake. She wasn't going to make more of this than there was.

"Is Kiefer still worried about rumors of you and Isabella?" she asked, moving on.

"We seem to have an ally in Ridley Sinclair."

"We do?" Charlotte hadn't even met the man yet.

"I hear he generally has an affair with his costar."

Interesting. "And he's staying in the same villa as Isabella?"

Alec nodded. "That he is."

"You think they'll have an affair?"

"Rumor has it they already are," said Alec. "Though that rumor may have been started by Kiefer."

Charlotte laughed. "I think I'm starting to like Kiefer."

"You be careful of Kiefer." There was a serious note in Alec's tone that caused Charlotte to twist to look him in the eyes again.

"What do you mean?"

"I mean Kiefer has a way with women."

"And you don't?" She glanced down at her naked body, the twisted sheets, the comforter that had been kicked off the bed an hour ago. If she needed to be careful of anybody here, it was Alec.

"I hear your father's due tomorrow." Alec changed the subject. She didn't blame him. What more was there to say?

"I heard that Lars has a few more days of second-unit work," said Charlotte. "But they want to start rehearsals for the major scenes."

"Will it bother you?"

"The major scenes?" Charlotte expected it to become even more chaotic at the château. But they'd known this was coming.

"Seeing your father. Is it worse than seeing Jack?"

"It's nowhere near the same," said Charlotte, burrowing farther beneath the sheet to combat a growing chill from the open window.

Alec reached to the floor and retrieved the comforter, spreading it over both of them.

"Thanks." She sighed as their body heat formed a warm cocoon.

"Your father?" Alec prompted.

"It's funny," she admitted. "I think I always knew David was a terrible father. Even when my mom was alive, he was never around. When she died, I honestly thought it would be Jack who took care of me."

"How old was Jack?"

"Nine. But he seemed very worldly wise. He used to pour me juice, make me sandwiches and read me bedtime stories." She smiled wistfully at the memory.

"And then he abandoned you."

"No, he didn't." She knew none of it had been Jack's fault. "But for years, I expected him to come and get me. I don't know what I thought, that he'd turn eleven, get a paper route and we'd live happily ever after. Pretty absurd, huh?"

Alec straightened the comforter around her. "You were a little girl."

"Who took a very long time to wake up to reality."

"Do you think you might be angry with him?"

She shook her head. "I missed him. That was all." She still missed him. She wanted a brother, and what she had was an acquaintance.

"Tell me about you and Raine." Charlotte knew she should go back to her own room before anyone else got home, but she didn't want to leave. She didn't want it to end just yet. "Did you protect her? Tease her? Gang up with her against your parents?"

Alec chuckled. "I was Raine's worst night—"

A deafening boom shook the château. Orange flames lit up the sky. Alec instantly threw himself on top of Charlotte, bracing her protectively against the bed.

"What the hell?" he ground out, glancing to the window behind him.

Charlotte blinked at the fire, smoke and ash rising toward the dark sky.

"You okay?" he demanded.

Her ears were ringing, and she'd experienced an adrenaline shot strong enough to stun an ox, but she nodded jerkily.

Alec sprang from the bed, crossing to the window while he stuffed his legs into his slacks. "Good God. One of the trailers is on fire."

"It blew up?" Charlotte stated the obvious as she

clambered out of bed herself, glancing around for her dress and shoes.

He dialed his cell phone with one hand, pulling his dress shirt on with the other as he headed for the bedroom door. There, he paused. "Will you be all right?"

"I'll be fine," she called. She could hear sirens in the distance, and people were shouting down on the lawn.

She prayed that nobody had been hurt. But the sirens were getting closer, and the shouts were getting louder. She struggled into her dress and into her shoes, then she clattered down the stairs to find out if she could help.

The front lawn looked like a disaster zone. Staff members and crew rushed to the aid of those lying on the ground. Alec was in the middle, shouting to his staff to bring blankets and first aid, while helping the gardeners to set up hoses to soak the semitrailers and a small cottage that were next to the fire.

Charlotte stopped, unsure of what to do.

She glanced at the man next to her. His face was black with soot, and he was cradling his left arm, his sleeve covered in blood.

"You're hurt," she stated, moving closer.

He looked down at his arm. "It's just a cut."

"Anything else?" She gingerly supported him on the uninjured side, helping him to the porch where he could sit down.

"It was the FX trailer," he rasped.

She separated the torn sleeve, revealing a long, deep cut on his forearm.

"They were getting the pyrotechnics ready for the battle scene." The man seemed to be in shock.

Charlotte's gaze shifted involuntarily to the burning

trailer. Alec was silhouetted against the flames. The fire trucks arrived, and he signaled them forward, clearing people out of their path as the firefighters jumped down and began connecting hoses.

If anybody had been inside…

A member of the housekeeping staff appeared, and Charlotte quickly latched on to a couple of towels and a bottle of water. She soaked one towel, carefully cleaning around the wound. Then she pressed the other towel against the cut, applying pressure to stop the bleeding.

"Am I hurting you?" she asked.

The man barely shook his head, his attention fixed on the firefighters and the approaching ambulances.

The attendants ran to a couple of people lying on the ground, and Charlotte wasn't sure whether she should flag them down.

"I can wait," the man said, guessing her thoughts.

"Are you sure?" The towel was soaking up a lot of blood.

"Charlotte?" It was Raine's voice.

Charlotte looked into Raine's stark expression.

"What *happened?* We just got back—"

"Can you get us a paramedic?"

Raine's gaze jumped to the injured man. "Of course."

She scooted across the lawn in her skirt and high heels. She stopped a woman in uniform and pointed to Charlotte. The woman grabbed a black case and trotted toward them.

"Thank you," said Charlotte as the woman knelt down.

"I'm fine," said the man.

"Let's take a quick look," said the attendant, swiftly removing the towel.

She opened the case and retrieved gauze, disinfectant and medical tape.

"I'll be sending you in for some stitches," she told the man.

He simply nodded, looking exhausted.

"What happened?" Raine repeated.

"The FX trailer blew up," Charlotte told her.

Raine's voice went hushed. "Anybody inside?"

Charlotte looked to the ambulance attendant.

The woman shrugged.

"We made it out," said the man, and all three women looked at him.

"We…" His eyelids fluttered rapidly, and the blood drained from his face.

"Mon dieu." The attendant quickly laid him prone, raising his feet. "Shock," she told them, then lifted her radio mic. "Etienne? Can you bring a stretcher?"

Her radio crackled something unintelligible in response.

"Have you seen Alec?" asked Raine as the stretcher clattered toward them.

"He was hosing down buildings." Charlotte peered into the gloom. The trailer was beaten down to a glowing pile of rubble. The other trailers and the shed were still standing. The lawn was a mud bog, and the surrounding flower beds were completely in ruins.

Charlotte's stomach turned hollow. She was causing the destruction of Alec's home. "I can't believe this," she whispered.

"Freak accident," said Raine, gazing around.

The man with the stretcher came to a halt.

"Fatalities?" asked the female attendant, attracting Charlotte and Raine's attention.

The man shook his head. "It sounds like there were three people in the trailer. They all got out. One broken arm. One concussion. Some superficial burns. And this one." He nodded to the man who was still unconscious on the porch.

"He'll need some stitches. We should start an IV and get a blood-pressure reading."

The two counted off, hoisting the man onto the stretcher, securing straps and hooking up tubes.

"He's going to be fine," the female attendant told Charlotte.

"Thank you." Too bad the same couldn't be said for Alec's front yard.

"It's not your fault," said Raine as they wheeled the man away.

"I *promised* him nothing would go wrong."

"Did you set off the explosion?"

"No."

"Then Alec will understand."

Charlotte watched Alec talking to the fire chief. His hands were waving, his face contorted and he was talking fast and emphatically. He didn't look as if he understood much of anything.

"We can replant the flowers," said Raine. "Haul away the rubble."

"Fire me," said Charlotte with a sigh of defeat. She really didn't want to face Alec's anger, particularly after she'd seen such a very different side of him.

"You're a volunteer," Raine pointed out. "I don't think we can fire you."

"Do you think he'll back out of the deal?" Butterflies formed in Charlotte's stomach as Alec started toward them, eyes hard, mouth pulled in a grim line.

"I think we're about to find out," said Raine.

Charlotte moved slightly closer to Raine for protection as Alec marched ominously toward them. Her heart rate seemed to increase with every step he took. His hands were dirty, his clothing soaked to his skin, and his face was streaked with soot and sweat.

He looked ruggedly sexy. Except for the scowl. Okay, even with the scowl, he looked sexy. She was hopeless.

He came to a halt. "No one was seriously hurt."

"I'm so sorry," said Charlotte.

Alec's eyes narrowed, and she assumed it was going to take a whole lot more than an apology.

"Do they know what happened?" asked Raine.

"Some kind of electrical malfunction with the pyrotechnics. It's going to put them behind schedule." He glanced around in disgust, and Charlotte figured the movie schedule was hardly his first concern.

He looked to Charlotte. "Can I talk to you alone?"

"It's not her fault," Raine jumped in.

Alec gave his sister a look that questioned her sanity.

Charlotte supposed it was her fault. And she didn't blame Alec for being angry. She was ready to face the music. But she was sorely disappointed at having let the Hudsons down.

Alec reached for her arm, then he seemed to remember his filthy hands, because he pulled back, nodding toward a quiet corner of the porch.

"I feel terrible," she began as soon as they were out of earshot. "I should have thought about security. I should have thought about safety—"

"I need to ask," said Alec, coming to a halt, turning to face her. He didn't look angry. In fact, he looked concerned.

"What?" she asked bravely, watching his expression closely.

"What happened earlier—between us."

Ahh. Now she got it. She shifted gears. This was the it-was-a-good-time speech, the we're-both-adults speech, the no-expectations speech.

Okay. She was prepared for that. They *were* both adults, and neither of them were under any illusions.

Charlotte squared her shoulders. "You don't have to say it, Alec. I understand. And I agree with you completely." They'd go on as if nothing had happened. If he'd let them stay and complete the movie, that was a huge win for her. She wasn't going to sit around and cry over a one-night stand.

Well, maybe she'd cry a bit. But only because it was such an incredible one-night stand. It would have been nice for it to be two nights or three. But that wasn't the way Alec operated. Or so she'd read in the tabloids.

"You agree with me?" he asked.

She nodded. "And it'll stay our secret."

He folded his arms over his wet shirt. "We already established that."

"Right." She nodded. "Of course we did." So what was left to talk about?

"What I wanted to ask you…" He glanced around. Then he moved in closer. "Do you want to do it again?"

Charlotte blinked. "I don't understand."

He moved closer still. "I don't dare even touch you out here, never mind pull you into my arms and kiss you. But I'm asking, do you want to make love with me again?"

"*And* finish the movie?"

"What does one have to do with the other?"

"Well, I'm here because of the filming, and now we've destroyed your yard."

He glanced over her shoulder. "They did a pretty good job of that."

"Are you kicking us out?"

"No."

"Why not?"

He sighed. "Do you have any idea how hard it is for me to stand here and keep my hands off you?"

Charlotte had a pretty good idea, since she was fighting the same battle to keep her hands off him. She smiled.

He frowned in return. "Answer the damn question."

"Yes."

"Good."

"Raine is staring at us."

"You let me worry about Raine."

Six

Charlotte changed out of her dress and took a long, hot shower. Afterward, she was still too keyed up to sleep. It was past midnight, but people were still working in the yard. Equipment roared to life, and a few firefighters stood by the smoking rubble with shovels and a hose.

She slipped into a pair of jeans and a short T-shirt, stuffing her feet into a pair of low sandals and pulling her damp hair into a simple ponytail.

Maybe she could find some brandy in the kitchen. A strong drink might help her sleep.

She padded down two flights of stairs, past the film sets in the entryway and the great room, along the hall toward the back of the house. She heard voices through the open door of a library.

Alec, Kiefer, Jack, Lars and three other crew members sat around a large table.

"David will be here in the morning to do an assessment," said Jack, slipping his cell phone into his pocket.

"We'll lose two shooting days at least," said Lars with a scowl. "Somebody's ass is on the—"

"I can pull a construction crew off the project in Toulouse," Kiefer said to Alec.

Charlotte cringed. Alec had been clear that none of his employees were to be impacted.

"I don't think it's necessary to fire anyone," said Alec, staring directly at Lars. "Seems to me you're going to need all the skilled labor you can find."

The three crew members stilled, and Lars's mouth worked as his face went ruddy. "How is it any of your—"

"It's my yard that was burned to a crisp," said Alec. "And I don't intend it to become a permanent movie set."

"We move on," said Jack, nodding in Alec's direction, clearly overruling Lars. "Accidents happen."

It was the first time Charlotte had seen her brother pull rank. Maybe it was because she didn't particularly like Lars. Or maybe it was because he was backing Alec. But she was proud of Jack.

Alec caught sight of her. He gave her a little smile and motioned her in, indicating an empty chair next to him.

"The construction crew?" Kiefer asked Alec.

"If we can spare them," said Alec, letting his thigh come to rest against Charlotte's as she sat down. He had also changed, into a pair of black slacks and a royal-blue, pin-striped dress shirt. He hadn't bothered with a tie, and she discovered she liked the casual look on him.

"Send me the bill," Jack told Kiefer.

Kiefer gave him a nod.

Lars was silent and sullen, his jaw clenched where he'd pulled back from the table.

One of the other crew members flipped through a clipboard. "If we switch scenes thirty-five and sixteen, and move up the party sequence, we can make up some time," he said.

"Can you get the extras in tomorrow?" asked Jack.

"On it," said the man, making a notation.

"The story editor isn't finished with thirty-five," said Lars.

"He has eight hours to *get* finished," said Jack.

"Unacceptable," Lars retorted.

"You want to duke it out with David tomorrow?" asked Jack, a tightness around his mouth. "Because I'm not about to tell a man coming off a string of low-budget independents that our story editor is a prima donna."

Alec leaned over to Charlotte and whispered, "I think Jack has this well in hand."

She tried not to smile. She'd always assumed Jack's laid-back persona meant he wasn't as strong as some of those around him. He might disguise it, but her brother seemed to have a backbone of steel.

"Charlotte?" came Raine's voice from the doorway.

Charlotte guiltily snapped her leg away from Alec's and pushed back her chair.

"I was looking for you," she said to Raine, coming to her feet. She crossed the room without looking back. "I was hoping to find some brandy," she told Raine in an undertone.

"Right this way," said Raine, pointing to the kitchen. She was still wearing the kicky little black skirt with a fitted, purple tank top. Charlotte couldn't help wondering what Raine had been doing for the past hour.

She settled into a breakfast nook, while Raine rattled through a cabinet.

The bay window faced east, so the destruction of the front yard was out of sight. The moon was full, the stars in multiple layers. Pot lights outlined a few of the garden pathways, and the pool was just visible down the slope, beyond an oleander hedge.

"I know I won't sleep, either," said Raine, curling onto the semicircular bench seat across from Charlotte. She set down a bottle of cognac and two thin crystal snifters.

"I'm so glad nobody was seriously hurt," said Charlotte.

"Now that out there," said Raine, pouring the amber liquid into the glasses, "that was more like the real Alec."

"He took it very well," Charlotte agreed. Though she supposed two hours of vigorous sex might have mellowed him out a little. "What were you doing with Kiefer?"

"We're renovating the head office in Toulouse. The architect wanted to change the configuration of my offices."

"Problem?"

Raine grinned. "Not really. But don't tell Kiefer."

"You're making him sweat?"

Raine nodded.

"Just recreationally?" Charlotte took a sip of the cognac, letting the warm liquid ease down her throat.

"You bet," said Raine with a toss of her bobbed hair. "Life's too easy for Kiefer."

"And it's not for you?"

Raine frowned. "It's not the same thing. I don't have every woman in France laying out the red carpet for me."

"You're his boss."

"Ha! I'd love to hear you say that when Kiefer's in the room."

"Say what when Kiefer's in the room?" Kiefer appeared from the hallway.

Charlotte glanced to Raine, unsure of what to say.

"Go ahead." Raine laughed. "Tell him."

Charlotte cleared her throat, trying to guess what kind of a hornet's nest she was walking into. "That she's your boss."

Kiefer scoffed out a strangled laugh. "Not until she can read a balance sheet, write a contract or take me in a fistfight."

"I own fifty percent of Montcalm Corporation."

"We both know that's an honorary thing." His gaze zeroed in on the bottle, and he helped himself to a snifter from a glassed-in cupboard.

"See what I have to put up with?" Raine asked Charlotte.

"Do you have signing authority?" asked Charlotte, taking Raine's side. She liked Kiefer, but she assumed he could take care of himself.

"I have plenty of signing authority." Raine nodded briskly.

"Alec is the CEO," Kiefer pointed out. "And I have absolutely no problem reporting to him."

"I don't know, Kiefer," Charlotte teased. "If she can sign your paycheck, I think you work for her."

Kiefer poured himself a measure of cognac. "When she has the power to fire me, I'll get worried."

"You're fired," said Raine.

Kiefer just chuckled, holding up his brandy in a toast. "You just keep publishing the pretty little puff pictures, sweetheart. Let me worry about the serious stuff."

Raine's jade eyes flared, and she jumped to her feet. "I can't get any respect. I swear, I am getting an MBA."

But Charlotte's attention stayed on Kiefer, watching his expression, catching that unguarded second when his gaze dipped to Raine's clingy, low-cut top and his nostrils flared.

Charlotte sat back. *Interesting.* The crackling energy between them was a lot more than just antagonism.

"Good luck with that," Kiefer drawled.

"If only to shove it in your face."

"Your degree is in what?" he asked mildly. "Fashion? Fine art?"

"*That's* why I'm a magazine publisher."

He swirled the cognac in his wide palm, pretending to study it. "By the way—" he looked up "—circulation was down last quarter."

"You're an ass."

"Hey—" he feigned innocence "—don't shoot the messenger."

"Don't ask me to do this, Alec." On the balcony of Alec's office, Kiefer gazed down at the construction crew swarming over last night's fire rubble.

"It's a couple of days," said Alec from the open doorway, struggling to understand why Kiefer would refuse. "Take her to the distribution offices. Meet with the executives."

"Raine doesn't need me there."

"I want you to get a feel for the magazine business. You said yourself distribution was down."

"Marginally."

Alec stepped out onto the balcony, moving next to Kiefer at the rail.

"You need me here," said Kiefer.

"No, we don't."

"Or in Toulouse."

"What good are you in Toulouse? The office is a mess, and the construction crew is working here."

"Tokyo, then. Send me to Kana Hanako."

"I want you to help Raine." Truth was, Alec wanted Kiefer to make sure Raine stayed away from the château for a couple of days. It was the only way he was going to get any time alone with Charlotte.

Underhanded, maybe. But he had used Kiefer for less noble purposes in the past.

Kiefer's jaw set in a line, and his hands smacked down hard on the rail. "Well, you might as well fire me, then." He turned to stalk back into the office.

What?

Alec gave his head a shake.

"What?" He shifted to stare at Kiefer.

Kiefer rounded, his hands on his hips. "Go ahead. Fire me for refusing an order."

"I'm not—" Alec stepped inside. "Listen, I know you're not wild about Raine."

Kiefer started to laugh.

"What's funny?"

"I'm not *wild* about Raine?"

Okay, so Raine made Kiefer nuts. They'd always sparked off each other, dragged one another down into the most petty of arguments. But they'd worked together for years. Alec assumed the relationship was at least tolerable.

Kiefer took a step forward, shaking his head in

amazement. "You think I'm refusing an order because I don't like Raine?"

"Why else?" It was not as if traveling to Paris, London and Rome was some kind of hardship. Particularly if they took the corporate jet.

Kiefer stared hard at Alec, a debate obviously going on inside his head.

"Kiefer?" Alec prompted.

"I *am* wild about Raine."

Alec didn't understand.

Kiefer gave another cold laugh. His fists clenched by his sides. "I'd rather you fired me for refusing an order than fire me for sleeping with your sister."

"Huh?" Alec was honestly speechless.

"Your sister's hot, Alec. She gorgeous. She's sexy—"

"But you two fight all the time."

"That's because if we stop fighting—" Kiefer clamped his jaw.

Alec struggled to reframe his thoughts. Kiefer and Raine? Raine and Kiefer? "You've known her for years. Surely you can keep your hands off her for a few more days."

"We've never traveled alone together."

"That's just crazy," said Alec, refusing to believe Kiefer would completely disregard his professional ethics.

"She's had a crush on me since she was eighteen," said Kiefer. "I'm not stupid. She hides it, because she hates herself for it—"

"Then she'll say no," Alec pointed out. "And I know you'll respect that. If you make a move, Raine will simply turn you down."

"Don't count on her saying no."

Alec struggled with a sudden burst of temper. His vice president was actually standing there telling him he planned to seduce his sister?

"Just fire me now," said Kiefer, throwing up his hands in disgust.

"Nobody's getting fired."

"Then forget about the trip."

"I can't forget about the trip."

"Why the hell not? Circulation took a minuscule dip. If you insist, we'll follow it up. But we can call the offices. It's not even worth the jet fuel—" Kiefer stopped. His chin suddenly dipped to his chest. He stared at Alec out of the tops of his eyes. Then he shook his head in disgust. "You need Raine out of the house."

Alec couldn't lie, so he stayed silent.

"It's Charlotte, isn't it? You want me to babysit Raine so that you can seduce Charlotte." Kiefer rapped his knuckles on the desktop. "Charlotte has a brother, too, you know."

"Jack has nothing to do with this. Charlotte's a grown woman."

"Yeah," said Kiefer. "So is Raine."

Alec was forced to agree. And that was a sobering thought for both men. It meant Raine's love life was none of his business. It meant Kiefer had held back all these years for no reason. It meant if Kiefer took Raine off in the jet, whatever happened between them was entirely their business.

"Yes," Alec finally answered. "She is."

The two men stared at each other in silence.

"And you still want me to take her around Europe?"

"If what you say is true, it's about time you two settled it one way or the other."

Kiefer gave a nod.

"I can count on your ethics?" Alec confirmed.

"*Everything* will be her call."

"Something to give me confidence," said Charlotte, staring into the depths of Raine's massive clothes closet.

"How about a jacket?" asked Raine, reaching for a couple of hangers. "Cropped? Classic?" She held up two.

"You have anything in white?" asked Charlotte. "I think white makes a statement."

"I'm not afraid of getting dirty? Even in the aftermath of a fire?"

"Exactly." Charlotte moved to get a better view of the skirts hanging in Raine's closet. The two women were close enough to the same size that she could borrow clothes. "I'd like to look crisp and professional."

Raine lowered her voice. "Are you nervous?"

Charlotte shrugged. "Isabella and Ridley are due on set today. David will show up, for sure—"

"Your father, David?"

"Right. My father, David. And Devlin and Max—two cousins—won't be far behind."

Raine turned and cocked her head. "You know, Charlotte, you are an incredibly successful, intelligent, beautiful woman."

"Thank you."

"I mean it. You've got nothing to prove. You shouldn't let them do this to you."

Charlotte turned her attention to a white, pleated skirt, trying to formulate her thoughts.

"*They* should be worried about impressing *you*," said Raine with staunch loyalty.

Charlotte laughed. "They're the Hudsons of Hollywood. They impress people simply by breathing."

There was a knock on the bedroom door.

"Come in," Raine called.

The door opened and Charlotte saw Kiefer. "You decent in there?" he called to Raine in the depth of the closet, studiously focusing on a bay window.

"No. I'm naked," stated Raine. "That's why I called you in." She brushed past Charlotte, her demeanor instantly prickly.

Charlotte hid a smile at Raine's habit of going overboard to hide her attraction to Kiefer.

Kiefer frowned at her sarcasm. "I was merely trying to be a gentleman."

"Why start now?" Raine responded tartly.

Charlotte made her way out of the closet.

"Your brother wants us to go to Rome."

Raine's brows went up. "Us?"

"You and me. And to Paris and London. He's worried about the circulation numbers."

"Tell him I'll get more data. Charlotte's here. I'm not going to Rome."

"He insists," said Kiefer. "Believe me when I tell you, I'm less thrilled than you."

"I doubt that," said Raine.

"He wants us to talk to the *Intérêt* distributors and come up with a game plan."

"Why now?"

"Because *now* is when the numbers are slipping."

Raine heaved a sigh.

"Buck up," said Kiefer, glancing at the three jackets draped over Raine's arm. "Maybe you can fit in a little clothes shopping."

Raine suddenly smiled. "What a great idea." She turned to Charlotte. "You can come with us to Rome. Via Condotti, Via Frattina. We'll have a blast."

"I don't—" Kiefer began. But Raine held up a hand to forestall him.

"It's decided," she pronounced. "If you're going to drag me to Rome, Charlotte and I will make a shopping trip of it."

Charlotte had to admit, the idea had merit. While she could borrow Raine's clothes, they wore different shoe sizes. When she packed for this trip, she'd expected to be staying two or three days. She definitely needed to upgrade her wardrobe.

Besides, getting out of Provence for a few days would mean she could put off meeting up with the Hudson clan. Although she told herself she could handle it, her stomach had been churning all morning. A few new outfits from Italy couldn't hurt her confidence.

Alec appeared in the doorway, his gaze darting from Raine to Kiefer, then settling on Charlotte. His expression stayed neutral, but gold flecks flared in his brown eyes, sending a shiver of remembrance zipping along her spine.

"Great news," said Raine, and Alec's expression turned puzzled.

"Charlotte's coming on the trip with us. We're going *shopping*."

Alec's horrified gaze shot to Kiefer.

"Raine's idea," said Kiefer defensively.

"Charlotte can't go with you," Alec quickly put in. "She has to stay with the film."

Raine waved a dismissive hand. "She's not in jail. Besides, what's left to blow up?"

"I really wish you hadn't said that," Kiefer deadpanned.

"I need Charlotte here," Alec insisted, and it instantly dawned on Charlotte that Alec was staying here.

Another look passed between Alec and Kiefer, and Charlotte realized it was a setup. Kiefer had been assigned to get Raine out of the way, so Alec could spend time with her.

Charlotte wouldn't lie to herself, she was keen to spend time with Alec, too. But talk about an over-the-top move by a self-indulgent man—sending his own sister on a wild-goose chase.

"I'd really rather go to Rome," she put in, giving Alec a defiant stare.

"See?" Raine jumped in. "The poor woman needs a wardrobe."

"Yeah," Charlotte agreed, "this poor woman needs a wardrobe."

Alec glared at her, clearly trying to transmit a message. She understood just fine. She simply wasn't going to be a party to his machinations.

"Fine," Alec ground out. "I'll come, too."

That surprised Charlotte. And judging by their expressions, it surprised Raine and Kiefer, as well.

"That's ridicu—" Something in Alec's eyes stopped Kiefer cold. "Great idea," Kiefer said instead. "The four of us, shopping together in Rome. What could be more fun?"

Charlotte wasn't sure about fun. But it was definitely going to be interesting.

Charlotte showed Alec no mercy. While Raine and Kiefer visited the magazine distributor in Rome, she dragged him to the shopping district. They visited Versace, Dolce & Gabbana, Ferragamo and Biagiotti, along with a dozen other shops and boutiques on the famous Italian streets.

Enjoying herself, she found beachwear, jeans, a couple of funky little jackets, three great party dresses and a formal gown for an upcoming event with her grandfather. She also picked out a new purse and a few pieces of jewelry. She'd fought Alec for the right to pay at every store. He was quick on the credit card draw, but she managed to either outsmart or outmaneuver him every time.

"Intimate apparel?" he asked, glancing skeptically at the discreet sign above the glass door on the stone face of the building.

He'd been patient so far, but she considered this the ultimate test. "A girl does need underwear."

"You think this is funny?"

In fact, she did. "You intimidated?"

"By women's underwear? Bring it on." He pulled open the door and stood back to let her enter.

Alec found a seat in a small lounge area and picked up a magazine. A sales associate quickly appeared and offered him coffee, which he accepted, hoisting the cup in a toast to Charlotte.

She held an elegant, full-length, white satin gown up against her body.

He frowned and shook his head.

She pointed to a frivolous pink bra and panties, decorated with white fur.

He rolled his eyes.

Scanning the small racks in front of her, she chose a short nightgown of subtly patterned purple silk, with a lace-inset front and spaghetti straps.

Alec gave her a thumbs-up. Then he waggled his eyebrows and pointed to a low-cut, lacy black camisole with a matching thong. It was obviously his turn to try to embarrass her.

She sauntered defiantly over and whisked the hanger from the rack.

He laughed silently and looked down at his magazine.

Charlotte moved farther back in the small store, selecting some more practical, though equally beautiful lingerie for everyday wear, then headed for a fitting room.

When she brought her selections to the saleswoman, Alec was there with his credit card.

"Not a chance," she muttered to him.

"My turn," he insisted.

"You're not buying my clothes," she told him, as the clerk glanced from one credit card to the next.

"I'm going to enjoy them every bit as much as you."

"Not if you keep this up," said Charlotte, and the clerk was forced to fight a grin.

Alec hesitated, and Charlotte moved quickly, pressing her credit card into the clerk's palm.

"I win," she sang.

He gazed down at the black camisole and thong on the counter. "Not necessarily."

As they had with her other purchases, they arranged to have them delivered to the hotel.

"Are we done?" asked Alec on the way out the door.

Charlotte pretended to consider. "That should keep me for a few days," she allowed.

"We still have London and Paris," he reminded her.

"Then I'm done for now," she said decisively.

"Thank goodness." He gently steered her south on the busy street.

"If you don't like shopping, why did you come?"

"Because *you*..." He smacked her smartly on the bottom.

"Hey!"

Two passing Italian men whistled their appreciation.

"...wouldn't stay home with me," Alec finished.

She blinked innocently up at him. "I was supposed to stay home?"

"Do you have any idea how much trouble it was to get Kiefer to take Raine out of our hair?"

"I can't believe it was hard at all. He's got the hots for her."

"You knew that?"

Charlotte scoffed out a laugh. "It's pretty obvious. Well, to everybody but Raine. She likes him, too, you know."

"So I hear."

"You playing matchmaker?" she asked.

"I wanted to see you alone. Those two can take care of themselves."

"And, here we are," noted Charlotte.

"You made me work hard enough."

"Serves you right. Pimping out your sister like that."

"Clearly, I'm shameless when it comes to you."

"Let's hope I'm worth it."

His voice lowered to an intimate tone. "Oh, I already know you're worth it."

While Charlotte told herself not to read too much into his words, they walked in silence along the narrow, cobblestone street amongst other couples and families out enjoying the sunshine and shopping. They came around a corner to the Tiber River.

Alec pointed to a marina of large, expensive-looking yachts. "We should rent a boat."

"You're joking." Talk about an extravagance.

"You have to see the river, particularly at sunset. The bridges, the statues. St. Peter's Basilica and the Castillo de San Angelo are absolutely magnificent."

"Look." It was her turn to point. "There's a patio café. We can see the river for the price of a cup of coffee."

Alec turned to stare at her in confusion. "You don't want to cruise?"

"I don't want to rent a yacht!"

"It's only money."

She took his hand. "Let's get a cup of coffee, then we'll walk a ways."

"Coffee?" he confirmed with obvious disappointment.

She nodded and pointed them toward the little café.

They found mesh, metal seats and a little metal table by the rail. The breeze was cool off the water, and a barge floated by, while compact cars made their way over an ancient stone bridge.

Before sitting down, Alec removed his jacket, putting it around Charlotte's shoulders. She smiled her thanks.

While he spoke to the waiter in Italian, Alec pulled out his own seat.

He sat down, his gaze soft on her face as he seemed to consider her. "You're different," he finally told her.

"Different from what?" The coat was still warm from his body heat, and it felt comforting around her body.

"From other women."

She toyed with the silverware on the table. "Is that a good thing or a bad thing?"

He sat back in his chair. "Ever since they estimated my net worth in *Forbes,* it's as if I have a bull's-eye painted in the middle of my back. A great big target for every woman who thinks her life would be improved by money."

"Were they right?"

His forehead creased. "The women?"

A tourist barge sounded its horn, and a group of partyers waved and shouted.

Charlotte waved in return. *"Forbes."*

"Why? Did you read it?"

"No. But your château and your jet plane have me convinced you're a pretty good catch."

He shook his head. "Do you have any idea how long it's been since I've had a date pay for her own clothes?"

Charlotte couldn't help but smirk. "You buy your dates clothes?"

"I buy my dates many things."

"You ever stop to think you're bringing this on yourself?"

"You ever stop to think most women in the world are mercenary?"

Charlotte wasn't sure how to answer that. He was probably right. At least, he was probably right about the women he'd been hanging out with most of his life.

"Not all women are interested in your money."

The waiter stopped at their table, placing clear mugs of espresso on little blue saucers. He added a tray of sugared and chocolate-drizzled pastries in the center of the table.

The aromas hit Charlotte, reminding her that she was hungry. She pushed her arms into the sleeves of Alec's jacket and reached for a tiny cream-filled, cherry-topped morsel.

"These," she told him, "you can buy me any old time."

"That's the secret?" He chose a sugared croissant.

She nodded enthusiastically. "Pander to my sweet tooth, and I'm yours for life."

Something flickered in the depths of his brown eyes, and she instantly regretted her choice of words. They might have moved past one-night stand, but they hadn't gone anywhere beyond a fling. She was fine with that, and she didn't want Alec to worry that she had any other expectations.

She wondered if she should explain. Or would protesting just make things worse?

He considered her for a second longer. "Good to know," he said simply.

"Of course," she put into the silence, waving her pastry, "the downside is, I won't fit into the clothes for much longer."

He smiled. "I'm not worried. Your derriere's a little on the skinny side, anyway."

"Are you serious?" She twisted to look at her backside. She exercised quite extensively to keep her derriere fitting into designer clothes.

Alec laughed. "There's nothing wrong with a curve or two."

"Don't let Lesley Manichatio hear you say that."

"I already told her."

"Right."

He shrugged.

"You actually know Lesley Manichatio?"

"We carry her brands at Esmee ETA."

"Wait a minute." Charlotte set her pastry on the edge of her plate, wiping her hands on a paper napkin. "You own Esmee ETA?"

"Yes."

"The stores? The chain?"

"Uh-huh." He nodded.

"Alec?"

"Yes?"

"You really are a catch."

"You want to rethink the river cruise?"

"Not on your life."

He grinned. "At least eat your pastry."

She picked it up again.

No wonder the man was paranoid. How would he ever know if a woman fell in love with him or his money? He could write a prenup, sure. But he'd still never know. A woman could fake love for a very long time if Alec was paying the bills.

Seven

The sun slipped below the horizon, and Alec watched the lights come on up and down the Tiber River. He was in no hurry to leave the café. He didn't want to share Charlotte with Raine or anyone else just yet.

Over her empty coffee cup, she sighed at the sight. "It really is beautiful, isn't it?"

Alec reached for her hand, smoothing his thumb over her soft knuckles, moving to her palm. "Let me take you on a cruise."

She gave him a pained, wistful look.

"Don't fixate on the cost," he whispered. Then he raised her hand to his lips, turning it over to place a soft kiss on the inside of her wrist. "I want to get you alone, and I can't think of anywhere more alone than in a boat on the river."

Her glance slid to the marina below, and Alec knew he had her. He seized the opportunity, signaling the waiter. "Do you have a number for the marina?" he asked.

The man nodded and withdrew.

"I didn't say yes," Charlotte pointed out.

"Not with your lips," Alec agreed. "But you said yes with your eyes."

"That's a stretch."

He shook his head. "I've been reading women's eyes for many long years."

"Bragging?"

"Merely supporting my position."

The waiter returned with the number written on a small piece of paper, and Alec retrieved his cell phone. He made a quick call, arranged for a yacht and crew, then flipped the phone shut.

He stood from his chair and came around to hers. "We have to eat dinner somewhere," he told her.

"It's a dinner cruise?"

"It's whatever we want it to be."

The only available boat, the *Florence Maiden,* was ninety-five feet from bow to stern. She had a chef, a fully stocked galley, three luxury staterooms, a formal dining room, a hot tub on the aft deck and five crew members to ensure the entire evening ran smoothly.

Charlotte drew a deep breath. "I guess a girl's got to eat."

Alec held out his hand, helping her to her feet. "That's the spirit."

He kept her hand as they made their way down several staircases to the marina gate. There, he gave his name to a uniformed security guard.

"Berth 27B," the man informed him. "Enjoy your evening."

Still wearing his jacket, Charlotte slipped her arm into his as they moved onto the bobbing dock. It was full dark now, and the lights of Castle St. Angelo seemed even brighter across the river.

Alec noted a sign on the wharf and pointed to their left. "This way."

Charlotte turned, and they started past several dozen gleaming-white yachts berthed nose-in. "Tell me it's not the one on the end."

Alec could already see the name painted near the bow. "It's what they had available."

"You truly can't be trusted." But there wasn't a trace of anger in her tone. In fact, she sounded pleased. Well, he was feeling pretty pleased himself.

The captain greeted them at the bottom of the gangplank, welcoming them aboard. With Charlotte climbing in front of him, Alec's spirits lifted with every step upward.

They settled in padded, teak deck chairs at the bow of the boat. The steward provided a wine list, and Alec chose a merlot.

"We should call Raine."

"Why would we do that?" Alec had finally succeeded in separating Charlotte from the herd; he wasn't about to make contact.

The ship's whistle sounded and the engines rumbled as they reversed out of the berth, drawing back from the traffic, trees and buildings along the bank.

"She might be worried," said Charlotte.

"She's got my cell number. And yours, too, I imagine. She'll call if she needs anything."

"They probably expected to join us for dinner," Charlotte continued.

"They'll get over it."

The steward arrived to uncork the wine. He offered Alec a taste and, at Alec's nod, filled their glasses.

"The chef can offer you a seven-course Italian dinner, featuring *gamberi al Limone* and *rigatoni alla Caruso*. If you prefer French, he has a lovely *petits tournedos aux poivres vert* accompanied by *la salade du Montmartre*. Or he can prepare a grilled filet mignon, Portobello mushrooms, with a traditional Caesar salad."

Alec looked to Charlotte. "When in Rome?"

"The Italian dinner sounds perfect," she said to the steward.

As the man walked away, she leaned closer to Alec. "We can only hope the pasta will improve the size of my derriere."

Alec leaned toward her, keeping his voice at a conspiratorial level. "I'll let you know later."

"Feeling pretty sure of yourself?"

He glanced at the moon, the water, the lights of the city and Charlotte wrapped in his jacket lounging back amongst the subtle lights of the yacht's deck. "So far, so good," he admitted, taking a satisfied sip of the merlot.

"It is nice to get away from the crowds," Charlotte agreed. "The noise."

"The explosions."

"Sorry about that."

"Did you see your father this morning?" asked Alec.

She shook her head.

"He was due in, right?"

Her gaze went to a cloud wisping across the moon. "Yes, he was."

"But you didn't stay to say hello?"

She watched straight over the bow. "I didn't want to hold everybody up."

Alec considered her profile for a moment. "You didn't want to see him," he concluded.

"I told you, it's not the same as Jack. With David, I don't care one way or the other."

"What about the rest of the family?"

"What about them?"

"Your cousins Dev and Max were coming in today. And Isabella would have been on set. Don't you want to get to know them?"

Charlotte's expression tightened.

"You escaped, didn't you?" Alec guessed.

She waved a dismissive hand. "I needed clothes."

"You could have had some shipped from home."

She mustered a cocky grin. "And where would be the fun in that?"

"Charlotte," Alec pressed. "Are you afraid of your family?"

"It's not the same as for you."

"Blood is still blood," said Alec. He had dozens of aunts, uncles, cousins and second cousins in and around Provence. Montcalm family occasions were large, boisterous and entertaining. It didn't matter how seldom he saw some relatives, they always meant something.

She gathered his jacket closer around her.

"You said you missed Jack," Alec pointed out, struggling to figure out her feelings. "Now's your chance to get to know him."

Storm clouds gathered behind her blue eyes. "It's complicated."

"That's just part of the package. You want to hear about my Uncle Rudy and his affair with cousin Giselle's next-door neighbor? Or the time Uncle Bovier disinherited his eldest son, Leroy, because he was gay? Talk about a crisis. My phone rang off the hook for weeks." Alec took a breath.

"At least you know them," said Charlotte.

"Not that well." There were members of his family he saw only once a year.

"And." She gave a hollow laugh. "They didn't give you away."

Alec stilled.

Her voice went hard. "Nobody looked at you and Raine, and said, 'We like Raine better. Give Alec away.'"

"I'm sure it wasn't—"

"I have one father, an aunt and uncle, two grand-parents, a brother and four cousins on the Hudson side of the family, and not one, not *one of them* thought I was worth keeping." She closed her eyes, shook her head and took a swallow of her wine.

"I was wrong," Alec put in softly, drinking in the intense emotion on her face. "You're not scared. You're angry." He nodded to himself. "That makes sense. You have every right to be angry with them."

She waved her glass for emphasis. "My grandparents took wonderful care of me."

"You waited your whole life for Jack to come and rescue you. He never did."

"Jack was a little boy."

"Emotions have nothing to do with logic." Alec rose from his chair, crossing the polished, redwood deck. He crouched next to Charlotte's chair. "If you could control your emotions with logic, would you be here?"

She gazed silently into his eyes.

"It's a risk, you and me. For you, it's your reputation. For me…" He gave a short laugh. "Well, all the usual reasons. Plus, you're Raine's friend, and she's going to kill me if you get hurt."

"I'm not going to get hurt."

"I'm counting on that," Alec said honestly. He might be narcissistic and self-centered, but he didn't deliberately set out to hurt anyone. He tried hard to choose independent, worldly women. That they were mostly gold diggers was regrettable, but then the breakup disappointed them on more of a financial level than an emotional one. And that was good.

He heard the steward behind him with the first course.

Alec came to his feet. He'd hold Charlotte in his arms later and try to chase away her demons. It was a temporary fix for both of them, but it was all they had.

The water in the aft-deck hot tub swirled around Charlotte's naked body. Soft, underwater lighting reflected on the blue walls, highlighting her pale skin and Alec's arms where they wrapped around her waist to anchor across her stomach.

Angry at the Hudsons? At first she'd dismissed Alec's theory. Schooled by her diplomat grandfather and gentle, compassionate grandmother, Charlotte always had her emotions completely under control. She wasn't given to outbursts of anger. She was analytical and empathetic. Anger was a self-indulgent emotion that was never productive.

But as dinner moved on, something pricked at her brain: Could Alec could be right? Had she spent the past twenty-one years repressing her anger? Was that why her stomach churned at the thought of seeing the Hudsons?

She'd always felt like an outsider. And she'd long since admitted to her jealousy of her cousins and their easy familiarity with each other. But was there more?

"Stop thinking," Alec rumbled in her ear, giving her a quick kiss on the temple, his arms tightening for a split second around her waist.

She was cradled in his lap beneath the warm water. He'd asked the ship staff to give them privacy, so they were alone on the dark deck, surrounded by a smoked-glass guardrail. Clouds had been moving in for an hour, and the city lights turned blurry as the first rain-drops plunked into the tub.

Charlotte snuggled against the cocoon of Alec's body. She didn't feel like an outsider now. In fact, for the first time in her life, she was at the center of the universe—hers and Alec's. She recognized the danger of those feelings and vowed they wouldn't get out of control. But for now, for tonight, Alec was a welcome break from the reality she'd have to face back at the movie set.

The rain grew heavy, fat droplets splashing into the hot tub.

"You want to go inside?" asked Alec.

"I like it here," she responded, reluctant to break the spell.

"I like it, too." He kissed her neck, tracing a trail to her damp shoulder and back again.

"You taste good."

"It's the rainwater."

"No, it's not."

She tipped her head to one side, giving him freer access. His large hands slipped up her stomach, covering her breasts. "You're soft," he muttered. "So soft."

She dropped her head right back, and he placed a warm, wet kiss on her lips.

"Have you stopped thinking?" he asked.

"I think you're magic," she answered, and he smiled.

"It's nice to be magic."

He kissed her again, more seriously this time. Then he carefully turned her so she was facing him, straddling his lap, her arms loosely around his neck.

He shimmied her close. "Do you want anything?"

"Besides you?"

"Coffee, brandy, dessert?"

"You're going to call the steward?" She glanced meaningfully down at their naked bodies.

"We can have it delivered to the stateroom."

"I assumed you had something else in mind for the stateroom."

He smoothed back her wet hair. "I'm in no rush." Then his expression turned serious. "We've got all night."

"What about Rai—"

He put an index finger across her lips. "Nobody's called. Nobody's going to call. It's just you and me." His gaze trailed from her neck to her breasts, her stomach and below. "You are astonishingly beautiful. I could sit here and stare at you all night."

"That's only because you can't see my skinny derriere."

"Turn around."

"I don't believe I will."

"I've grown fond of your derriere." He slipped a hand beneath her and gave a squeeze. "Plus, you ate all that pasta."

She struggled not to wriggle under his hand. But it was strong and warm and oh-so-sensual. "The pasta was delicious."

Alec kissed her mouth. "A dismal second."

"To?"

He drew back. "You fishing for more compliments?"

"Oh." She pretended to suddenly understand. "A dismal second to *me*."

He chuckled low. "You are shameless."

She gave in, shifting her body so that his hand touched the sensitive spot between her legs.

"Pretty much," she agreed in a husky voice.

His eyes darkened, and he leaned in for a very serious kiss, his fingertips setting out on an exploration that made her gasp, even as cool rain water trickled down her spine.

"Inside?" he rasped, and she quickly nodded her agreement.

He lifted her out of the tub, wrapped them both in thick, white robes and carried her the short distance to the master stateroom.

The room was huge, with a cushioned, cream-colored carpet, gleaming cherrywood paneling, a massive bed with a rose-colored comforter, eight pillows and a padded bench at the foot. There were mirrors on the ceiling, oil paintings on the walls and a subtly textured, cream wallpaper that wrapped around a sitting nook with overstuffed furniture and porcelain lamps. Several flower arrangements gave the room a sweet, subtle scent.

Alec set her down on the soft carpet, dragging back the comforter to reveal crisp, white sheets. He tossed most of the pillows, then tugged at the sash of her robe. With warm hands, he brushed the terry-cloth from her shoulders, easing the fabric down her arms, until it cascaded to a pool at her feet.

"Amazing," he whispered, drawing back to gaze at her naked body.

Charlotte felt amazing. She loved the warm look in his eyes, the hiss of his indrawn breath, the power of his muscled body as he tossed his own robe and stood naked before her.

She reached out to touch his chest, his skin warm under her fingertips. "Amazing," she echoed.

He stepped forward. His palm cupped the curve of her hip, drawing her in. His other hand touched her chin, tipping her face ever so gently as he bent toward her for a soft kiss.

"I don't want tonight to end," he told her.

Neither did she. "What if we keep sailing? Into the Mediterranean, through the Strait of Gibraltar and out into the Pacific."

"Don't tempt me."

"They'd probably send a search party."

He raised an eyebrow. "But I wonder how many times we could make love before they found us?"

"I wonder how many times we can make love tonight?" she countered.

"Now there's a challenge." He backed her into the edge of the bed, kissed her soundly, his hands roaming, while she gave up any pretense at control, dragging him onto the bed, kissing his mouth, tasting his skin, running her hands down his back, his thighs, kneading his hard muscles, before sitting up to straddle his body.

They both groaned at the contact, staring into each other's eyes. His hands bracketed her hips, easing inside her. He was huge and hot, and she gasped as sparks spread out to touch her fingers and her toes.

He locked his hands with hers, and he flexed his hips. She matched him thrust for thrust, her head tipping back, and the world sliding into a cataclysm of color until she cried out his name and he wrapped her in an engulfing hug.

Hours later, they lay side by side, he on his back, she sprawled on her stomach. She felt as though she might never move again.

Through bleary eyes, she watched him liberate a long-stemmed rose from the vase beside the bed. He stroked its soft petals along her shoulder, down the indent of her waist, over the curve of her hip then across her derriere.

"I've changed my mind," he said, "your derriere is perfect."

She couldn't help but smile. "You do know how to show a girl a good time."

"I try."

"You didn't have to do all this," she continued. The yacht, the hot tub, the amazing dinner. "I'd have slept with you again anyway."

His voice was a low rumble. "You mean I could have checked us into the Plaza Della Famiglia for thirty euro and had my way with you?"

She smiled. "Yes," she answered honestly.

He stared, not moving, at the ceiling for a while.

There was a funny catch to his voice when he spoke

again. "That means a lot to me." He paused. "Knowing that you mean it."

Then he rose on his elbow to gaze down at her. "But it's also important to me that I didn't do that."

She nodded, understanding, touched by his point. And, quite frankly, a luxury yacht made for better memories than a cheap motel.

He gently brushed a lock of hair back from her cheek. "Of all the women…" He went silent for a long minute. Then he leaned forward to kiss her mouth.

He pulled her almost fiercely to him, kissing harder and deeper. Her energy returned in a rush, and their naked bodies meshed together. The rain drummed steadily on the window and lightning flashed in the sky, while the yacht, droning steadily, made a lazy turn to head back up the Tiber River.

They made it to the airport just in time to greet Raine and Kiefer and jump on the jet to get to London. The Montcalm Gulfstream had two seating areas, four armchairs facing each other at the front of the cabin and a couch, table and two side-facing armchairs at the back.

Raine seemed uncomfortable as they boarded, moving to the back and buckling in on the white leather couch. Charlotte followed, wondering if she'd somehow offended her friend by staying out all night. She and Raine were sharing a hotel suite, so Raine had to be fully aware that Charlotte had spent the night with Alec.

Alec and Kiefer sat down in the second row, on opposite sides of the aisle, facing forward. The captain came back to talk to Alec, while a steward offered drinks all around. Charlotte said yes to champagne and orange juice, steeling her courage to face Raine.

"You all right?" she asked Raine as the jet taxied for takeoff. Alec and Kiefer had immediately settled in to a work discussion.

"Yeah." Raine nodded without glancing Charlotte's way.

"The meeting?" Charlotte forced herself to ask. "It went well?"

Raine gave another nod.

The engines whined to full throttle, the jet gaining speed before smoothly lifting off the runway, climbing fast and banking north.

As they leveled, and the noise subsided, Charlotte gathered her courage. "Raine, I have to—"

"You're probably wondering," Raine interrupted, glancing worriedly at the two men in the front of the cabin. She leaned close to Charlotte. "You're probably wondering why I didn't show up last night."

Charlotte was confused. "Show up?"

Raine nodded. "At the hotel. I—" Her eyes darted to Alec for a split second. "I was with Kiefer."

Charlotte raised a hand to her lips to cover up the smile. "You spent the night with Kiefer?"

Raine nodded, looking pained. "I wasn't going to—" She twisted her hands around her clutch purse. "I know I said I wouldn't—"

"I slept with Alec," Charlotte admitted in an effort to lessen Raine's embarrassment.

Raine drew back. "Huh?"

"I didn't go back to the hotel suite, either."

"You slept with Alec?" Raine hissed.

"Shh." Charlotte checked out the backs of the men's heads to make sure they weren't listening. "Yes."

"So you didn't even *know* I wasn't there?"

"Didn't have a clue," said Charlotte.

"I could have gotten away with it?"

Charlotte nodded. "But you *slept* with Kiefer? What happened?"

"After the meeting," said Raine, keeping her voice down, "we went to dinner. I wondered why you guys didn't call, by the way."

"I wondered why you didn't call us."

"There was dancing," said Raine. "And, well…"

"He now knows you think he's hot?" Charlotte suggested.

"He knows now."

Both women stared ahead in silence for a moment.

"And Alec?" asked Raine.

"Knows I think he's hot, too."

Raine nodded, a grin growing rapidly on her face.

Suddenly, both women burst out laughing.

The two men turned to stare.

"Nothing," Raine assured them.

"Girl talk," said Charlotte.

Alec's eyes narrowed in suspicion, but Charlotte gave him a benign shrug. It wasn't her place to give away secrets. After a minute, the men went back to their conversation.

"What now?" asked Raine.

Charlotte didn't know how to answer that. Last night had been magic, from shopping to coffee to the yacht. But in the cold light of day, she had no idea what Alec would expect.

"What now for you?" she asked Raine, stalling for time.

"Honestly? I think it's going to get really awkward, really fast," said Raine. "It was great, but now we have to work together." She folded her arms over her chest and leaned her head back on the seat. "There's just no way this ends well."

Charlotte nodded, understanding completely. *Really awkward, really fast,* was a good way to put it. It was some consolation that she'd be done with the movie in a few weeks. After that, she and Alec's paths didn't need to cross. But for Raine, a fling with Kiefer was a whole lot more complicated. She wished she had some helpful advice to offer. But she had nothing.

Alec rose from his seat and moved down the aisle, his expression serious. He nodded to Raine. "Kiefer would like to talk to you."

Without meeting her brother's eyes, Raine scrambled to her feet and moved up the cabin.

Alec stayed behind, taking the seat next to Charlotte. And when he turned to her, his expression softened.

"Hey." He smiled.

"Hey." Despite the circumstances, she couldn't help but smile back.

"How are you feeling?"

"I'm fine."

"Tired?"

"A little."

Between their bodies, he took her hand in his. "So, what do you want to do in London?"

She didn't want to be presumptuous. Though she'd happily spend more time with him. "What do *you* want to do in London?" She put it back on him.

Unexpectedly, he cupped her cheek, raking spread fingers back into her loose hair, pulling her forward for a kiss.

"Kiefer," she warned in an undertone, as Alec's lips closed over hers.

"Kiefer knows," said Alec against her mouth. Then he kissed her deeply. "*This* is what I want to do in London."

"For two whole days?"

"Yes."

"Did Kiefer say…anything?" Charlotte asked carefully.

Alec nodded toward the front of the cabin. "Take a look."

She twisted her head to see Raine sitting across Kiefer's lap in the big armchair. They were whispering and giggling together.

"I feel like I'm in high school," she told Alec.

He agreed with a nod. "But with much better transportation and a platinum card."

"You're going to try to spend money on me in London, aren't you?"

"*Try?*" he scoffed, cocking his head and giving her a smirk. "I've already booked a suite at the Ritz and a box on the Grand Tier at Covent Garden."

Eight

By the time they made it through London and Paris, Charlotte felt like a spoiled princess. She'd given up arguing with Alec about money. She even gave up trying to pay for her own clothes. He'd simply worn her down.

But now they were back in Provence. One of Alec's drivers had delivered the Lamborghini to the airport. So they'd stowed the luggage in the limo with Raine and Kiefer and were speeding under the streetlights, top down, along the highway with jazz pouring out of the sound system. She'd dressed casually for the trip, in a new pair of designer jeans and a cropped, peach tank top with flat lace insets.

Alec was a steady, confident driver. And as their speed increased, she kicked off her sandals and tipped her head back, letting the cool wind flow over her skin.

"Almost home," said Alec, shifting out of Sixth as the turnoff to Château Montcalm came into view.

She tried to formulate the right sentiment. She watched Alec's profile as the aspen and oak trees flashed by.

"What?" He glanced over.

Straightforward seemed like the best choice. "I had a really great time, Alec."

He grinned. "Me, too."

Their gazes caught and held.

"Thank you," she told him sincerely.

"Anytime," he breathed, turning his attention back to the road, slowing down further as the château's driveway loomed.

Charlotte let out a sigh, sliding her feet back into her sandals. As the headlights caught the semitrailers, the scarred lawn and the open-air buffet tables that provided craft services to the crew during the day, she tried to smooth her hair into some sort of order. But she quickly gave up. And when Alec brought the convertible to a halt at the front door, she decided a shower would be first on her list. She might as well get rid of the dust along with the tangles.

Alec swung around to open her door, and Charlotte came to her feet, stretching out her neck and back after the long journey. The film set was quiet as they crossed to the front door, with just a few grips, production assistants and security guards putting things in place for the morning.

Alec pushed open the wide door, and the quiet of the yard disappeared. Chitchat and music wafted out from the great room. Several people laughed, while Lars's unmistakable voice proposed a toast to Isabella.

Charlotte's stomach clenched in alarm. The Hudsons wouldn't, they would *not* hold a party in Alec's château while he was away. She cautiously glanced up at him. His mouth was set in a firm line, and before she could even register the anger in his eyes, he was marching toward the archway leading to the great room.

Though Charlotte dreaded what she'd find, she felt compelled to follow along.

"Monsieur Montcalm?" Henri hustled out from the hallway to ambush Alec.

"Not now, Henri," Alec growled, brushing past.

"But, *monsieur.*"

"Save it." Alec kept walking. It was the first time she'd ever heard him utter a sharp word to a member of his staff, certainly not to Henri.

"Madame Lillian Hudson arrived this afternoon."

Alec didn't react, but Charlotte certainly did. Lillian was here? Her grandmother had shown up on the set?

"Given her age and *illness,*" Henri stressed, striding along beside Alec, "I thought it wise to invite her to stay in the château."

Alec's steps faltered.

"I was certain, were you here, you would insist," said Henri, a wealth of meaning in his tone.

"She's ill?" Alec asked, a muscle twitching near his left eye.

"She has cancer," Charlotte supplied in a pained voice. They'd done it. Her family had actually thrown a party in Alec's home.

"I put her in the Bombay room with her son, Markus, next door. The rest of the family is with Jack at the hotel."

Alec's nostrils flared as he sucked in a sharp breath.

"I'm so sorry," Charlotte whispered.

Alec glanced at her, but said nothing.

Henri's voice went to an undertone. "Dinner tonight is to welcome Lillian to Provence."

Alec was silent a second longer. But then he gave a sharp nod. "Thank you, Henri."

Henri nodded in return. "Of course, *monsieur*."

Then Alec held out his arm to Charlotte. "Will you introduce me to your family?"

Charlotte's stomach clenched tighter. Judging by the noise level, the entire family, along with assorted production staff, were in Alec's great room. She was tired, trail weary, dusty and disheveled. She didn't want to see the Hudsons or anyone else right now.

But she couldn't say no to Alec. He'd been extraordinarily patient under some very trying circumstances. So, instead of protesting, she nodded and took his arm. They walked through the archway to the stone-walled, high-ceilinged great room. Its polished hardwood floors, Aubusson rugs and Louis XV furnishings were covered in wall-to-wall Hudsons— Charlotte's grandmother Lillian, her uncle Markus, her father, David, her brother, Jack, and cousins Dev and Max, and Isabella chatting intimately with Ridley Sinclair.

Jack was the first person to notice Alec. As he came forward, Charlotte quickly disentangled herself from Alec's arm.

"Alec," Jack stated heartily, extending his hand. "Great to have you back."

"Thank you," Alec intoned, but Charlotte could hear the tension in his voice.

Jack turned. "Everybody, this is Alec Montcalm, our host."

There was a chorus of greetings and a surge forward that halted when people realized Lillian was making her way to Alec.

Everyone, including Alec, waited as the frail-looking woman approached him.

"Mr. Montcalm," came Lillian's steady voice.

Alec took a few steps forward to close the distance.

"Mrs. Hudson," he nodded, gently taking her hand between his. "A pleasure to meet you at last."

"My thanks, on behalf of my entire family, for your hospitality."

"No thanks are necessary," said Alec. "It is my pleasure."

No one listening could have guessed at the trials and tribulations Alec had been through with the film so far.

Charlotte's glance caught Jack's, and when his gaze slid along her outfit, she remembered her appearance. If only the archway or even the patio door were a little closer, she'd slip out. But the last thing she wanted to do was call attention to herself.

"As you may know," said Lillian, "this film is near and dear to my heart."

Alec stood to one side and gestured to Charlotte. "Your granddaughter expressed that quite eloquently."

Lillian and the entire family turned their attention to Charlotte.

Charlotte's hand went reflexively to her messy hair. Then she wondered if dust was smudged on her cheeks or if every wrinkle in her clothing was visible under the great room lights.

"Hello, Lillian," she managed.

"Lovely to see you, dear." Lillian nodded regally.

"It was Charlotte who convinced me to allow Hudson Pictures to use my château," Alec continued.

Charlotte could see what Alec was trying to do, and it was admirable. But she could also see he was making Markus uncomfortable. It was his project, and he didn't seem used to other people taking the spotlight.

Sure enough, Markus stepped forward. "Markus Hudson." He offered his hand to Alec and shook heartily. "CEO of Hudson Pictures."

With everyone's attention on Alec and Markus, Charlotte took a step backward. She was escaping to the shower just as soon as humanly possible. She could always come back for a drink later and say her hellos. Hopefully, by then, her new clothes would have arrived in the limo. They would boost her confidence.

While Alec and Markus talked, she eased carefully backward.

But then Jack appeared by her side. "I hear you were in London," he opened.

Charlotte gave another hopeless swipe at her hair before answering. "And Rome and Paris."

Jack nodded, a glance straying to Alec.

"Raine wanted to go shopping," Charlotte quickly put in. "You met Raine, right? It was mostly her who helped me convince Alec to let you film here. She should be right behind us." Charlotte glanced toward the hall. "With Kiefer, the vice president of Montcalm."

"You okay?" Jack wedged in.

"Fine." Charlotte clamped her mouth shut.

Jack nodded across the room at their father. "You going to say hello?"

"I'm not in a rush." If she could avoid it, she would. Her emotional state was better if she simply avoided her father altogether.

At the moment, David was working on a martini—no surprise there. He was also watching his brother, Markus, through squinting eyes, his lips pursed in obvious annoyance. She knew the two brothers didn't get along. She might be out of touch, but that much family gossip had come her way.

Again, no surprise. David might be a talented director, but he was also narcissistic and egotistical. And from what she'd been able to glean, Markus had little patience for difficult personalities.

"Show him you're not intimidated," Jack suggested.

"I'm not," she lied. She was intimidated by the entire family, particularly en masse. And she knew talking to David would have the power to zap her back to the unwanted little girl at the airport.

"Glad to hear it," said Jack, taking a sip from his crystal tumbler. Then there was a sneer in his voice. "Because he's definitely not worth it."

Charlotte simply nodded.

"You will say hello to Cece, right?" Jack referred to his new wife.

"After I shower," Charlotte agreed. "I really need to get cleaned up."

"Theo's a great kid," Jack put in, voice softening as he gazed across the room once again. "And I'm going to be a wonderful father. And that man…" The hard voice came back in force. "That man will *not* influence me in any way. I am not him."

Charlotte felt an instant admiration for her brother. He'd obviously come to terms with his childhood. She was happy for him, but she couldn't help but feel even more lonely.

"I won't let him define me," Jack finished.

Charlotte wished she could be that strong. But she was a long way from not letting her upbringing define her.

Alec was right when he said she was angry. But she was also hurt. And she was also lonely. And being around the Hudsons, especially David, made her wonder if anybody in the world would ever choose her, ever truly love her, just for herself.

Alec saw Charlotte leave the great room. His initial reaction was to go after her, but Markus was still talking, and he was curious about her father, who was sitting off to one side, looking sullen as he watched his older brother through narrowed eyes.

Lillian had said good-night, and was being helped back to her room. Alec had been introduced to Isabella and Ridley Sinclair. Judging by their expressions and body language, he'd bet the affair rumors were true. He wondered if he should alert Kiefer. It wasn't too late to sneak a tabloid reporter onto the property, or give them a heads-up on the location of the stars' villa rental.

Markus had also introduced his sons Dev and Max. Both seemed hardworking and intelligent. Dev was planning to leave with his father and Lillian within the next few days. Max planned to stay to work with David on a daily basis. It was easy to see there was no love lost between Markus's side of the family and his brother, David.

In fact, Alec wondered why David was directing the film at all, until he overheard Isabella comment on

David's artistic and dramatic vision. Apparently, vision was a difficult thing to come by in Hollywood. That would explain why everyone put up with Lars's temperamental nature. Alec would have fired the man weeks ago.

At a lull in the conversation, Alec excused himself and approached David.

"Alec Montcalm." He offered his hand.

David had the grace to stand up from the armchair in front of the stone fireplace. "David Hudson."

"I understand you're directing the film?"

"Is that all you understand?" David's gaze slid to Markus; he was obviously wondering if his brother had been badmouthing him to Alec.

"Can I freshen your drink?" asked Alec, nodding to the near-empty glass.

David glanced down. "It's the Glen Klavit. One ice cube."

Alec gave a brief nod to a staff member, and indicated David's glass. "I'll have the same," he told the waiter.

"A man with good taste in scotch," David commented.

"I visited Klavit Castle last year," Alec said conversationally. "Almost inaccessible, and damn cold. But there's no better place on earth for distilling coastal whiskey."

David nodded as the waiter presented their drinks on a silver tray.

"Charlotte and I were in London last week." As a segue, it was a stretch, but Alec didn't want to be at this all night.

"I was wandering through your pool house," said David, as if his daughter's name hadn't even been mentioned. "And I was wondering, would you be open to a minor renovation?"

"We stayed at the Ritz," said Alec. "Took in the Royal Ballet."

David's eyes narrowed, as if he was assessing Alec's mental competence. "Uh, right. Always a treat. There's a lighting problem with the pool house. We'd like to add a window in the front. When we pan left, we're going to lose the natural light on Isabella, and the mood can't be too somber. It's the pivotal scene where Lillian and Charles pledge their love. I thought about backlighting." David's eyes lost focus. "But we're going for realism, not some overly romanticized—"

"As long as you don't use explosives," Alec cut in.

David drew back with a frown, obviously missing the joke. "It's a love scene."

"I see."

"It's midway thought the script. The conflicts have been well set up, and the central characters are—"

"Sure," said Alec, taking a bracing swig of the scotch, wishing he'd gone for something that was cask strength. "Put in a window."

"That's good," said David with a distracted nod. "Then I can talk to wardrobe about Lillian's hat."

"Whatever," said Alec, realizing Charlotte had nothing in common with her father.

He glanced across the room to where Jack was talking with his cousin Max. David and Jack both had dark hair and blue eyes. But there was nothing definitively similar about their appearances, either.

"We might need a few extra shooting days," David put in. "I have Cece working on script revisions."

"No problem," said Alec. As long as Charlotte stuck around with them, the film crew could stay here as long as they liked.

Charlotte had missed breakfast. Exhausted from lack of sleep in Rome, London and Paris, and battling butterflies in her stomach at the proximity of all those Hudsons, she'd buried her face under the covers and dozed until nearly ten.

The house was quiet as she wandered into the kitchen, the noise from the film set filtered by the thick stone walls. Cece was in the breakfast nook, script pages spread out in front of her, with her two-year-old son, Theo, playing trains on the floor. Cece had recently revealed the fact that Theo was Jack's son, making him Charlotte's nephew.

For some reason, Cece and Theo weren't nearly as intimidating as the rest of the clan. Maybe it was because they were new to the family.

"Good morning," Charlotte offered, pouring herself a cup of coffee from the big island counter.

"Morning," Cece returned with a smile, her brown hair flowing softly around her delicate face, coffee-toned eyes warm and welcoming.

Charlotte immediately relaxed, her stomach calming down for the first time in hours. "Am I disturbing you?"

Cece shook her head. "David's being a jerk this morning. He can damn well wait for the new pages."

Then she seemed to remember who Charlotte was. Her face flushed slightly. "Oops. Sorry."

"For insulting the man who abandoned me and made my mother's life a living hell?" Charlotte plunked down on the bench seat across from Cece. "Wow. Don't know where that came from."

"It was well earned. I hope it was cathartic."

"I take it you and Jack have discussed our *father?*"

"Jack and I have discussed quite a lot of things in the past couple of months."

Charlotte was hit with an unwelcome pang of jealousy. She squelched it. "I'm glad you found each other," she said in all honesty. "And I'm sorry I missed the wedding."

"It was very short notice," Cece allowed.

"We were in China," Charlotte explained. "I couldn't leave the ambassador."

"Jack told me." Her attention suddenly shifted. "Not in your mouth, sweetheart."

Charlotte glanced down at Theo. His cherubic little face was scrunched up in a grin as he gnawed on a section of wooden train track.

"He's adorable," she told Cece.

"He looks just like his father," said Cece, and Charlotte's eyes suddenly burned.

She quickly blinked, raising her coffee for a sip to cover up. "Are you thinking about brothers or sisters?"

Cece smiled. "You bet. We're a little behind on timing, but we're planning to make it up in effort."

Charlotte laughed. Jack's children, growing up in a stable, loving home. It was a wonderful turn of events.

Two figures passed by the window outside. It was Max and his assistant, Dana Fallon.

"They're moving around back today. Shots in the garden, I think," said Cece.

Max shouted a question across the lawn to the assistant director. The man answered with hand gestures.

Dana started to say something, but Max strode away.

Charlotte caught an unguarded look of longing on Dana's face.

"Oh, dear," she whispered under her breath, cradling her warm, stoneware cup.

"I know," said Cece. "She's got it bad for Max."

"Does he know?"

Cece shook her head. "The man is oblivious to everything but work. And she's such a great girl."

"Should somebody clue him in? Maybe Jack?"

Cece raised her brow. "If you were her, would you want somebody to clue the guy in?"

Charlotte couldn't help thinking about her growing feelings for Alec. Alec was a playboy, a womanizer; he didn't have the slightest interest in a serious relationship. Would she want some helpful soul telling him that she was falling for him?

Not on your life. As long as she kept her secret, she could have a few more weeks of paradise. The second it was out, he would run for the hills.

"No," she admitted. "I suppose Dana's best chance is if Max notices himself. You suppose there's anything we can do to help that happen?"

Cece gave a sly grin, and Charlotte felt her first true connection with a member of the Hudson family.

"Morning, all," came Raine's sleepy voice.

"Hi, Raine," Charlotte answered. "Have you met Cece? She's the screenwriter and my new sister-in-law." The title felt odd on Charlotte's tongue, but she forced herself to use it anyway.

"We haven't met," said Raine, holding out a hand to shake.

"You have a lovely home," said Cece. "It's going to give the picture such authenticity."

"I only hope it's standing when you're done," said Raine, pouring herself some coffee and selecting a pastry, before hopping up on one of the bar stools at the island counter.

"I heard about the explosion," said Cece. "And I saw the aftermath. You do know they'll pay for it."

"As long as no one was hurt," said Raine, taking a big bite of the beignet.

Cece glanced down at the script pages. "I'm trying to keep the rest of the battle scenes to a minimum."

"We appreciate that," said Charlotte.

"But you have to admit," Raine put in, "it was exciting."

"It was definitely exciting," Charlotte agreed. As had been the preceding hours in Alec's bed. That was the first time they'd made love. It was fantastic, and it had actually improved with time.

Not that his technique had needed one iota of improvement. But she knew him better now, knew him and liked him. Liked him a lot.

Oh, no.

This was bad.

"I think I'll go change," she told the other two women, coming to her feet.

A sudden wave of dizziness flashed through her brain, and she grabbed the edge of the table to steady herself.

"Too many sleepless nights?" Raine teased.

And Cece's interest perked.

"Parties in London and Paris," Charlotte quickly explained, resisting the urge to glare at Raine. "I slept great last night."

"We're not as young as we used to be," Cece chimed in.

"Speak for yourself," said Raine. "I can still party like a nineteen-year-old."

"Not if you want your circulation numbers back up," came Kiefer's voice. He gave Raine a mock stern look as he entered the room.

Then something passed between them, something strong and intimate that made Charlotte jealous. Which was silly. If Raine and Kiefer were happy together, it was nothing but good news. And if Jack and Cece had found joy together, Charlotte was thrilled for them.

Still, an indefinable emotion clogged her throat, and she mumbled something more about getting dressed, then she quickly left the kitchen. Alec had been too nice to her the past few days. She was beginning to read things into it that simply weren't there. He was a decent guy who had a lot of experience in dating. He also had an unlimited credit card, which helped him entertain in style.

She had to stop confusing his innate class and hospitality for deeper feelings.

Nine

Two days later, Lillian, Markus and Dev, along with Dev's fiancée, Valerie Shelton, left Provence. Alec finally felt as if he had a little privacy. He waited until after midnight, until the set was quiet and the staff had retired for the night. Dressed in a pair of jogging shorts and a simple T-shirt, he padded down the hallway to Charlotte's room.

He silently cracked open her door. Moonlight shone through the billowing sheer curtains, reflecting off her soft skin and blond hair. Her covers were half off in the warm evening, revealing the lace-inset, purple silk nightgown she'd bought in Rome.

He'd wanted to buy it for her. He still wished he'd bought it for her. He wanted to feel some ownership of the garment. And, he admitted to himself, he wanted to feel some ownership of the woman wearing it.

It was a ridiculous and inappropriate emotion. Charlotte didn't need him in her life. Everything she'd said and done for the past three weeks told him she wanted stability. She wanted family. She wanted a man she could count on.

Nobody could count on Alec.

Still, it didn't stop him from wanting her.

He crossed the room, crouching down beside the big bed.

"Charlotte?" he whispered.

She stirred in her sleep.

He brushed a hand gently over her hair. "Charlotte?"

She groaned. "Did they catch the château on fire?"

He smiled. "No. Everything's still standing. You asleep?"

"I was." She blinked her eyes open in the dappled light.

"I was lonely," he confessed.

After a silent moment, she smiled sweetly up at him. "Me, too."

"Thank goodness."

She slid over, and he slipped into the bed beside her.

He wrapped an arm around her waist and pulled her backward against his body. "I like you in silk." He nuzzled against her neck, kissing her hairline, breathing in the intoxicating scent of her skin. "I like you out of silk, too." He slipped his hand below the hem of the short nightgown, sliding it up to her flat belly, letting it rest against the softness.

Then he kissed the side of her neck, drawing her earlobe into his mouth.

"Are we sleeping or making love?" she asked.

"Do you have a preference?" He did. But he was

willing to compromise anything if it meant he could hold her in his arms tonight.

"Just getting clarification."

"Any reason we can't do both?"

"I've been having a little trouble getting up in the mornings."

"I can be quick," he offered. "And then you can get right to sleep."

He felt her body quiver with laughter. "Such a gentleman."

He moved his hand to the curve of her breast. "Does fast work for you?"

She turned onto her back, and he could just make out her expression in the moonlight. She was such an incredibly beautiful woman, and his heart did a funny flip-flop as he gazed into her eyes.

"Slow works for me," she told him, slipping her small, soft fingertips under the hem of his T-shirt and stretching it off over his head.

"Slow it is." He leaned in for a full-on kiss.

Her warm lips softened and parted. He was instantly lost in their magic. A cool breeze danced over his bare back, while his blood heated to a boil. But still he kissed her, holding her close, worshipping her body, moving ever so slowly, ever so patiently into more intimate kisses, more intimate caresses, making love to her until they both collapsed from exhaustion.

Even then, he held her close. Less than half-awake, at the first streaks of dawn, he longed for things he knew could never be.

Charlotte woke up alone. It was late, and the film set below on the front lawn was a hive of activity.

Equipment was humming. People were shouting. And the greasy smells from the catering-truck breakfast grill permeated her bedroom.

Her stomach roiled.

She jumped out of bed and rushed to the bathroom, vomiting briefly into the toilet.

She sat back on the cool tiles, rubbing a sheen of sweat from her forehead. No matter how amazing it was with Alec in the middle of the night, she had to start getting some sleep. Raine might feel like a teenager, but Charlotte's system was clearly rebelling.

She rose shakily to her feet, splashing water on her face and brushing her teeth at the sink. Now that the dizzy spell had passed, she was hungry. Really hungry.

Maybe she'd grab a snack first, then get a shower later. She reached for the robe hanging on the back of the bathroom door.

Suddenly, she froze.

She was incredibly hungry, and not the least bit ill.

This was four mornings now that she'd felt temporarily nauseated.

She did some quick math in her head, then she dropped weakly to sit on the edge of the tub.

No.

It couldn't be.

They'd used a condom, and the odds against it were astronomical.

Still.

She cringed and dropped her face into her palms.

Her period was five days late, and she'd just vomited at the smell of bacon.

She had to get her hands on a home pregnancy test.

* * *

Positive.

Charlotte stared at the parallel magenta lines on the little plastic wand. She was pregnant. She was going to have Alec Montcalm's baby, angering him and disgracing her grandfather all in one fell swoop. Alec hadn't signed up for this.

And what would the Hudsons think? They'd realize she'd been carrying on an affair right here under their noses. Any respect she'd hoped to gain from Jack was gone. And Lillian. Lillian was from another time, another age. Charlotte barely knew her grandmother, and *this* was what Lillian would learn about her. Especially after learning of her brother Jack's wife Cece's pregnancy. She kept that a secret from Jack for two years. How would Lillian cope in another scandal?

She swiped at a wayward tear.

She was pregnant.

She had to be strong.

There was—

She glanced down at her stomach, and her hand moved reflexively over the flat surface. There was a baby inside her. A baby that would need love and care and protection, despite any circumstances of its birth. A little girl, like her. Or a little boy, like Jack, who would count on Charlotte to take care of him.

She sat up straighter, knowing what she had to do.

She'd keep her pregnancy a secret—at least until the film finished shooting. The Hudsons would never have to know it had happened here. Then she could quit her job with her grandfather, and go away, somewhere private, where nobody knew her and nothing could hurt her child.

She'd have to tell Alec eventually, of course.

Alec.

Her stomach tightened with dread.

How was she going to sleep with Alec again? She couldn't do it with such a huge lie between them. And he would be back to her room, probably tonight. And she'd have to look him in the eyes and…

She groaned out loud.

"Charlotte?" It was Raine.

Charlotte grabbed at the plastic wand. "I'm…" she called out. "Just a…" She scrambled to her feet.

"Are you okay?"

"I'll be…"

But it was too late.

The en suite door was open, and Raine had crossed the bedroom.

"Cece and I were—" Raine stopped cold, with Cece nearly barreling into the back of her.

Charlotte could feel the blood drain from her face.

The cardboard package was strewn across the countertop. The wand was in her hand, with its damning positive result glaring up in living color.

Raine reached for the wand, confirming what she had already seen.

In a split second, Raine had pulled Charlotte into her arms. The dam burst loose, and Charlotte's tears flowed freely.

"It's okay," Raine crooned.

"It's a disaster," moaned Charlotte.

Raine grasped her firmly by the shoulders, pulling her slightly away, speaking firmly. "No. It's not. Babies are *never* a disaster."

"Alec doesn't want to be a father," Charlotte hiccuped. "He doesn't even want a relationship. All he wants—"

"Don't sell Alec short."

But Raine didn't understand. She had rose-colored glasses when it came to Alec. Though, who could blame her? He was a wonderful brother. He was willing to fight people for her.

The memory brought fresh tears, and the bathroom blurred around her.

She felt an arm on her shoulders, and it was Cece's voice this time. "I know how you feel," Cece stated. "I've been exactly where you are. You're scared. You feel all alone. You're desperately struggling to get your bearings."

Charlotte nodded. Cece had it exactly right.

"Now, here's what you're going to do." Cece led Charlotte to the bed, sat her down on the edge and sat next to her, taking her hand. "You are going to tell Alec immediately."

Charlotte's entire body clenched at the mere thought of that conversation.

Even Raine took a couple of reflexive steps across the bedroom. "I'm not so—"

"You have no choice," Cece continued. "You know, and he deserves to know, too."

Charlotte shook her head. It was too soon. Like Cece said, she needed to get her bearings before she did anything at all. "He doesn't need—"

"The longer you wait, the worse it gets. He'll want to know why you waited, and you will not have a good explanation."

"He doesn't need to know when I knew."

"Charlotte," said Cece with exaggerated patience, "look at me."

Charlotte did.

Raine sat down on the other side of her, rubbing one shoulder.

"I waited two years," said Cece. "First I waited a week. Then I waited two more. And then I was in Europe, and nobody had to know. And then I came back, and I had Theo to explain. I very nearly kept my son from his father."

"It won't be like that." Charlotte would tell Alec. She just needed a bit of time.

"It won't get easier," said Cece. "Every day after today, it'll get harder."

"She could be right," Raine said. "Starting the minute we walk out that door, we're all going to have to lie to him."

Cece nodded. "Can you lie to him, Charlotte?"

Charlotte shrugged, her eyes dampening again. Could she lie to Alec? She didn't want to lie to him. But she didn't want to tell him the truth, either. Because telling him the truth would mean the end. And she had so counted on things not ending just yet.

Another week. Another day. Even another night in his arms. Because once he knew, he'd never hold her tight again. He'd never whisper in her ear, nuzzle her neck, wrap his strong arms around her body. And she'd never be able to pretend, not for one more second, that they had a future together.

Not that she'd be able to pretend, anyway.

Cece was right.

She couldn't lie to Alec.

* * *

"I have to be honest," said Kiefer, as they replaced their mountain bikes in the rack in Alec's garage. "It's worse than I thought."

Alec squirted a stream of water into the back of his throat, wiping the sweat from his forehead. "You two back to fighting?" It wasn't surprising. It was damned inconvenient from a business perspective. But Alec had only himself to blame. He was the one who sent them on the trip.

Kiefer shook his head, leaning back and bracing his elbows on a workbench. "Not fighting."

"What's the problem then?" Alec didn't understand.

"All that fighting we *used* to do?"

"What?" Alec glanced at his watch. He had a conference call with Japan in an hour, and he'd hoped to see Charlotte before then.

"Turns out it was foreplay."

Alec dropped his water bottle back into the holster. "Seriously, Kiefer. Too much information. She's my sister."

Kiefer reached into his hip pocket and pulled out a small metal object, tossing it to Alec.

Alec caught it in midair. It was a scrolled silver box, hinged at the lid. He popped it open, revealing a large, diamond solitaire.

His gaze flew to Kiefer.

"It's not like I'm asking your permission or anything." Kiefer sobered. "But I wanted to give you a heads-up. I'm proposing to your sister."

"It's not about the money, is it?"

Kiefer scowled, and Alec saw a flash of genuine anger in his eyes.

"I can't believe you even asked that."

"Story of my life," said Alec.

"Not the story of mine. And you know better." Kiefer glared at him for a loaded moment.

"I know better," Alec admitted. Kiefer was a man of integrity. Alec snapped the box shut and tossed it back. His lips curved in a grin. "You think she'll say yes?"

"She damn well better," Kiefer growled. "Or else become a nun. Because that woman is never, *ever* getting near another man as long as I'm breathing."

Alec rocked forward and stuck out his hand, clasping Kiefer in a strong, thorough shake. "Then congratulations, brother. We'll talk later about reorganizing the company structure."

Kiefer held his palms up. "Hey, I'm not looking for—"

"I know you're not. But, trust me, you'll be sharing the pain the minute the honeymoon is over."

Kiefer grinned, and Alec grinned broadly in return. He couldn't imagine a better husband for Raine. He couldn't imagine a better business partner for himself.

A door opened on the far side of the garage.

Kiefer popped the ring box back in his pocket. "Better go get showered. I've got a hot date tonight."

"Good luck," said Alec. "You'll both come and see me after?"

"You bet." Kiefer gave a jaunty salute as he backed away.

"Alec?"

It was Charlotte, and Alec weaved his way through the parked cars toward her. Something deep inside him settled to contentment as he took her hands in his, drawing her into a hug.

She clung to him for a long minute, burying her head against his shoulder. But there was a tension in her body, a strain in her breathing.

He pulled back to look into her luminous, almost frightened blue eyes.

"Hey?" he asked, going on alert. "What's wrong? Your father? Jack?"

She shook her head, stepping farther away.

He reached for her, but then something held him back. He got a horrible feeling in the pit of his stomach.

"Charlotte?"

She turned her head, focusing on the small windows at the top of the bay doors where stark sunlight filtered through. "I…" She closed her eyes.

"You're scaring me," he told her honestly.

She nodded, swallowed, then looked back at him. "I'm so sorry, Alec."

"What?" He took a reflexive step forward, but she shrank back.

"Spit it out, Charlotte," he demanded. Nothing could be worse than standing here wondering what had put that look in her eyes. And nothing could be worse than getting signals that his help wasn't welcome.

"I'm—" She took a breath. "I'm pregnant."

Alec felt as though he'd been punched squarely in the gut. How could she…? When did she…?

"Who?" The question burst out of him with absolutely no eloquence whatsoever.

Her eyes squinted down. "Who what?"

"Who's the father?" He wasn't going to rail. He wasn't going to judge. She was a grown woman when she arrived on his doorstep. He hated that she had a past, but she did.

Her face contorted with anger. "How can you even *ask?*"

"You think it's none of my *business?*" Okay, now he was starting to judge. And now he was starting to get angry. He couldn't help it. The thought of another man's hands on Charlotte made him want to break something.

"You, you idiot. *You're* the father!"

Alec jerked back. "How—"

"The usual way." Her hands curled into fists by her sides.

"But it's only been—"

"Three weeks. Nearly three weeks."

"The first time?" Not bloody likely.

Her voice went hard. "I'd say so."

"We used a condom," he pointed out.

"We did."

There was a loud buzzing in his ears. She couldn't be lying. DNA tests were too easy to come by these days. She'd actually gotten herself pregnant. With his willing participation.

Here he'd thought she was different. He'd thought she was honest.

"What?" He sneered. "Did you poke holes in it?"

She blanched, but he honestly wanted to know how she'd pulled it off.

Many women had tried to trap him many different ways. He'd let his guard down with Charlotte. A mistake, obviously. But she'd seemed different, genuine, uninterested in his money. He'd been certain it was safe to enjoy a fling. But now he could almost hear his late father's admonition in his ears.

Across from him, Charlotte appeared speechless.

"What's your explanation?" he pressed.

And then they started. The big, shimmering crocodile tears he'd seen a hundred times. Next would be the protestations of innocence, the near-Oscar-quality denial that she'd been involved in any kind of plot whatsoever to get her hands on his money.

Damn.

He felt so hollow this time.

The betrayal was so much worse when he wasn't prepared.

"No explanation?" he asked.

"An accident," she managed in a halting rasp. "I didn't mean—"

"Yeah. An accidental pregnancy. Oldest trick in the book."

She shook her head.

"I guess I'll see you in court." He shook his head, turning for the door.

"Alec." His name seemed torn from her soul.

But he didn't turn back. As he made for the door, fury bubbled up inside him, both at her and at himself. He'd been a fool, and it was going to cost his family big-time.

It was all Charlotte could do to say upright. Her legs were wobbling and her broken heart was shooting pain to every corner of her being.

She'd expected to Alec to be angry.

She certainly hadn't expected him to declare his love and propose marriage. Although a small corner of her soul had hoped for that. But she hadn't expected his accusations. And she'd been completely unprepared for his cruelty.

She gripped the corner of a Mercedes. She had to walk out of here. There were a hundred people making a movie on the front lawn. Somehow, she had to hold her head up and make her way back to her room.

There, she'd pack. Hopefully, she wouldn't see anyone before she could call a taxi and make it to the airport. Home to Monte Allegro. She'd explain to her grandfather, quit her job and disappear. There was absolutely no way she'd be meeting Alec in court or anywhere else.

He could take his money and choke on it.

She heard a sound. Then Raine and Cece appeared. They rushed to her side.

"Oh, dear," said Cece.

"Bad?" asked Raine.

Charlotte nodded, valiantly fighting her tears. "I have to get back to my room. He thinks I got pregnant on purpose."

Both women gasped.

Raine growled. "I am going to—"

"No!" Charlotte grabbed Raine's arm. "Please don't say anything to him! Just let me leave. All I want to do is go home."

Raine searched Charlotte's expression for a long moment. Then she nodded. "You should go home. Take care of yourself. I'll ream my brother out later."

Alec couldn't get Charlotte's image out of his head, her tears, her confusion, her vulnerability. Obviously, she'd been certain her plan would work. Just as obviously, he couldn't let it. Even if he had been plagued with second thoughts for the past two hours.

He brought his fist down hard on the desktop.

He couldn't marry a woman who'd set him up, no matter how much he wished it could work between them. And what kind of a fool was he for even considering it?

Suddenly, his office door burst open. He spun around, ready to shout. Not even Kiefer and Raine walked in on him without knocking.

It was Jack, and before Alec could react to the shock, Jack drew back his fist.

Alec's first reaction was to duck the punch. But he forced himself to hold his ground, taking the shot straight to his jaw.

He grunted at the pain, which felt strangely good. Setup or not, he'd slept with Jack's sister and made her pregnant, and he deserved the other man's anger.

Jack stepped back, shaking out his hand, blue eyes near black with anger. "You son of a bitch," he spat.

"Yeah," Alec agreed, staring levelly into Jack's eyes.

"We'll see you in court."

Alec shook his head. "You won't have to. Your niece or nephew will have everything they could ever possibly need."

Jack snorted. "Except for a father." Then he turned for the door, and a pain worse than a cracked jaw shot through Alec.

His child would have a fractured family. Just like Charlotte. Damn.

He hated this.

He hated every single thing about it.

"Do me a favor," he called to Jack.

Jack halted. After a moment, he turned, looking ready to throw another punch.

"Tell her you decked me for it."

Jack's brow furrowed. "Why?"

Alec inhaled, taking a moment to make sure he said

it right. "Because Charlotte doesn't believe you love her. She's been waiting twenty-one years for you to start acting like a big brother."

Ten

Charlotte stared at the pile of designer clothes on the bed. Half of her wanted to forget Alec ever existed. The other half wanted to cling to every scrap of a memory.

She ran her fingertips over the gold, beaded dress she'd worn the first time they made love. Then she lifted the strap of the evening gown she'd worn to the Royal Ballet. Alec had booked the director's box, and their seats were second only to the royal family.

They'd eaten dinner overlooking the Thames, danced to an orchestra, then laughed their way through sweet treats in their bedroom at the Ritz. Alec was convinced she'd fallen in love with his lifestyle. Truth was, she'd fallen in love with Alec. She'd wear rags and live in a hut if it proved it to him.

She heard the bedroom door open, but she didn't

bother turning around. It would be Raine, back with a bigger suitcase. But it didn't matter. Charlotte had pretty much decided to leave the clothes behind.

The bed creaked, and she realized it was Jack sitting down beside her.

She hurriedly swiped her cheeks, pasting a smile on her face. "Leaving a little early," she said, gesturing to the scattered clothes. "Raine's out looking for a bigger—"

Jack's strong arm curled around her shoulders. "Oh, Charlotte."

Charlotte gasped out a sob.

Jack's other arm went around her, and he pulled her close, rocking her against his broad chest. "Cece told me. I am *so* sorry."

Charlotte shook her head, embarrassed by the fresh tears. "It's okay." She sucked a painful breath into her burning chest. "I knew… It wouldn't…" She gave up trying to talk.

Silence rose between them.

"I have loved you," Jack finally said, emotion thick in his voice, "every second of every day since they took you away from me."

Charlotte stilled.

"You were my baby sister. I thought they'd bring you back. I thought he'd—" Jack struggled with a breath. "I thought he'd come to his senses. I mean, how could anybody not love you?"

Charlotte clung to her brother, pressing her cheek against his chest while he stroked her hair. Her chest burned even more painfully. "I love you, Jack."

"I'll always love you, Charlotte. I'm here. For anything, *everything*. Whatever you need. I'm here, and Cece's here, too. And Theo. Theo will be the best cousin ever."

Charlotte nodded, a small sigh of relief coming through her wall of pain.

"I punched him out," said Jack.

Charlotte drew back.

"I punched Alec out. He doesn't mess with my baby sister and get away with it."

"Is he okay?"

Jack frowned. "Not 'thanks, big brother'?"

"Oh, yes. Thanks, big brother. But is he okay?"

Jack closed his eyes for a long second. "Uh-oh."

"What?" Not that everything wasn't colossally wrong at the moment.

"You're in love with him."

Charlotte couldn't admit it. But Jack obviously saw it in her eyes.

"Of course you're in love with him." Jack nodded. "Why else would you make love with him."

"I knew it was temporary," said Charlotte.

"But you fell for him anyway."

Charlotte closed her eyes. "Yes," she admitted quietly.

"I know how that goes," said Jack in a sympathetic tone. "When I realized I loved Cece—"

"It's not the same thing," Charlotte quickly pointed out.

"Are you sure?"

"Oh, I am sure." She nodded, voice shaking with conviction. Alec Montcalm didn't fall in love with anybody. He was honest and up-front, and he meant every syllable when he told a woman it was temporary.

"What can I do?" asked Jack.

"You can be an uncle."

He gave her another hug, and it felt good. Despite the fact that her world was falling apart, it felt so good to hug her brother again.

"I'm only a phone call away," he told her.

Charlotte glanced around. "I think I'm just going to leave. I don't need these clothes. What I need is to set up a life for a baby."

"California is nice," said Jack. "You don't have to be right in L.A. to be close by."

Charlotte managed a smile. "Thanks for that. I have to talk to the ambassador first. But I really will give it some thought." There were definitely worse places in the world than California.

Alec needed to get away, and Tokyo seemed like it might just be far enough.

He had to get Charlotte out of his head. He had to stop thinking about his baby. And he had to purge the ridiculous idea that his being in love with Charlotte, and Charlotte being in love with his money, was a recipe for happily ever after. It wasn't, and it never would be.

In the driveway, he tossed his briefcase onto the passenger seat of the Lamborghini. Then he opened the driver's door and dropped down on the seat, slamming the door and stuffing the key into the ignition.

He'd check in with Kiefer and Raine while the jet refueled in New Delhi.

"You were right," came Jack's mild voice as he appeared in Alec's rearview mirror. "She didn't know I loved her." He brought his hand down on the top of the Lamborghini's door, and rounded on Alec. "But after that, your theory fell way apart."

Alec didn't get the point. But he waited for Jack to explain.

Jack placed his other hand on the door and leaned in. "She would have given anything for it to be you who said it instead of me."

"Said what?" Alec reached for the ignition key.

"That you loved her."

Alec scoffed. That statement made absolutely no sense. "It's the money," he reminded Jack.

Jack's eyes narrowed. "Would you repeat that?"

Hell, yes. Alec would repeat it as many times as Jack liked. "Charlotte and every other woman I've ever dated are in love with my money. M-O-N-E-Y. To get it, they're willing to put up with me."

Jack suddenly looked as if he might laugh. "You actually believe that? You actually think it's the money?"

Alec didn't bother answering this time.

"Charlotte doesn't need your money," said Jack. "The family has money."

"Charlotte's not involved in Hudson Pictures." Alec knew that for a fact. Even if she hadn't told him herself, Kiefer had researched the corporation before letting them anywhere near Château Montcalm.

"I'm not talking about the Hudsons," said Jack.

What the hell else could he be talking about?

"The real money's on the Cassettes side." He shook his head as if he pitied Alec. "Charlotte is the presumptive heir to Ambassador Edmond Cassettes's fortune. And even if she wasn't, her trust fund is big enough to buy a small country."

Alec's stomach clenched around nothing.

"My God, Alec. To her, your money's probably nothing but a tax burden."

Jack might as well have slammed him in the head with a brick this time.

Charlotte had money?

Serious money?

She wasn't, *couldn't* be after Alec's.

"Then why…" He stared at Jack in confusion. What was this all about then? Why did she sleep with him? Why did she get pregnant?

Jack smacked his hands down on the car door and jerked back to standing. "Grab a clue, Alec." And he turned and walked away.

"Son of a bitch." Alec flung open the door.

None of this was making any sense. None of it. But he had to talk to Charlotte. She had to help him understand.

Charlotte came to the bottom of the main staircase with a small suitcase in her hand. Filming had finished in the foyer a few days ago, and it was back to normal again.

Raine was arranging for the limo, and Charlotte had called ahead for a plane reservation to Monte Allegro. By midnight, she'd be back in her own bed.

Then the front door burst open, and Alec strode through. Her stomach clenched, and for a second she felt a wave of dizziness.

Alec glanced from side to side. There were voices in the great room, and footsteps in the hall. On the landing above, two housekeepers chatted as they dusted the wooden railing.

Alec clenched his jaw.

He stepped determinedly forward, grasping Charlottte's hand. "Come with me."

In surprise, she dropped the suitcase, spinning around, her legs reflexively taking up a near trot as she struggled to keep up with him.

Behind the stairs, he jerked opened a thick door.

"Alec? What—" And then they were pacing down a flight of stone stairs. They rounded a corner into a cool, dimly lit wine cellar. Old racks stretched away on both sides, covered in thousands of dusty bottles of wine.

Then the aisleway widened out, revealing a hewn beam tasting table, a rack of clean glasses and several antique chairs.

Alec turned on her, letting go of her hand. "I don't understand."

Charlotte glanced around. She wasn't exactly scared, but she was more than a little confused. "I don't understand, either. What are we doing? Why did you bring me here?"

"Why did you get pregnant?"

Charlotte stood up straight, determined to maintain her composure. She had another chance to give Alec a final memory of her. And it was going to be dignified, or she would die trying.

"Did you miss eighth-grade biology?"

"That's *not* what I meant."

"Well, that's exactly how it happened. We had sex. Birth control is not foolproof, and we were in the bottom, or is it the top two percent?"

He took a few steps, in a half circle around her, eyes narrowing like a predator. "What do you want from me?"

"You're the one who dragged me down here."

"Do you want my money?"

"I never wanted your money. If you'll recall, I tried my damnedest to get you to stop spending it."

"I thought it was part of the plot." He paced back the other way.

"The *plot?*" The only plot she'd ever had was to keep away from Alec. When that became impossible, she convinced herself to have a fling. Falling for him was entirely accidental, and it would have been the stupidest plot in the world.

"To convince me you were different, so I'd let my guard down."

"Did it ever occur to you that I *was* different?"

He continued pacing. "Only every second we spent together."

"*So?*" What was this all about?

He came to a sudden halt. "You can't love me, Charlotte."

A chill poured over her body.

"It's not possible," he said. "It makes no sense." His expression was totally and completely sincere.

"Why not?" she dared ask.

"I'm self-centered and suspicious. I have no depth of character. And I've skated along on my family's legacy my entire life."

Charlotte couldn't believe what she was hearing.

"I accused you of sabotaging our condoms," he continued. "And, and at the time, I *meant* it." A note of desperation came into his voice. "If it's not my money— Without my money—" The question seemed torn from his soul. "What is there to love?"

Charlotte's shoulders slumped, half in astonishment and half in abject relief. "I love *you,* Alec."

He shook his head.

"I don't want your money."

"I know," he admitted.

"Then there's no other explanation, is there?"

"There could be," he argued.

She moved toward him. "Then come up with one."

He watched her in suspicious silence.

She moved in closer. "Come up with one," she dared him.

Then she stopped less than a foot away, tipping her chin to gaze at his tense expression in the dusky light. She gathered the final shreds of her courage, going for broke. "Come up with a logical explanation, or tell me that you love me back."

He stared at her, and something flickered in the depths of his dark eyes. "Are those my only choices?"

"Yeah."

"Can I propose instead?"

The burning weight lifted off Charlotte's chest, and she blinked against tears of relief. "Only if you say you love me first."

"I love you first." He reached for her. "I've loved you since I saw you on that dance floor in Rome."

"I didn't love you then," she admitted, and he laughed.

"Just so long as you caught on eventually."

"I caught on a few weeks ago." She smacked him in the shoulder. "Why weren't you paying attention?"

"Ouch." He rubbed his shoulder, pretending she'd hurt him. "You're as bad as your brother."

She peered at Alec's face. "Where'd he hit you?"

Alec pointed to his jaw.

She came up on tiptoe and kissed it better. Then she leaned forward to kiss the shoulder she'd smacked.

"I was paying attention," said Alec. "But all I could tell was that I wanted to be with you more than any other woman, other person, ever in my life. I was afraid it wasn't real." He paused. "So I guess I took steps to make sure it couldn't be real."

"It's real," she whispered, looping her arms around his neck.

His hand slipped between their bodies to rest on her stomach. "Our baby," he whispered, "is going to be loved and protected and cared for by two very happy parents."

Charlotte smiled, hope and joy flowing freely through her veins. Their baby would have loving parents, and Jack and Cece and Theo. Raine and— *Raine!*

"Raine was getting me the limo," said Charlotte. "She'll wonder—"

"Don't you worry about Raine." Alec settled his arms around Charlotte's waist. "Kiefer's taking her on a date tonight."

"That's nice." Charlotte smiled.

"He's bringing along a pretty impressive diamond solitaire."

"Really?" Charlotte was thrilled for her friend.

"He's a good man," said Alec.

She nodded in return.

"So, what about you?" he asked.

"What about me?"

He cocked his head to one side. "What are you doing tonight?"

She pretended to ponder. "Well, I do have this plane reservation."

"Canceled," he said, settling his arms more firmly at her waist.

"Then I guess I'm free."

"Care to join me for dinner?"

She smiled and pulled up for a quick kiss. "Love to."

"There's a safe in my bedroom."

"Really, Alec, condoms are no longer necess—"

He laughed. "I mean a jewelry safe."

"I thought I'd made it pretty clear that you didn't need to bribe me," she teased.

"I was thinking we could look for an engagement ring. There's no end of heirloom jewelry up there. As I recall, my grandmother— Charlotte?"

She couldn't stop her tears this time. "You were serious?"

"About marrying you? Hell, yes. Right away. Right now. As soon as we can get a license." He sobered. "You're carrying my baby, Charlotte. My heir. I'm not giving you a chance to change your mind."

"I won't change my mind," she told him sincerely. In Alec's arms for the rest of her life was exactly where she wanted to be.

In a secluded corner of the Montcalm garden, screened by cypress trees, with the scent of lavender wafting through the air, Charlotte and Alec stood next to Raine and Kiefer as the priest intoned their vows.

Charlotte wore a strapless white dress, three-quarter-length satin with flat lace over a fitted bodice, with a white satin bow tied over one hip. Raine's dress was slightly fuller, more formal, with clouds of soft tulle following to just below her knees. She had cap sleeves and a princess neckline. Both women carried bouquets of lavender and white roses.

Jack and Cece served as witnesses and, along with Theo, were the only guests. Dressed in a little gray suit, Theo played in the grass, picking wildflowers as the ceremony wore on.

Alec slipped an antique gold band onto Charlotte's

finger, snuggling it up to the two-carat, princess-cut solitaire once worn by his grandmother. As they were pronounced man and wife, he drew her to him for a long, tender kiss. When it ended, Charlotte had to force herself to let go.

Then Kiefer kissed Raine, and Jack popped the cork on the bottle of Montcalm champagne.

"Welcome to the family," Jack told Alec, pouring the pale, bubbly liquid into the waiting champagne flutes. "I trust this means we'll get a discount on renting your château?"

"Discount?" asked Alec, brows raised as Cece caught Theo's hands going for the small white and lavender wedding cake.

"Surely you won't charge your own family full price." Jack held up his glass to propose a toast.

"Surely," Kiefer echoed.

"To the brides," said Jack, his soft gaze catching Charlotte's, transporting her back to being four years old, when her big brother walked on water.

"The stunningly beautiful brides," he finished.

"The brides," the small group echoed.

"We won't charge you for the château," said Alec.

Jack nearly choked on his champagne. "I was joking," he sputtered, while Cece patted him on the back.

Charlotte gave Alec an astonished look. "But the damage."

He shrugged. "We'll—"

A loud crack rent the air, and the entire group reflexively cringed. Then something groaned, and there were far-off shouts. The wedding party rushed to the pathway in time to see Isabella, Ridley and three crew members dash out of the pool house.

A cameraman scrambled to the bottom of a stately old oak tree. The oak groaned a second time, keeling over in slow motion, falling with increasing speed until it landed on top of the pool house, squashing it flat.

David shouted something unintelligible, arms waving as he stomped toward the cameraman. But he missed a step, tripped on a cable and fell headfirst into the pool.

"Wow," said Alec, taking a sip of his champagne and resettling his arm around Charlotte's waist.

"Don't see that every day," said Kiefer.

"Yeah, that'll be coming out of David's fees," Jack put in, lifting his glass to his lips.

Charlotte anchored her arms around Alec's waist, tipping her head up. "Welcome to the family, sweetheart."

He kissed her soundly on the lips, the sweet champagne on his tongue tickling her senses and making promises for the night ahead.

He drew back, gazing into her eyes with raw longing. "And welcome to mine."

* * * * *

Wonder what's going on in the lives of
Devlin Hudson and his new fiancée, Valerie Shelton?
Find out in this exclusive short story by
USA TODAY *bestselling author Maureen Child.*

Scene 2
by
Maureen Child

Valerie Shelton walked through the production offices of Hudson Pictures and simply shook her head in amazement at the level of energy surrounding her. At every desk, someone was on the phone, gesturing wildly as if the person they were speaking to could see them. There were movie posters on the wall, the scent of stale coffee in the air and a sense of urgency that pulsed in the room like a rapid heartbeat.

She smiled to herself and realized she was excited to be a part of it all. Even just a small cog in the giant wheel that was Hudson Pictures. She was engaged to the man who made this all work. To the man who had taken her to France to see for herself the inner workings of a movie being made.

Still walking across the crowded room toward Devlin's office, Val thought back over the last week.

Their stay in Provence had been thrilling despite the fact that she and Dev hadn't gotten as close as she had hoped for.

But he was busy, she reminded herself. The man seemed to be constantly working. She admired that, even as she told herself it would change once they were married—once they were a team.

The busy room faded away as her mind took her back to the mansion in Provence where filming was taking place. The atmosphere had seemed almost magical and watching Devlin at work, seeing him handle money men and actors with the same even-handed treatment had only made her admire him more. He was a man who carried power easily. Not like her father, who ran his newspaper empire with a tight fist and a raised voice.

If there still was a small voice in the back of her mind warning her away from a man who didn't love her, she silenced it by promising herself that love would come. Eventually. She could wait. She would be the woman he wanted. The woman he needed. Until Dev finally realized that she was in his heart to stay.

After all, they'd shared at least one nearly magical moment at the château. The night before they were to fly home, they'd strolled in the darkness, their only company moonlight sliding through the thick stand of trees surrounding Alec Montcalm's estate.

"Did you have a good time?" Devlin watched her as if her answer were all too important.

"Yes," she told him, linking her arm through his. "It's exciting being behind the scenes of a movie."

He gave her a half smile and a shrug. "Exciting? Watching take after take? Hearing the actors grumble about the writing, the writers complain about rewrites and the director demanding perfection?"

"You're used to it, that's all," she said, loving the feel of his body beside hers. He was tall and strong and, in the moonlight, his blue eyes shone with wicked promise. A promise that sent her stomach in a hard spin and made heat rush through her body in response.

She hadn't thought it would be difficult to wait for sex until their wedding night, but suddenly, Val wanted Devlin to take her. To take her right there in the moonlight. She wanted them to begin their lives together in this most amazing place—to feel a connection between them that had seemed to be missing for the week they'd spent in France.

He hadn't had much time for her and though she'd expected that, she hadn't realized how hard it would be to be with him and yet apart. She'd seen how some of the film crew had watched her with sympathy in their eyes, as if they knew that she was in love—alone.

As if hearing her thoughts, Devlin stopped, turned her to face him and ran his big hands up and down her arms. He gave her a smile, and bent to press a kiss on her forehead as if she were a distant relation. "This was supposed to be a fun trip for us. I'm sorry I had to spend so much time dealing with problems."

She swallowed her disappointment. She would be the woman he needed. The woman who understood. "It's okay, really. I had a wonderful time, even though I would have liked to have more time with you."

His hands squeezed her shoulders briefly. "You're not getting much of a bargain in marrying me, Val."

Here was the man she wanted. The man who took the time to walk in the moonlight with her. The man who worried that she might regret her choice in marrying him. The annoying doubts in the back of her mind were silenced by his words and her own confidence in the decision she'd made.

"Oh, I don't know," she said, lifting one hand to lay it gently on his chest. She felt his heartbeat, slow, steady beneath her hand. "I think we'll do very well together, Dev. Here we are, in this beautiful spot, beneath the moon and right now, everything seems perfect."

He looked at her for a long thoughtful moment, and something she couldn't quite define flashed in his eyes briefly. He lifted one hand from her shoulder to cup her cheek, his thumb sliding across her skin in a caress. "You're too understanding. You know that, right?"

"Am I?"

"Yeah. Any other woman would have been complaining about being left to her own devices so often. Would have wanted to tour Provence and would have expected me to join her."

She covered his hand with hers, holding his touch to her face. "I knew this was a working trip for you, Dev…."

He studied her again, his gaze moving over her features as if committing them to memory. Then he whispered, "You really are beautiful, aren't you?"

With her hair loose around her shoulders, wearing a red, long-sleeved sweater and sleek blue jeans, she felt anything but stylish. Still, hearing him say those words fed the fires already simmering inside her.

Then he slowly lowered his head to hers. Her heartbeat kicked into a gallop, her breath stilled in her lungs and the very core of her went hot and liquid. His mouth neared hers, only a breath away now. She went up on her toes to meet him—

And his cell phone rang.

He jolted, as if lurching backward from the edge of a cliff, and mumbled, "Sorry," as he reached into his shirt pocket for the demanding phone.

Coming back to the present, Val was almost surprised to find herself standing stock-still in the middle of the production room. Her memories had been so vivid, the recollection of that near kiss in the moonlight so profound, that she'd completely lost track of where she was or what she was doing there.

Now she remembered. She'd come to surprise Devlin with a lunch date. Smiling to herself, she walked toward his office and idly noted that his assistant, a forty-something woman named Audrey, wasn't at her appointed post. Which, Val told herself, only made it easier to surprise Dev.

She strode past Audrey's desk, opened the office door and stepped inside. Devlin had his back to her, staring out the wide windows at the incredible view of Beverly Hills and the mountains beyond. Just looking at his broad back, muscles defined beneath his crisp white shirt, something inside Valerie turned over helplessly. Before she could speak, though, a disembodied voice floated out of the speakerphone on his desk.

"Looked like Val had a good time in Provence."

"Guess so," Devlin answered noncommittally.

"Well," the masculine voice countered with a half laugh, "don't get too excited."

"Let it go, Luc," Dev said and Valerie knew the man on the other end of the line was Devlin's brother Lucian. "It was what it was. A business trip. Val had a good time. I'm glad. Let it go."

"She loves you, you know."

Valerie sucked in a breath. Had she been that obvious to everyone? Was she really wearing her heart on her sleeve so openly? And was that necessarily a bad thing?

"I know," Devlin said, and turned from the window. His gaze locked with hers and a jolt of something wild and fierce and unexpected passed between them. Never taking his gaze from her, Devlin took a step toward the desk, said, "Gotta go, Luc," and clicked the disconnect button.

"Val." Devlin couldn't stop looking at her. In her trim, sleeveless green dress, she looked as cool and welcome as a cold drink at the end of a long, hot day. His body stirred and he noted his own reaction to her absently. He didn't love her, but he wanted her. That was good. Wouldn't be much of a marriage if he didn't want his wife in his bed.

The fact that she loved him worked in his favor, too, he reminded himself.

"I didn't expect to see you today."

"I thought I'd surprise you by abducting you for lunch."

He gave her a smile as he came around the edge of the desk and walked toward her. He caught her perfume in the air-conditioned office and he dragged that now-familiar scent into his lungs as he reached her. Her eyes looked huge, and he wondered if she was embarrassed to have overheard his idiot brother's comments.

"Luc didn't mean anything," he said, just in case.

"It's all right." She smiled up at him and the light in her eyes seemed to slice through him. "He wasn't wrong. I do love you, Dev. Otherwise, I wouldn't be marrying you."

Guilt tried to rear up inside him, but Devlin squashed it back down. He'd never pretended to love her, so there was no reason for guilt. With that thought firmly in mind, he mentally brushed aside the production meeting he'd scheduled for lunch.

He didn't love the woman he was about to marry, but that didn't mean he couldn't give her what she needed once in a while.

"Lunch is a great idea," he said, turning from her to go snag his suit jacket off the hanger in his closet. Slipping it on, he walked back to her, took her hand and threaded her arm through his. The touch of her skin sent a scorching need of lust staggering through him and Devlin welcomed it. Need he could deal with. Lust was welcome. Love wasn't on the table. "What do you think? The Ivy?"

"Really?" Her pleased smile lit up her face and, just for a second, Devlin thought about letting her go for her own sake. Letting her find someone who would be able to love her back. But then he remembered why he was marrying her. The Shelton newspaper dynasty and Hudson Pictures were going to be a great team. Best to keep that in mind.

"You're not too busy?"

Shaking his head to clear his wandering thoughts, he gave her a smile. "I think Hollywood can get along without me for an hour or so."

* * * * *

BARGAINED INTO HER BOSS'S BED

BY
EMILIE ROSE

Dear Reader,

Hollywood – one single word that evokes dozens of images of glamour, glitz, fairytales, movie stars and dreams that come true.

Being invited to write Dana Fallon and Max Hudson's story allowed me to learn about what happens behind the scenes in movie production and to focus on the filmmaking process. Lucky for me, I have Screen Gems Studios, Wilmington, North Carolina, nearby to make the learning process accessible.

And, as always with a continuity series, I was blessed with an opportunity to work with some of my favourite Desire™ authors, to allow my characters to play with theirs.

I hope you enjoy taking a peek at Hollywood from the other side of the camera with Max and Dana.

Happy reading!

Emilie Rose

To LaShawn, a woman who truly embodies the phrase "dance like nobody's watching." You go girl!

One

"What is this?"

Dana Fallon flinched at the irritation and impatience in Max Hudson's voice. She couldn't blame him. Hudson Pictures was up against an immovable deadline in shooting their current project, and her leaving now wasn't the nicest thing she could do to them.

But she had her reasons. Good ones.

Stand by your decision. Execute your plan. Her big brother's booming "coach" voice echoed in her head even though he was on the other side of the Atlantic Ocean.

She reined in her retreating courage, brushed the dark curtain of overgrown bangs out of her lashes and tucked the ends behind her ear. Her gaze bounced off the disbelief in Max's vivid blue eyes and focused instead on the V of tanned, muscled chest revealed by the three unfastened buttons of his white Joseph Abboud shirt. Dangerous territory.

"It's my resignation. I'm quitting, Max. You'll need to advertise for my replacement as soon as we return to the States. I've already drafted the ad for your approval."

"You can't quit." He wadded the paper one-handed and pitched it toward the trash can in the corner of the hotel suite he'd been using as a temporary office for the past several months. He missed. In the five years she'd worked for him, Dana didn't think he'd ever managed to hit a wastebasket with a paper ball regardless of which continent they were on. Max might be a creatively brilliant producer and film editor, but despite his killer body he had no athletic talents of the team sports variety.

She loved him anyway, and didn't that make her an idiot since her attachment was completely one-sided and unlikely to ever be returned? It was time she admitted Max would love his deceased wife until he joined her in the grave and move on.

He went back to shuffling papers as if his pronouncement settled everything, and she was tempted to scuffle back to her hotel room with her metaphorical tail between her legs. But she couldn't. Not this time.

When a job offer from a friend had coincided with the anniversary of her brother's accident, Dana had realized she was no closer to attaining her goals today than she'd been when she'd taken this job. Her brother had never quit pursuing his dream despite setbacks and staggering odds, and she owed it to him to find the same courage.

That morning she'd promised herself that as soon as she left France behind and returned to California with the rest of Hudson Pictures' cast and crew she'd seize control of her life and go after the career and family she wanted.

"I have to go, Max. I want to produce my own films, and you're never going to let me do that here at Hudson.

Like my letter says, I have an opportunity with an indie film company—"

"You misunderstood me. You *can't* quit—not to work for another filmmaker." His inflexible tone warned her not to argue.

She'd known this wouldn't be easy. That was the main reason it had taken her weeks—until the day before her departure from France—to work up the courage for this conversation. "I'm not asking your opinion."

"Because you already know what I'll say. It's a stupid decision and a step backward to leave a major player like Hudson to go to a fly-by-night independent studio. That aside, read your contract. You're forbidden to work for another film company for two years after you leave us."

Surprise snapped her shoulders back. She didn't remember signing a noncompete clause, but she'd been so thrilled to be offered a position at Hudson that she hadn't read the contract as carefully as she should have. The document in question was in her file cabinet at home. She couldn't verify or disprove his words. "Two years?"

"Yes. It's a standard clause in Hudson contracts. It keeps people from taking proprietary information with them when they go."

He stabbed his fingers through his short dark hair and moved a pile of papers on his desk as if he were looking for something and was irritated at not being able to find it. She fought the urge to spring forward and locate the missing item for him the way she always had in the past.

Helping him and taking care of him wasn't just her job, it had become something of an addiction—one she needed to kick.

"The timing of your tantrum sucks," he added without looking up.

She gasped and tried to put a lid on her anger. Hasty words and emotional outbursts never solved anything, and it wasn't like him to be rude. But then he wasn't often under this much pressure. The film had to be wrapped and ready before his grandmother Lillian Hudson died from the cancer consuming her body. They were getting close to completion since they'd already begun the postproduction phase, but the clock was ticking. Time was short and Lillian's remaining days were limited. Everyone involved was working around the clock and tense enough to crack.

Still, anger flushed any lingering reservations Dana might have had about hurting Max's feelings from her system. When she'd taken this job five years ago she'd intended only to get her foot in the door, gain a little experience and then move onward and upward in a year or two. She was overqualified to be the executive assistant to a producer and film editor—even one as acclaimed as Max Hudson. She had credentials—even if they were of the East Coast variety instead of the West Coast.

She'd always dreamed of producing her own films. But then Max had turned out to be an amazing boss. She'd found herself learning more from him than her years at university and her internships back home had taught her.

And then like a dummy, she'd fallen for him, which made leaving impossible. Until now. After watching him waltz off with yet another blonde last week, she'd realized that if the romantic setting of Chateau Montcalm in Provence, France, couldn't make Max see her as a woman instead of just an office accessory, then he never would.

She had put her life on hold to be near him for too long. She had to move on. Her brother often said that treading water did nothing but maintain the status quo, and she'd been treading and going nowhere. That had to end. Now.

She struggled to get control of her emotions so she wouldn't end up shrieking at him, and when she thought she had, she took a deep breath. "This is not a tantrum, Max. This is my career."

He looked up from his desk, his blue eyes glacial. "You'll have no career if you try to find work elsewhere in the film industry."

Shock slipped beneath her ribs like a sharp sword. Shock, hurt and betrayal. Max had a reputation for being ruthless in pursuit of his vision for a film, but he'd never been that way with her. "After all I've done for you, you'd blackball me?"

"In a heartbeat. Your leaving now would destroy our chance of finishing before—" He bit off the words and turned his head toward the storyboard hanging on the wall. But she didn't think he was focusing on the graphic depictions of each scene from the movie.

His jaw muscles bunched and his lips flattened. Watching him struggle with his feelings gripped her in a choke hold. She knew he was crazy about Lillian. They all adored the Hudson matriarch. And the knowledge that they would soon lose her was difficult to handle. But Dana knew Max was wrong about one thing. He could finish this film without her.

He visibly pulled himself together and his eyes found hers again. This time they were hard with determination and devoid of emotion. This was the face of the man she'd seen reduce misbehaving cast or crew members to Jell-O with a few terse lines. She locked her knees to prevent the same thing from happening to her.

"Dana, I won't let you make me fall behind schedule.

My grandmother wants to see the story of her romance with my grandfather on the screen. I will not disappoint her. And I will do whatever it takes to prevent you from sabotaging this project."

"Sabotaging!" She couldn't believe what she was hearing. She'd known he wasn't going to take this well, but to threaten her? When she'd started working for him five years ago he'd still been reeling from his wife's death. She'd done everything except breathe for him until he'd surfaced from his grief. And she'd continued to be his right hand ever since.

This was the thanks she got?

Fury simmered inside her. If she stayed in this suite one more minute she was going to say something she'd regret.

"I am going back to my room." It had taken everything she had to work up the nerve for this confrontation, and she'd crashed and burned because he was being an idiot. She needed to regroup, to replan. Because she couldn't go on. Not like this.

She pivoted on her boot heel and stomped out of his suite. A stream of Max's muttered curses followed in her wake. He called her back, but she didn't stop and she didn't go to her room. She couldn't. A sense of claustrophobia engulfed her. She bypassed the elevator, jogged down the emergency stairs and slammed out the side exit of the hotel. Her long stride covered the parking lot as she headed…*somewhere*—she didn't know where, but anywhere away from the infuriating, selfish bastard in the hotel was preferable to here.

"Dana," Max called from behind her. She ignored him and lengthened her stride. "Dana. Wait."

She heard his footsteps quicken as if he'd broken into

FREE BOOKS OFFER

To get you started, we'll send you
2 FREE books and a FREE gift

There's no catch, everything is **FREE**

Accepting your 2 **FREE** books and **FREE** mystery gift places you under no obligation to buy anything.

Be part of the Mills & Boon® Book Club™ and receive your favourite Series books up to 2 months before they are in the shops and delivered straight to your door. Plus, enjoy a wide range of **EXCLUSIVE** benefits!

- Best new women's fiction – delivered right to your door with FREE P&P

- Avoid disappointment – get your books up to 2 months before they are in the shops

- No contract – no obligation to buy

2 **FREE** books and a **FREE** gift

We hope that after receiving your free books you'll want to remain a member. But the choice is yours. So why not give us a go? You'll be glad you did!

Visit **millsandboon.co.uk** to stay up to date with offers and to sign-up for our newsletter

---

D0CIA

Mrs/Miss/Ms/Mr _____   Initials _____

BLOCK CAPITALS PLEASE

Surname _____

Address _____

_____

_____   Postcode _____

Email _____

MILLS & BOON®
Book Club

FREE BOOK OFFER
FREEPOST NAT 10298
RICHMOND
TW9 1BR

NO STAMP
NECESSARY
IF POSTED IN
THE U.K. OR N.I.

a jog and then he caught her elbow as she reached a corner, pulled her to a standstill and swung her around to face him. "Give me a couple of months. Let me get *Honor* in the can. And then we'll talk."

"There's nothing left to talk about, Max. I've asked you for a bigger role and been refused so many times I've quit wasting my breath. I didn't spend all those years and all that money getting a degree in filmmaking to be an executive assistant."

"I'll give you a raise."

She tilted her head back and glared at him. He could be so obtuse sometimes she wanted to scream. "It's not about the money or even the project. I believe in this movie with all my heart, and I want to help you finish it. But the chance to produce the indie film won't wait for me. My friend's company needs me *now*. The only reason I have this opportunity is because their last producer died unexpectedly. I've already made her wait three weeks for a decision. If I turn them down or try to stall them any longer they'll find someone else. If anyone understands budget and time constraints as a producer, you should, Max. You know I have to move now."

She could practically see the wheels turning in his brain. His hand slid from her elbow to her bicep to her shoulder, his long, warm fingers infusing her flesh with heat that seeped through the fabric of her blouse and straight into her bones. It wasn't a sexual thing on his part. But it was on hers. She felt the noncaress deep inside.

She had a love-hate reaction to his touches. She loved how each caress made her feel all excited and jittery and breathless, but she hated how a simple brush of his fingers could weaken her knees—and her willpower—and turn her into putty in his hands.

And he didn't even notice.

Talk about adding insult to injury.

"Stay, Dana. I'll give you associate producer credits on *Honor*. That will give you better credentials whenever you decide to move on. Not that I intend to make it easy for you to leave. You're the best assistant I've ever had."

His praise filled her with a warm glow, and then reality hit her with a cold, sobering shower. He was talking about her work, not her personally. He'd never see her as anything more than a coworker. And she wanted more—so, so much more. But right now, with his fingertips gently massaging her shoulder, she was too addled to make a decision.

She shrugged off his hand. "I'll think about it and get back to you before we touch down in L.A."

"I won't be returning with you tomorrow. I need another week here, maybe two or three. I want your decision now."

Frustration and a sense of entrapment made it difficult for her to breathe. He knew if she agreed she wouldn't go back on her word. Unlike most of the inhabitants of Hollywood, her word was her bond. But if she stayed with him…how would she ever get over him and move on with her life? And if she couldn't do that, how would she ever have the family or the career she craved?

James, her older brother, her idol, would be so disappointed in her for waffling.

"We both know 'associate producer' is a pretty useless title, often no more than a boon given because someone did somebody a favor. I want more than credits, Max. I want hands-on skills. And I know you. There's enough control freak in you that you'd give me the title but none of the producer's responsibilities. I'd come away with a slightly better-looking résumé, but without any new abilities."

A nerve in his upper lip twitched, drawing her attention to the mouth that had monopolized so many of her dreams—a mouth she had yet to feel against hers in her waking hours. A September breeze cooled her skin and stirred his thick hair. She fisted her fingers against the need to smooth those dark glossy strands back into place.

"With the deadline we're facing, you'll be working around the clock if you take this position, and I promise you, this won't be a meaningless title. You'll get your new skills." *And you'll regret it,* his challenging tone implied.

She could feel herself slipping toward acquiescence and tried to pull back from the ledge to weigh the positives and negatives. As he'd said, any Hudson Pictures product carried clout and a guaranteed cinematic release. An indie film did not. The best she could hope for was acclaim at the Sundance or Toronto film festivals and possible success if that happened and the movie got picked up. But the market for independent films was exceptionally tight right now. Few were selling without big name stars. Her friend's flick had no box office draws in the cast.

Slim-to-none chances versus a sure thing. Some choice.

Focus on the outcome, her brother always said. In this case, the outcome was a chance to get named credit for working on a major feature film, one she truly believed in, and a credential for her résumé.

She sighed in defeat. She was only twenty-eight. Her dream of a family, of someone to come home to and a career she could be proud of, could stand a few months' delay.

Although she'd probably live to regret it, this was a chance she just had to take.

"I'll do it."

* * *

Friday evening Dana palmed the key to Max's Mulholland Drive house in her damp and unsteady hand, but she hesitated to slot the key into the frosted-glass-and-iron front door.

It was stupid to be nervous. She'd been to Max's house dozens of times since he bought the place four years ago, but never while he was here. He usually sent her to pick up or drop off something while he was tied up at his office, on a set or away on location. She'd been here several times since the day two and a half weeks ago when she'd left him in France. But tonight felt different.

Should she let herself in or ring the bell? He had to know she'd arrived. Not only had he summoned her the moment his plane landed and told her to drop everything and get over here, but she'd had to stop at the end of the driveway and punch in the security code to open the electronic gates. Whenever the gates were activated a chime sounded in the house. Had he slept through the summons? Or was he working? Either way, she didn't want to disturb him. She lifted the key.

The door opened before she could shove it in the slot and her heart tripped. Max, with a dark beard-stubbled jaw, a faded blue T-shirt and a pair of snug, worn jeans, stood barefoot in front of her. She'd never seen him dressed this casually before. He tended to dress for success at work, and he'd always demanded the same of his staff. Today's sleepy-eyed, just-out-of-bed look made her want to drag him right back to the rumpled and possibly still-warm sheets.

Don't go there.

She dragged her brain back from taboo terrain and studied his pale, drawn face and mussed hair. His body was probably still nine hours ahead on French time and thought it was the middle of the night. After several months in France it had taken her a few days to adjust. "Jet lag?"

"I'm fine. Come in. We have a lot to do."

Typical male. Refusing to admit weakness and stupidly ignoring the fact that he needed rest. "I take it you didn't sleep on the plane or nap when you got home?"

"No time. I could use a pot of coffee."

"You don't drink coffee, Max."

"I will tonight."

"I'll make it." She instantly wanted to kick herself. Taking care of him was her past role, not her current one. If she wanted him to give her new duties, then she had to stop doing the old ones.

"Thank you." He turned and headed back into the house, leaving a subtle trail of his cologne, Versace Eau Fraîche. She knew because she'd had to buy a bottle when he'd forgotten to pack his for a previous trip, and she loved the lemon, cedar and herb notes.

Her gaze traced the tired set of his broad shoulders. When she caught her eyes taking the old, familiar journey down his straight spine to his tight butt, which looked totally yummy in the jeans, she abruptly averted her eyes, tightened her grip on her briefcase handle and mentally shook herself.

Get over this obsession already. He's not yours. He never will be yours. Move on.

The two-story marble foyer echoed her footsteps as she followed him toward the elevator with her gaze firmly fastened on the back of his head. The doors enclosed them into the paneled space. She focused on the numbered panel until he leaned against the wall—another testament to his exhaustion. Max never leaned on anything. He was too dynamic for slouching.

"Max, you'd think more clearly if you slept a few hours."

"Later."

The doors opened onto the second floor. His multi-level house clung to the side of a hill. She knew the layout from her previous visits. The kitchen, living and dining rooms were on this level. His office, the screening room and his private den occupied the third. His massive bedroom and two others sprawled across the fourth floor.

She'd had a few brief stints in his bedroom, but sadly only to pack his suitcase or retrieve a file or a forgotten PDA. She'd never even dared to sit on his king-size bed, let alone crawl between the sheets the way she did in her dreams. And she knew from being asked to pack for him in the past that he didn't own any pajamas. Did he sleep nude or in his boxer briefs?

Not a journey her mind needed to take.

When she reached the sunlit kitchen she headed straight for the high end stainless-steel coffeepot sitting on the black-marble countertop. She'd overheard Max tell one of his brothers that he'd bought the appliance because most of the women who slept over couldn't wake up enough to leave without their caffeine. She didn't want to think about the parade of anorexic blondes through his life. Or his bed. They were a reminder that with her dark hair and eyes and olive skin she could never be what he desired.

"Where's the coffee?" she asked.

"Freezer." He sat in a chair at the glass-topped table with his back to the extraordinary view of the city, the distant ocean and the heated pool and spa below the window. Most of the rooms in his house overlooked the same spectacular vista. He dropped his head into his hands, exhaustion dragging his frame downward. The evening light streaming through the glass highlighted every tired crease in his handsome face.

She squashed the sympathy rising within her. He was the one who'd chosen not to sleep. But honestly, sometimes he reminded her of her two-year-old nephew who pushed himself harder when he started to tire rather than risk collapsing if he stopped moving. "The filters?"

He pointed to a dark wood cabinet above the machine and massaged the back of his neck. She yearned to step behind him and do that job for him, to tangle her fingers in his short dark hair and massage the warm skin of his neck. But she didn't dare. She'd done a lot of personal stuff for him as his assistant, but nothing *that* personal.

Instead, she retrieved the coffee and then opened the cabinet and located the paper filters. Within moments the energizing aroma of coffee filled the air. She heard the rumble of his stomach from across the room over the gurgling pot.

"Have you eaten, Max?"

"On the plane."

Apparently, even first-class food hadn't sated his hunger. "Can I fix you something?"

Old habits died hard. She'd have to work on breaking them after he recovered from his trip. Better yet, she'd hand those duties over to her replacement, if personnel ever found someone who could meet Max's exacting standards, and then she wouldn't have to worry about him anymore. That thought made her stomach twinge in an odd way. Who was she trying to fool? She'd always worry about Max.

"There should be some food in the fridge," his deep voice rumbled without its usual resonance.

"Max, we've been out of the country for months. I canceled your catering service, remember? And when I left you in France, you weren't sure when you'd be home. Since you didn't let me know you were returning until your plane touched down today, I haven't reinstated the caterers."

She checked the Sub-Zero refrigerator even though she knew she'd find none of the precooked meals she used to have delivered on a biweekly basis. As expected, the unit was empty except for condiments and a few bottles of beer. Nothing edible occupied the shelves or bins. The cleaning crew would have followed her instructions to remove any perishables the day after the film team left for France.

She'd have to take care of reinstating the caterers and the maid first thing in the morning. For money, which Max had in abundance, anything could be had—even on a weekend.

"Let me see what I can whip up." She raided his freezer and found only old chocolate ice cream, which she tossed in the trash, and a bag of meatballs. The meatballs held possibilities. Turning to the cabinets she searched and discovered a box of whole wheat pasta and a jar of marinara sauce. It wasn't the gourmet fare Max was used to, but it would have to do.

She located a pot for the pasta and another for the sauce and wondered who'd bought the items. One of his women? He didn't usually date the domesticated variety. He went for the leggy, actress wannabes who had banned carbohydrates from their vocabularies and their diets. Not that he practiced the old clichéd casting couch— she'd learned from observation that sleeping with him pretty much guaranteed a woman would never work with him. That didn't stop them from lining up.

She shoved the pot under the faucet and turned on the water. "Do you think you have everything you need to complete postproduction?"

"If I don't, then the second unit will deal with it once I make a list of my requirements."

The second unit filmed establishing shots that didn't require the principal actors. They'd make clips of the chateau or the landscape or distance pieces in which less expensive doubles could fill in for the actors.

With Max's editing talents and the magic of colored filters and computer software, those clips could be cut in between closeups and no one would ever know the scenes hadn't been filmed in sequence, in the same month or even on the same continent.

Dana had never been around for the second-unit shooting, since, like this time, she was usually sent home to clean up what had accumulated while they were away and to prepare for his return. She'd love to see how the second unit worked.

As producer, Max was usually the first on the scene and the last to leave. But with *Honor*, because he was also the film editor and the family wanted him to assure quality by doing the postproduction himself, he'd left the location before the second unit came in.

She loved the way Max gathered all the pieces of the movie puzzle together to make the final product seem like a seamless picture, and she'd learned a lot watching his process.

"Max, I know you like to be there till the last clip is filmed, but the rush job on the editing is forcing you to be here. I could go back to France to oversee the second unit filming for you."

"You're needed here. What's the status on the sound stages?"

From practice, she followed his jump in topic and poured the jar of sauce into the smaller pot. "They're ready for anything you might need. I checked and the sets look exactly like the photographs of the interior rooms of the chateau."

It always amazed her to see how the prop master and set dressers could identically re-create any place by using film, photographs and measurements. If she hadn't driven herself to the studio yesterday and fought the obscene Burbank traffic, she would have sworn she was still thousands of miles away in France when she'd toured the sound stages. But the real rooms of the chateau didn't have the soundproofed panels that the imitation sets on the movie lot had. Audio recorded here would be much clearer and have fewer outside interferences like airplanes flying overhead.

"Good. Have you eaten?"

His question surprised her. "No, Max. I jumped and came running the moment you called."

Like she always had. It was not as if she had a Friday night date to cancel or anything. Her feelings for Max had killed her dating life for the most part. She tried every now and then, but what was the point in dating a man who could never measure up to her boss? That was going to change. As soon as this movie was finished she would date again—lost cause or not.

"Make sure to fix enough food for two."

His consideration made her heart squeeze up into her throat. He was a nice guy, charismatic and confident…when he wasn't being a demanding perfectionist.

"You'll need your energy," he continued. "We'll probably be up all night. And keep the coffee coming."

Her hopes and optimism crashed. She turned away to hide her disappointment. She should have known Max's concern for her wasn't personal. All he cared about was work—the only mistress, other than his late wife, to whom he'd ever been faithful as far as she knew.

Would she never learn?

She couldn't bend over backward to please him at every turn the way she used to. That wasn't her job anymore. She had to find a way to remind him—to remind *both* of them—of the boundaries of her new role as associate producer.

And then once *Honor* was completed she would tender her resignation. Again. This time she wouldn't let him talk her out of it. She had more important things to accomplish in her life than being someone's invisible assistant, and wasting her time pining for her boss was not going to get those items checked off her list.

She squared her shoulders and stared at the man who'd played the starring role in her fantasies for the past few years. Beginning now, her actions were going to be all about her. Her life. Her dreams. Her success. She was going to go after the family and career she craved.

And no one was going to stand in her way. Not even Maximillian Hudson.

Two

Max fought the sensation of being trussed up in an invisible straitjacket Sunday morning. Having a woman move into his house even temporarily broke his twenty-four-hour rule, and he had that rule for a reason. Never again would he allow a woman to be more than a one-night stand.

But when Dana had fallen asleep sitting in the spare chair in his study just before sunrise yesterday he'd realized he couldn't ask her to work eighteen-hour days and then make the drive home. It wasn't safe. Instead of waking her and sending her on her way he'd let her sleep and left for the office so he wouldn't be around when she awoke. He'd barricaded himself in his office at Hudson Pictures all day Saturday.

He would not be responsible for another woman falling asleep at the wheel and ending up dead. His gut clenched as the memories rained down on him. His wife was gone, and he knew from experience that rehashing and regretting that night would not bring Karen back. Nothing would. He slammed the floodgates on the past the way he always did.

Reminding himself that his cohabitation with Dana was a temporary measure and nothing more than a way to squeeze more working hours out of each day, he brushed aside his disquiet. He wasn't doing this for Dana's benefit. It was a purely selfish action. If something happened to her, it would be close to impossible to finish editing *Honor* on time.

He shoved open the door to the first-floor guest suite, entered and dropped the small suitcase he carried beside the bed. "Leave your stuff in here."

Dana rolled her shoulders stiffly and yawned as she followed him into the room. She covered her mouth and the muscles in her arms shifted, revealing her excellent physical condition. He'd heard that she, like several of the employees, often made use of the personal trainers Hudson Pictures had on location for the lead actors. It showed.

Why had he never noticed that before?

He yanked his gaze back to her face. She looked tired. Not surprising since he'd called and woken her far earlier than most people got up on Sunday morning and demanded she pack a bag and get over here.

He should be exhausted, too, but he was charged by adrenaline, too much caffeine and too much to do. He'd snatched a couple hours sleep here and there, but he'd have to wait to catch up once he had the first cut of the film put together.

There were a lot of pieces to this project that would

normally be farmed out to others, but the family wanted tight control on the finished project. That meant he had more responsibilities than usual. But thanks to digital nonlinear filming he could do most of the work here on his computer instead of in the office where constant interruptions would slow him down.

He caught his gaze wandering over Dana again. Her usual work wardrobe was professional, conservative. Today's snug, ribbed orange tank top clung to her breasts, and she'd cinched her low-rider jeans with a wide leather belt, drawing attention to her rounded hips. She'd dressed too casually for the office, but they weren't going leave his house today, so he wouldn't waste time complaining or waiting for her to change.

She usually wore her long, dark hair up in a neat, no-frills style, but this time she'd clipped the strands up in one of those messy, I'm-getting-ready-to-shower styles that left her neck dusted with loose tendrils—the kind a cameraman loved when shooting a love scene or any other scene requiring a shot of a woman's vulnerable nape.

She hadn't bothered with makeup, but her smooth olive skin and thickly lashed dark eyes made cosmetics unnecessary. A makeup artist would love her, and if the male crew members saw her like this they'd be salivating over her. She looked approachable instead of her usual cool as ice.

Despite her skills in the office, Dana could easily be in front of the camera instead of behind it. Another thing he'd missed.

The fact that she had never used her womanly shape, big chocolate-brown eyes and lush red lips to wheedle her way out of hard work was a point in her favor. He'd experienced enough vain, demanding actresses to lose patience with high-maintenance attitudes long ago. The last thing he needed was more behind-the-scenes melodrama. Movie sets were always full of drama of the unscripted and unwanted variety. The *Honor* set had been no exception.

During the winter his younger brother Luc had become engaged, knocked up his fiancée and decided to leave Hudson Pictures for a horse ranch in Montana. In the spring his cousin Jack had discovered a son he didn't know he had and married the kid's mother. About the same time the family had learned of their grandmother's cancer after she'd had a frightening collapse. And then this summer his cousin Charlotte had become pregnant by the owner of the chateau where they'd been filming *Honor*.

If Max had his way, autumn would not yield any more real-life drama for the cast and crew and definitely not for him.

He shook off the past and focused on Dana. "I want you staying here until we finish the locked cut."

Her eyes widened and then her teeth pinched her bottom lip. "But the final cut could take months."

"We don't have months and you asked for this position. I warned you that you'd be working around the clock." He regretted letting her back him into a corner. But he hadn't had a choice. He needed an assistant to pull this off, and he didn't have time to train someone new on his methods. Dana knew how he worked. "If you can't handle it, speak up."

Her chin rose at his challenge and her cheeks flushed peach. "I can handle it. But when you said pack a bag I only packed enough clothing for a couple of days. I'll have to swing by my apartment and pick up more later."

"Fine. Let's get started." He headed for the stairs, hoping the climb would chase away his grogginess.

"Max, I need coffee first. It's not even six yet. And in case you don't know it, I stayed here until ten last night."

Thanks to his security system's ability to text his cell phone he knew how late she'd stayed. He'd deliberately avoided coming home until after she'd left, and then he'd rolled in around midnight. The pile of completed work she'd left on his desk proved she hadn't been sleeping on the job all day. But then Dana had never been one to shirk even the dirtiest assignments.

"You know where the coffeepot is."

"I left messages with the caterers and the housekeeper and asked them to resume services immediately," she said from close behind him. "They should return first thing Monday morning. Hudson's personnel director is trying to hire my replacement. In the meantime, unless you quit being so critical of every résumé you receive, you might have to work with a temp."

He stopped and turned on the stairs. From the tread above her he looked down at her upturned face, and against his will the swell of her cleavage drew his gaze. The sight hit him with an unexpected punch of arousal.

What the heck?

Dana worked for him. That made her off limits. He ripped his attention from her smooth skin. Only then did he notice she carried several canvas bags looped over her wrists in addition to her ever-present briefcase. "Is there a reason why you're telling me this?"

"Yes. I've run your office without a glitch for five years, Max. You need to know the effort that goes into that because you're going to notice some rough spots during the transition. I'll do my best to smooth them out, but you might just have to suck it up and deal with a few irritations."

The fire in her eyes and voice surprised him. Had Dana ever talked back to him before? He didn't think so. In fact, she'd almost been invisible in getting things done without drawing attention to herself. More than once he'd almost run into her because she was by his side before he even called for her.

"Nothing can slow us down."

"Max, I can't guarantee that, but I'll try to make sure nothing does. Let me unload the groceries and then we can get started. You may be able to work without breakfast, but I can't."

A subtle floral fragrance reached his nose. Dana's perfume? Why had it never registered before? And why was it intruding now? Not intruding, just distracting. She smelled good. He shook off the unnecessary awareness. He didn't have time for distractions.

"Give me those." He pulled the bags from her arms, carried them to the kitchen and set them on the counter. She immediately withdrew a covered rectangular dish from one and popped it into the microwave.

"What is that?"

"A breakfast casserole. I made it last night." She methodically unpacked the remainder of the bags while the microwave hummed, and she stored each item in the cupboards or fridge—fruits and vegetables, juice, milk, bread, eggs, a wedge of the cheese he preferred, two thick T-bone steaks, his favorite cut of meat.

The other night he'd had to escape to the balcony while Dana cooked the spaghetti. The domestic scene had brought back too many memories. Karen had loved to cook. During their brief marriage they'd spent many hours together in the kitchen of their old house laughing, loving and eventually eating whatever she'd whipped up.

That was back in the day when sharing a meal with his bride had been one of the highlights of his day, second only to making love with her.

Damn.

Karen had never set foot in this house, but he felt her presence everywhere he went these days. He blamed the disturbance on the script. Shooting the story of his grandparents falling in love reminded him of falling for his wife and the despair of losing her. He'd known he wanted to spend the rest of his life with his red-haired beauty within three days of meeting her, but he'd had only three years—years that had passed faster than a blink.

And now she was gone.

And it was his fault.

"When was the last time you ate?" Dana's voice plunged into the depths of his dark memories and yanked him to the surface.

He drew air into his tight lungs and searched his mind. "I don't know. Your spaghetti, I guess."

She scowled at him. "Max, that was thirty-six hours ago."

He shrugged. "I was working."

She rolled her eyes and made a disgusted sound. "And you always forget to eat when you're working."

Did he? Was that why she was always shoving food in front of him?

She filled a tall glass with ice and some of the pineapple juice she'd brought with her and set it on the counter in front of him. He sipped the sweet liquid while she bustled around. Moments later the scent of coffee brewing filled the kitchen.

"You don't need a new executive assistant. You need

a keeper," she muttered under her breath as she banged more items into cabinets.

The quiet anger in her tone raised his hackles. "What did you say?"

She turned, brown eyes flashing with temper, and parked her hands on her hips. "I said you need a keeper. I have your food and dry cleaning delivered and your house cleaned. I run your office, pay your bills and schedule your car maintenance and even your dentist and doctor appointments. You're a brilliant producer and film editor, Max. You can schedule a multibillion dollar project down to the dime and edit it down to the second, and heaven knows, you can work miracles with film and the cast and make sure everyone else's needs are met. But you can't manage your own life."

"What?" Karen had often said the same thing. That without her he'd be lost. She was right. That's why he had Dana.

Dana pushed her bangs off her forehead and sighed. "That's not your fault. You've never had to. You had your family and an army of servants and then your wife and now me to do all that for you. But you're going to have to learn. Your next executive assistant may not be willing to manage your personal life, and I won't be around forever."

"We've been over that. You can't quit."

Her gaze met his dead on, steady and determined, dark brown and serious. "I promised to see you through the end of *Honor*. And I am leaving Hudson Pictures once we're done. I negotiated the noncompete clause out of my new contract. You can't give me what I need, and I'm not going to let you hold me back anymore."

Her comment took him aback. Man, she was full of surprises today. None of them good. "I'm not holding you back."

"Yes, you are."

The sadness in her voice caught him at a loss. He didn't understand all this emotional crap, and he was too tired to try to figure it out. Was she PMSing or what? "What exactly is it you want, Dana? I gave you the promotion you demanded."

She glanced toward the doorway and shifted on her feet. "I need a life."

"You have a life and a job most people would kill for. You travel the globe and frequent five-star hotels and restaurants. You wear designer clothing to premieres and work with movie stars others only dream of meeting. The films we create make history, damn it."

"No, Max. You make history. I just watch from the sidelines." She dug in her briefcase, extracted her PDA, a pen and a pad of paper and then rapidly filled the page with her neat script. When she finished she pushed the sheet toward him.

"What is this?" Whatever it was, he knew from her expression that he wasn't going to like it.

"This is a list of people who make your world turn. Your caterer, dry cleaner, housekeeper, dentist, doctor, barber and the like. Until your new executive assistant is hired, you'll be dealing with these people yourself."

"Why won't you?"

"Because it's not my job anymore."

Speechless, he stared. Where was the efficient, quiet woman who'd worked for him for the past few years? "What in God's name happened to you in France?"

"I had a wake up call from my brother. He made me realize that my life was passing me by while I ran yours."

"You have a brother?" How could he not have known that? Come to think of it, did he know anything about

Dana's personal life? He searched his mind and came up with a blank slate. She didn't share; he didn't ask. He liked it that way.

But then he realized he didn't even know where she lived or where she was from originally. Going by the slight accent that slipped out now and then he'd guess she'd come from a southern state. He'd have to have personnel fax over a copy of her résumé.

"My brother, James, is two years older than me. He's a football coach at the university back home. Coaching was his dream, and he didn't let anything stop him from attaining it."

She pulled out a manila folder and slid it across the countertop. "Here's the schedule of your current appointments and a selection of the caterer's sample menus. Mark your choices, add anything else you want and then fax the sheets to the number on the top of the page. They'll coordinate the delivery times with Annette."

Confused, he frowned. "Who is Annette?"

She sighed as if she'd lost patience with him. "Your housekeeper. She's worked for you for four years."

He should have known that. But when was he ever home during the day? "What in the hell is going on, Dana?"

"I'm your associate producer now, Max. I won't be your caretaker anymore."

Caretaker.

He stiffened at the insult. "I'm thirty-three years old, not a child who needs a nanny. I can take care of my own damned needs."

A daring sparkle glinted her eyes and the edges of her mouth slowly curved in a mischievous smile. One dark eyebrow rose. "Really? Care to wager on that, Hudson?"

Something inside him did a queer little twist. He'd

never seen this side of Dana before, and he wasn't sure what to make of the change or if he liked it. "Oh, yes, I'll bet on it. Put your money where your mouth is, Fallon."

She shook her head. "Money means nothing to you."

Drumming his fingers on the folder, he ticked through the possible stakes. What did she have that he wanted? The answer was obvious. "If I handle all my personal junk without asking for your help, then you'll stay on as my assistant after we wrap *Honor*."

She bit her lip and shifted on her feet. "Your executive assistant, not an associate producer?"

"That's right. After this project you return to your old duties."

"And if I win?"

"I'll give you the best damned reference you've ever seen. I'll even make a few calls to help you get your next job."

Her lips parted and her chest rose as she took one deep breath and then another. Her bright orange top kept drawing his attention to her breasts. Her sedate, conservative clothing had never had that effect on him. He forced his gaze back to her face. Should he insist she go back to her professional clothing? No. That would be a sign of weakness.

"Be sure you want to wager this, Max. Because you won't win."

He was sure he didn't want to have to train someone new. Dana might have been around for a long time, but he remembered how many assistants he'd hired and fired before finding her. As she'd pointed out, she made his life run smoothly. She'd fit in from the first day she stepped into his office.

"I'm sure you won't win. Do we have a deal?"

He'd give her the responsibility she wanted with this picture, and if he played his cards right and showed her the harsh reality of an associate producer position, she'd see her job as his executive assistant involve a hell of a lot less work and stress. She'd beg to have her old job and her old hours back. Then his life would run smoothly once more.

She held up one finger. "If you win, I'll stay on for one year. That's the most I'll promise. Not that it's going to happen."

His competitive spirit kicked in. She ought to know better than to back him into a corner. He thrived on working under pressure. And he would do his best to change her mind about the one-year stipulation. "You have yourself a deal, Dana."

He held out his hand and she put hers in it. The contact of her warm, soft palm and long slender fingers against his sent a surge of electricity up his arm. He'd felt that jolt only once before.

The first time he'd kissed his wife.

He yanked his hand free.

Man, the *Honor* script was messing with his head.

He didn't have those kinds of feelings for Dana. Or anyone. And he never would again. Because the last time he'd let himself care about a woman she'd ended up dead.

Three

Max pulled away from Dana so abruptly he yanked her off-balance. "I'm going for a swim."

"What about work? You're the one who called me before sunrise and said we needed to get started. And what about breakfast?"

The microwave dinged as if to reinforce her point. Glad to have a distraction from the residual tingle in her palm, Dana wiped her hand on her jeans and then opened the door. The delicious smell of the ham, zucchini and mushroom strata filled the air.

"Later."

New job. New rules. No more passivity. She was part of his team now—not his support staff—not his gopher.

She grabbed his forearm before he could escape. His muscles knotted beneath her fingers. Heat seeped from his skin to hers. How would she ever get over him if she couldn't stop this instant awareness? She'd have to find a way. Somehow.

"Listen, Max, if you want to starve yourself and go without sleep when you're alone, that's fine. But hunger and tiredness make you cranky, and that makes dealing with you less than pleasant. When I'm around, you need to eat and sleep."

The stunned expression on his face made her want to take the words back. She'd jumped so far across the line of proper boss-employee conduct that she'd be lucky if he didn't fire her. But something her brother had said in his pep talk about putting up with the garbage you had to endure and eliminating the annoyances you could had struck a chord with her.

If she couldn't leave Max, then she had to make an effort to make her remaining time with him bearable. What did she have to lose? She'd already given up on winning his heart. "You can swim after breakfast."

He pulled his arm from her grip. "That's not safe. It causes cramps."

"Oh, please. That's an old wives' tale, and you know it. Stop making excuses. Sit down. I'll get you a plate."

She watched him mentally debate his reply and then, surprisingly, he nodded. "Let's eat outside."

A victory of sorts. She'd take it. She grabbed a tray and piled on the dishes, flatware, coffeepot and casserole. Max took the tray from her and headed outside to the wide patio.

After taking a moment to admire the flex of his thick biceps, she raced ahead to open the sliding-glass door and then closed it behind them. Today he looked more like the smartly dressed, composed boss she was used to seeing in his crisply pressed Pal Zileri trousers and a short-sleeved shirt. Thanks to dealing with his dry cleaning, she knew more about his favorite designers than she needed to.

A steady breeze blew her bangs into her eyes. She impatiently brushed them aside. Now that she was home she needed to make time for a trim. "You should probably find time to visit your grandmother today. She's asked about you."

He set the tray on the table and shot her a questioning look. "You've talked to her?"

The cool morning air smelled fresh instead of smoggy. She caught a whiff of his cologne and inhaled deeply before she could stop herself. "Of course. I've visited Lillian twice since we've been back. She's a bit frail, but her attitude is good, and she's as sharp and witty as ever."

He gave her a strange look. Dana shrugged and sat. "My family is on the other side of the continent and I miss them. So excuse me if I've adopted some of yours."

"Where?"

She blinked in surprise. "Where is what?"

"Your family."

How unusual. Max didn't ask personal questions. He kept the lines between business life and personal life very clearly drawn. "North Carolina. My father teaches filmmaking at the university in Wilmington and my brother coaches there."

"That's where you caught the movie bug."

"From my father? Yes. He always talked about coming to California and making movies, but family obligations kept him on the East Coast." Why was she blabbering this stuff? Max hated useless chitchat.

"So you're doing this for him."

"No, I'm doing it for me. He and I used to edit our old family movies together. It was a hobby we loved and shared. During high school and college I used to write screenplays, but—"

Shut up, Dana. You're blabbering again.

"But what?"

"Screenwriting's not exactly a secure occupation."

"Nothing in the entertainment industry is."

"No." That was why she'd been so thrilled to land a job with a heavyweight like Hudson Pictures.

She lifted the serving spoon to dish up the food, but hesitated when she realized she was about to fill Max's plate. It was a bad habit—one she had to break. How many times had she fixed his lunch when she prepared hers? In fact, if she knew he was going to be working at his desk instead of out schmoozing for lunch, then she usually spent the evening before preparing something special and then packed enough for two the next day. No more of that.

She served herself and set the spoon back in the casserole dish, letting him get his own.

He did so. "You'll have to send your family tickets to the *Honor* premiere."

Her fork stopped short of her lips. Who was this man? Usually exhaustion made Max grumpy. It never made him likeable and approachable. "They'd like that."

"I didn't know you and my grandmother kept in touch."

A chuckle escaped before she could stop it. Lillian had been a regular contact since the first day Dana set foot on Hudson property as Max's executive assistant. The eighty-nine-year-old might be subtle, but she was effective.

"Are you kidding me? I run your world and she checks to make sure I'm doing it correctly and to her standards.

She has a soft spot for you. Don't tell her I said so, but I think you might be her favorite grandson."

A tender smile curved Max's lips and the love in his eyes made Dana's breath hitch. If he ever looked at her like that, her new resolution to get over him would crumble.

No, it won't. You're past that. Remember?

Right. She'd promised to say yes to the next guy who asked her out. She might even sleep with him because it had been…forever since she'd had sex. Well, a couple of years anyway.

Step one in her twelve-step guide to getting over Max Hudson was to immerse herself in another man…or three.

Yeah, right. You never learned to juggle men.

Maybe it was time she tried. At least her heart would be safe that way.

Except for one fizzled relationship, she hadn't dated all that much since taking the Hudson position. Luckily she lived in an apartment building populated by attractive actors waiting for their big break. When she had to attend a Hudson Pictures function she asked one of her neighbors to accompany her. That way she always had a good-looking guy on her arm, and she did them the favor of giving them exposure and introducing them to a few powerful people in the biz. A win-win situation.

She pulled herself back to her present. "In all the years I've worked with you, you've never worked with an associate producer. What will my duties be?"

He seemed to ponder as he ate. "You'll liaison with the cast and crew."

"I've done that before."

"You'll be responsible for checking location details, making sure each of the cast has what he or she requires and you'll be troubleshooting."

Not what she had in mind. "This is beginning to sound like my old job."

"And until I have a new executive assistant it's my job. I'm delegating."

"Max—"

"Don't 'Max' me. You asked for this, Dana."

"If you'd look at the résumés piled on your desk, you might find a new E.A."

"I have looked and none of the applicants has your qualifications."

"That's because I was overqualified."

He frowned. "I don't have time to train anyone right now, and neither do you."

"But—"

"I'll also need you to check the log sheet."

She blinked at his change of subject and nearly groaned. Writing down each scene as it was filmed was mind-numbing. Checking it against the film was doubly so. She sighed. "What else?"

"Make an edit script."

Boring desk work. But, okay, she knew that was part of the process. She forced herself to keep eating although he was killing her appetite.

"Capture the footage and back it up. You do know how to work the editing software, don't you?"

"Yes."

She'd spent a lot of her nonwork hours learning the computer program that stored the dailies digitally on a hard disk. A good producer knew how to get his hands dirty in every phase of production. Putting the clips in order was busywork, but at least she'd get to see the raw footage and get a feel for how the film might come together. That part was exciting.

Max's vision for the story would determine the final product. His editing would set the pace, tone and emotional impact of the film and a million other things simply by the clips, shots and angles he chose to include or cut. Even the sound he chose would affect the final product. While editors might not get much of the credit, the editor could make or break a film.

And then something struck her. "Wait a minute. This is beginning to sound more like editing than producing. And why are you giving me the tedious jobs?"

Max didn't even blink at her accusation, nor did he deny it. "Because right now that's what I need you to do. The producer's primary job is to keep everyone happy, on schedule and under budget. Someone has to do the grunt work, and you need to learn from the bottom up."

She sat back, her appetite and her enthusiasm gone. "I have a degree in filmmaking, and I served several internships with Screen Gems at the Wilmington studios."

"You haven't used any of that knowledge since you graduated, and the technology has completely changed in what? Six, seven years?"

"About that. But I've done my best to keep up."

"Good. Then maybe you won't slow me down. We'll move faster if I don't have to stop and explain things every step of the way." Max took a few bites of his breakfast. "I'll also want you checking for continuity errors, specifically the clocks, candles, setting, cigarettes or anything else that might be an issue. Make sure they haven't changed from shot to shot. No short candles that suddenly get tall."

"That should have been done during filming."

"Right. And yet slipups make it into even megabudget films—even the ones that aren't rushed through postproduction. But I won't have them in mine."

He finished his breakfast and rose. "Time for that swim."

She watched him climb the outdoor, circular iron staircase in the corner of the patio to the master suite and exhaled a pent-up breath when he disappeared inside.

He'd finally given her the job she wanted. But he wasn't going to make it easy. But if he thought he was going to force her back into her old job he was going to be sorely disappointed.

Because like her brother, she was no quitter. She might have gotten sidetracked from her goals for a while, but once she set her mind to something she stuck to it.

Like saving Max. Or saving herself.

Dana turned away from the sight of Max's tanned, muscular shoulders and arms cutting laps through the long pool below the window. No way could her brain function with that kind of distraction.

She was determined not to let Max or herself down, but when she stared at the overwhelming mountain of work on her desk and the long list she'd made of her assigned duties, she had to wonder if she was up to the task. Sure, she'd asked for the responsibilities, but Max had piled them on. His pointing out that she was a bit…rusty in her production skills hadn't helped her confidence any.

But she wasn't above cheating by calling on an expert for guidance if it meant keeping on top of her workload. She picked up the phone, dialed and pressed the receiver to her ear.

"Y'ello?" The deep southern drawl comforted her almost as well as one of her daddy's big bear hugs.

"Hi, Daddy."

"How's the new job, sweet cakes?"

She wished she could lie and say work was a breeze. "I'm feeling a little overwhelmed at the moment. I've e-mailed you a list of the duties Max has assigned me. Have a minute to take a look?"

"You betcha. Hold on a sec." She heard him tapping on the keyboard over the phone line and then the greeting from his e-mail provider.

Seconds later he whistled. "You're going to be earning that pay raise."

"It looks like I'll doing mostly grunt work and a lot of editing tasks."

"Yep. But you wanted to polish your skills, and he's going to make you."

"I have a question for you. What do I need to do next to keep ahead of things?"

She'd kept him posted via e-mail every step of the way because he was living vicariously through her. Today's list was just an update. She knew that if she failed in this position he'd be just as disappointed as she, maybe more so.

"You've been his right hand for years, so this isn't too different. Put every tool Hudson needs at his fingertips. With him juggling two jobs—producer and editor—his time is going to be tighter than ever. Help keep others on schedule for him whenever you can, and run interference with the troublemakers and squeaky wheels. Every project has them. Identify 'em as soon as you can and be proactive, otherwise their poison can spread."

"Got it."

"When you finish the capturing he'll start editing, and remember, an editor's job goes faster if he doesn't have to wait for the components."

She scribbled as fast as she could and hoped she could decipher her notes later. "After the basic editing the next editing components he'll need will be…" she searched her mind, "Sound, right?"

"If he's not calling in an independent sound designer, that's it. And you know where to find what you need, don't you?"

"I do." During college she'd been shocked to discover that most of the movie's soundtrack was added during the editing phase. Quite often the audio recorded on location wasn't up to par and dialogue or sound effects were added later.

There were audio libraries where film companies could buy or rent the sounds or background ambience they needed for a film. The roar of a passing subway train or the hum of a busy city street corner might be used in a dozen other films, but the typical moviegoer would never recognize it as one he'd heard before.

"I'll get right on it, Dad."

"That's my girl. Give him what for. Show him that a steel magnolia can whup a California girl any day. Have they hired the composer for the musical score yet?"

"Yes. It's not anyone I'm familiar with."

"Get familiar. You want to be on a first-name basis, so that glitches can be smoothed over quickly and painlessly."

"Got it." She wandered to the window and looked out to see if Max was still in the pool. He was pulling himself out, his muscles flexing under wet, tanned skin. Using both hands, he slicked back his hair. His wet trunks clung to him like a second skin, outlining his masculine attributes in ex-cruciating detail. Her mouth dried and her pulsed skipped.

"Miss you, sweetheart." Her father's voice pulled her out of the lust zone. She turned away from the window.

"I miss you, too. Thanks for your help."

"Make sure home is your first stop after you put this one in the can. You're due a vacation, aren't you?"

She smiled. He father had never been anything but supportive of her career choice. Of course, that might be because they shared the same dream.

"Past due. I'll come home for a visit after this is all over. I'll see you then. Love you, Daddy."

"Love you back."

She disconnected and headed for the spare desk in Max's office. Thirty minutes and six phone calls later she had a list waiting when Max walked in. He looked refreshed from his swim. His dark hair was still slightly damp, and he'd donned her favorite DKNY outfit of gray pants and a white shirt with subtle gray stripes.

She rose and handed him the pages and a memory stick containing the audio files from the library. "I've contacted the sound library and found the items on your list. They're downloaded onto your flash drive. I also have the Foley artist on standby. I'll call when you're ready for him."

She loved watching Foley artists work. Once they opened their little briefcase of "toys" the sound specialists could re-create just about any noise to be perfectly synced to the audio tracks and inserted during the editing phase. Dubbing in voice audio wasn't nearly as interesting, but it still beat the monotony of logging and making edit scripts.

Max paused, his eyebrows raised in surprise. "Thanks. You've been busy."

She shrugged. "That's my job."

"Yes, it is." But there was a new respect in his eyes that hadn't been there before. His approval made her stomach turn somersaults and her entire body flush with pleasure.

Uh-oh. Getting over him wasn't going to be nearly as easy as she'd hoped. She'd just have to try harder.

"You have to trust me, Max. I won't let you down."

"We'll see about that."

And that's when it hit her. Max might be extremely charismatic, but he was also a loner. He didn't let anyone in, not even her. If he couldn't trust her after five years, would he ever?

"Give me ten minutes," Dana said over her shoulder Monday morning as Max followed her into her apartment.

He ripped his gaze from her butt, but not before registering her nice shape in a pencil-slim black skirt.

What was his problem? Finding her in his kitchen early this morning wearing skimpy shorts-and-camisole pajamas with her dark hair rumpled and streaming over her shoulders had clearly messed up his thinking. She'd been waiting for the coffee to brew or, more likely judging by her worshipful expression, praying to the coffeepot gods to send deliverance from her boss's brand of evil.

Maybe having her stay at his place wasn't such a good idea. He liked his space and his privacy. But they were getting more accomplished than they would have in the office.

He checked his watch. "We have a conference call in two hours."

"Max, I'll have my suitcase packed in no time." She dropped her purse and keys on an entry table made from glass and irregularly shaped but sturdy grayed branches. Driftwood? "Come in and make yourself comfortable."

He did a whip pan of the apartment, soaking up details

in a flash. He never would have taken his superefficient executive assistant for the relaxed beach-cottage type, but her rustic white-painted furniture with its bright blue cushions and citrus colored pillows combined with the box-framed seashells and artwork on her walls definitely looked as if he'd just walked in from the beach. Even the straw mats on the hardwood floor resembled the types he'd seen in coastal homes.

Not that he'd had time to see a vacation home recently.

He tried to sync the casual decor with the woman he knew and it didn't work. He was used to seeing Dana in conservative suits with her hair tightly pinned up—like she was now. He crushed the memory of her long, bare legs, flushed cheeks and heavy-lidded eyes. But damn, she'd looked sexy in his kitchen.

Forget it, Hudson.

Easier said than done. No matter how hard he tried to erase the memory, it kept popping up on his mental movie screen.

He ran a finger under his tight collar. "Did you rent this place furnished?"

She turned in her small living room, her brown eyes finding his. "No, it's all my stuff. Did you want something to drink while you wait?"

She spoke quickly, as if she were uncomfortable having him in her home. They'd decided to carpool today, since her apartment complex was on the way to the Hudson Pictures studios. It was too hot to wait in the car, so he'd followed her in.

"No thanks."

"Have a seat then. I'll be right back." She hustled down a short hall, and his gaze stayed focused on her hip-swinging gait until she turned a corner out of sight.

The golden, orange and red hues of a large beach scene hanging behind the sofa drew him closer. He could practically feel the warmth of the setting sun reflecting off the water and glistening on the ivory sand. He moved on to a second painting on an adjacent wall of a bright yellow hang glider sailing above the blue ocean. A third picture had caught the infectious grin of a child in a ruffled orange swimsuit playing on the beach with buckets and shovels beneath a colorful umbrella. The pictures, similar in style and technique, were well executed and looked so real he could almost hear the waves and smell the salt air.

He checked the artist's signature. All three were by a Renée Fallon. Fallon? A relative of Dana's? He'd have to ask.

A cluster of twenty or so framed photographs drew him to the opposite wall. He recognized a much younger Dana with an older man and woman and a preadolescent boy. She looked enough like the trio that he guessed they were her family. He turned back to the painting of the child, noting the similarities, the same big brown eyes, same smile and same coltish legs and long, dark hair. Dana without a doubt. So the artist did know her.

He scanned each photograph, and it was as if he were watching a much less serious Dana grow up in front of him. It wasn't until she hit what he would guess were her college years that her expression turned serious and her smile looked forced. What had caused the transition from carefree girl to serious woman?

In the next photo a group of young men in football jerseys surrounded a guy in his late twenties or early thirties. The guy grinned up at the camera, a trophy in his hands. He had Dana's coloring and a more masculine version of her features. She'd said her brother was a football coach. This had to be him. And then Max realized the boys crowding around him almost obscured a wheelchair. Her brother was disabled? She'd never said.

His gaze returned to the previous pictures where the guy had been a tall, muscle-bound athlete wearing a football uniform. What had happened?

You don't need to know. Your employees' personal lives are none of your business unless they impact their work.

But Dana had said a wake-up call from her brother sparked her decision to leave Hudson. That made the topic fair game.

A yawn surprised him. He blamed it on lack of sleep combined with Dana's decor. The space with its pale blue walls and beachy furniture made him think of kicking back barefooted with warm sand trickling between his toes and a cold tropical drink sweating in his palm. The room was surprisingly soothing.

Exhaustion hit him hard and fast. When had he had a vacation last? Maybe after *Honor* was finished…. No, after his grandmother… He snuffed the thought, rubbed a hand across his face and sat on the sofa. He didn't want to miss any of his grandmother's remaining days.

He glanced at his watch and leaned his head against the tall backrest. He'd give Dana two more minutes and then he'd yell for her to hurry up.

But visiting her apartment had stirred his curiosity. Who was the real Dana Fallon? The hyperefficient quiet assistant in business suits or the sexy, mouthy, tank-top-and-jean-wearing woman who'd arrived at his house on Sunday?

He suddenly had a strong desire to find out.

The urge to kiss Max awake was almost too strong for Dana to resist. Too bad *almost* didn't count.

"Max," she called quietly.

He didn't stir.

Two hours ago she'd come out of her bedroom and found him asleep. She couldn't remember ever having seen him so relaxed before. He'd practically dissolved into the cushions of her couch. But she shouldn't be surprised. She'd be shocked if he'd had more than two hours' sleep last night. He was pushing himself too hard—exactly the way he had after he'd lost his wife.

Why did men always think drowning themselves in work would cure a problem? It didn't. It only delayed dealing with the issue. And exhaustion made any problem much harder to handle.

While watching Max sleep, something inside her had melted, and she'd known she was in trouble. She'd wanted to cover him, tuck him in and kiss his smooth-for-the-first-time-in-forever forehead. Instead, she'd studied the shadows beneath his eyes that even his tan couldn't hide and decided not to wake him. She'd known he'd be irritated at himself for falling asleep and even more irritated with her for not waking him, but too bad. He'd needed the rest. Everyone at the studio would benefit if he had a nap, and he'd be sharper for the upcoming meeting.

She told herself she had nothing to feel guilty about, and it wasn't as if she'd been wasting time. While he'd slept she'd worked from her laptop at her kitchen table. But now his respite was over.

"Max," she tried again, a little louder this time. He still didn't stir. Dana dampened her lips and eased onto the cushion beside him. The warm proximity of his leg beside hers made her heart race. Touching him both appealed to her and repelled her. She flexed her fingers. She wanted to stroke his smoothly shaven jaw—ached to actually—but that would only make leaving him all that much harder. And she was going to leave. Eventually.

She debated her options. Shake his leg? She checked out the long, muscular thigh beside hers and discarded the idea. Tap his arm? No, she'd always hated being poked awake—her brother's favorite method when they were schoolkids and had to catch the bus.

She cupped a hand over the shoulder closest to her and gently shook him. "Max, wake up."

His eyelids slowly lifted and his unfocused gaze found hers. His mouth curled in an easy, delicious, breath-stealing smile. "Morning."

The groggy, rough timber of his voice made her stomach muscles quiver. Wouldn't she love to wake up to that every day?

"Good morning." Had he forgotten they'd already played out this scene in his kitchen? She hadn't. How could she forget his catching her looking like a ship-wreck victim washed up on the beach? She'd been em-barrassed to be caught in her pj's, but she'd thought he was still sleeping when she'd staggered toward the cof-feepot. He might survive on a couple of hours sleep, but she couldn't—not without a few gallons of coffee to lu-bricate her mental wheels.

His hand painted a hot path up her spine. She gasped. Then his fingers cupped her nape and he pulled her forward. Too stunned to react, she let him move her like a rag doll. Warm lips covered hers. Her heart stopped and then lunged into a wild beat as his mouth opened over hers.

Shocked, but thrilled, she responded, meeting the slick, hot glide of his tongue as he stroked her bottom lip for just a second before reality smacked her upside the head.

Who does he think he's kissing? One of his blondes? His dead wife? She jerked free.

Max stiffened and blinked, the fog vanished from his eyes instantly and clarity returned. His hand fell away and his lips compressed. "I apologize. That shouldn't have happened."

She fisted her fingers and fought the urge to press them to her tingling mouth. "It's okay. You must have been dreaming."

His jaw shifted. "Must've been."

He lifted his arm, checked his watch and swore. "I've missed the conference call. You shouldn't have let me sleep."

Coming on the heels of her fantasy desire to kiss Max coming true, his accusatory tone rubbed her the wrong way.

"You needed the rest. I've called everyone involved and rescheduled the call until noon. It was no big deal, and no one was inconvenienced. If they had been I would have woken you. That's why I'm waking you now. We need to go."

She stood, removing herself from the temptation of kissing him again even if he did think she was someone else, and pressed her hands to her thighs to still their trembling. "I've left you a new toothbrush on the bathroom counter if you want to freshen up."

Not that he needed to. He'd tasted delicious.

Stop it, Dana.

He rose, standing so close his scent filled her lungs and his body heat reached out to encircle her. She told herself to move away, but her legs refused to listen. Instead, she found her head tipping back and wished he'd kiss her again, this time fully awake and cognizant of what he was doing and who he held.

As if he'd read her mind, his gaze dropped to her lips. Her pulse rate skyrocketed and her mouth dried. His eyes returned to hers, but while his pupils dilated, his lips settled into an almost invisible line of rejection. "Again, I apologize. It won't happen again."

Disappointment settled like a fishing weight in her stomach. "I—it's okay, Max. No harm done."

His gaze bounced to her wall of photos. "Is that your brother?"

Another abrupt subject change. But then he did specialize in them. It had taken her a while after she first started working with him to keep up. "Yes."

"What happened?"

"You mean what put him in the wheelchair?"

He nodded.

"James went swimming at a rock quarry with his college teammates. He dove in where he shouldn't have. We're lucky he's alive. He'd planned to play pro football after he graduated and then coach. He had to abandon the first part of his dream, but he never gave up on the coaching part, and he didn't let his disability stop him. He's the defensive coordinator and has plans to keep moving up."

"And the paintings? Who is Renée Fallon?"

He'd been busy while she'd been packing, and why did he have to ask personal questions now when her brain was still too stuck on that kiss to function? "My mother."

"She's very good."

"Yes, she is. We're all very proud of her."

Without another word, he swept past her and down the hall.

Dana quit fighting and pressed her fingers to her mouth. *Forget that kiss happened.*

He wasn't kissing you. Not in his head, anyway.

But that kiss, accidental or not, wasn't something she could ever erase from her memory.

In fact, she wanted another one.

And that blew her goal of escaping Max and getting a life of her own right out of the water.

Four

Hudson Pictures' studios in Burbank reminded Dana of home.

The property had a forties vibe that was both nostalgic and quaint. She loved everything about the place from the large, well-maintained buildings housing the sets and equipment to the small bungalows that made up the offices. It was the architecture of those bungalows that reminded her of her grandparents' waterfront community in Southport, North Carolina, which had been constructed in the same era.

She squashed a wave of homesickness and reminded herself she was living hers and her father's dreams. Not many people got a chance to do that.

As she hustled through the studio grounds beside Max she couldn't help getting mushy and emotional. When Dana had first started at Hudson Pictures, Lillian had personally guided her through the maze of buildings recounting the story of her life with Charles Hudson.

Oh, sure, Dana had recognized the subtle grilling the older lady had hidden behind the fairy-tale romance, but she'd been too enthralled by Lillian's exciting past to resent the inquisition. Lillian's blue eyes, eyes so like Max's, still came alive when she'd talked about those days.

Lillian had told Dana that it had been Charles's dream to make the story of their lifelong romance into a movie, but he'd died back in 1995 before seeing it to fruition. And now Lillian had adopted her husband's dream as her own—one last gift to him before she joined him, she'd told Dana over their last tea. She wanted the world to know what a wonderful man Charles had been.

Looking at the Hudson matriarch now, no one would guess the older woman had led a secret life as a spy masquerading as a cabaret singer in France during World War II. That's how she'd met Charles and their courtship had begun, and it was where they'd secretly married. When France was liberated, Charles had been ordered to fight in Germany, but he'd promised to return for his bride as soon as he could. He'd kept that promise, and then he'd brought Lillian here to the home and studios he'd built for her and made her a star. Lillian in turn had made Hudson Pictures a megasuccess, a privately owned filmmaking dynasty.

Dana sighed and pressed a hand to her chest. Every woman should have a larger-than-life romance like that. Her eyes grew misty just thinking about a lover who would cross the globe for her or stand by her through the difficult challenges of life. But so far, she hadn't been that lucky. She'd had boyfriends in high school and college, but nothing with forever written on it—not even close, but not for lack of looking. She found either friendship or passion, but she'd never managed to find a man who brought her both. And that was what she wanted more than anything.

She was determined to hold out for a true love like her parents', her brother's or Lillian and Charles's. With three excellent examples you'd think she'd have better luck.

"Dana."

She startled at Max's firm tone. "What?"

He stopped outside their office bungalow and stared down at her through narrowed eyes. "Did you hear a word I said?"

Her cheeks burned. "Um…no. I'm sorry. I was thinking about the *Honor* script and how lucky you were to convince Cece Cassidy to write it. She did a great job."

"Jack convinced her."

Upon Lillian's request, Max's cousin Jack had approached his former lover for the job. "He ended up with a great screenplay from her and found a son he didn't know he had—a double blessing."

Jack and Cece's romance was just one of several connected to *Honor*'s cast and crew. Was it too much to hope for one of her own before they wrapped? Apparently.

And then she noticed Max's scowl. "Lillian is thrilled to have a great-grandchild."

His frown deepened. "Is there anything else you'd like to share with me before we go into this meeting?"

She winced at the bite of his sarcasm, and then she wanted to smack her forehead. Duh. She'd forgotten that according to the Hudson rumor mill he and Karen had been trying to get pregnant when Karen died. Mentioning his younger cousin Jack's son had not been a good idea.

"No. I've made a list of bullet points that require attention and action right now, but I'm not exactly sure why your uncle David is calling this meeting, and he wouldn't say. I don't know if what I have is relevant."

She hurried through the door he opened for her and bolted toward her old desk, where she dropped her briefcase and withdrew a folder, which she passed to him. They had yet to sort out a new office for her, and since her replacement hadn't been found, there was no rush to vacate the space. Max had rejected each of the applicants' résumés personnel had sent over. He'd yet to call one single person in for an interview.

"Everything you need should be in here. Do I get to sit in on the meeting?"

"Yes. But I'll do the talking."

"Understood."

He'd barely spoken on the drive in. Was he still thinking about the kiss that, she suspected in his opinion, shouldn't have happened? She couldn't stop rehashing it. If only she hadn't jerked away…

What would he have done?

Nothing. He wasn't kissing you. He was kissing whomever he'd been dreaming about.

But what if she was wrong? What if he had known it was her?

Excitement made her shiver.

Get real.

All right, so chances were he hadn't been thinking of her. Should she tell him she'd enjoyed the kiss? Probably not. If she played her hand and he rejected her, it could get uncomfortable. Would she be able to handle the humiliation of running into Max at one Hollywood event after another? The Hudsons were powerful people. One word from any of them whispered in the right ear and she'd have a hard time ever finding a job anywhere in the movie biz.

That would be a disaster because the last thing she wanted to do was tuck her tail between her legs and run home, disappointing herself, her father and her brother.

But what if she could find a way to make Max notice her as a woman…?

She thought about her brother fighting the odds and winning, and about her father who'd found a way to achieve his dreams on the East Coast instead of the West, and her mother who made a living sharing her color-drenched view of the world with others. She'd faced rejection head-on daily until she'd finally found success.

Dana asked herself how she could be any less courageous.

She watched Max's stiff spine as he headed for his office.

Every member of her family took risks on a regular basis, with their hearts and their careers. She was the only one who always, *always*, played it safe. Coming to Hollywood was the only real risk she'd ever taken…and she'd done that only after she'd landed the job as Max's executive assistant.

It was time she found the courage to gamble on something that really mattered. And what really mattered was Max.

"We have a problem," David Hudson's voice said over the speaker.

Dana wasn't crazy about Max's uncle. He might be charming on the surface, but in her opinion he was a womanizer who never had time for his children. The only reason she didn't hate him was because he treated his mother, Lillian, well.

"What problem besides a shortage of time?" Markus Hudson, Max's father and the CEO of Hudson Pictures, countered.

Dana liked Markus, and she saw a lot of him because he was close to Max and often stopped by the office to chat. Markus was a wonderful husband, father and son.

While only Dana and Max occupied the office, Max's oldest brother Dev, the COO of Hudson Pictures, plus Luc, Max's younger brother who acted as PR director, had joined them on the conference call but had been silent thus far.

"What kind of trouble, David?" Max asked.

"Willow Films is making a World War II picture scheduled for release just prior to *Honor*."

Dana gasped and nearly dropped the pen she held for note taking. Willow was Hudson's biggest rival. There wasn't a lot of good feeling between the two film companies. In fact, the competition sometimes turned ugly.

"Worse," David continued, "rumor has it the story has some similarities to Lillian and Charles's. But I can't get anyone to tell me how similar the two films are."

"How accurate is your source?" Dev asked.

"I trust it," David replied.

Dana could feel Max's tension and see it in the lines on his face. His fingers fisted on his desktop. "Even if we could swing an earlier release at this late date, I don't think I can finish *Honor* any faster."

"We're not asking that of you, son." Markus's voice filled the room. "But we might need to put a PR spin on this to make our film sound bigger and better and different or Willow will kill our momentum."

"I'll get on it," Luc said. "But it would help to know more about their product."

"I'll see what I can get," David said, "but they're pretty damned tight-lipped."

Adrenaline rushed through Dana's system. One of her past boyfriends was an assistant director for Willow, and she and Doug had parted on good terms. In fact, he owed her a favor….

She sat up straighter as she turned an idea over in her mind. Could she get the information this group needed out of Doug?

She opened her mouth to volunteer, but sealed her lips without saying a word. Why make promises she wasn't sure she could keep? Best to test the waters first.

But the chance to do something to make Max notice her had fallen right in her lap. And she was determined not to blow it.

"Long time no see, babe," Doug said as he joined Dana at The Castaway in Burbank on Tuesday evening.

Dana had invited Doug to the restaurant in the hills overlooking the golf course because it had been his favorite back when they were dating. Once the sun set and the city lights twinkled below, the setting would be magical. Too bad it had never sparked romance between them.

"I'm glad you could make it on short notice." She rose from her seat and leaned forward to kiss his cheek. As usual, the doofus turned his head at the last second and she caught him square on the mouth. He was one of those people who kissed every female, young or old, on the lips, and because he was the total package—smart, ambitious, charming and attractive in a golden-boy kind of way—he could get away with it. Unfortunately, there had never been any chemistry between them, not even a tiny fizz. But they'd given it their best shot.

"Lucky you called when you did. The boss and I leave on recce at the crack of dawn tomorrow. I won't be back for at least two weeks, longer if it doesn't go well."

"*Ooh,* I'm jealous. I love scouting out potential locations. Where are you headed?"

"Can't say. Top secret. But it's somewhere warm and sunny with umbrella drinks." His blue eyes, shades paler than Max's, glimmered with amusement. He took his seat. "Congrats on the promotion."

"You heard?"

"Tinseltown is a small, gossipy community. Besides, you were once my girl, so I keep tabs on you. Liking the job so far?"

"Most of it. It has a steep learning curve, but I'm learning from the best." She wasn't going to tell him Max was working her fanny off, and she was lucky to get six hours of sleep each night or that she loved every minute of the torture.

"I'll bet it's a load of pressure with *Honor* nearing completion."

She smiled. He'd opened the subject, which made her job easier. As an assistant director, Doug assisted the director much the way she assisted Max. Doug didn't actually direct and he was okay with that. She'd have preferred the more creative position. But his job meant he knew a lot about ongoing projects.

"Yes, there is a lot of tension at the moment. I hear Willow has its own World War II film coming out soon."

"You heard correctly."

"Is it a romance?"

One corner of his mouth rose in a teasing smile. "Could be."

"Oh, c'mon, Doug."

He leaned forward and caught both of her hands in his on the table. It was a familiar gesture, one he'd done dozens of times before. "Why should I share with you? You work for the enemy, remember?"

"What do you have to lose? Everyone in Hollywood already knows the gist of Charles's and Lillian's story, and your picture is coming out first. Besides, I introduced you to the person who ended up hiring you for this job you adore, *remember?*"

Doug used to live in her building and had been her premiere date on more than one occasion before they'd tried and failed to be more than just occasional stand-in dates. She'd made the job connection for him at an after party.

"Good point." He released her, waved down the waiter and ordered a bottle of champagne. They had been together for about a year, and he hadn't forgotten her preference for Krug Brut Grande Cuvée. "Yes, it's a romance. I know how much you love sappy love stories."

"How similar is it to *Honor?*"

"It's similar."

She grimaced. That wasn't good. "That's going to make marketing on our end difficult."

"Not if you play up the differences."

That's exactly what Markus had said. "How are we going to know what those differences are?"

The waiter returned with the champagne. Dana impatiently waited for the whole tasting ritual thing to pass and then opened her mouth to repeat her question. Doug halted her with a raised finger.

"First we celebrate your promotion." He lifted his glass. She dutifully clinked her rim to his and sipped. The golden liquid bubbled down her throat leaving a nutty, toasted finish behind, but it failed to sooth her agitated nerves. She didn't need alcohol. She needed answers.

Doug covered her free hand with his. "Dana, relax. I didn't work on the film directly, so I don't know the details, but I might have a copy of the script at my place. You can follow me home and I'll check. If I don't, then I can probably get you a copy when I get back. After all, as you said, what could it hurt? It's too late in the game for any espionage stuff."

Surprise made her gasp. She couldn't possibly ask for any more. "Will that get you in trouble?"

"I don't think so. I'll test the waters first."

"I don't want to get you fired."

He winked. "I don't want that, either."

"I could kiss you, Doug."

"Please do."

That stilled her for a moment with a twinge of discomfort. "But you know—"

"Dana, just shut up and kiss me. I know it means nothing. But it raises my value to be seen with a hot chick."

Chuckling, she rose and leaned over the table without bothering to argue about his "hot chick" comment. She gave Doug a quick peck. It was like kissing her brother only Doug wore pricier cologne.

"Celebrating something?" Max's voice said behind her.

She froze an inch away from Doug's lips and then straightened and turned. The icy look in Max's blue eyes made her uneasy. "Uh…hi, Max."

Max wore his black Jack Victor suit with a white shirt and a black-and-white patterned tie. He looked delicious in a forbidding way.

Doug's chair scraped as he pushed it back and rose.

"We're celebrating Dana's promotion. I'm glad you were finally smart enough to recognize her worth."

She shot Doug a warning glance. Doug ignored her and offered Max his hand. "I'm Doug Lewis. We met a couple of years ago at the *Legions* premiere."

Max gave him a brief, hard shake. "I remember."

Max no doubt did. Dana didn't think he ever forgot a name or face. But at the time Doug hadn't been working for Willow. Should she tell him Doug had promised her a copy of the Willow script? No, better not. She didn't want to get Doug in trouble, and she didn't want to raise Max's hopes in case Doug couldn't deliver.

"Thanks for stopping by to say hello," Doug added in clear dismissal. "We won't keep you."

Aghast, Dana stared. Did the man have a career death wish?

Max's cold eyes found Dana's again. "My appointment is waiting. Don't stay out late tonight. We have a full schedule tomorrow. I'll meet you in the kitchen at six."

Having dropped that bombshell, he strolled across to the dining room. Her gaze followed him to a table where he joined his older brother.

Dana turned on Doug. "Are you crazy?"

"Whoa. He'll meet you in the kitchen?"

She sighed. "Until *Honor* is finished I'm staying at Max's house. It allows us more working hours if I don't have to commute."

"You've had it bad for him forever."

Her cheeks warmed. "He is my boss and I like and respect him."

"It's more than that and you know it. Opportunity is knocking, babe. Why not see if we can stir up a little heat?" He reached for her.

Groaning, she evaded him and sank back in her chair. "That's why you asked me to kiss you? You saw Max coming?"

He shrugged. "Maybe."

Doug had stirred up something all right. Max's anger. Max had looked furious to find her out partying when she should be at home working on *Honor*. She had a mountain of work on her desk and not enough hours in the day to get it done.

She prayed the copy of the Willow script came through. Only then could she fully explain to Max why she was consorting with the enemy.

"You look ready to breathe fire," Dev said as Max joined him at their table.

"My assistant is wining and dining when she should be at home working." That was the only reason seeing Dana kiss the guy had pissed him off. The urge to knock the kid back into his chair had nothing to do with the fact that she'd been kissing Max thirty-two hours ago.

For God's sake, she worked for him. The kiss had been a mistake—one he shouldn't, couldn't, *wouldn't* repeat. Had he learned nothing from his marriage? Business and pleasure were a volatile combination.

"You're out tonight, too."

"This is work. We're here to develop strategy to counteract the Willow competition. Damn, this time crunch is killing us."

"Rushing the film through production and postproduction has definitely added some pressure. But you can't expect her to work around the clock."

"Until this film is done we're all working around the clock. She knew what she was getting into before she signed on as associate producer, and she's being paid accordingly. If she'd wanted nine-to-five, she should have kept her old job."

Dev looked beyond Max's shoulder and his eyes narrowed. "How well do you know Dana?"

Obviously not as well as he'd thought given the discoveries he'd made in the past few days. Had he ever seen her smile the way she'd been smiling at her date? "Why?"

"Her dinner date is Doug Lewis."

"I've met him."

"He's Trey Jacob's assistant."

A knot jerked tight in Max's midsection. "Lewis works for Willow."

"That's right. And we have a possible leak. Think there's a connection?"

Instant denial sprung to Max's lips. He'd trusted Dana with everything for the past five years. But Dev had planted a seed of doubt and tendrils of mistrust took root. Would Dana betray him? Would she betray Hudson Pictures? If so, why? What possible motive could she have?

Money? He'd seen no signs of excess spending in her apartment, and she drove a four-year-old economy car. She wasn't into jewelry or designer shoes and handbags like so many of the actresses he dealt with.

A promotion? She'd have less of a chance of producing anything at Willow than she had with Hudson, and she was smart enough to know it.

Max scrolled through his memories. The *Legions* premiere hadn't been the only time he'd seen Dana with Lewis. "She's been dating him for at least two years."

"I'd say that needs looking into."

"I agree. I'll talk to her tonight."

"Tonight?"

He wished his brother hadn't picked up on that. "When I get home."

"You'll call her that late?"

"No. I'll see her. She's staying with me."

Dev's eyebrows shot up. "She's living with you?"

"No. *Staying* with me until *Honor* is completed."

"Same difference."

"Not at all. It's business. Working from my home office means fewer interruptions and a way to squeeze more hours out of the workday. She's downstairs in the guest suite. It's nothing personal."

That kiss had been pretty damned personal. His reaction to seeing her with bed head, no makeup and in her skimpy pajamas had felt personal. Why else would he have been dreaming about her when he crashed on her sofa? A seriously hot dream.

Planting one on her when he'd still been in that hazy half-awake state had not been one of his finer moments. He'd be lucky if she didn't cry sexual harassment. That would give the PR department a serious issue to work on.

"You're sharing a house. Trust me, women have expectations when that happens. Everything changes."

"Dana knows the score."

"I hope you're right." Dev got an *ah-ha* look on his face. "I get it. This is about Karen."

"No," Max denied quickly.

"Yes. You don't want Dana on the road late at night because of what happened to Karen. It's the same reason you always make your bimbos sleep over after sex instead of kicking them out like a smart man would. Better yet, you could go to their place, leave when you're done and avoid the messy mornings after."

"You're trying to connect unrelated incidents."

"Liar." But the insult was hurled in a brotherly tone. "The accident wasn't your fault, Max."

He didn't want to rehash this. Not now. Not while they had so much other garbage on the table. "I need a drink."

He scanned the area, searching for their waiter. It was because he'd had too much to drink that night while he was wheeling and dealing that he'd made Karen drive.

Is there a lesson here, buddy?

A familiar knot of tension balled between his shoulder blades. *Forget the drink.* "I shouldn't have let her drive."

"She was old enough to make that decision herself, Max."

"She was tired."

"Karen could have called for a driver. Wouldn't be the first time one of us has done that. Or she could have had a couple cups of coffee. God knows she had guts enough to speak up for what she wanted on the job. That night shouldn't have been any different."

Another reminder not to get involved with someone he worked with. He and Karen had had a great marriage most of the time, but when they had one of their rare arguments the bad mood had followed them into work and hung over the entire studio like a dark cloud. She'd been his executive assistant until he'd convinced her to quit, stay at home and try to get pregnant.

"Forget it. That's history. We have a current crisis to manage." He didn't need to be raking over old, cold coals tonight. If he did he'd end up drinking too much. Again. His pity parties didn't happen often, but when they did, they weren't pretty. That's why he usually carted himself out of town for the event. This year his tight schedule wouldn't allow it.

"You're right. Max, the similarity between Willow's film and ours might be coincidental. Congruity happens. And if it were any other film company I wouldn't think twice. But it's not another company, and if we have a leak then you have to consider Dana as the source."

He'd already come to that conclusion. "If I fire her, I'll never get the editing done on time."

"Then you won't fire her. Yet. You'll just watch her like a hawk. Can you handle that?"

She was already living under his roof. All he had to do was find a way to control the hours when she wasn't working or sleeping and since those would be few and far between until November, it shouldn't be too difficult.

"I have it covered. And I'll find out if she's leaked anything and if so, how much."

Five

Dana closed Max's front door and locked it behind herself as quietly as possible, then she turned and spotted a big shadow in the dark foyer. She startled and fumbled for the security panel, intent on setting off the alarm if she had to.

The light flicked on, identifying the shadow as Max. She pressed a hand over her racing heart. The gate chime would have alerted him to her arrival. "Max, you scared me."

"What did you tell Lewis about *Honor?*"

She smothered a wince. She'd been afraid he'd think the worst. "Nothing."

"He works for Willow."

She heard accusation in his tone, but until she had the script in hand and she was sure delivering it wouldn't get Doug fired, she couldn't give Max the whole story. Doug hadn't had a copy of the script in the pile at his condo. She'd have to wait until he could look around the office when he returned from recce.

"Yes. He works for Willow. He's been there a couple of years. And you might as well know now that I helped him get the job."

"So that you could exchange information?"

"No."

"Did you leak details of the *Honor* script to him?"

She pushed off the door and met his gaze straight on. "No, Max. Why would I do that?"

"You tell me."

That he didn't trust her ticked her off. "You think I sold information to our competitor?"

"Did you?"

The accusation stung. "I was trying to *get* information from Doug tonight, not give it to him. You wanted to know about Willow's upcoming film. I've known Doug a long time. I was hoping he'd tell me what we needed to know."

"Did he?"

"Not yet."

"You kissed him."

She shrugged. "Doug kisses everybody. It means nothing."

"Yesterday you kissed me."

Her mouth watered over the memory. She swallowed. "No. *You* kissed *me*. But I get that you didn't know who…you weren't awake or aware…that it wasn't me you were thinking of."

She was so uncomfortable with this conversation she could barely look him in the eyes.

"He's your lover."

She grimaced and curled her toes in her shoes. "He was. He isn't anymore. That ended years ago."

"Before or after he went to work at Willow?"

Why did he need to know this?

"About the same time. We didn't want to be accused of a conflict of interest, so we ended our relationship." By then they'd figured out they were better friends than lovers anyway. And yes, Doug had figured out she was looking for someone who could make her forget her boss. But Doug hadn't been that guy. No way was she going to tell Max that.

"Did you promise to meet him again?"

Heat crawled up her cheeks. Not in the way he meant, but she wasn't going to lie. "We didn't set a date."

"But you are going to see him again."

"I might. He's a friend." If he got the script, they'd definitely meet. He was supposed to call if/when that happened and set up a rendezvous. Waiting a week or three seemed like an eternity.

Max moved closer until he loomed over her and she had to tilt her head back to hold his gaze. "I could fire you for that conflict of interest you mentioned."

Her stomach sank. "You don't need to do that, Max. I swear I'm not sharing company secrets. I'm trying to help, not hurt Hudson Pictures."

"Will you sleep with him to get the information?"

She flinched and gasped. "No."

"Will you kiss him again?"

This was a weird conversation for a man who avoided personal exchanges like he would stepping on a fire-ant hill. "Probably. I told you Doug kisses everybody."

"Do you?"

She couldn't gauge his mood. She'd never seen him

like this…all edgy and male with a hint of aggression just below the surface. He wasn't drunk. His words and eyes were clear and she didn't smell liquor on his breath.

"No. I'm pretty selective who I kiss."

His eyes narrowed. "Are you?"

He closed the gap between them. Only an inch or two separated their torsos. Her breath stalled in her chest. "Max?"

"I knew who I was kissing yesterday. I always know who I'm kissing." He lifted her chin with his knuckle and covered her mouth with his.

Dana stood frozen with shock. Fast on the heels of that hair-raising circumstance came a potent cocktail of heat, arousal and adrenaline. His lips pressed hers open and his tongue sought and found hers in a slick, hot caress. A whimper of need slipped up her throat. Her nails bit into her palms as she struggled for sanity and fought the urge to wrap her arms around him.

She didn't have a clue what was going on or why he was kissing her. And she didn't care. She'd dreamed of this moment too often to question or fight it. His chest pressed her breasts and their thighs touched, and then his arm hooked around her and yanked her against him. Her heart raced and her skin flushed.

His heat scorched her, winded her, aroused her. The pressure of his mouth on hers intensified, bending her back over his arm, opening her mouth for deeper possession. She dropped her purse on the floor and gave in to the need to wind her arms around his middle for support as the room spun around her.

The warmth of his palm splayed over her hip and rose with torturous slowness to rest on her rib cage with his thumb just below her breast. Her nipple tightened in anticipation. She wanted him to touch her, ached for it. But he didn't.

His hold loosened and he stepped away. "Don't see Lewis again if you want to keep your job."

Dana struggled to catch her breath and unscramble her brain. "Wha-what if I can't promise that?"

"I'd think long and hard before I refused if I were you. Your job won't be the only one on the line."

And then he pivoted and climbed the stairs, leaving her alone in the foyer. Dana sagged against the front door with her heart pounding a deafening roar in her ears.

If she did as he ordered, she wouldn't get the answers Hudson needed. Surely once she had the script Max would understand and forgive her for ignoring his command?

It was a risk she had to take.

When he saw Dana smother a yawn, Max pushed away from his desk and stood. "Take a break."

Dana's brown eyes found his. "It's not even noon."

He couldn't think for the distraction of having her only yards away. He heard each shift of her body, every sigh and even the quiet rumble of her stomach, for pity's sake. Working in close proximity to her had never been an issue before. Why now when he didn't have time for this?

"We don't have time to correct mistakes that slip by because you're tired."

She snapped upright. "If I were that tired I'd take a break. I know my limitations. Do you, Max?"

"Of course." Had she changed perfumes? Her scent seemed stronger. Or maybe he was just more aware of it since that kiss last week.

Why had he kissed her?

Why had she kissed him back?

He plowed a hand through his hair and turned toward the window. He hadn't slept worth a damn since that night because he couldn't help wondering what she had been doing during those two hours after she'd left the restaurant with Doug Lewis. He'd worried about her driving on his twisty road after drinking champagne.

But mostly he'd wondered if she'd been in Lewis's bed.

And why did the idea of her naked and sweaty with Lewis make his gut burn? Must be because of the possible betrayal of Hudson secrets. If she'd shared the *Honor* script details, what else would she share?

The air inside the office suddenly seemed stuffy. He had to get out of this room. "I'm going for a swim."

Dana blinked, her long lashes briefly concealing the confusion in her eyes. "Okay, I'll cover the phones."

"No, you'll join me. We'll both be more alert after a break." And maybe the chlorine in the pool would kill her scent.

"But—"

"It's Saturday, Dana. No one important is going to call. Put on your suit. I'll meet you outside."

He left before she could argue and jogged upstairs to his room. Changing into swim trunks took only seconds and then he was outside on his private deck sucking up the fresh air and letting the sun bake his skin. Neither did anything to cure the restlessness riding him.

What was his problem?

He descended the circular stair to the flagstone patio. The blue pool water glistened, but a swim wasn't really what he needed. It was just a way to physically exhaust himself so that he could concentrate.

The door from the guest room to the patio opened, and Dana strolled out wearing a black bikini. He nearly choked on his tongue. She was toned where it counted, but soft where she needed to be. Honey-golden skin wrapped her curves in a mouth-watering package. Hunger hit him like a fist in the gut. How had he missed that she had a fantasy-worthy body?

He shook himself, trying to break the spell. This was Dana, the woman who'd been right under his nose, his right hand, for the past five years.

A woman who'd stood by him through some tough times.

A woman who might have betrayed him.

An idea infiltrated his brain like smoke slipping under a door. What better way to end the pillow talk between Dana and Lewis than by keeping her out of the other man's bed?

And the best way to do that was for Max to keep her so busy in his bed that she wouldn't have the time or energy to think about her ex-lover.

The idea sent a rush of heat through him, but his conscience countered with a warning prickle up the back of his neck. Sleeping with an employee was never a good idea. He'd learned that lesson the hard way. But he wasn't going to marry Dana. She'd already stated her intention of leaving Hudson as soon as possible—if she won the bet. The complication would be a problem only if she stayed on as his E.A.

Deliberately seducing her for personal gain wasn't the decent thing to do, but it would serve dual purposes. One, having her would satisfy his curiosity so that he could quit obsessing about her and get the damned film completed on time. She'd been interfering with his concentration since she'd moved into his house. Two, by getting closer to Dana he could find out exactly what she'd shared with Lewis and what Lewis had told her about Willow's upcoming flick.

He walked toward her and saw the exact moment she figured out something was amiss. She froze. Her lashes fluttered and her lips parted—her soft, delicious lips. He couldn't wait for another taste. God knows, the last two kisses had only whetted his appetite.

"Max?"

As he drew nearer he let his gaze devour the sleek curtain of her long, dark hair and the round curve of her breasts swelling above the black triangles of her top. Nice. Probably real. Real wasn't something you saw too often in Hollywood. Her chest rose and fell as if she were drawing quick, shallow breaths.

A glint of gold caught his eye, drawing his attention down her midline to just above her modest-by-Hollywood-standards bikini bottom. A tiny piece of jewelry glimmered in her navel. Closer inspection revealed a heart dangling over the dimple of her belly button, its swing agitated by the fine tremor of her body.

Dana, his conservative assistant, had a navel ring?

He searched her face. Who was this woman who had completely hidden her true personality from him for so long? She stared back at him, eyes wide, pupils expanded, but not with fear or rejection. He saw hunger, a hunger almost as great as his own in her dark brown eyes.

If she'd given him one back-off signal, he'd respect it. The last thing he needed was an employee crying foul. But she gave no such signals. Instead she licked her lips and tilted her head to the side, sending a cascade of thick dark hair across her shoulder to semi-conceal one breast and shoulder. "I—I thought we were going to swim."

Her whisper swept over his skin like a caress, leaving goose bumps behind. Goose bumps? When had he last experienced those? And she hadn't even touched him yet. "Later."

He reached for her. She met him halfway, their bodies colliding with a gentle slap. The fusion of her smooth, hot, golden skin to his forced the air from his lungs. He paused to catch his breath, to wrestle for some measure of control, to remember why he was doing this.

She might have betrayed him.

She might be planning to betray him further.

But the knowledge didn't kill his appetite. He wanted her kiss so badly he deliberately denied himself the pleasure, grasped her upper arms and backed her toward the house. Anticipation made his mouth water.

Their bare legs brushed against each other, their bellies sliding with each step. Her breasts nudged his chest, her nipples tightened and prodded him, and her quickening exhalations puffed against his chin. Desire pooled in his groin and his muscles clenched. He could feel himself hardening against her. If she had any doubts where this was headed before, she couldn't possibly now.

He paused on the sun-warmed flagstones outside her room, giving rational thought one last chance to derail him from this irreversible course of action, giving her one more chance to object to crossing the boss-employee line.

"Dana, if we go through that door, I am going to be inside you."

She took a quick breath. Her hands cupped his shoulders and for a moment he thought she'd push him away.

But then she looked at him through her lashes with those passion-darkened eyes and coasted her palms down his biceps and back up to his neck. With agonizing slowness, she scraped her short nails lightly down his arms, over the insides of his wrists, across his palms, before the tips of her fingers hooked his. Sauntering backward with a hip rolling gait, she tugged him toward her room, making it clear she wanted this as much as he did.

Dana wanted him.

The knowledge rocked him, shocked him. When and how had that happened? Before she'd returned his kiss, he couldn't remember her ever giving him those kinds of signals. In fact, if anything, she'd mothered him, pampered him. Spoiled him, he admitted.

He reached past her to slide open the door. Cooled air rushed out of the house and over his skin, but did nothing to cool his desire. Once they'd crossed the threshold—literally, figuratively—there would be no going back. His feet sank into the carpet. He closed the door behind him, sealing them into the silent house.

The room smelled like her, looked like her. The *other* her. This woman he didn't know. She'd added candles and framed photographs of her family and potted plants to the room.

Who was this other woman? he asked himself not for the first time.

He caught her face in his hands and stroked her smooth skin and then threaded his fingers through her thick, silky hair. Her head tilted back, but he ignored the silent invitation. He caressed her neck, her shoulders, her arms, and then he transferred his hands to her hips and drew circles over her hipbones with his thumbs. She shivered and gasped. The sound hit him low and hard.

Easing his hands upward, he outlined her narrow waist and the bottom edge of her rib cage, savoring her warm, satiny skin. Her lids fluttered closed. He bent to kiss one, then the other. Her thick lashes tickled his chin, and her back arched, pressing her pelvis into his. Need stabbed him. He sucked a sharp breath through his gritted teeth.

Dipping his head, he sipped from the shadowy warmth beneath her ear. She angled her head to give him better access. This time he didn't refuse. The hot press of her hands at his waist jolted him. The unhurried caress of her soft hands up and down his sides urged him to rush, to push her onto her bed and bury himself inside her. He wanted her hard and fast. For that reason he kept a tight-fisted grip on his control.

Mindless passion was for college kids. Smart passion, delayed satisfaction brought greater rewards. And purpose. He reminded himself he was doing this for a reason, but that reason was a little hazy when she tasted so good on his lips and on his tongue.

Nuzzling the fragrant spot behind her earlobe made her shudder in his arms. Her nails raked his back and ripped an unexpected groan from deep in his chest. He drew back, putting space between him and fighting the temptation to say to hell with slow and easy.

He traced the V-neck of her top with one finger, his eyes focusing on the nipples beading beneath the thin fabric. He wanted those tight buds in his mouth, needed to roll them around on his tongue and taste her. Instead he circled the band of black around her ribcage and drew a line down the center of her belly. He repeated the circle around her navel and then the top of her bikini bottom.

She shifted impatiently, her smooth, warm thighs sliding against each other. "Max."

The half cry, half whimper got to him. He'd bet his Lamborghini she'd sound like that when he slid inside her the first time. And that couldn't happen soon enough. His patience evaporated. He reached for the knot at her nape and fumbled it free. The ties dropped and the fabric slid downward with excruciating slowness before finally baring her breasts. He swallowed hard at the sight of the dusky centers.

Dana reached one arm behind her back and loosened the other tie. The top floated to the floor. He flexed his fingers in anticipation and then cupped her warm, soft flesh in his palms and buffed her nipples with his thumbs. Her breath hitched. She bit her lip. He bent his head and took a puckered tip into his mouth.

Her taste was like nothing he'd experienced before. He savored her unique flavor and her scent filled his nostrils. Her fingers threaded through his hair, holding him close as she arched into him, her free breast branding his bicep. But he wasn't trying to escape. Not until he'd had his fill of her and cured this damned sudden and irrational obsession that had hit him like a bad case of the flu.

He shifted his mouth to the neglected soft globe and used the moisture he'd left behind to lubricate his massaging fingers on the first. Dana's fingers tightened, her nails scraping an arousing pattern on his scalp. He wanted more.

"Mmm. That feels good," she whispered brokenly.

Planting one knee on the floor, he hooked her bikini bottom with his thumbs and yanked it down her legs. She gripped his shoulders as she stepped out of her swimsuit, her touch hot and firm on his skin. He wanted her hands all over him, the sooner, the better.

Letting her nipple slide from his mouth, he looked up at her, at her red lips and heavy-lidded eyes, at the curve of her damp nipples, her small waist. But it was the tiny cluster of dark curls that beckoned him. He needed to taste her. Her golden skin, her sweet center, the essence of her arousal. But not yet. Not when his hunger was sharp enough to cut him.

He pressed a kiss to her breastbone, laved his way down her belly, toward the golden heart. He circled the jewelry with his tongue and she hiccupped a series of short fast breaths. As he strung kisses along her bikini line he used his hands to caress from her hips down the outside of her legs to her feet.

He curled his fingers around her ankles, grasped the delicate joints and urged her legs apart, widening her stance for balance because he intended to rock her world.

"Max?" she breathed.

He worked his hands upward on the insides of her legs this time, his palms coasting over warm, smooth soft skin. She was so damned touchable. The scent of her excitement grew stronger as he neared his target and his own desire pounded through his veins, urgent and unrelenting. He forced himself to take it slow when what he wanted to do was shoot to his feet and bury himself deep inside her with a single thrust.

He reached the back of her knees. She shivered at the scrape of his fingernails along the sensitive crease. He did it again with the same results. She clutched his hair and then released, clutched and released. Her short nails lightly outlined his ears, sending stimulating ripples cresting through him.

He finally reached her thighs and massaged their sleekly muscled length, working his way from her tensed quadriceps and hamstrings to her softer, warmer inner thighs. He traced her panty line with his thumbnails and her knees quaked. Encouraged, he leaned forward and traced the same path with his tongue, simultaneously finding her center with his fingers. She was hot, wet and ready for him. Her hands cupped his head holding him close.

Her fragrance filled his lungs and surged straight to his groin. The selfish urge to flip her on her back on the bed and ride her hard crossed his mind. Instead, he replaced his fingers with his tongue and laved the swollen flesh waiting for him, circling it, tasting it, exploring it until he found the spot that made her cry out and curl her toes into the carpet.

Her taste filled him with a desperate, ravenous hunger for more. More. More. His pulse hammered in his head, almost drowning out the sexy-as-hell sounds coming from Dana's mouth.

"It's too much. I can't." Her nails dug into his scalp. She tried to pull away.

He clamped his hands on her buttocks and intensified his oral caress. Her legs shook. She tasted so damned good, smelled so good, felt so good. He sucked her into his mouth and pumped his fingers deep inside her. Even without her moan to clue him in, he registered the exact second she quit fighting and went over the edge. Her cries filled the air and her internal muscles clenched his fingers.

He rode the wave with her, savoring each squeeze, each whimper, each spasm. And when her knees buckled, he held her upright. He kissed the pale skin between her curls and the twinkling heart and looked up at her. Her pleasure was a sight to behold. Dusky peach painted her cheeks and her lips were red and swollen from her biting them.

Her eyes slowly opened halfway and found his. The hand she had gripping his shoulder slid up the side of his neck, under his jaw and then she lifted his chin. "Thank you."

"My pleasure." And it had been. He rose and kissed her hard on the mouth.

Reality check. He'd been so eager to lose himself inside her he'd almost forgotten a critical component. "I've barely started. But we need a condom."

Her lashes fluttered and she lowered her chin. "I have some."

She bit her lip as if embarrassed by the confession, and then walked across the room. He enjoyed watching her move, and the tight curve of her bottom made him grit his teeth. Delicious.

Dana was a beautiful woman. How could he have been so blind?

She withdrew a plastic packet from her purse and turned. Despite the blush on her cheeks, there was a sexual sparkle in her eyes that grabbed him by the hormones and demanded his attention. But there was also a contradictory reticence lurking in the way her gaze bounced from his and the way she chewed her bottom lip. Her tight body language and a slight hesitation snagged his curiosity. He didn't know what to make of this from his confident executive assistant who handled conniption-fit-throwing actors and on-set disasters without breaking a sweat.

He took the package from her, pulled her close and covered her mouth with his. Her response started out tentative but quickly became so wild and uninhibited she pushed him close to the edge of control. He nipped her bottom lip. She bit him right back—not hard, just playful. Sexy. Enticing as hell. Hunger bolted through him like lightning.

He stroked her smooth back, her soft bottom, and she mimicked his every move, squeezing where he squeezed, scratching where he scratched. He tightened his arms around her, pulling her flush against his erection for one brief moment before bringing his hand between them to find her center. She whimpered into his mouth as he thumbed her still swollen flesh.

She yanked her mouth free. "Max, I want you."

"And you're going to have me as soon as you do one more thing for me."

"What?" Her body tensed in his arms and her nails dug into his shoulders. He quickened his caress. Orgasm overtook her.

"That's what I was waiting for," he whispered against her temple once she stopped shuddering.

Her lips and teeth found his shoulder, surprising him with a gentle love bite and punching him with another arousing jolt. She impatiently shoved his swim trunks down his legs and wrapped her fingers around his length. She stroked him long and slow from base to tip and back again.

His teeth clamped shut on a furnace blast of desire. It slammed him like a runaway trolley, winding him, making his head spin. He struggled to right himself and then kicked aside his trunks and tore the condom open with his teeth. She tried to take it from him, but he was so triggered he didn't dare let her. He grabbed her hand and redirected it to less dangerous territory—his waist. Only that ended up being more hazardous than he'd anticipated as her nails traced havoc-wreaking patterns on his skin with devastating results.

He rolled on the latex with an unsteady hand, ripped back the comforter and backed her onto the mattress.

She lay down and he caressed her long, luscious legs apart. He wanted to feast on her, to nibble from toes to earlobes, lingering and making her cry out again and again. He wanted that too much.

How could he want Dana this way when he'd never had a sexual thought about her before that kiss? He brushed aside the question and positioned himself. He intended to take it slow, to control his passion and keep his head the way he always did, but then she wrapped a hand around his nape, pulling him down for a kiss, and simultaneously hooked a leg behind his butt and pressed him forward. Slow and rational ceased to be an option.

He sank deep into her mouth and into the hot, slick glove of her body simultaneously. Hunger grabbed him by the groin and the throat, and a groan of pleasure barreled its way out of his chest. Instinct took over. He couldn't slow the thrust of his tongue or his hips. She met him stroke for stroke, engaging in a mental and physical tug of war for control. Reining himself in was no longer a sure thing. It was a damned risky proposition.

He fought through the animalistic drive riding him and tried to focus on her pleasure. This was about her, about keeping her from Lewis's bed. But damned if he gave a flip about his motives at the moment.

He swiveled his hips against her. She broke the kiss. "That f-feels g-good."

Her breathy, broken words drove him to repeat the maneuver again and again until her back bowed and her nails raked his back, his thighs, his chest. She nipped his shoulder—another gentle love bite—and that was all it took. He crossed the line, the point of no return. He pounded into her. Deeper, harder, faster. Again. Again. Her gasps and cries fueled him.

When he felt her tense, heard her breath catch, he did the same. Fighting his way back from the brink became a lost cause. Orgasm ripped through her, making her body squeeze his and forcing the air from her lungs in a sexy groan. And he lost it. His own release battered him over and over until he was spent. His lungs burned. His arm muscles quivered and then collapsed. He landed on her. It took seconds to regain his strength and lift himself from the warm, damp, soft cushion of her body. Not that he wanted to leave. And that worried him.

Her eyes remained closed, her lashes a dark fan on her flushed cheeks. But it was the smile curving her lips that nailed him right in the chest. He leaned down and brushed his mouth over hers.

What the…?

His arms snapped straight and then he rolled off her and landed on the bed. The bed that smelled like Dana. Like Dana and hot sex.

Why had he kissed her that way? He didn't do tender gestures. Not anymore. Sex was sex. Basic. Primal. Satisfaction of a need. And in this case, a way to protect his assets. No emotion required or desired.

But damn, he wanted to ask her about that smile. If it meant what he thought it did—that this was more than just physical release for her—then he needed to warn her. Temporary was his MO. His *only* MO. He would never marry again.

But if he warned her off and she got huffy, then his honesty could cause problems. One, she might quit. Two, she might pout and refuse to speak to him—the way Karen sometimes had. Three, anger might drive her back to Lewis. None of those options would help him get *Honor* completed on time.

So he'd have to suck it up and hope like hell she didn't get emotionally attached. Because happily ever after might make for a great film, but it had no place in his life.

Six

Dana couldn't stop smiling.

She lay flat on her back, eyes closed, fighting the urge to grin like a fool. Max lay beside her. She could hear his rapid breathing, feel his body heat and smell him. She inhaled deeply. Correction, she could smell *them* and the intoxicating aroma of their lovemaking. The urge to grin grew stronger.

Making love with him had exceeded her fantasies. And she couldn't ask for more. She was so happy they'd finally taken this step—even if she didn't know what had precipitated it.

The mattress shifted. She forced her heavy eyelids open in time to see Max leaving the bed. She soaked up the sight of his broad shoulders, tight butt, and long, muscled legs as he bent to scoop up his swim trunks from the floor. Yummy.

He disappeared into the adjoining bathroom without looking back. Something felt a little off. She chalked it up to the awkwardness of the first time with a new partner. Not that she had a whole lot of experience with that circumstance. And he did have the condom to deal with.

Rolling out of bed, she gathered her suit and shifted on her feet as she tried to figure out what to do next. Put the suit back on? Get dressed? Climb back in bed? She still hadn't made up her mind when Max returned dressed in his trunks.

His gaze rolled over her, lingering on her breasts, which tightened in response to his widening pupils and intense expression. His gaze coasted past her waist and hips to her legs and then slowly returned. His eyes stalled briefly on her navel ring before gliding up until they locked with hers once more. She saw suppressed passion but also caution in his eyes.

Her fingers tightened on the fabric of her swimsuit. A sudden and unexpected wave of insecurity made her want to cover up. He dated some of the most beautiful women in the world. How did she measure up? She certainly wasn't as skinny as his usual type. And she wasn't blonde.

"I'm going to take a quick swim and have lunch before getting back to work. Shall I cook enough for two?"

She blinked in surprise. He'd taken her to restaurants for working lunches, but he'd never prepared anything for her or even offered to fetch anything for her from the Hudson Pictures canteen. And while all he'd be doing was heating up something the caterer had left, that he'd offer to include her now made her feel all warm and fuzzy and cherished.

"I could make lunch." She'd rather stay here and cuddle with him. But they really didn't have time for that.

"I can handle it. You take a shower or…whatever it is women do after…sex."

Sex. She'd rather he called it making love. But he was a guy. A commitment-phobic guy. "Maybe I, um, could join you in the pool and then we could make the meal together."

"I'm going to swim laps." He turned on his heel and exited through her patio door.

Confused, Dana stared after him. Had that been a statement or a dismissal? Did Max regret what had just happened?

How could he regret what had been one of the best moments of her life?

And where did they go from here? Because for her, everything had changed. She no longer wanted to get away from Max, and she no longer wanted to win the bet. She wanted to win his heart.

Only the hum of the electronic equipment disturbed the silence of the room.

Dana sat at her desk in Max's home office and tried to focus on work, but her mind kept straying. She wasn't dumb enough to delude herself that Max was in love with her. Yet. His cool demeanor throughout lunch had proven that. There had been no tender, reminiscent smiles, no wicked glances promising more lovemaking to come later.

But he did desire her. She knew good acting when she saw it, and Max hadn't been faking his passion earlier.

So why the oppressive silence now?

Max's office chair squeaked as he twisted to face her. Her heart skipped in anticipation of what he'd say.

"How is the capturing coming?"

Work. She'd expected something…personal. She tried

to mask her disappointment. "It's going well. I should be finished in a couple of days."

He swiveled back and then stopped. "My family is having a dinner tonight. I'd like you to join me."

Happiness welled in her chest. He was including her—like a real date. That had to mean something. "I'd like that."

"We'll leave at seven."

She glanced at her watch. She had just over an hour to get ready. And then she realized she wasn't prepared—not to go to Hudson Manor as Max's date. "I didn't pack anything that would be appropriate for a night out. I'll need to go to my place to change."

"Back up your work and go. I'll pick you up in an hour." His neutral tone lacked enthusiasm and again, that niggling feeling that something wasn't quite right hit her.

She brushed it aside. They'd made love and he was taking her to his family dinner. As her brother had always claimed, as long as you're making forward progress, you're headed in the right direction.

And Max was picking her up at her house. It would be almost like a date. Their first date.

Dana's palms moistened and her pulse quickened as Max pulled his car to a halt in front of Hudson Manor. She'd been here several times before for functions related to work and to visit Lillian.

But tonight was different. Her role had changed.

Or had it?

It was hard to tell from Max's demeanor. He hadn't taken her in his arms and kissed her when he'd arrived at her place. In fact, he was acting as if they hadn't been lost in each other's bodies this afternoon.

She shook off her insecurities and looked up at the

Hudson's home through the car window. The French provincial mansion Charles had built for Lillian on Loma Vista Drive in Beverly Hills never failed to impress her. The gray stone facade with its wrought-iron decorative accents tripped every romantic switch she had.

Set on fifteen acres with two swimming pools, four tennis courts, stables plus a carriage house and a guest house, the estate had a fairy-tale quality that made it impossible for Dana to imagine living in such grandeur.

Charles and Lillian had filled the place with antiques they'd bought on their world travels, but the place didn't feel in the least like a museum. Every other time Dana had come for a visit she'd been very comfortable. Tonight, not so much.

Max came around to her side of the car and opened her door. He offered his hand to assist her out. She grasped him tightly, glad for the reassurance under the changed circumstances. What would his family think about him with *her*?

She climbed from the car, took a deep breath and squeezed Max's hand. She deliberately stepped into his body. "Thanks for including me tonight."

He held her pressed against his length for a moment, but then released her without a kiss, leaving her feeling a bit adrift. "You're welcome."

She kept pace beside him as they headed for the front door. Why hadn't he kissed her? Maybe he wasn't into public displays? "I can't imagine what it must have been like growing up here. It's quite different from my home."

"You get used to it."

She laughed at his dismissive tone. "I don't think so. According to Lillian when she gave me a tour, your house has fifty-five rooms. Mine had ten. There's a bit of a discrepancy."

He opened the front door and motioned for her to precede him. She entered the grand foyer with its marble floors, double-wide staircase and soaring ceiling. Until she'd visited Hudson Manor she'd had no idea there was such a thing as hand-painted wallpaper. Back home she and her mother had bought the stuff in rolls and redone the entire house themselves. It wasn't the same. Not even close.

"Who'll be here tonight?" She hoped he didn't notice the nervous quiver in her voice.

He shrugged. "Probably everybody except Luc, who's in Montana. He and Gwen are too close to the baby's due date to travel."

"Hudson Pictures will miss him as the PR director, but retiring to raise a family on a ranch does have its appeal."

His gaze sharpened. "You're interested in leaving L.A.?"

She shook her head. "Oh, no. I love the bustle and edginess of the city, but I was raised in a smallish town. I understand the appeal of a less hurried lifestyle."

The quick shuffle of feet drew Dana's attention. Hannah Aldridge, the sixty-something housekeeper who'd been with the family forever, hustled toward them. Her hazel-green eyes glowed with a warm welcome. "Good evening, Mr. Max, Ms. Dana. The family is in the front salon."

"The salon?" Max sounded surprised.

"Appears there's something to celebrate tonight."

Excitement stirred in Dana's belly. Was Max planning to surprise her by announcing their new coupledom to the family?

"What's the occasion?" he asked, dashing her hopes.

"That I don't know. You look lovely tonight, Miss."

Dana felt the heat climb her cheeks and smoothed a

hand over her black cocktail dress. She'd bought both the minidress and shoes at a studio wardrobe clearance sale. That was the only way she'd ever be able to afford designer apparel.

"Thank you, Hannah." A part of her wished Max had been the one to issue the compliment. Yes, his gaze had gobbled her up when she'd opened her door to him earlier, but he hadn't said a word about her appearance even though she'd taken extra care to look good tonight. "How is Lillian this evening?"

"She's well, and you're a peach for asking. Go on through. They're waiting for you."

On the short walk to the salon Dana tried to rally her courage. She told herself she knew these people and they knew her. She had nothing to fear. But the bats swooping and diving through her stomach didn't get the message.

The room fell silent the moment they crossed the threshold, tightening her nerves even more. How would Max explain their new situation? If he'd simply take her hand, everyone would get the message. But how would they react?

A chorus of welcomes greeted them. Dana forced herself to smile and wave at the nine people gathered in the room. Max broke away immediately to cross the room to his grandmother's side, leaving Dana by the door. Lillian looked as good as could be expected for her age and her condition. Her blue eyes twinkled and her expertly tinted auburn hair was perfectly styled. Her private nurse stood just behind her shoulder.

Dana felt a twinge of loss. Lillian's terminal illness was hitting them all hard, and while having time to prepare for her passing was a gift, that day was still going to be hard for everyone.

Max knelt, kissed Lillian's cheek and held her hands as he spoke to her so quietly Dana couldn't hear him. His gentleness and genuine affection for his grandmother tugged at her heartstrings.

At a loss, Dana tried to decide whether to join Max and interrupt his private moment with his grandmother or to impose herself on another group's conversation. Before she could decide Markus and Sabrina, Max's parents crossed the room toward her.

Sabrina, looking as elegant as ever in a designer evening pantsuit with her dark blond hair twisted in a French plait and her blue eyes sparkling, embraced Dana and kissed her cheek. "I'm happy you could join us, Dana."

"Thank you for including me."

Markus took her hand in both of his and gave it a squeeze. He looked to be in one of his jovial moods tonight. "It's the least we can do since our son is working you around the clock."

Her smile wobbled. Max must not have said anything about their being a couple now. But what could he say? He could hardly call his mother and say, "I slept with Dana today, so I'd like to bring her to dinner tonight as my date."

Okay, Dana admitted, maybe her expectations had been a little skewed. "I'm enjoying the challenge of my new position, and Max is teaching me a lot."

"May I fix you a drink?" Markus offered.

She did a quick scan of the room. Everyone seemed to be holding a glass. "A glass of white wine would be nice. Thank you."

"Sweet or dry?"

She wrinkled her nose. Living in California hadn't made a devoted wine fan out of her yet despite her vacation through Napa Valley on an educational winery tour. She'd learned a little about wine, but only enough to get by. "The sweeter, the better."

"I have something you might like."

Markus went one way. Sabrina took Dana's hand and led her in the opposite direction toward Max's brother Dev and the very slender brown-haired woman by his side.

"Dana, did you get a chance to meet Valerie Shelton, Dev's fiancée, in France?"

"I did, but only briefly. It's nice to see you again, Valerie." Dana shook her hand. Valerie was Dana's age, but seemed much more reserved. Dana had yet to figure out what about the cynical Dev appealed to the innocent and reserved Valerie other than looks and money. He was as rich and handsome as the rest of the Hudsons. But she'd always considered the COO of Hudson Pictures to be a bit aloof.

"It's nice to see you, too." Valerie gave her a shy smile. "I heard you've had a promotion since returning."

Sabrina nodded. "Dana is *Honor*'s associate producer now."

"That sounds exciting." Valerie glanced at Dev. The adoration shining in her violet eyes made Dana's breath catch. She hoped her feelings toward Max weren't as obvious to everyone around them. She'd have to be more careful.

Dev didn't seem to notice Valerie's tender regard. In fact, his cool blue eyes were watching Dana. Was he also concerned about her dinner with Doug? She prayed Doug would come through with the script so she could put both Dev's and Max's minds at ease.

Dana forced her attention back to Valerie. "It's a

dream job, but it's also hard work. No one wants to disappoint Lillian."

Markus returned to Dana's side and offered her a wineglass of pale gold liquid. "Try this, Dana. It's a German Riesling, 2006 vintage."

She accepted the glass and dutifully sniffed and sipped and rolled the wine around on her tongue as she'd been taught before swallowing. "It's very good. Nice and fruity. Thank you."

"Excellent. Let me know if you need a refill."

A tap on the shoulder made Dana turn. Bella, Max's baby sister, stood beside her. She had Max's blue eyes, and her grandmother's auburn hair. "Doesn't look like Max has you tearing out your hair yet."

"Not yet." Dana's gaze tracked him to the opposite side of the room where he now stood talking to his cousin Jack and David, Max's uncle and Jack's father, with his back to her. David was *Honor*'s director. She tried not to feel hurt by Max's neglect, but she had expected to be by his side tonight, not on opposite sides of the room.

Dana returned her attention to Bella. They'd known each other superficially for years because of Hudson Pictures, but not all that well until they'd gotten to know each other better while on location in France. Bella was not only beautiful, she was feisty and a lot of fun—when she wasn't wrapped up in her costar.

Dana scanned the room for Bella's man of the moment. Bella had played Lillian in *Honor*. Ridley Sinclair, a box-office star and Bella's current beau, had played Charles. Dana wasn't crazy about Ridley and thought Bella could do better than a guy so self-absorbed, but their off-screen romance had burned pretty hot.

"Is Ridley joining us tonight?"

"No. He's off doing…whatever." She waved a dismissive hand, but sounded a bit put out.

Markus patted his daughter on the shoulder. "I'll leave you ladies to catch up." He left to rejoin his wife.

Bella hooked her arm through Dana's. "Excuse us, Valerie and Dev. Dana, do you remember Cece, Cousin Jack's wife?"

"Yes, I do. Max worked quite a bit with Cece on fine-tuning the script." But Dana let herself be led to Jack, Cece and Max's side, hoping Bella hadn't seen the same lovestruck expression on her face that Valerie had displayed earlier. David stood on the fringe of the group.

Cece was a petite brunette, a brilliant scriptwriter and obviously in love with her husband. She grimaced as Dana and Bella approached. "They're talking shop again. Didn't Lillian forbid that tonight?"

"I did," Lillian called out. She winked at them and beckoned Dana.

"Excuse me," Dana said before going to Lillian's side. She kissed the papery cheek.

Lillian squeezed her hand. "You've made progress."

Dana drew back. "I'm sorry?"

"He was watching you while he was talking to me."

Dana's heart skipped a beat. She started to turn and look at Max, but Lillian caught her hand. "Don't look, dear. Never give all your secrets away. It gives a man too much power."

"Max was watching me?" she whispered.

Lillian nodded.

A blush scorched Dana's cheeks. "We're spending a lot of time together. Working," she added hastily, because there were some things you just didn't share with a man's grandmother.

On one of Dana's recent visits Lillian had confessed she'd known about Dana's crush for years and kept hoping her grandson would wise up. But she'd also warned Dana that Max's love for Karen had been all-consuming and her loss devastating. She wasn't sure Max would ever love that deeply again.

"Of course you are, dear. I'm glad he's giving you a chance to pursue your dream and that he brought you tonight. Keep up the good work. And remember, Dana, the best things in life are worth waiting for."

"Yes, ma'am. I'll try not to forget."

"Take care of him." The *after I'm gone* remained unspoken. But those silent words put a lump in Dana's throat.

"You know I'll do my best as long as I'm with him."

Lillian shooed her back to Max's side. Dana desperately wanted to take his hand, but didn't know if the gesture would be welcomed.

"No little man tonight?" she asked Cece.

Cece and Jack both smiled at the reference to their son—the son Jack hadn't known about until he'd tracked Cece down to ask her to write the script.

Cece shook her head. "We left Theo at home. This would be too late an evening for him."

"Good point." Dana had seen Theo only a few times, but he looked exactly like his black-haired, blue-eyed daddy, and he was completely precious. An old familiar ache squeezed her chest. Way back when, she'd believed she'd have several children of her own by the time she reached twenty-eight. "Let me know if you ever need a babysitter."

Cece grinned mischievously. "Don't make that offer lightly. I know your number."

Bella, her eyes brimming with excitement, shifted on her heels. "So is everything ready for the sixtieth anniversary bash and the movie preview?"

Jack nodded. "My staff has everything under control."

Bella looked at Dana. "I can't wait to see the first cut to see if I did Lillian proud. I mean, I saw the dailies, but…"

Dana touched her arm. "Bella, from what I've seen so far, you have nothing to be worried about. And once Max works his magic…"

Bella gave her a quick hug. "The three of us, you, me and Cece, are going to have to do some serious shopping. Oh, and we should probably include Valerie. I want a drop-dead gorgeous dress for this."

David rolled his eyes. "Shopping. That's one topic guaranteed to run any man away." He excused himself and went to his mother's side.

Max's gaze followed him and then he turned to Jack once David was out of earshot. "Is everyone behaving tonight?"

"Yes. Your father and mine are keeping it civil. For a change."

David Hudson did not get along well with his older brother or his brother's wife. There was a tension between them that Dana hadn't figured out yet despite the numerous interactions between David and Max. As director and producer they worked closely together.

Max scanned their little gathering. "Hannah said there was going to be a celebration. Anybody know what's going on?"

Jack shook his head. "No clue. Cece and I have no news. You?"

Dana tensed and waited, holding her breath, but Max shook his head. "Not me."

Her hopes sank like lead. She'd waited so long for it to happen that she really wanted to share the news that they were a couple. It was practically bubbling inside her.

Dev joined them with Valerie trailing behind. "I can answer your question." Dev turned to the room and used his key to tap on his glass. "May I have everyone's attention?"

He waited until the room fell silent. "Valerie and I eloped yesterday."

Gasps and surprised grunts filled the room. After a startled moment, Sabrina and Markus made their way across the room. Sabrina hugged her son and then her new daughter-in-law. Markus shook Dev's hand and then briefly embraced Valerie.

"Valerie, darling, welcome to the family," Sabrina said, and then turned her hurt eyes on Dev. "I wish you'd let me arrange your wedding. Your father and I would have enjoyed sharing such a special moment."

Dev shrugged. "We didn't want fanfare."

"A wedding on the estate grounds would have been nice," Lillian added.

"Oh, that's a lovely idea," Valerie gushed, but then seemed to regret her words. "But Dev and I couldn't wait."

Dana thought Valerie looked as if she would have liked some pageantry.

"Are you pregnant?" Bella asked bluntly, but not unkindly.

Valerie's cheeks turned crimson. She dipped her chin. "No. Oh, no. That's not what I meant."

An awkward silence descended. Dana moved forward to hug Valerie and break up the uncomfortable moment. "Congratulations. Perhaps I could arrange a belated bridal shower for you?"

Valerie's eyes filled with gratitude. "That would be nice, Dana. Although I'm sure we won't require any wedding presents. Dev tells me he'd like to live here in his suite of rooms."

"Every woman needs gifts. Sexy lingerie, for example," Bella said with a wicked smile that made Valerie blush more.

"I'll call next week and we'll work out the details." Dana stepped aside and let others offer their good wishes.

She glanced at Max and found his narrowed eyes focused on her. What was he thinking? From his forbidding expression she'd bet he wasn't remotely interested in following in his brother's footsteps to the altar.

All she had to do was find a way to change his mind, because there was nothing she'd like more than to marry Max on the grounds of Hudson Manor and begin her own fairy-tale romance.

Seven

"**H**ow did you know?" Max asked Dev after dinner when the men had retired to the patio for cigars and left the women inside to yap about the sixtieth anniversary gala.

"Know what?"

Max divided his attention between the women on the opposite side of the French doors and the far end of the patio where his father and uncle looked to be having another tense discussion. Jack was with them, running interference, Max would guess. "How did you know Valerie was the one?"

Dev puffed on his cigar. He exhaled long and slow as if the answer might be found in the smoke slowly dissipating in the air above their heads. "You're not expecting something sappy and romantic, are you?"

From his brother the cynic, who seemed to believe women were put on this earth only to procreate and provide entertainment? No.

"I just want an answer. Why Valerie? Why now?"

"I'm thirty-five. It's time to settle down. Valerie's well connected. Her father's a newspaper mogul and that could work in Hudson Pictures's favor when we need publicity in the future. She and I suit each other, and she won't give me a lot of backchat."

Like Karen had. His brother didn't say it, but he didn't need to. Max's wife had been quite opinionated. That she hadn't been a suck up or a pushover was one of the things Max had liked and respected about her. But she'd had a tendency to get in people's faces when crossed. Sometimes that had caused friction.

Dana was a hell of a lot more diplomatic.

He nixed the thought. There was no comparing the women and no reason to, especially now when the anniversary of Karen's death was just around the corner.

His gaze wandered to the woman in question on the other side of the closed glass doors. Her dress tonight had nearly knocked him to his knees. She'd gone from conservative, figure-concealing clothing to the kind that accentuated every curve of her luscious figure.

The wrap top of her black dress cupped her breasts and showed just enough soft skin to make him want to bury his face between the smooth globes and slip his hands beneath the short hem to see if she wore panties.

But he was stronger than that. No woman would make him weak with wanting again. He kept his head these days. No more getting swept away by passion. Reason ruled.

He forced his attention back to his brother and practical matters. "If you'd made a spectacle of the wedding instead of secretly sneaking off, it would have been great PR for *Honor*. Romance While Filming the Romance, or some similar headline. The press would have eaten it up. You know you wasted that opportunity."

Dev shrugged. "I know. But Valerie is an only child. You know what kind of production a traditional wedding would have turned into. Months of planning, too many trivial, irritating decisions… You know the drill. You did it."

Max knew. Karen had been an only child, too. Their wedding had taken a year to plan, and there had been times when the process had spiraled so crazily out of control he'd wanted to say to hell with it and elope. By the time they'd walked down the aisle he'd been relieved to have it over with and not to have to make any more decisions about stupid stuff like the color of the napkins and the like.

"Besides," Dev continued, "I didn't want to deal with the paparazzi, and we don't have time right now for all the cloak-and-dagger theatrics necessary to pull off a Hollywood wedding. Tents, helicopters, security."

"Amen to that."

"I preferred to close the deal as quickly as possible."

"That's it? Convenience? You weren't swept away by passion?"

Dev exhaled a smoky plume. "You do remember who you're talking to, don't you?"

Funny, he'd expected more from his big brother. But he shouldn't have. "Do you love her?"

"Like love worked so well for you." And then Dev winced. "I'm sorry. That was a low blow."

Love had worked for him. For a while. "Forget it. Did you at least get a prenup, so she won't take us to the cleaners?"

"What? You think I'm stupid?"

"No. I'm just looking out for our assets."

"While you're covering Hudson assets, what have you found out about Dana and Doug Lewis?"

"Nothing yet. I'm working on it."

"Any progress?"

He wasn't about to share his strategy. "Some."

"Let me know what you discover."

"As soon as I know it myself." And that meant he needed to turn up the heat and steam some information out of Dana.

And the desire to do so had nothing to do with how hot she looked tonight in that low-cut dress and those killer high heels.

Nothing whatsoever.

But damn, she looked amazing.

Good thing his hunger for her was temporary and could be turned off as soon as *Honor* hit the screen.

Otherwise, he'd be in trouble.

"The wedding announcement was a surprise," Dana said from beside Max in the darkened car on the way home from the dinner party.

Max kept his eyes on the winding road. "Yes."

"Did you know? Did Dev mention his plans at lunch?"

"No."

He heard her sigh and then the rustle of her dress as she shifted on the seat. Her scent and each sound she made seemed amplified in the quiet confines of the dark car. But the lack of light also kept him from checking out her legs the way he had on the way over to Hudson Manor. He was damned lucky he hadn't run them off the road.

How had he never noticed she had great legs before tonight?

"Does he realize what an amazing PR opportunity he missed? We could have had free airtime on every network and in a substantial number of magazines and web pages."

That's what he liked about Dana. Not only did she think like him, she reacted with logic rather than emotion. Karen had tended to go the opposite— He choked off that thought. He had to stop comparing the women. He'd promised Karen forever. The most he could offer Dana was for now, and then only because she might have the information he needed.

"He knew and he chose not to exercise that option."

"We could still use it to create a buzz. It could be our slant on making *Honor* stand out from Willow's film in case we can't find out what theirs is about."

She had a point—one too good to ignore. "I'll ask Dev to talk to PR. What do you know about Willow's film?"

He caught her sideways glance in the glare of an oncoming car's headlights. "You could have asked me that the other night instead of accusing me of sharing information."

She didn't miss a beat at his abrupt change of subject. She never did. It was as if she could follow the convoluted twists of his mind. No one else had ever done that. And she was right. He could have asked, but wondering if she'd betrayed him combined with seeing her kiss Lewis had crushed any tact Max might have had.

"I apologize. I should have asked."

"Doug said Willow's film is a romance. He didn't work on the project directly and hasn't read the script, but from what he's heard, there are quite a few similarities to *Honor*. I'm working on—" She stopped abruptly and turned to stare out the dark passenger window.

"You're working on what?"

"Nothing," she replied too hastily. "If I find out more, I'll let you know."

Dana was lying or holding something back. He wanted to know what and why. "When will you see Lewis again?"

Moments ticked past where the only sound was the car's tires on the road. "I'm not sure. He's on recce."

"But you plan to see him when he returns." He liked the idea even less now than he had before.

"Yes, Max. I'm going to see him. And you're going to have to trust that I won't share Hudson Pictures's secrets. If you can't trust me, then you need to fire me."

Trust her.

He'd trusted her for five years. Why was doing so now suddenly so difficult? Because Hudson Pictures very likely had a leak, and all indicators pointed to Dana as the most likely source. She had the info, the opportunity and the connections.

But did she have the motive?

If so, he hadn't yet figured out what it was. But until he knew for sure, he couldn't afford to give her anything that could be used against them.

The stroke of Max's hand down the length of her hair as they entered his darkened house just before midnight pleasantly surprised Dana.

But when he grasped a handful at her nape and pulled her to a halt he shocked her. Her breath caught. "Max?"

She heard the deadbolt click and then Max slowly reeled her backward, tugging just hard enough to make her nape prickle, but not enough to inflict pain. She never would have thought such caveman antics to be sexy, but the way her body instantly responded proved her wrong. Her skin tingled and her breath and pulse quickened.

He didn't stop until her back pressed against the length of his front. His chest and thighs were warm, hard and strong as she leaned into him. His breath steamed her cheek a second before his jaw, rough with evening beard, took its place. "Take off your clothes."

A lightning bolt of hunger made her gasp. "Here? Why?"

"We're going to take a moonlight swim."

Not a bad idea, but— "M-my suit is—"

"You won't need it." His free hand skimmed from her hip, over her waist to cup her breast. His thumb found her nipple and circled. Her flesh hardened beneath his caress. "Have you ever been skinny-dipping?"

She could barely think with the tangle of desire forming in her belly. "Um…no. What about your neighbors?"

"We won't turn on the lights." He released her hair and cupped her other breast with his hand. The dual massage melted her resistance, her arguments, and her ability to form sentences. He gave her a gentle shove into the center of the foyer. "Strip for me, Dana."

Moonlight streamed through the high windows, angling down on the floor, onto her, like a soundstage key light. Max remained in the shadows.

"Have you ever stripped for a man?" he asked when she hesitated.

Her heart pounded a path up her throat. "No. Not…um like this."

"Start with that sexy black dress. Take it off."

Adrenaline hit her with a dizzying rush. Her spinning head had nothing to do with the wine she'd drunk with dinner and everything to do with the words he'd just uttered. But nervousness dried her mouth. Her purse slipped from her fingers and landed at her feet.

She bent to pick it up.

"Leave it, and get naked for me."

But she just wasn't ready to do as he asked. "You first."

She heard him chuckle, low and sexy. She'd never heard that sound from him before and she liked it. She liked the way it rippled over her skin and made her quiver.

He stepped forward just enough to cast his body into the murky light, but kept his face in the dark. He shrugged out of his suit jacket and tossed it toward a settee. Next he worked the knot of his tie loose, and then yanked it free with a quick whip of sound.

"Shall I keep going?"

She'd had no idea Max had a naughty side, but that teasing tone was definitely the looking-for-trouble variety. She dampened her lips and nodded. "Please."

He unfastened his cufflinks and dropped them on the credenza. His watch followed. The clunk of metal hitting wood echoed in the high-ceiling space. He unbuttoned his shirt from the top down, revealing a widening wedge of his tanned chest with each passing second. He peeled off the shirt and tossed it on top of his jacket.

His hands settled on his leather belt, but stilled and then dropped to his sides. "Your turn."

She ripped her gaze away from the rippled definition of his muscles. Why would a man who looked like this work behind the camera instead of in front of it? She had no clue. The women of America would certainly appreciate the view she currently had.

"I—I—" She didn't know what to say. Feeling both excited and completely out of her element, she reached behind her back for the zipper. The tab slid down a few inches and then snagged. She tried to reverse it, but it wouldn't budge. "It's stuck."

"Turn around." He stepped into the light, giving her a glimpse of the hunger stamped on his face. His desire sent a thrill through her. Her legs trembled as she turned.

His hands cupped her shoulders, stroked down to her wrists and then back up. Her insides went all shivery—the way they always did when he touched her.

He brushed her hair forward over her shoulder. His warm breath on her nape was her only warning before his teeth lightly grazed her skin. A shudder quaked through her. His fingers manipulated the stuck zipper, his short nails scraping her spine as he worked. She had no idea how he could see with the lack of light. And then the tab rasped down. Cool air swept her back seconds before his palms, hot and strong, slipped beneath the fabric to grasp her waist. He held her in place while he strung a necklace of kisses along her shoulders and beneath her ear.

"Turn around and drop the dress," he ordered huskily in her ear.

Her entire body flushed with heat. On unsteady legs she pivoted only to discover Max had moved back into the shadows. But the glimpse of desire she'd seen earlier gave her the courage to be bolder than she'd normally be. She folded her arms at her waist and dipped her left shoulder. That side of the dress slid down to her elbow. She heard him inhale and repeated the action on the right side leaving her bare from the waist up except for her sheer black lace push-up bra. Only her crossed arms kept the dress up.

She straightened her shoulders and then slowly lowered her arms. The dress floated to the floor, leaving her in the bra, matching lace bikini panties and black heels.

His breath whistled out and he stepped forward into the light, but abruptly stopped. His nostrils flared and his hungry eyes burned over her, filling her with a sense of empowerment.

She lifted her hand and eased down one bra strap and then the other. Max watched through unblinking eyes. She opened the front clasp and peeled back the cups of her bra. His Adam's apple bobbed. She shrugged and her bra fell to the floor behind her.

Max's gaze devoured her breasts. The growing ridge beneath his zipper made her mouth dry. She dampened her lips, and then taking a deep breath, she stroked her hands from her rib cage to her waist and then her hips.

A quiet growl rumbled from him. She needed him to touch her, but he waited. Dana hooked her thumbs under her string bikini panties and pushed them over her hips. They slid down her legs and Max's eyes followed. She stepped out of them, but kept on her shoes.

When his gaze met hers again, her knees went weak at the barely controlled passion she saw in the hot blue depths. His hands returned to his belt buckle, made quick work of loosening the leather and unfastening his trousers. He kicked off his shoes and shoved his pants and boxer briefs to the floor. Next, he ripped off his socks and straightened.

The size of his erection shouted his desire more clearly than words. Max Hudson wanted her. That was something she'd prayed for for years and all that mattered at the moment. She'd work on making him love her.

He prowled toward her. "Do you have another condom in your purse?"

She barely heard his low growled question over her pounding pulse. She believed in miracles, in happily ever after and love at first sight, but mostly she believed in being prepared for all three. That was the reason she carried condoms. "Yes."

"Get it."

She crouched to reach the purse she'd dropped on the floor. Max surprised her by kneeling behind her. He curved his body around hers, wrapping her in a tight, hot hug. His arousal slid between her buttocks and came to rest against her wet center. She gasped. His palms caught her waist and his thighs flanked her hips as he stroked his length against her damp folds, moistening himself with her arousal. Then he leaned away, but only far enough to caress her shoulders and arms and length of her spine.

"You are beautiful, Dana," he murmured, "and very sexy."

Her heart squeezed with love. She'd waited what felt like forever to hear those words from him. She smiled at him over her shoulder and reached back to caress his bristly jaw, but she couldn't make out the emotion in his eyes in the darkness. "Thank you. So are you."

He cupped her bottom and lifted her upright as he stood. His sex remained pressed between her cheeks. His hands found her breasts and kneaded them.

"Get the condom. Now."

She was so turned on and her hands were shaking so badly she had trouble holding on to her purse, but she located the protection and dropped her bag again. The smack of it hitting the floor echoed off the walls.

He hooked an arm around her middle and yanked her backward. His chest blanketed her back with heat. He caught her jaw with his hand, turned her head toward him and took her mouth as if he couldn't wait another second.

The kiss was rough, hard and deep, with no warm-up

preliminaries, and the odd angle with him behind her made her feel a little powerless. But the vulnerability aroused her so much she could barely stand, because Max never lost control. That he was clearly on the verge of doing so now had to mean something.

Slightly off balance in her heels, she reached up and looped her arms around his neck, holding on as tightly as she could. His hands briskly raked her torso.

"To hell with the pool," he growled against her lips and walked her deeper into the darkness.

"Max, I can't see." Afraid she might run into a wall, she stretched her arms out in front of her.

"I know the way." With his hands on her waist he guided her forward only a few feet and then stopped. His short nails scraped the middle of her back. He grabbed her hands and lifted them. "Hold on."

Dana made out the shape of a door frame with her palms. Where was she? The doorway to her bedroom hall? "Max?"

His hands found her breasts. He kneaded her, tweaked her tight nipples and then buffed the stiff tips, causing an ache deep in her womb. A hot, open-mouth kiss scorched her neck, followed by another and another while his hands worked magic on her body. His touch was hurried, but sure and devastatingly effective.

He caressed her belly, circled her navel ring, and then finally, finally, slipped his fingertips into the curls between her legs. She was already slick for him.

He traced a devastating path over and around her sensitive flesh. She cried out as he found the right spot only to abandon it. At first she thought he just didn't realize what he was doing, but then he did it over and over, bringing her to the brink and then letting her fall back. Her breath came in pants and her legs trembled.

He strung a line of nips and kisses down her spine. His hot breath on her buttocks preceded an open-mouthed kiss that rocked her in her shoes. He rose and tugged the condom from the hand she had fisted against the door-frame.

"Hold on," he repeated, and then clutched her hips and drove into her from behind.

Dana gasped in surprise, in pleasure. This position took him so deep it stole her breath. He adjusted her stance and went deeper still, bending his knees and then rising to fill her again and again. She groaned out his name as desire stronger than any she'd ever experienced took hold of her.

Max had her off balance and confused, but he also had her unbearably aroused. How could she like this fast and furious coupling in the dark? It wasn't tender or romantic or any of the things she thought she needed from him. But she did like it. She liked the out-of-control passion, the unrestrained hunger. And she loved that Max was on the verge of losing control. She could tell by the ragged breaths steaming her nape, the tremor of his body against hers, his groans and the increasing pace of his thrusts.

He kissed and nibbled her neck. His hands caressed her breasts, her center. This position with him covering her like a stallion was so blatantly sexual, so primitive. He crossed her magic spot again, but this time he didn't tease her and move on.

He circled with devastating effectiveness and pressed his cheek to hers. "Let go for me, baby. Let go."

His roughly voiced command made her shiver, and then tension knotted into a ball. She imploded. Wave after wave of white hot heat shimmered through her. She cried out and dug her nails into the wood. It took everything she had to remain standing, everything and Max's support. His hands clamped on her hips and he plunged faster. He muffled a groan against her neck as he shuddered against her back and again as the aftershocks worked through him.

Dana fought to catch her breath and find her balance. Once she did, she smiled.

Max had lost control. With passion like that, love was sure to follow.

Max awoke suddenly. Something wasn't right. The bed. The light filtering though his eyelids. He opened his eyes and surveyed the room, trying to get his bearings.

Dana's room.

He turned his head. She lay curled beside him with a hand tucked beneath her cheek and the other resting on his chest. The corner of the sheet barely covered her torso, and her dark hair streamed across the pillow.

A strong need to escape crawled over him. Why had he stayed with her last night?

Because your legs were too weak to carry you upstairs.

His blood flow detoured at the memory of taking her in the doorway and again when they'd finally staggered to the pool sometime before dawn.

Why hadn't having her once satisfied his hunger the way it did with other women? Even now he had to fight the urge to tug the sheet away from her breasts and taste her, slide into her, ride her into wakefulness. Why hadn't sex in the dark been as anonymous as it should have been?

But there had been nothing unidentifiable about her scent in his nostrils, her taste filling his mouth or her body gripping his intimately. Not even the chlorinated water had masked who he held in his arms. She'd still tasted and smelled like Dana.

What kind of hold did she have over him?

Whatever the hell it was, he intended to break it.

But not at the risk of delaying *Honor*.

Not wanting to wake her, he carefully lifted her hand from his chest and placed it on the mattress between them before easing toward the edge of the bed. His leg and butt muscles protested every shift. Oh, yeah. He'd known from the muscle fatigue last night, from the way she'd made him weak and quivery, that he'd pay for the acrobatics. He wasn't twenty anymore.

"Love you," she mumbled.

He went rigid. He didn't want her love. He didn't want any woman's love. But especially not one whom he suspected had betrayed him.

He twisted and looked at her over his shoulder. Her eyes were still closed and her skin still flushed from sleep. She must be dreaming.

What makes you think she's talking to you?

But if not him, then who? Doug Lewis?

The twinge in his gut was due to last night's gymnastics. That's all it was. Too much exercise.

Lewis was welcome to her—once *Honor* had been released.

And then if she was the leak, Max would fire her. It would be inconvenient to train her replacement, but he'd survive. He always survived. Even when he shouldn't.

But a niggle of doubt dug into Max's side. What if he were wrong? What if Dana was falling for him?

He couldn't let that happen.

But how could he stop it?

He'd have to tread carefully. Keep her close. But not too close. Push her away. But not too far.

He could stand anything for a couple more months. And then it would be over and his life could get back to normal.

And Dana would be gone.

Eight

Dana entered the kitchen not knowing exactly what to expect after last night's wild passion.

The smell of coffee greeted her, and her pulse tripped. Max had made coffee for her? That seemed like a good sign. But the kitchen was empty. She poured a mug of coffee.

It was barely six. Was Max already at work?

Movement outside drew her attention. Max sliced his way through the water cleanly, efficiently. Excitement coursed through her body at the memory of swimming with him just hours ago. Of course, swimming was an exaggeration. He'd pulled her from the bed, led her outside and towed her into the pool. Naked.

The lapping of the cool water against her bare breasts and bottom had been as sexy as a lover's caress. The fact that they'd been outside with pale moonlight and a gentle breeze on their damp skin had only heightened the intensity of the sensations.

Her nipples and her internal muscles tightened at the memory, and her gaze went to the rounded stairs at the end of the pool where he'd taken her. She'd had no idea she was such a hedonist, but she'd loved every minute of their sensual play. He'd loved her with his mouth, his slick, wet hands and his hard body.

Fanning her warm face, she blew out a breath and then opened the door and crossed the flagstone patio to the pool. She dampened her lips and wished she had the nerve to strip off and join him. She ached to make love to him in the bright sunlight where she could see his face and his eyes while he was inside her.

Instead, she kicked off her sandals, sat on the edge and lowered her feet into the water. She sipped her coffee while she watched Max swim. His daily laps and the home gym down the hall from her bedroom on the first floor explained his killer body.

He pulled up short and turned to her. "You're up early."

She shrugged. "So are you."

"Habit."

"Thanks for making the coffee." She loved the idea of sharing quiet mornings together and discussing the upcoming day.

"No problem." He waded toward her with water streaming down his torso. "Time to get to work."

The abrupt shift from personal to business threw her. "Before we do, I just wanted to say…Max, last night was…amazing."

His pupils expanded. He jerked a quick nod.

"But I—I don't know what to tell your family about us."

He stiffened. "Why tell them anything?"

She fought to conceal a flinch.

"Because of this." She pointed to the tiny love bite on her neck. That Max had been carried away enough to forget himself thrilled her. "Bella and Cece grilled me last night about who I was dating."

"What did you say?" His guarded tone set off tiny alarm bells in her subconscious.

"I managed to dodge the question because I didn't want to lie. What are we going to tell them?"

He hefted himself from the pool and reached for a towel. "It's none of their business."

"But…" She wanted them to know. She wanted *everyone* to know.

He inhaled, glanced away and then back to her. "Dana, revealing anything now is premature. Let's hold off and see where this thing goes. No need to get their hopes up if we don't work out."

If they didn't work out.

She was head over heels in love with him and he was just testing the waters, so to speak.

A sobering reminder that they still had a long way to go.

"Which is the real you?"

Max's question shattered Dana's concentration. She looked up from the breakdown sheet, which detailed the requirements for the few remaining scenes to be shot on the Hudson Pictures lot. "I'm sorry. What did you say?"

"Which is the real you?" he repeated. "The buttoned-up executive or this?" He nodded to indicate her denim skirt and lace-trimmed tank top attire. His gaze lingered on her flip flops and peach-painted toenails.

She'd deliberately dressed a little more casually while staying at his place. The goal had been to remind both of them that her role had changed. She wasn't his superefficient executive assistant anymore. When they went to work at Hudson Pictures she still wore her office attire because it looked more professional.

But she considered the fact that Max had been thinking about her a plus—especially since he was always front and center in her thoughts.

His gaze lingered on her breasts, and of course, the body parts in question tingled. How could they not? Max had that effect on her. Since they'd been making love, he'd turned her inside out with ecstasy more times than she could count. She knew Max desired her, but she was afraid sex was all he wanted from her.

"I'm both."

"Impossible. They're contradictory. And for five years I've seen no hint of the navel-ringed beachcomber." His gaze dropped to the jewelry concealed beneath her shirt.

"Why is it impossible, Max? You, as a producer, juggle a multitude of personalities. You have to be creative and smart enough to recognize a marketable script when it hits your desk. In preproduction you have to be a salesman and a PR man to a get financial backing for your project if it's not in-house.

"During production you're a clock watcher, babysitter and a peacekeeper on the set. As an editor in postproduction you have to be a visionary who sees the true message in the script and puts the complicated puzzle pieces of video, audio and special effects together to reveal that message." She shrugged. "If you can be that complex, why can't anyone else?"

"It's not the same."

"It is. We're all what we need to be for the people around us at any given time."

A line formed between his eyebrows. "Don't put me on a pedestal, Dana, and don't fall for me. What we have is great, as you said, but I'm incapable of giving you what you need. I can't love you back."

Alarm trickled down her spine like melting ice. Had he guessed her feelings? She'd tried to keep things light because she knew that's what he wanted. "Who says I'm falling for you?"

"You did."

"I've never said any such thing."

"You said it Saturday night."

Panic shot through her along with a stiff shot of humiliation. She vaguely recalled saying something like that in a dream the night they'd made love in the hall and again in the pool. *Please tell me that was a dream.*

The only thing she could do was brazen her way through this. "I must have been dreaming. I don't even remember who or what about."

He didn't look as if he bought her story. However, protesting more would only make her look guilty. She decided to go on the offensive.

"But, Max, your editing work proves you feel the emotions you claim you can't. You know exactly which shot to use to convey the most impact, when to use sound and when to let the characters speak.

"I once read that a great movie needs no dialogue—that the expressions of the characters show the story. You do that, Max. With your editing choices, you reveal the story through the emotions on the characters' faces, and it's amazing to behold."

"Being able to edit film is not the same as being able to experience emotions."

"I don't think that's true."

His scowl deepened. "You have too much faith in people."

"And you have too little. Maybe it's time you tried to trust again."

"And maybe it's time you stop trying to psychoanalyze your boss and get back to work."

She winced at the bite of his words and turned back to her desk. But that didn't mean she was giving up on Max Hudson. She'd only just begun her campaign to win him over.

Dana shut the front door and stopped. The house felt eerily silent. Max had been here when she left to go shopping and his cars were in the garage. He must be here.

Juggling the shopping bags, she headed for the stairs. She rarely used the elevator because she preferred the exercise after sitting at her desk for most of the day. She'd noticed Max did the same.

The second level seemed equally still. "Max?"

No answer.

She headed for the kitchen and unloaded her groceries and then carried the office supplies up to the third floor. Max wasn't there, either.

Maybe he was sleeping? She glanced at her watch. Barely nine. That would be an extremely early bedtime for him, but maybe weeks of burning the candle at both ends had caught up with him…unless he wasn't well? That could explain the odd, silent mood he'd been in all day.

She dumped her bag on her desk and once again headed for the stairs. His bedroom door stood open. She hesitated. They'd made love almost every night since that first time six weeks ago, but never in his room. She tapped on the door, but when he didn't answer she made her way inside the darkened room and flipped on the light. The bedroom and the adjoining bath were empty, as was the private deck outside his bedroom. "Max?"

Had she missed him on the patio or in the hot tub? She leaned over the rail and scanned the shadowy tiled area. Unless he'd hidden himself in a spot that the landscape lighting didn't illuminate, then he wasn't there. Where could he be?

She turned to go back inside and noticed a spiral staircase leading up to the roof tucked in the far outside corner. She'd never been up there before, had never even known of the rooftop access. The gate at the bottom was ajar. With her heart beating a little faster she made her way to the stairs and climbed. The flat roof made a great observation deck, but had only a low wall, no railing. Max sat in a folding chair with his back to her, facing the light-sprinkled valley below.

She struggled against a sense of vertigo. "Max?"

"Go back inside," he said in an unnaturally flat voice.

Then she noticed the whiskey bottle on the ground by his chair. "Are you okay?"

"Fine."

He didn't sound fine. She carefully made her way across the twenty feet or so that separated them. "I didn't know you had a deck up here."

"Dana, I don't want company."

But he sounded like he needed it. There was a hollowness to his voice that she'd never heard before. "Why?"

"Go back downstairs."

"And if I refuse, will you push me over?" The height was getting to her. There wasn't a second chair, so she eased down onto her knees on the pebbled surface beside him.

He glared at her, and the rising moonlight revealed the pain on his face. Her heart clenched in sympathy.

"What's wrong, Max? I'm not leaving you up here alone, so you might as well tell me."

"For God's sake, I'm not going to jump."

The words sent a jolt of panic through her. "I didn't think you were. But something drove you up here in the dark."

"It's none of your business."

"It became my business when you forced me to move in with you and even more so when you scared the day-lights out of me by disappearing."

He swore. "She died three years ago today and it's my fault. Is that what you wanted to know?"

He turned his head away as if he wanted the words back. She'd known from old gossip that Karen had died in the fall, but she'd never heard the exact date. "Your wife?"

"Yes." He raked a hand over the back of his head and then reached down to recap the liquor bottle. There wasn't much missing. He must not have had much to drink, maybe a few sips.

"Why do you blame yourself? I heard she fell asleep at the wheel."

"We were at a party. She was tired and begged me to leave. But I was too busy wheeling and dealing to go home. So we stayed. I worked a few deals. Back then I was still busting my ass to prove I deserved my job."

He stared off into the distance. "When we did finally go, I'd had too much to drink, so I made her drive. I shouldn't have."

Dana covered his hand with hers. "If you'd been drinking, you did the right thing."

"She was pregnant. That's why she was so tired and why

she kept asking to leave early. She'd planned to tell me that night after the party. She wanted to celebrate. Privately."

Her heart ached for him. "I'm sorry, Max."

"She fell asleep at the wheel, ran off the road and hit a tree. She and our baby died and I walked away without a scratch."

She couldn't speak for the knot in her throat, so she squeezed his hand.

"When I got home from the hospital the next day I found the card and the pregnancy test, along with a non-alcoholic bottle of sparkling cider waiting in an ice bucket in the kitchen."

Tears stung Dana's eyes and put a burning lump in her chest. "That must have been like losing her a second time."

His gaze held hers in the semi-darkness. "Yeah. Exactly."

There was nothing she could say to lessen his pain, so Dana did the only thing she could think of. She climbed into his lap, hugged him and held him.

He stiffened at first, but eventually the tension drained from his muscles, and then his arms wound around her and he hugged her back. "No one else knows about the baby. Keep it to yourself."

That he'd shared such a painful secret with only her touched her and gave her hope.

"I will." She pressed her cheek to the warm raspiness of his beard-stubbled jaw. "You can't blame yourself, Max. You were doing your job by schmoozing and you were protecting her by not driving the car. It was an accident. A terrible, tragic accident. But it wasn't your fault."

His somber gaze held hers. "You'll never convince me of that. And that's why you can't love me. Because I will never allow myself to love you, or anyone else, back."

Her heart sank. At that moment she was very afraid that he might be right. And she was just as afraid she'd never get over him.

"Wake up." Max's voice jarred Dana from a sound sleep.

"What?" She blinked at the bright light in her eyes.

"Get up. You wanted to be a producer. Now you get to do one of the less desirable parts of the job."

"What's that?"

"Maintain the peace. We have to go haul Ridley's butt out of trouble."

She sat up in her bed and shoved her hair from her eyes. "Ridley's in trouble?"

"He's holed up in a nightclub getting drunk and obnoxious. We need to get him out before the paparazzi make paydirt out of him. *Honor* doesn't need the negative publicity. Throw on that black dress you wore to the family dinner and do it fast."

"I have to dress up to fetch Ridley?" And then she noticed Max was already dressed in black trousers and a white silk shirt left open at the neck to reveal a wedge of his great chest. He hadn't shaved, and the dark, beard-stubbled look was ravishingly sexy on him in a pirate kind of way. "You're going, too?"

"Yes."

"Because you don't trust me to handle it?"

"Ridley is unpredictable. You couldn't handle him alone."

"We have to go into the club to get him?"

"Yes, that means dressing the part or you don't get past the front door, which at this place is picky as hell. I stand a better chance of getting in with a beautiful woman on my arm."

The backhanded compliment made her all warm and fuzzy.

"You have five minutes."

She glanced at the clock. "It's three in the morning. Couldn't Ridley have partied at a reasonable hour? And is Bella with him?"

"No to both. Bella had the good sense to leave and call me when he turned ugly."

Dana threw back the covers and bailed out of bed. Max leaned against the dresser, arms folded, and watched her. Despite their intimacy, his scrutiny made her incredibly self-conscious. She hustled to her closet, snagged the dress in its plastic dry cleaning bag and debated locking herself in the bathroom.

But no. She wanted him to want her. That meant enticing him. It had been two weeks since the family dinner, two weeks in which he'd made love to her every night and then abruptly left her bed to sleep in his own.

She tossed the dress on the bed and dropped her chemise on the floor. Next she headed for her lingerie drawer and selected the black lace thong and matching push-up bra she'd bought in France on a whim but never worn. She stepped into the panties and then shrugged on the bra. Max's swiftly indrawn breath rewarded her bravado.

Digging deep for chutzpah, she paraded to the bathroom, but left the door open. When she checked the mirror, she found Max's gaze glued to her butt and bit her lip to hide a smile as she quickly washed her face, applied minimal makeup and ran a brush through her hair.

Returning to the bedroom, she dug out a pair of big, gold chandelier earrings and slipped on a gold heart-link necklace that fell between her breasts. Her nipples tightened under Max's scrutiny.

"You have one minute left." His voice sounded a tad huskier than usual and her pulse kicked in response.

She stabbed her feet into her highest black heels and felt a rush of adrenaline as Max's lids fell to half-mast and his nostrils flared. Fighting dirty was fun.

She removed the dress from the plastic bag and slipped it over her head, then twirled a slow circle. "Ready."

Max swallowed visibly, and Dana noticed the thickening ridge in his pants. Arousal slithered through her as he slowly pushed off the dresser and moved toward her. He didn't touch her but his eyes burned a path from her face to her toes and back.

"Grab your ID and let's go."

She would have liked a compliment on how she looked or acknowledgment that she'd dressed in under five minutes. But she'd settle for the obvious signs that he desired her.

Max strode from the room. Dana grabbed her purse, shoved the necessities into a tiny, beaded evening bag and hustled to catch up with him. In the attached garage he stood by the open car door—the silver Mercedes sedan this time instead of the black Lamborghini Roadster. She slid in and waited for him to round the car and climb into the driver's seat.

"Does this happen often?" she asked.

He shrugged and reversed out of the garage. "Depends on the actor. Some are more of a headache than others."

"And why don't their managers or agents babysit them?"

"Sometimes they go by the 'any publicity is good publicity' fallacy. At the moment we—Hudson Pictures—have more to lose if this turns ugly. And Bella called me."

The last line snagged her. Max adored his baby sister although he, like his father, tended not to be obvious about his feelings. That was one of the things it had taken her a good chunk of her five years with Hudson to learn. The Hudson men didn't show their feelings openly. She was used to her father and brother, whose bear hugs and obvious affection left you in no doubt of their feelings.

He exited the electronic gate, hit the road and accelerated. "The plan is to get in and get him out with as little fanfare as possible. The paparazzi will be lurking like vultures and may even get right in your face, so watch every move you make and every word you speak. If anyone asks, we're going to check out a new club we've heard about."

"I've heard about Leslie Shay. Does she have a personal vendetta against the Hudsons or something?"

"Or something. She's one of the worst paparazzi vultures. If we're lucky, she followed Bella, and we won't have to deal with her."

"If we're not?"

"Then the fact that you and I were seen together might be tabloid fodder tomorrow."

She couldn't exactly dread that. She wanted everyone to know they were an item.

"Thanks for including me tonight, Max. I want to learn every aspect of the business—the good, the bad *and* the ugly sides of it. I guess I just never heard you talk about this part."

"That's because I don't. This part of the job doesn't need to be discussed. It just needs to be handled and discreetly. Trust me, Dana, you do not want the babysitting part of the job. Actors are worse than children and they get in more trouble with bigger stakes. One stupid star can kill a movie's box office potential. Producing isn't a glamorous job."

"I never thought it was. I'm the one who handled the petty squabbles you were too busy to deal with. Remember the actor who complained that his trailer wasn't the biggest on the lot, the one who demanded only bat guano coffee and the actress who wanted five pounds of green M&M's delivered every Monday? You delegated those to me."

He grimaced. "This is bigger. This isn't going to be a back-lot headache. This has the potential to blow up in our faces."

"I understand, and you can count on me." She wanted to cover his hand on the gearshift, but didn't think the gesture would be welcome. To heck with it. She did it anyway.

His fingers, his entire arm, stiffened and then relaxed. "Thanks for coming without complaining."

She squeezed his hand and then put hers back in her lap. She didn't want to push him too far too fast. "I'm happy to help. Besides, I'll get to see the inside of one of the 'in' clubs."

A few moments later they arrived at a club Dana had only read about in the tabloids. Max pulled up at the front door, tossed the keys to the valet and circled to her side of the car.

"Don't make eye contact with the crowd," he cautioned as he assisted her from the car. "And remember, don't answer any questions."

Excitement hummed in the air from the minute she stepped on the sidewalk. People milled around the club entrance to catch a glimpse of the stars going and coming. Some looked like fans. Others were clearly paparazzi. Max swore under his breath, leaned close and pressed his mouth to her ear. The feel of his flesh on hers made her shiver.

"Shay is here. Tall, skinny brunette to your left. Keep moving. Keep your mouth shut."

Dana took a quick look from under her lashes to identify the woman. Flashbulbs went off, but she kept hustling to keep up with Max.

"Max," called a voice from the reporter's direction, "who's your new girl? Going to follow in your brother's footsteps with wedding bells?"

Max didn't comment. He stopped at the front door and spoke to the big, black-suited goon guarding the entrance. Dana couldn't hear the conversation, but the stiffening of Max's body didn't bode well. She leaned around him to see refusal stamped on the bouncer's face and knew she had to think fast.

"Please, it's my first time. Bella promised me I'd love it here." She batted her lashes for added effect. When that didn't seem to work on Stone Face, she winked. "She also bet me five hundred bucks I couldn't get her brother to bring me."

The guy looked her over from top to bottom, returning to ogle the cleavage her new bra had created. "Yeah, sure, go on in."

He shoved open the door and the sound of raucous music hit Dana like an explosion. The bass drum vibrated the fabric of her dress. She squeezed between Max and the bouncer and darted inside. The door closed behind them. She hesitated while her eyes adjusted to the darkness and the strobe lights. The smell of cigarettes and cigars permeated the air.

Max wrapped an arm around her waist and pulled her close. "You're good."

She grinned up at him. "Now let's go find our man."

"Bella said he was in the back room when she left." Max cut a path through the loitering clientele.

Dana tried not to gape at the famous faces they passed, but she couldn't help it. This was the A-list crowd, something she'd never be a part of, and while she was used to dealing with movie stars on the set, clubs like this were out of her realm.

She scanned the faces of the famous and the hangers-on and then bounced back to one. That looked like Ridley in the corner, but it was dark and hard to be sure, and the guy wasn't alone. Bella wouldn't like that if it was Ridley.

"Isn't that him? Kind of hard to tell with three women piled on top of him."

"That's him. Now let's convince him to walk out with us."

Ridley was dark haired, of medium height and handsome if you liked the type of guy who knew he was attractive and always had an agenda—Dana didn't—and he was totally oblivious to their presence until Max lightly kicked the toe of his shoe.

"How's it going, Ridley? I heard you needed a ride home."

Judging by his drunken glare Ridley wasn't happy to see them.

"Excuse us, ladies. Ridley has a prior engagement." Max peeled a pair of hundred dollar bills off his money clip and handed it to one of the women. "Next drink's on me."

The trio vanished. "You had no right to bus' up my party," Ridley slurred.

Max leaned down, said something in Ridley's ear Dana couldn't hear, grabbed his hand in what looked like a handshake—but judging by the bulge of Max's biceps was much more—and yanked the drunk actor to his feet.

Looking ticked off, the star of *Honor* gave Dana a lecherous look. "I'll go if I can sit in the back with her."

"Don't even think it," Max growled at him. His jealous tone sent a thrill through Dana. If he was jealous, he had to feel something, didn't he?

"Let's get the hell out of here without causing a scene."

The three of them left the club and piled in Max's car, Ridley alone in the back and Dana in the passenger seat. Max turned to glare at him. "If you want to work for Hudson Pictures again, you'll clean up your act."

Ridley sat in sullen silence for the next thirty minutes. Max dumped him at his home and headed back for Mulholland Drive.

"That went relatively well," Dana ventured.

"Just remember that if you read something in the paper tomorrow it doesn't make it true."

He meant the wedding plans the reporter had mentioned. "I wouldn't dream of trusting any information that didn't come directly from the source."

"Good. Let's go to bed. You're going to pay for tormenting me with that little performance you gave while getting dressed." The fire in his eyes lit a corresponding flame in her.

But making Max want her was the easy part. Making him trust her and want to keep her forever was going to be the real challenge.

Nine

Dana jerked to a stop on the patio Monday morning when she realized Max was on his cell phone.

He had his back to her and her gaze automatically took the familiar tour from his broad shoulders to his tight butt.

"Handicapped access to all premiere events." His words penetrated her lust. "Dana's brother is in a wheelchair, and I don't want him to have any difficulties while he's here. Make sure all obstacles are removed."

Emotion gripped her in a stranglehold. Max had mentioned making arrangements for her family to attend the premiere. She'd expected to have to handle the details herself, but she had been so slammed with her new duties that she had yet to get around to following through.

"I've already booked the airfare and hotel for all five of them."

Five? He had to mean her parents, her brother, her sister-in-law and their son, Dana's precious nephew. She couldn't wait to see them, but the premiere was months away. First they had to get through next month's first-cut showing at Hudson Pictures's private sixtieth anniversary party.

She clutched the phone in her hand to her chest. This was the man she'd fallen for, the one who cared enough to make sure the important people in his life—and hers, apparently—were taken care of.

"Thanks." He turned and spotted her. "Did you need something?"

She swallowed to ease the lump in her throat and held out the receiver. "It's Luc."

Max took the cordless phone. "Luc, what's the news?"

He listened for a moment and then a sad smile curved his lips. "Congratulations. How are Gwen and the baby?"

Dana walked to the edge of the patio to give him privacy. She scanned the cityscape below and the distant ocean. Today a haze hung over it all, diluting the sun. As much as she enjoyed living in California, she missed the cleaner air back home and the changing seasons. In Wilmington, October meant brilliant fall leaves and pumpkins for sale on every corner. Here, fall was just a word on the calendar. The temperature fluctuated only about thirty degrees all year.

Max joined her. "Gwen had the baby last night. A boy. They named him Charles after our grandfather, but they plan to call him Chaz. Luc will e-mail pictures when he gets home from the hospital."

Given what Max had told her about Karen's pregnancy, she wondered how he felt about the news. It was impossible to tell from his poker face and neutral tone. "Is everybody okay?"

"Yes. I need to send something."

"You mean *you* need to shop for a baby gift?"

He opened his mouth and closed it again as her emphasis on "you" sank in. "Yes."

In the past, as his executive assistant, buying gifts would have been her job. She waited for him to ask for help. If he did, she'd have to point out that he was losing that silly bet they'd made when she moved in three weeks ago.

"Would you like a list of appropriate shops?"

"And have you claim victory? No. I'll go online and see what I can find."

She should have known he wouldn't cave. The man was too stubborn to concede defeat. Thus far he'd handled each of his personal items without her assistance. Of course, there had been few of them, and he did have the cheat sheet she'd made for him that first day to help. But then again, Max budgeted money, schedules, cast and crew for his pictures. Juggling a few personal appointments shouldn't be too difficult.

And now that things had changed between them, did she really want him to lose the bet and give her a glowing referral to another movie studio? No.

She decided to switch to a safer subject. "You're making the travel arrangements for my family?"

He nodded.

Travel arrangements had been her job as his E.A. If she hadn't already been in love with him, she would have fallen head over heels at that moment. "Thank you, Max. I could have done it."

He brushed off her thanks with a dismissive wave. "They weren't the only ones I had to make. We have too much to do to waste time yakking. The first cut isn't the final cut, but I want it to be as perfect as possible for the anniversary party and we have only a few weeks left. Let's get to work."

And then he turned on his heel and walked away, leaving Dana feeling both elated and alone. At times like this when she needed to share her excitement and he turned his back, she wondered if she'd ever break through that tough shell he'd built around his heart, or if she should throw in the towel and admit defeat.

Click, click, click went the pen in Dev's hand. *Click. Click.*

The repetitive sound was beginning to get on Max's nerves. He rocked back in his home office chair and looked at his brother, who'd parked his butt on the corner of Dana's desk.

Dev stared back, tension drawing his features tight and making Max wonder if his big brother's honeymoon was over, and if he was regretting his month-old marriage.

Click. Click.

"Spit it out, Dev. What has your neck in a knot on a Saturday afternoon?"

"We're down to the wire for November's sixtieth anniversary party and the first viewing. You have only a few more weeks. Are you going to be ready?"

"The first cut will be ready." Thanks to Dana's help and more hours of overtime than he'd ever put in before. But for his grandmother he'd do anything.

"What about Dana? You have scripts and treatments for potential new projects rolling in daily. We need to know if we can trust her before we start making decisions on what to shoot next."

"I've kept her too busy to screen new projects. If she

knows anything about where Willow got their information, she's not talking. How's married life?"

"Don't change the subject. You've had weeks to find out if she's our snitch. If you haven't, then you're not trying."

"I am trying, damn it. The script similarities could be coincidental."

"We both know that's unlikely."

Yeah, they both knew it. If it had been any other film company, they'd have blamed the situation on coincidence. But not with Willow. There was too much bad blood between Hudson Pictures and their number-one rival, and the contributing incidents had escalated in the past few years—years since Hudson had employed Dana, a woman who had admitted she was overqualified for the position. So why had she taken the job?

Max shoved himself to his feet and walked to the window. Was Dana the leak? Given his suspicions, he couldn't believe he'd spilled his guts to her about Karen and the baby. He'd deliberately kept that shameful piece of information to himself. No one else knew. Not even Dev.

What was it about her that made everything so damned easy? Too easy. They shared work, meals, conversation and sex. Incredible sex. Like this morning in her tub. What had started as his offering to wash her back had turned into—

Damn. Had the air-conditioner quit working? He stepped into the hall to turn the thermostat down a few degrees and then returned to his seat.

Why couldn't he quench his thirst for her despite being with her almost twenty hours a day? He didn't want to want her. He sure as hell didn't want to like or respect her. But he'd given her his dirtiest producer duties, and she'd done them without question or complaint. Her willingness to do the undesirable jobs and her perspective on the editing impressed the hell out of him. She'd offered several damned good suggestions.

The more she gave, the more he demanded from her, and she delivered over and over, no matter how hard he tried to make her regret backing him into a corner.

If she'd betrayed him with Lewis, would she work this hard? Or was she busting her butt just to get him to let down his guard and uncover more she could use against him?

If so, for what gain? Was she on someone else's payroll?

He didn't want to believe it.

"Max, we need to know if she's the source. What are you doing to find out?"

His brother's surly tone, combined with Max's own frustration over the situation, hit him the wrong way. He scowled at Dev. "I'm sleeping with her to keep her out of Lewis's bed and to find out if she sold us out. What more do you want me to do?"

A gasp jerked his attention to the doorway. Dana stood frozen in the opening, her fist an inch from the wood as if she'd lifted it to knock. She looked at him through pain-flooded brown eyes as the color drained from her face.

"You—I—how could you?"

Regret clutched Max's chest and coldness seeped over him. He'd heard the front door close minutes ago, but he hadn't heard the gate chime, which meant she hadn't left and returned. Because she hadn't gotten around to it? Or because she'd stayed behind to eavesdrop on a private conversation?

He stood and started toward her. "Dana—"

She held up a hand to stop him. "Was I just part of the job to you? Just another mess Hudson's producer had to clean up?"

The hurt in her voice ripped him right down the middle. "No."

"You didn't want me to keep my job because you needed my help with *Honor*. You wouldn't let me quit because you didn't want me to take what I knew elsewhere. God, you even told me that in the beginning, and I was still dumb enough to fall in love with you."

Fall in love with him. The words crushed him like a fallen set wall, immobilizing him and making it impossible to fill his lungs.

She couldn't love him. He didn't want her to love him.

He didn't want to have this conversation in front of his brother. "Get out, Dev."

"What?"

"Leave."

Dana's chin rose. "Why don't I make it easy for both of you? I'll leave. I can be packed and gone in five minutes. Out of your life and off Hudson Pictures's payroll."

He couldn't let her go. Not yet. She knew too much. "If you walk out that door you'll never work in Hollywood again."

She gasped and paled even further. "You bastard."

"Max—" Dev started.

"Get out, Dev," Max repeated, and when his brother didn't move he added, "Now."

"Don't screw this up," Dev said low enough that Dana wouldn't hear him before he stormed out.

Max silently held Dana's gaze until he heard the roar of an engine racing out of the driveway. "You were going shopping. Why didn't you?"

She flinched as the accusation in his voice sank in, and then marched over to her desk, snatched up a piece of paper and waved it in front of his face.

"Because I forgot my shopping list. I was going to cook a special dinner for you because it's Halloween. It's a tradition my mother started when James and I outgrew trick-or-treating so we wouldn't feel as if we were missing out on all the fun. But forget it. Get your own dinner."

She crumpled the paper, threw it at the trash can and missed. Dana never missed. She folded her arms. "I can't work with someone who doesn't trust me."

"You have no choice. You signed a contract."

"The contract doesn't say I have to have sex with my boss or live in his house. From now on, I'm doing neither."

Her words hit him like a whip. "We'll have more interruptions at the office."

"Too bad."

Memories of fighting with Karen followed by days of her pouting silences forced their way forward. If Dana acted the same way, then completing *Honor* on time was in jeopardy. He'd have to cut corners and he never cut corners.

But he couldn't compel her to stay here or to work here. He didn't need the legal department to tell him that could be construed as kidnapping. "I'll help you pack up your work."

"I can handle it."

But he couldn't trust her to do so. "I'll help you and then I'll deliver the boxes to the office."

Comprehension dawned on her face. "You don't trust me not to drive straight to Doug or whoever it is you think is buying your secrets."

He couldn't deny it.

Her body went rigid. "I'll tell you what, Max. You pack up the office. I'm going to deal with my clothes. I'll see you at the office Monday morning."

"What about tomorrow?"

"Tomorrow is Sunday. I'm taking a day off." She turned on her heel and strode out of the room. Her footsteps clattered down the stairs.

He was going to lose her.

And considering he didn't know whether she was guilty or innocent, that realization bothered him far more than it should.

Dana sank down on her bed and then sprang right back up again to pace her bedroom. Anger, hurt and betrayal swirled inside her like a noxious cocktail.

She should have known her relationship with Max was too good to be true. She'd thought they'd been growing closer, especially after he'd confided in her about Karen and the baby.

But Max hadn't suddenly discovered he desired her after five years. He'd been using her. She didn't know how he could have made love to her—correction, had *sex* with her—so tenderly and so passionately, if he'd felt nothing.

But apparently, he had no problem faking it.

Or was she just too stupid to know the difference between real and pretend passion? She'd believed she knew what good acting was. But he'd been so good he'd fooled her.

She had to get out of his house—the sooner, the better. Her heart was broken, her career in jeopardy and her dream of having a career and family she could be proud of...*dead*.

All she wanted was to get through the next four weeks. When *Honor* was finished she'd… Darn that bet. Unless Max blew his end of it soon, she'd be trapped. Assuming he didn't fire her. And why wouldn't he if he didn't trust her? Getting fired for selling company secrets—even if she hadn't—would make it impossible to get another job in the industry.

She yanked open the closet, pulled out her suitcases and slung both onto the bed. She popped them open and stared at the gaping insides. When she'd unpacked them she'd been full of hope, full of love and dreaming of possibilities.

"Fool," she muttered, and grabbed an armload of clothes. She cramped them in the first case without worrying about wrinkles or removing the hangers. After mashing the mound flat, she added more and more until both the closet and dresser were empty and each piece of luggage overflowed.

How could you love a man who would treat you this way?

She marched into the bathroom and gathered her makeup and toiletries. The extra large box of condoms she'd bought after she and Max became intimate mocked her.

So much for being prepared for love.

After shoving her loot into luggage, she sat on one lid to squash it closed. Her hands trembled so badly she could barely get the latch to catch. She had the same problem with the second.

Next she dropped to her knees. The temptation to stay there on the carpet and sob grabbed her by the throat, but she forced herself to keep moving. She was not going to cry over this. She'd loved Max and decided to leave him once before. The world had not ended then and it wouldn't now. She would survive.

Although it might not feel like it.

Why hadn't she listened when her conscience and his grandmother warned her that Max might not ever get over his wife? Even Max had told her. But she hadn't believed him.

The collapsible crate she'd flattened and hidden under the bed was hard to reach, but after she pulled it out and wrestled it back into shape she loaded it with her pictures, candles and plants. She continued her frantic denuding of the room until no trace of her presence existed.

How would she face Max at work day after day knowing what he'd done? Knowing that he'd coldly and calculatingly penetrated her body, her mind and her soul and he hadn't cared?

Taking a deep breath, she rubbed her dry burning eyes. Only ten yards separated her from her car and escape. She didn't want to run into Max. She eased open her door and checked the hall. Empty.

Grabbing her keys and the crate, she hustled down the hall, through the foyer and out the door. She wedged the crate into the passenger seat of her car and straightened. She did not want to go back into that house. But what choice did she have? She would not give him the satisfaction of making her call and ask him to have her belongings delivered.

Bracing herself for a possible encounter, she put one foot in front of another until she reached her room. When she did so without incident, she closed the door, sagged against it and exhaled a pent-up breath. The bed drew her gaze like a magnet. For the past five weeks she'd been making love and opening her heart to Max in that bed. And he'd been taking her for a ride.

How ironic. He thought she'd betrayed him, but he was the Judas.

A knot expanded in her chest, making it difficult to inhale. She wanted to go home—not to her apartment—to North Carolina. Back to the loving arms of her family. But she couldn't disappoint them. And she wouldn't disappoint herself. And there was the bet. Part of her wanted to say to hell with it. But the other part of her had too much pride to welsh.

She swallowed to ease the lump climbing up her throat, grabbed both suitcases by their handles and turned her back on the memories. She would forget, and she would get over him. Eventually.

She checked the hall again and again found it empty. How stupid of her to think he might care enough to have anything else to say.

Dragging her luggage, she made one last pass down the hall and across the foyer. She paused at the front door. She'd never set foot in this house again and, despite everything, that realization left her feeling a little empty. She loved this house on the hill with the beautiful vistas from every room.

She loved its owner more.

Get over it, and get on with it.

She yanked open the door and jerked to a halt. Max stood beside her car, looking heart-stoppingly handsome in his Ravazzolo trousers and Canali shirt. A wolf in designer clothing.

Drawing a deep breath for courage, she strode forward.

He stepped between her and her car's trunk. "Dana, you don't have to go."

How could he say that? "Yes, I do. You used me, Max, and you don't trust me. That pretty much says it all."

She used her remote to open the trunk. "Excuse me."

After a tense, silent moment Max took the suitcases from her. His hands brushed hers on the handles, and she couldn't believe after what he'd done that her body dared to tingle from the brief contact.

After loading the cases he shut the trunk and just looked at her, searching her face with those dazzling blue eyes.

Lying eyes, remember?

She refused to let him see how much he'd hurt her. Turning her back on him so he couldn't see her unsteady hands, she removed his house key from her key ring and then pivoted and held it out. "This is yours. I no longer need it."

When he didn't take it, she reached out, took his hand and slapped the key into his palm. She felt the contact with his warm flesh deep inside, and that only angered her more.

Why him? Why love a man who would deliberately hurt her?

She wasn't capable of saying another word. Her voice box had burned up. She turned and climbed into her car. And then she peeled out of the driveway, barely missing the wrought-iron gates because they opened too slowly.

She didn't look back because she didn't want to remember what a gullible, lovestruck fool she'd been for Max Hudson.

But one thing was certain, she would never, ever let herself care for anyone like that again.

Falling in love had been eradicated from her goals list.

Max wasn't sure what he'd find when he reached his office Monday morning, but it wasn't the old Dana.

At second glance, he realized that was not the old

Dana sitting behind her desk. The previous version would have greeted him with a glass of orange juice and a smile that started his day on the right note.

This Dana had donned one of her conservative suits and scraped back her hair like before, but her pale face wore no welcome. Her eyes lacked their usual luster, and her movements were stiff and tight. There was no glass of juice.

Would she pout and make working conditions difficult the way Karen had when she was ticked at him? Either way, Dana had shown up and he had to be grateful for that. After the way she'd left him Saturday evening, he'd half-expected to never see her again.

Dana rose as he entered and offered him a large manila envelope. "Dev brought this by earlier. He needs you to look at it ASAP and get back to him."

Her tone was cool, but professional. No snit fit in evidence. "What is it?"

"I don't know. The envelope is sealed. I'm no longer your assistant. I didn't open it."

He wanted his assistant back. "Thank you. Any messages?"

"They're on your desk. And your two o'clock appointment has confirmed." He started to turn away. "Max, there's one more thing." She lifted a script from her desktop and handed it to him. "This is a shooting script of Willow's World War II film."

Surprised, he searched her expressionless face. "How did you get a copy?"

He knew the answer: Doug Lewis. And the burn in his gut was anger. Nothing more. She'd seen the guy again when he'd specifically asked her not to.

"It doesn't matter how. But next time, before you

accuse someone of selling company secrets, you should do your research first. The screenwriter is a former Hudson employee. He's using a pen name, but that was easy enough to penetrate with the online copyright registration site. I checked with human resources and he was fired seven years ago 'for cause.' I've written his real name right there." She pointed to the top of the cover page. Max recognized the name immediately. The guy had been a troublemaker.

"After you've read the script you might want to forward it to the PR department so they can put their spin on the promo."

He'd wronged Dana. Hurt her. Used her. Betrayed her.

"I'm sorry, Dana."

"It's a little late for sorry. Now if you'll excuse me, your associate producer has to solve a minor crisis on the back lot. I've asked human resources to get you an executive assistant temp. She should be here by nine."

Dana walked away without a backward glance, and it felt as if the energy in the room and his enthusiasm for the project followed her out.

But completing *Honor* wasn't about him. It was about his grandmother and granting her last wish. He gritted his teeth and peeled his gaze off the curve of Dana's departing butt. The answers he and PR needed might be inside the script he held, but the pages wouldn't give him what he wanted.

He wanted his former relationship with Dana back— the one they'd had before France. He wanted her trust. And he wouldn't mind more of the mind-melting sex.

But he had a feeling he'd lost both forever.

Ten

"**D**ana tells me she might be leaving us," his grandmother said when Max joined her on the settee in the sunroom. "Something about pursuing her career goals elsewhere."

Dana had been to see his grandmother again. Why didn't that news surprise him? "Yes, ma'am."

"I thought she had a career with Hudson Pictures—especially since you finally recognized her talent."

He wanted to get up and pace, but his grandmother's shrewd blue eyes pinned him in place.

"She might move on once *Honor* is completed." Unless he held her to that bet. It had been a struggle, but not once had he asked for her assistance on the day-to-day garbage of his life. He'd had no idea how much Dana did to make his life run smoothly both on the job and away from it. Her word was her bond. If she made a promise, she'd stand by it. He could make her stay.

But did he want her to, knowing how she felt about him? Was it fair to ask that of her when he couldn't give her what she needed?

"Do you have anything to do with that decision?"

He didn't want to talk about Dana. Didn't want to think about how empty his house had been these past sixteen days without her. Didn't want to think about the candle the maid had found in the guest suite bathroom or the fact that he kept it on his nightstand so he could smell the beachy scent as he tried to fall asleep.

And he wasn't interested in spilling his guts or getting a lecture about being stupid. "I might."

A small, reminiscent smile touched her lips. "Everyone believes your grandfather and I were a match made in heaven, but we didn't always get along. Like you and Karen, we fought, we made up. Love is like that—fire and ice. But you and Karen never had those warm, balmy days when it felt good to just float along together side by side. It was always one extreme or the other. Love that's going to last needs those restful days, too."

Not liking the direction of her conversation, he shifted on the cushion. "I came to talk to you about the film."

"I don't need to talk about the film. I know how the story goes. I'm trying to tell you the part I left out when I talked to Cece." She laid a pale blue-veined hand over his. "I won't be here much longer, Maximillian. I want to see you happy before I go."

Her words made everything in him clench in denial and then in loss. Soon she would be gone and there would be no more quiet conversations like this one.

"I am happy," he insisted automatically.

"No. You *were* happy. For the most part. And then Karen died. I know that hurt. I know you wished you could have taken her place and that you didn't want to go on without her. I know, because I felt the same when your grandfather left me.

"But it wasn't my time, and it wasn't yours. We still have work to do here. I had my sons and my grandchildren, and Charles's story to tell. That kept me going. You might want to think about what or who kept you going."

"My job."

"Oh, it was much more than work that made you get up each day."

"What are you talking about?"

"That's for you to figure out, Maximillian. But remember, those who loved us, Karen and my Charles, would want us to be happy—even if it's not with them."

She waved for the nurse who stood behind her shoulder at all times.

"Grandmother—"

"I'm tired, dear. Go back to work. I know you have a lot to do and only a week to do it in. And while you're there, consider convincing Dana to stay."

"Dana, would you come in here, please?" Max's voice said via the intercom.

The summons was the last thing Dana wanted to hear. Seeing Max every day and working with him despite the canyon between had been painful and difficult. She'd clung to her professional demeanor by a fraying thread, but she missed the old warmth between them.

"Yes, sir." She pushed herself to her feet.

In the three weeks since she'd moved out of his house she'd gone through the motions. She worked herself to the point of exhaustion only to wander around aimlessly at home too tired to sleep. On the positive side, she'd lost that ten pounds that had stubbornly clung to her hips despite diet and exercise, but she couldn't seem to work up any excitement about it. Other than making dress shopping for the anniversary party easier, the weight loss was irrelevant.

She tapped on Max's door. In the past she would have automatically gone in after knocking, but not anymore.

"Come in."

She took a bracing breath and opened the door.

He rose as she entered. Before, he wouldn't have. His gaze took in her scraped-back hair and tailored cinnamon-colored pantsuit. "Sit down."

She sat. He did the same. She hated the new stiff and formal atmosphere between them.

"I've finished the first cut. I want you to take a look at it."

He'd been putting in a lot of hours. She wasn't surprised he'd finished early. "To check for continuity errors?"

"To prepare yourself to introduce the film at the anniversary bash."

Surprise stole her breath. She searched his face, but then suspicion took over. "Why me?"

"You've gone above and beyond the call of duty since this project began, and your dedication deserves a reward."

"That's not necessary, Max. I was only doing my job."

His blue eyes showed remorse. But it was too little too late. "Dana, I owe you."

The only thing she wanted from him was something he couldn't give. "You don't owe me anything except a good reference."

His eyes narrowed. "I haven't lost the bet."

Dread filled the pit of her stomach. "You wouldn't hold me to that."

He rocked back in his chair and laced his fingers over his flat abdomen. "Why wouldn't I?"

Her heart raced and her palms dampened. She *had* to get away from Hudson Pictures when *Honor* was done. She couldn't stay. "Because you don't trust me."

He shrugged. "I made a mistake."

She licked her dry lips. "I don't want to stay here, Max. Release me from the bet."

"No. You're mine for a year."

Max was late.

Dana couldn't remember the last time he'd been late for anything. She scanned the people milling about the room again, wondering if she'd somehow overlooked him in the gathering of *Honor*'s cast and crew and special guests waiting for the unveiling of the film's first cut. But she didn't see Max among the expensively garbed guests.

The rest of the Hudson family was already here. Even Luc and Gwen had flown in from Montana with the baby, but they'd left the baby at Hudson Manor with a sitter tonight. Dev, Luc and Jack were with David. Sabrina and Markus were sharing a glass of champagne by the piano where a musician played music from the movie score. The other Hudson women, Cece, Valerie, Gwen and Bella, had clustered around Lillian, who'd been determined to come tonight despite her declining health.

Dana supposed she could join them, but she was too agitated. She'd heard the phrase "alone in a crowded room" before, but until tonight she hadn't understood it. Now she did. In this group of perhaps a hundred guests she felt like an outsider, but that was probably because her conscience was bothering her and she'd isolated herself. She'd never broken a promise in her life, but she was seriously considering welshing on her bet with Max.

Could she live with herself if she tucked her tail and ran home after the *Honor* premiere next month?

Probably not.

But she might have to learn to.

She needed her parents, needed her father's bear hugs and her mother's gentle wisdom. Talking over the phone just wasn't the same as a face-to-face discussion, which was why she hadn't told them what was going on in her personal life. At the very least, she would take a long vacation and go see them. She'd earned it.

But first, she had to get through the next few weeks.

She exhaled what she hoped would be a calming breath and brushed a hand down her silk gown. She'd wanted basic black for the evening, but Cece and Bella had convinced her to buy a burnt orange halter dress with beading around the straps and the gathered bodice. The gown was attention-getting and form-fitting and not at all her usual style.

An air of excited anticipation hummed in the air, but nothing could get started without Max. Where was he? She considered digging her cell phone out of her evening bag and calling him. Before she could, Max strolled through the entrance. Her heart and lungs simultaneously contracted. He looked devastatingly gorgeous in his Armani tux. Of the three tuxes he owned, this one was her favorite.

He turned and spoke to someone behind him. Dana forced her gaze from his tall, lean form to see who'd accompanied him. She wasn't sure she could get through her presentation tonight if he'd brought one of his vapid blonde dates. Seeing her replacement in the flesh would be hard to take.

But her parents stood behind him. Surprise made her gasp and press a fist to her chest. What were they doing here? They weren't supposed to come until the premiere. There was no one she wanted to see more right now.

She hurried across the room, dodging hors d'oeuvres and champagne-carrying waitstaff and other guests. Max spotted her as she approached and smiled. That tender, indulgent twist of his lips made her stomach flip-flop. She forced herself to look away, brushed right past him and threw her arms around her mother first and then her father.

Her eyes burned and her throat clogged up. As if her father sensed her inner turmoil—he always had in the past—he squeezed tighter.

"What's going on, baby girl?" His gruff whisper made her chest tighten. With colossal effort, she pulled herself together, gave him one last hug, pasted on a smile and drew back. Bawling now would not be a good thing.

"What are you doing here?" She hoped they wouldn't notice or comment on the shakiness of her voice. But the tightening of their expressions said they'd taken note.

Her mother took her hand in both of hers, offering silent support. "Max thought we might enjoy sharing your big night."

Max. Dana's eyes found his. How could she ever stop loving him when he did wonderful things like this?

"Thank you, Max." She was proud she managed to keep her tone level.

"You're welcome. I'm only sorry your brother and his family couldn't make it. They'll be here for the premiere." His gaze traveled over her. "You look beautiful tonight, Dana, and as vibrant as one of your mother's paintings."

Her breath caught. That was exactly the reason she'd

allowed herself to be talked into this dress. It reminded her of home, of peaceful long walks on the beach at sunset gathering shells with her mother. The color was exactly the same shade as the sun's reflection off the water just before it slipped into the ocean.

Stop being so nice. She wanted to scream the words at the top of her lungs, but she bit her tongue. She wanted to hate him, to walk away without feeling guilty and then forget him.

Tall order.

"Thank you," she mouthed, but the words just wouldn't come out.

He checked his watch. "It's almost showtime. Are you ready?"

She cleared her throat. "Of course."

"Good. Let's introduce your parents to my grandmother and my parents then I'll show them to their table."

Before they could do as he suggested, raised voices yanked their attention to the far side of the room. David and Markus stood toe-to-toe, at it again. The brothers' arguments were legendary, but Dana had expected them to be on their best behavior tonight.

David took a swing at Markus and missed. Shocked, Dana watched as Dev and Jack, who stood nearby, jumped into the fray.

"Excuse me." Max took off across the room.

Dev grabbed his father. Jack did the same with his, but David struggled, and shouted, "Tell him, Sabrina. Tell him you slept with me. Tell him we were lovers."

Gasps rent the air and then the crowd went quiet as if holding their collective breaths and waiting for more. Markus cursed his brother and struggled, but Max and Luc joined the effort to keep the men apart.

"Tell him his precious baby girl is mine," David shouted. "Tell him Bella is mine."

A shocked silence descended. A woman's pained cry broke it. Dana looked toward the sound. Bella paled and pressed a hand to her mouth. She staggered forward to her mother. "Is that true? Is David my father?"

Tears streamed down Sabrina's cheeks. She cast an apologetic glance at her husband and then her daughter. "I—I—yes."

Well, that explained the tension between David and Markus.

Even from yards away Dana could see the pain on Bella's crumpling face. Bella turned on her heel and raced from the room. Dana's heart ached for her. She turned to her mother.

"I need—"

"It's okay, baby, go to her."

Dana didn't ask twice. She took off after Bella, raced outside and caught the sight of her blue gown going behind one of the office bungalows. Dana followed and found Bella leaning against the building gulping air and obviously fighting tears.

"Bella?"

Bella waved a hand as if to say either go away or she was okay. Dana knew she wasn't okay. She recognized when someone was hanging on to their composure by a thread. She'd been doing the same just moments ago. But as painful as her broken heart might be, it seemed trivial compared to Bella's shattered world.

Without a word, she put her arm around Bella's shaking shoulders, offering support.

"I can't believe…I mean…*David*." Bella shuddered. "How could she? He's a jerk."

Dana shook her head. She'd been thinking the same thing. What could Sabrina have possibly seen in her brother-in-law? "You'll have to ask your mother that. But you know David can be quite charming when he wants something."

Bella gulped several breaths. "My father—I mean, *Markus*—is he going to hate me?"

"Markus is still your father in every way that counts. I'm sure he's shaken up by this, too. He looked shocked, and you'll probably have some stuff to work through. But Bella, he's loved you for twenty-five years. He's not going to stop just because of David's big mouth. Daddies don't do that. Daddies love their baby girls no matter what."

It was as if a lightbulb went off in her head when she heard herself say the words. Her father would always love and support her—even if she disappointed him by letting go of their dream of making it big in Hollywood.

She couldn't work for Max anymore. And if that meant she couldn't work in Hollywood, then she would find work elsewhere. There were production studios all across the country. She'd build her credentials elsewhere and then when she was strong enough emotionally and professionally, she could return to Hollywood—if she still wanted to.

"This is just not my day." The ironic humor in Bella's voice caught Dana's attention. "First Ridley. And now this."

"What about Ridley?"

"He dumped me. Can you believe that? The jerk actually dumped *me*."

Good riddance. She kept the words to herself, but she understood Bella's pain. "Isn't he here tonight?"

"He will be. But he's coming with someone else."

Dana gave Bella an empathetic hug. "Men can be idiots."

"No kidding. I don't want to go back in there, Dana."

"I'm sure everyone will understand if you don't."

"But I can't hide out here. *Honor* means everything to Grandmother. I can't let her down. And I can't let those morons know they hurt me. But as soon as this is over I swear I'm heading somewhere until the gossip dies down. I'll go back to Europe and find a quaint little Italian village to hide out in…or something."

"That's the fighting spirit. And who knows, I might go with you."

Bella's big blue eyes searched Dana's. "He hurt you, didn't he? My dolt of a brother—*half* brother."

"Heartbreak isn't fatal. I'll survive. You and I both will." And she knew it was true—even though it didn't feel like it at the moment. "My office is just around the corner. I have makeup in my desk if you want to drop in and do a repair job."

"Ugh. I need it, huh?"

Dana wrinkled her nose. "A little touchup wouldn't hurt. I'll go with you."

"I'm keeping you from introducing the film."

Dana smothered a wince. "If they can't wait, then Max can introduce it. It's his masterpiece, after all."

"Is it a masterpiece?"

"Bella, you did an amazing job. Lillian will be proud. So let's go back in there and, as my daddy would say, let's show 'em what we're made of."

The crowd was getting antsy. Max glanced at his watch.

His father and David had been sent to opposite sides of the room like spoiled children. His mother sat pale and

drawn by his father's side. Bella and Dana had disappeared during the fracas. He hoped Bella was okay with
the bombshell. But checking on her would have to wait.

Canceling the showing of the first cut wasn't an option.
They needed feedback from tonight's viewing for the
final edit. The film was already scheduled for the
premiere and the theatrical release. Those dates were set
in stone.

Surely Dana would come back since her parents were
here. He'd promised her the opportunity to introduce the
film, but he could see his grandmother's energy flagging.
He couldn't wait much longer before he'd have to begin
without Dana.

Dev gave him a "get on with it" signal. Max realized
time was up. He was on the verge of taking the stage
when the doors opened and Dana and Bella strode in
with their backs straight, their heads high and their hands
linked. They made a striking picture in their jewel-
colored gowns. Bella wore cobalt blue and Dana car-
nelian.

He'd seen Dana in premiere finery before, but he'd
never seen her look more beautiful, more confident or more
determined than she did right now. Her dark hair draped
her shoulders like a dark satin curtain, the ends teasing the
cleavage revealed by her low-cut dress. His fists clenched
in memory of the silky strands threading through his
fingers, dragging over his skin and wrapping around his—

He cut off the thought as a bolt of desire shot through
him, and he looked away from the tempting sight of her
womanly shape.

His grandmother beckoned and Dana and Bella immediately went to her side. The rest of the Hudson women
closed ranks around them.

His grandmother grasped Dana's hand and pulled her close. He couldn't make out what she said, but suddenly, one thing became very clear. Dana hadn't just adopted his family, they had adopted her. She was a part of them, one of them. She belonged.

Why in the hell was he the only one afraid to let her in?

Who was he kidding? He'd already let Dana into his life. As she'd pointed out, she'd been running his life for him for years. And lately he woke up thinking about her each morning and lay in bed at night thinking of her while he waited for sleep to give him a few hours of oblivion.

Her smile was like his personal ray of sunshine.

Sap.

Sad, but true. When had she become so important to him? He didn't have a clue. She'd become an integral part of his life. There was only life before Dana and life since.

He didn't want there to be a life after Dana. The idea of her leaving opened a crater of emptiness in his chest.

But she was right. He was holding her back. She was too smart and too talented to waste her skills in an executive assistant position. She'd proven she knew how to look at the big picture, see all the components and juggle them the way a producer has to. Her hard work had made it possible for him to finish the first cut with days to spare.

Hell, who was he kidding? Dana had made it possible for him to get through every day since—

Then it dawned on him. That was what his grandmother had meant when she'd asked him who kept him going each day. Dana did. How could he have missed it? She'd prodded, challenged, and even fed him to keep him from crawling into a hole after Karen's death.

Dana had resurrected him.

And even if it was the right thing to do, he didn't want to let her go. She'd claimed she'd fallen for him. If he hadn't killed her feelings with his distrust, could he appeal to her romantic heart and convince her to stay and give them a shot at the kind of love his grandparents had shared?

Dana straightened, nodded at his grandmother and then strode across the room. Like a woman on a mission she climbed the stairs to the stage and stepped behind the microphone.

"Good evening, everyone. I hope you've enjoyed our entertainment thus far."

A scattering of laughter broke the tension in the room. This was the Dana he'd come to love.

Love.

He shook his head at the realization. He'd been so busy avoiding the intense instant attraction he'd had with Karen that he'd missed the simmering volcano of his relationship with Dana slowly building up pressure until it finally erupted in white-hot passion.

How long had she loved him? How long had she waited for him to wake up?

He zoomed in on her beautiful face and hoped he wasn't too late.

She smiled at the crowd. "I promise the night will only get better from this point, and the only drama you'll see will be on the screen. Tonight Hudson Pictures brings you an amazing tale of bravery, heroism and true love— the kind of love that we all aspire to have one day. A love that withstood the test of time and every challenge the world threw at it.

"Ladies and gentlemen, may I present *Honor,* the one

and only true, authorized story of Charles and Lillian Hudson's lifelong adventure."

"Wait," he shouted before the lights went dim and raced for the stage.

Dana's shocked gaze found his as he jogged up the stairs. The crowd rumbled as he crossed the platform toward her and stopped behind the microphone. When she tried to leave, he caught her hand and held her by his side.

He turned to the crowd. "Every movie has a message, and the message you'll find in *Honor* tonight is that true love is worth waiting for. It holds strong through adversity and stands the test of time.

"A love like my grandparents' is a rare and special thing. It's easy to find someone who'll stand by you during the highs, but not nearly as easy to find someone who has the fortitude to stand by you during the lows or keep speaking to you when the road gets a little rocky.

"The credits will tell you Dana Fallon was the associate producer on this film. What they won't tell you is that she's become part of my family, part of my life. And I can't imagine a day without her by my side. She has been my true partner for the past five years."

He heard Dana gasp, but kept going. "My grandmother asked me recently who or what made it possible for me to get up every day. What kept me going? The answer is Dana kept me going."

He turned to face her and saw tears brimming in her beautiful brown eyes. She tried to tug away, but he wouldn't let go. He didn't ever want to let her go.

"A very wise woman told me that a great love not only has fire and ice, but warm, balmy days where you drift along happy and content just to be with the one beside you. Dana, you are the only woman who has ever brought me all three.

"What we share is that same unbreakable bond my grandparents had. And I hope I haven't been so slow on the uptake that you've given up on me."

She hiccupped in several breaths and a few tears spilled over—tears that couldn't hide the love shining out at him like a warm beacon.

"You were right. You have too much talent to waste as my executive assistant. You've proven you deserve to be a producer, and you'll be a damned good one. But I'm selfish enough to hope you'll make room for me in your life as you shoot to the top."

He dropped to one knee. She pressed her fingers to her trembling lips. "I've been a blind, stupid fool. But please allow me to share not only the good times with you, but also those days when you're challenged."

He carried her knuckles to his lips. "I love you, Dana. You've made me a better, stronger person. And I want to spend the rest of my life with you. Marry me and let me give you that romance of a lifetime that you dream about."

She cupped his chin, stroked his jaw and then traced an unsteady finger over his lips. "I love you, too, Max. And nothing would make me happier than sharing my life with you. Yes, I'll marry you."

He shot to his feet, pulled her into his arms and swung her around. He kissed her and tasted tears and happiness, but mostly he tasted love. It felt good not to hold back, not to be cautious or afraid.

Applause rocked the room, and then a shrill whistle rent the air. He reluctantly pulled back, lowered Dana to her feet and turned toward the direction he'd heard the sound.

His brothers were laughing and pointing at their grandmother. She beckoned them over to her table.

Holding tightly to Dana's hand, he led her off the stage to his grandmother's side. "Did that whistle come from you, Grandmother?"

"Of course it did. I may be old, but I haven't forgotten all my tricks yet. It's about time you came to your senses, Maximillian Hudson."

She tugged off her diamond engagement ring and offered it to Max. "You could not have said it better. Dana is family, and I would like for my future granddaughter-in-law to have this, the ring from the man I love."

A shocked squeak of noise bubbled from Dana. "Lillian, I couldn't."

"Unless you hate it, you can and you will."

"Of course I don't hate it. It's beautiful."

"Then let the boy put it on your finger."

Max took the ring, kissed his grandmother on the cheek and knelt before the two women he loved. "Dana, may I?"

She offered her trembling left hand.

"With this ring, I promise to always try to be the man you need me to be."

Dana's smile lit up the room like sunshine. "You already are, Max. You have been for a very long time."

Max wanted to be alone with Dana. He wanted to drag her back to his place and make love to her without the emotional barriers between them. But there were two-hundred-plus people, including his grandmother, waiting for their first viewing of *Honor*.

"Roll the tape," he shouted, and seconds later the lights dimmed.

He dragged Dana to their table as the opening score swelled. Reluctant to release her for even a moment, he shifted their chairs so that they sat shoulder-to-shoulder and thigh-to-thigh. Her warmth, scent and love seeped into him.

He knew each frame crossing the screen backward and forward, but this time he viewed his grandparents' love story from a new perspective.

He realized love didn't make a man weak. It empowered him, made him braver, stronger and better as part of a whole than he had been alone.

The film that he and Dana had created together was easily the best work of his life because he had shared the burdens as well as the triumphs with her. They made a damned good team.

And as the credits rolled at the end and the house lights came up he saw the happy tears streaking down his grandmother's face, and knew he'd done her and himself proud because in telling her story he'd found the courage to live and love again.

* * * * *

*Wondering if Valerie's marriage to the
infamous Devlin Hudson is what she dreamed?
Then don't miss this exclusive short story
by* USA TODAY *bestselling author
Maureen Child.*

Scene 3
by
Maureen Child

Vegas weddings had always brought to mind tacky little chapels, Elvis impersonators as the justice of the peace, and plastic bouquets.

But when Valerie married Devlin, he somehow managed to make it both quick and beautiful. They'd been married in the chapel attached to the brand-new luxury resort, Treasures. Surrounded by stained glass, a glorious garden and the soft sigh of classical music, they'd exchanged vows with the last rays of a beautiful sunset spearing into the flower scented chapel.

It had all seemed so perfect a few hours ago, Valerie mused, sitting in the dark of Treasure's penthouse suite. She stared out the wide bank of windows and the brightly lit sprawl of Las Vegas, some thirty stories beneath her. Life pulsed down there, frantic, eager, desperate. But here, alone in the luxury of a darkened suite, she felt none of it.

"God, I was an idiot," she muttered quietly.

She should have told Devlin she was a virgin. Should have let him know that he was her first. That she was nervous as well as excited. Maybe if she had, things would have turned out better. For both of them.

Pushing up from the low slung couch, she walked barefoot to the wall of glass, put her hands on the cool panes and stared directly down at the street below. Neon shone back at her like fallen stars from an alien sky. She stared so hard, the lights began to blur and she closed her eyes, instantly opening a mental doorway to her memories.

The wedding had been so lovely. Devlin so handsome. So tall and strong and quite simply, mesmerizing. Valerie had been swept along on a thick tide of romance. Running off to Vegas instead of doing what society would have expected and throwing a huge, elegant wedding had seemed…romantic. And it had been. For a while.

Valerie's forehead rested against the glass and she squeezed her eyes shut even more tightly. Memories crowded her mind and made her squirm with discomfort.

She'd wanted Devlin. Her body had been achy for weeks as if in expectation of her wedding night. But nervousness it seemed, was much stronger than excitement. At the dinner they'd shared in one of the hotel's private dining rooms, she'd tried to drown the flocks of butterflies in her stomach with champagne. But the nervous flutters had only grown, expanding with the alcohol to make her clumsy, tense and more edgy than ever.

Devlin had been smooth and kind and gentle. As if he'd sensed her uneasiness, he'd kept conversation light, almost impersonal. Then, on the elevator ride to their suite, he'd kissed her, stealing her breath and briefly stilling the frantic worries racing through her mind.

But once in their suite, alone together in the palatial bedroom with its massive bed and flickering candlelight throwing dancing shadows on the walls, Valerie's body had betrayed her completely. She'd locked up so tight, it was a wonder she hadn't given off sparks.

She wanted him, but fear and nerves and anxiety had just been too much to conquer. Plus, the champagne had made her head fuzzy and her stomach unsteady. When he came to her, unbuttoning her dress, sliding it off her shoulders, taking her mouth with his even as his fingers tweaked at her hardened nipples, Valerie had started shaking. Shaking so badly she could hardly stand up and she'd batted at his hands like a crazy person. She'd just needed air. Some time to think. To get used to everything he was making her feel.

But he kissed her deeper, longer and want began to win the battle over anxiousness.

In seconds they were on the bed and Devlin was leaning over her, positioning himself between her legs and Valerie had opened for him, sure that once he was inside her, everything would be fine.

It hadn't been.

"Are you all right?" Devlin's voice came out of the dark, from somewhere behind her.

Oh, no. She couldn't face him. Couldn't look into his eyes and see regret over marrying her. But it wasn't as if she could avoid facing him forever. Valerie shut off the flood of painful memories, swallowed hard and whispered a lie. "Yes. I'm fine."

"Then why are you in the dark?"

Because she didn't want the light. She wanted to lick her wounds and that was better done in the shadows. Alone. How was she supposed to face him? How could she look him in the eye knowing that he was remembering everything she was? That the image of their botched lovemaking was no doubt overshadowed by the fact that he'd had to hold her hair back for her while she threw up every drop of champagne she'd consumed?

Could there ever have been a more disastrous wedding night?

"Dev, can we not talk about this?"

"Why? Are you still sick?"

"God, no." Her head pounded and her mouth felt like the Sahara, but the nausea was gone. "I just don't want to have to discuss it, okay?"

"That's the problem, isn't it? You not wanting to talk about it. Damn it, Val, you should have told me you were a virgin."

She laughed softly. "Well, I'm not now, am I?"

"If I'd known, it could have been different. It didn't have to be like that."

Slowly, Val turned her head to look at him. Standing across the room from him, he was mostly hidden in darkness, the dim reflection of the city lights not bright enough to reach him. Even now, even remembering the pain and embarrassment of their first time together, Valerie's body hummed with need.

She hadn't found that magic she'd heard so much about. But that was her fault and she knew it. If she hadn't had so much champagne. If she hadn't kept her virginity a secret. If she hadn't been so damn nervous—worried about doing something wrong—everything might have been better.

But it was too late now to get a second chance at a first time. That moment was lost forever.

Wrapping her arms around her middle, she held on

tightly and tried to sound matter-of-fact. "It's okay,
Devlin. I'm fine. You're fine. I'm sure it'll be better the
next time."

It *had* to be, she thought. After all, there was nowhere
to go but up. Besides, she loved him. Wanted him. Wanted
this marriage.

Devlin took a step toward her and stopped when he
saw her back up almost instinctively. He felt like some
raving caveman. Damn it, he hadn't had a virgin in his
bed since he was fifteen and had coaxed Debbie Colucci
into the back of his father's limo.

How the hell could he have possibly guessed that Val
would be a virgin? He hadn't even known there were any
virgins left. *Until* he'd entered her small, tight body and felt
her stiffen in reaction to the pain he knew he'd caused her.

Shoving one hand through his hair, he sighed heavily
and shook his head. He'd let his own need take control,
that was the problem. If he'd been paying more attention,
he'd have noticed the way she was drinking their champagne. The subtle signs of nerves she'd displayed as soon
as they entered the bedroom.

But he hadn't been thinking at all. He'd been feeling.
The roar of lust, the rush of desire. He'd seen her, wanted
her and taken her. Not realizing until it was too late that
she was an innocent.

Well, he couldn't give her back that innocence, but he
for damn sure could give her some space now.

"Look, I'm going downstairs. Hit the blackjack tables
for a while. You…" He shook his head again and turned
for the door. "There's a Jacuzzi in the bathroom. Go have
a soak. It'll help."

"You're leaving?" She sounded surprised.

But hadn't she been the one to leave their bed and

come to the living room alone? Hell, he told himself, she didn't know what she wanted. Why would she? So he'd make the decision for her.

"Yeah," he said. "I'll be downstairs an hour or two. Give you some time to yourself."

"Devlin—" Now she took a step toward him, and he was the one to retreat.

Dev didn't want to talk about their disastrous lovemaking session. He didn't want to explore what he was feeling, didn't want to look into her wounded eyes any longer. What he wanted was copious amounts of scotch and the impersonal feeling of getting lost in a crowd.

"Just try to relax," he told her. "Get some sleep. We can talk in the morning."

"I can't believe you're leaving. On our wedding night."

In the dim light, her eyes looked shattered and confused and Devlin almost changed his mind about leaving her. And that wasn't a good idea.

He didn't want to hurt her, but he also didn't want to be dragged into an emotional debate he had no interest in. They were married, yes, but he'd never pretended that this was a love match. He'd never promised that soul-deep connection. And now, he knew that the best thing he could do for her was to back off, whether she knew it or not.

"Valerie," he said softly, "the wedding night's over. Why don't we just leave it at that and move on? All right?"

When he left, he closed the door quietly behind him, but not before he heard her begin to cry.

* * * * *

Turn the page for a sneak preview of
Dakota Daddy
by Sara Orwig.

This fantastic new story is available from
Mills & Boon® Desire™
in April 2010.

Dakota Daddy
by
Sara Orwig

June

That old saying about a woman scorned was too damn true, Jared Dalton thought.

He thought back to when he'd first learned that old man Sorenson had died and that Megan had no apparent interest in keeping the family ranch. Jared assumed he could buy it easily. To his surprise, the minute Megan had learned who intended to buy the ranch, she'd withdrawn it from the market. Now he was here to get her to sell.

With a disturbing skip in his heartbeat that overrode a simmering anger, he saw Megan emerge from the Sorenson barn, carrying a saddle to the corral. She was too far away for him to see if her looks had changed. Her red shirt was as noticeable as her long-legged, sexy walk, which still revealed the years she had studied dance before she'd left for college. Her black hair was in a thick braid that lay on her back. Setting the saddle and blanket on the fence, she turned to the approaching horses to give each a treat. Within minutes she had saddled and mounted a sorrel.

The sight of her brought back too many hurtful memories. Vengeance was sweet. He just wished her father had lived to be part of the intended payback.

Jared intended to encounter her out on the ranch, where she would have to talk to him. He'd spent the night in a comfortable log guesthouse on her ranch without her knowledge in order to watch for her this morning. Before dawn he had dressed in jeans, a blue Western shirt and a wide-brimmed black Stetson.

Now he went to the barn to saddle a bay to follow her without haste.

The vast, grassy land made it easy to see in all directions except along the river, where trees could hide a rider from view. He knew he could catch her when she stopped at the river to let her horse drink. Until then, he didn't want to alert her that he was trailing behind. Thunder rumbled in the distance, and a glance at gathering clouds told him rain seemed imminent.

As soon as she reached the line of trees, she vanished from view. Watching, he could remember meeting her at the river—and their steamy kisses. Since their split, he rarely thought of her without bitter feelings surfacing.

Unwanted memories enveloped him. He had known her all his life. Even as their dads battled over water, he'd paid no attention to her because she had been six years younger—the skinny little kid on the neighboring ranch. The first time he'd ever noticed her was when he was getting his master's degree and she'd entered his same university in Chicago.

Too clearly he could recall that initial encounter. Her black hair had cascaded in a cloud over her shoulders and her startling turquoise eyes sped his pulse. She filled out a white cotton blouse that tucked into the narrow waistband of a tan skirt. When she'd smiled broadly at him and said hello, he'd thought he was looking at a stranger. If a beautiful woman greeted him, however, he had no intention of not responding.

"You don't know me, do you, Jared?"

Surprised, he'd stared at her and frowned, trying to recollect. "Did you go to UT?" he asked, referring to the University of Texas, where he'd gotten his undergraduate degree.

She laughed and stuck her tongue out at him and he sucked in his breath. All her pink tongue had done was make him think about kissing her. He was getting turned on and he didn't have a clue how he knew her.

"Jared, for heaven's sake!" she said. He shook his head, touching a lock of her soft hair.

"Okay, I give. I can't believe I don't remember a gorgeous woman. Where have we known each other?"

"I'm Megan Sorenson," she'd said, laughing at him. He stared in astonishment, seeing it now in the turquoise eyes. But that was all. Gone was the skinny little kid, replaced by a luscious, curvaceous woman.

"You grew up," he said, and that sparked a fresh burst of laughter.

"I didn't know you're going to school here," she said. "I thought I'd heard you'd graduated."

"MBA," he said slowly. "Have dinner with me tonight."

She tilted her head to study him. "You know how our dads fight. You and I should keep a distance."

"C'mon, Megan. Their fight isn't our fight. I've never in my life had anything against you."

"Oh, liar, liar!" she accused with amusement again dancing in her eyes. "You thought I was a pest. You wouldn't even say hello if you saw me."

He felt his face flush. "I'll make it up to you. I promise to give you my full, undivided attention," he said, and saw a flicker in her eyes. The moment between them sizzled and his heart raced.

"Dinner it is," she said breathlessly.

"About seven," he'd replied. And from that moment on, he'd thought he was in love. He'd hoped to marry her. They'd talked about it and planned on it, and then that summer after her freshman year, when Megan had gone to Sioux Falls to stay with her aunt and uncle, Olga and Thomas Sorenson, her dad sent one of his hands to summon Jared.

The old man had run him off by threatening harm to Jared's dad. He'd always wondered how much Megan had known about what her father was doing. For over a year he'd hurt, pain turning to anger that had grown when she wouldn't answer his letters. It pleased him enormously to buy her ranch. This payback was long overdue, and again he wished he'd offered to buy the ranch when Edlund Sorenson had still been alive, just to watch the old man's face.

Most obstacles weren't insurmountable, he'd discovered. Not with the wealth he had accumulated. He didn't expect this one to be, either.

2 FREE BOOKS
AND A SURPRISE GIFT

We would like to take this opportunity to thank you for reading this Mills & Boon® book by offering you the chance to take TWO more specially selected books from the Desire™ 2-in-1 series absolutely FREE! We're also making this offer to introduce you to the benefits of the Mills & Boon® Book Club™—

- **FREE home delivery**
- **FREE gifts and competitions**
- **FREE monthly Newsletter**
- **Exclusive Mills & Boon Book Club offers**
- **Books available before they're in the shops**

Accepting these FREE books and gift places you under no obligation to buy, you may cancel at any time, even after receiving your free books. Simply complete your details below and return the entire page to the address below. You don't even need a stamp!

YES Please send me 2 free Desire stories in a 2-in-1 volume and a surprise gift. I understand that unless you hear from me, I will receive 2 superb new 2-in-1 books every month for just £5.25 each, postage and packing free. I am under no obligation to purchase any books and may cancel my subscription at any time. The free books and gift will be mine to keep in any case.

Ms/Mrs/Miss/Mr_____ Initials _____

Surname _____

Address _____

_____ Postcode _____

Send this whole page to: Mills & Boon Book Club, Free Book Offer, FREEPOST NAT 10298, Richmond, TW9 1BR.